Harry Bowling was born in Bermondsey, London, and left school at fourteen to supplement the family income as an office boy in a riverside provisions' merchant. Called up for National Service in the 1950s, he has since been variously employed as lorry driver, milkman, meat cutter, carpenter and decorator, and community worker. He now writes full time. He is the author of twelve bestselling novels, *One More for Saddler Street*, *That Summer in Eagle Street*, *Waggoner's Way*, *The Farrans of Fellmonger Street*, *Pedlar's Row*, *Backstreet Child*, *The Girl from Cotton Lane*, *Gaslight in Page Street*, *Paragon Place*, *Ironmonger's Daughter*, *Tuppence to Tooley Street* and *Conner Street's War*. He is married and lives with his family, dividing his time between Lancashire and Deptford.

'What makes Harry's novels work is their warmth and authenticity. Their spirit comes from the author himself and his abiding memories of family life as it was once lived in the slums of southeast London' *Today*

D0582426

Also by Harry Bowling

One More for Saddler Street
That Summer in Eagle Street
Waggoner's Way
The Farrans of Fellmonger Street
Pedlar's Row

The Tanner Trilogy
Backstreet Child
The Girl From Cotton Lane
Gaslight in Page Street

Paragon Place
Ironmonger's Daughter
Tuppence to Tooley Street
Conner Street's War

Down Milldyke Way

Harry Bowling

HEADLINE

First published in 1996
by HEADLINE BOOK PUBLISHING

First published in paperback in 1997
by HEADLINE BOOK PUBLISHING

10 9 8 7 6 5 4 3

ISBN 0 7472 5543 1

Typeset by
Letterpart Limited, Reigate, Surrey

Printed and bound in Great Britain by
Mackays of Chatham PLC, Chatham, Kent

HEADLINE BOOK PUBLISHING
A division of Hodder Headline PLC
338 Euston Road
London NW1 3BH

To Lydia. With Love.

Prologue

January 1946

The weak wintry sun hardly penetrated the high, grimy windows of the courtroom, and the lights that had been switched on cast a yellow pall over the proceedings. It was mid-afternoon on a bitter day, and outside snow was threatening to fall as soon as the east wind dropped.

The oak-panelled Hall of Justice was warm and stuffy, but Kate Flannagan shivered as she stared down at her white hands clasped tightly in her lap. She was stricken with a cutting sense of loneliness and isolation, and she raised her eyes slowly, glancing down from her front-row seat in the visitors' gallery to the crowded area beneath. The people sitting around her and down below on the rows of hard wooden benches were there for many reasons. Friends and relatives of the accused waited with anxious expressions, rubbing shoulders with bland-faced or bored-looking court reporters and casual visitors, who came to observe, to learn, to satisfy their own curiosity, and to gloat.

Kate Flannagan felt compelled to be there in the courtroom on that dark January day, compelled by the pressing need to sever the last strand of her attachment and so set herself free forever. Only then could she pick up the pieces

1

of her life, gather her children closer to her and face the long winter ahead.

A hush had come over the court, and as the presiding judge looked up over his gold-rimmed glasses and cleared his throat gruffly there was little doubt in anyone's mind that the sentence would be severe. The summing-up by the prosecution had been delivered with clarity and forcefulness, a telling contrast to the weak and unconvincing performance of the defence counsel, and when the jury left the courtroom to deliberate no one had been left in any doubt as to the verdict.

Kate sat tense and dry-eyed as the words rose from the well of the court. 'William James Flannagan, the sentence of this court is that you will serve seven years' imprisonment.'

There was some delay after the court was cleared, and while she waited in an adjoining room Kate Flannagan thought about her two children. Her elder sister Mary would be giving them their tea about this time and both Jimmy, who was twelve, and nine-year-old Jenny would be quite happy in the company of their cousins.

They had shown little more than mild interest in their mother going to the Old Bailey, and it was understandable. Their father was not like their uncle John, who came home every night at the same time and would sweep his youngest child up into his arms and playfully ruffle everyone's hair. Their father was a shadow, a stranger who passed in and out of their young lives, leaving no mark, no abiding memories to cherish.

'Mrs Flannagan?'

Kate stood up quickly, and with a dry mouth and a knot in her throat she followed the policeman through the open door into a small room. It was windowless and smelled of tobacco smoke, and in a corner a chair had been placed in front of a two-foot-square grille. The constable closed the door as he went out, leaving her alone, and she sat down and peered through the grille's fine mesh. Two men were sitting on a narrow bench in the passageway beyond, staring glumly at their feet, and a police sergeant stood guard, his face expressionless. Then she saw her husband being led through the far door. He sat down facing her through the grille, his hands forming two large fists on the small ledge.

'I didn't expect yer ter come,' he said gruffly.

'Yer didn't expect 'er ter come, did yer?' Kate replied bitterly.

William Flannagan's eyes dropped for a moment, and when he looked up again Kate saw nothing in them, nothing but a remote coldness. His face too showed no warmth, only a blankness, as though he was facing a total stranger.

'I didn't wanna come, but I 'ad to,' Kate said, her eyes fixed on him. 'I've got a life ter lead, an' there's the children.'

'What are yer sayin', Kate?' he cut in. 'Are you askin' me or tellin' me?'

'I'm tellin' yer, Will. It's over fer good. It was over the day yer took up wiv that woman.'

'So yer wanna divorce?'

'I can get it. Desertion, adultery.'

Will Flannagan smiled sardonically. 'I won't challenge it,' he said quietly. 'As far as I'm concerned, it's finished. It's over between us.'

Kate swallowed hard. There was so much she had been prepared to say, so many scathing words that had festered inside her like a clot of venom she would spit in his face, but now she could only pity him, as she would an animal

3

caught in a trap. He had changed out of all recognition from the man she had loved and married. He was a drunk, a womaniser, a convicted criminal who had shown no compassion to the Hatton Garden jeweller he had robbed, and now in a few minutes he would be transported to prison. He was paying the penalty for his crime, but she was being punished too, and so were her children. Deprived of a husband and father to provide and care for them, they would have to fight hard to survive in the harsh world outside, but survive they would.

'Time's up,' the police sergeant said firmly.

'I wish yer well, Kate,' William said in a low voice.

'I wish yer well too,' she replied, like a stranger in her own body as she stood up to leave.

Across the River Thames, eastwards and beyond the grimy wharves, the chamber of Bermondsey Borough Council was illuminated by two iron chandeliers hanging high above the gathering. The session had lasted all day and it showed on the faces of the councillors.

'Mr Chairman, I feel that we have exhausted all arguments and it is time we took a vote.'

Councillor Bradley nodded in agreement. He was beginning to feel the strain, and tiredness hung around his neck like a heavy weight. Chairing the housing committee was a burden he had found to be taxing to the extreme and there was so much to do, so many unpalatable decisions to carry the can for, in a borough which had borne the brunt of the Blitz. 'I agree, Councillor Smythe,' he replied in a flat tone. 'We'll vote by a show of hands on the proposal. All in favour.'

Ten minutes later the housing committee meeting was wound up and the members slowly dispersed. Councillor

Bradley made his way to the nearby Swan pub along with his old friend Tom Smythe, and in the comfortable saloon bar the two men sat by the coke fire sipping their drinks.

'It's a shame it had to go the way it did, but what else could we do?' Bradley sighed. 'I'd like to see the end of the damn place just as much as anyone. Milldyke Buildings is a blot on this borough of ours but with money as tight as it is we've just got to suffer it until the lease runs out.'

'I agree,' Smythe replied, staring thoughtfully into the fire. 'Another five years though – it's no comfort for the poor souls living there.'

Bradley nodded. 'When I think of the carnage wrought on Bermondsey and the homes destroyed I'm tempted to ask why those particular buildings were spared, but it's wickedness even contemplating it. Every bomb dropped took lives and a bomb on those buildings would have taken quite a few. I know for a fact that a lot of the tenants preferred sheltering there as against using the public shelters.'

Councillor Smythe forced a tired smile. 'I've got to face those tenants tomorrow,' he said in a soft voice. 'I'm not relishing it one little bit. They're looking for a compulsory purchase order, not another five years living in the bloody place.'

'Perhaps they won't have to, if we can bring it to the Government's attention,' Bradley remarked. 'Putting some decent modern flats in the place of that slum should be made a top priority.'

Councillor Smythe lifted his glass. 'I'll drink to that sentiment, Joe, and I'm sure the Milldykers would too,' he said smiling.

Chapter One

June 1946

She saw them as soon as she stepped out into the bright
morning sunshine in Weston Street: Mrs Barnes and Mrs
Miller, along with Fanny Harrington, her fat arms folded
over her ample bosom. They were fifty yards down the
turning outside Mrs Miller's house but they had already
spotted her, or rather Fanny had. Her body movements gave
her away: the sweep of her head, and the way she crossed
one leg over the other and pointed the tip of her shoe on to
the pavement. They were all looking towards her now and
Kate Flannagan sighed in resignation. One more day and
she would be rid of the lot of them.

'Mornin', Mrs Flannagan. Nice day.'

Kate forced a smile as she drew level. 'It certainly is, Mrs
Miller.'

'Yer leavin' us termorrer then,' Fanny said, leaning her
large bulk against the brickwork.

Kate did not slacken her stride. ''S right.'

'She'll be sorry,' Fanny remarked to her cohorts, loud
enough for the young woman to hear as she turned the
corner into Tower Bridge Road.

The market hubbub and the cries of the stallholders lifted

Kate's spirits somewhat and she allowed herself a brief smile. Fanny Harrington would be saying her piece and the other two would be nodding dutifully and grimacing for effect. She could hear the virago now. 'Bloody good riddance, that's what I say. That ole man of 'ers was never any good an' people like that give the street a bad name.'

Perhaps she was being a little too hard on the woman, but she doubted it.

When Kate arrived at her sister's house in Abbey Street she could see that Mary had been busy. There was a smell of disinfectant in the passage and fresh net curtains were hanging in the parlour.

'I've got the kettle boiling, make yerself comfortable,' Mary urged her.

Kate flopped down in the armchair beside the black-leaded grate and kicked off her tight shoes while her sister busied herself in the scullery. A shaft of sunlight filled with motes of dust filtered into the room, picking out the frayed patch of carpet beside the chair.

'Are the kids all right?' Mary called out.

'They're fine,' Kate told her. 'Jenny's bin askin' questions but Jimmy seems to 'ave accepted it wivout much fuss.'

'Well, at least they'll still be near enough ter stay at their school,' Mary said. 'That's the worst of a move when kids 'ave ter change schools.'

Kate sighed downheartedly. Moving out of Weston Street was the last thing she wanted, despite Fanny Harrington and her cronies, but she had no option. Belton Estates had been patient and even sympathetic, but the rent arrears had risen to an unacceptable level and the notice to quit had finally been served.

Mary came into the parlour carrying a tray with two cups

of tea and a sugar bowl. ''Elp yerself ter sugar,' she said, putting it down on the table.

Kate stood up and took a large spoonful. 'They're comin' at nine o'clock sharp termorrer,' she remarked.

Mary sat down gingerly on the edge of the armchair facing her sister, still managing to slop tea into the saucer. 'I wish there was somefing I could 'ave done,' she said sighing, 'but it's bin a struggle this last few months, what wiv the way fings 'ave bin at the docks. I don't fink my John's 'ad a full week's work since Gawd knows 'ow long.'

Kate smiled appreciatively, watching her elder sister as she sipped her tea. Mary was forty years old but she still appeared to have the bloom of youth. Her deep-blue eyes shone out of a round face and her fair hair was cut short and shaped around her head. She had a good figure too, with hardly any stomach bulge, despite having had four children. Mary was one of life's optimists and it was always nice to visit her, Kate thought. What did Mary think about her visits though? Every time she called it was gloom and doom, what with William getting arrested, then the trial, and now the eviction notice. If only she could call with some good news for a change.

Mary sipped her tea noisily and then put the cup and saucer down on the table, giving Kate a bright smile as she reached across to a small cigar box lying on the shelf at her elbow. 'I dug this out o' me wardrobe last night,' she said. 'They're Mum's bits an' pieces.'

Kate took the box and opened it. She stared down at beads and brooches, hatpins and large bone buttons, and then she saw the ring, a thin gold band with a high shoulder holding five tiny rubies. She drew it out almost reverently and slipped it on the tip of her little finger. 'I remember Mum wearin' this,' she said softly.

'Only on 'igh days an' 'olidays,' Mary reminded her. 'She used ter say it was too good ter wear as an everyday ring.'

Kate nodded. 'It's beautiful. Why don't yer wear it?'

'It won't fit any o' my fingers. You might as well wear it,' Mary told her.

Kate smiled affectionately. She knew that her sister had spotted her bare hand and she rubbed her wedding finger self-consciously. Along with her engagement ring the wedding ring was now tucked away somewhere in Dawson's pawnshop; and this was Mary's way of saying that she had permission to pawn the ruby ring as well. 'I couldn't wear it,' she replied. 'Mum gave it ter you, an' besides, it wouldn't fit any o' my fingers eiver.'

Mary felt a tinge of annoyance at her younger sister's tactful answer. The ring would only have raised a few shillings, but it would certainly have helped. That was Kate though and she would never change. Even as a child she had always shown a fierce independence. She took after her father in that. He was a proud man who had worked on the river all his life: tall, dark, and powerfully built, with a smiling face that hid a fiery temper when he was put out. Yes, Kate certainly took after him. She had his complexion, with raven hair and large hazel eyes, though a sunny expression had been little in evidence over these last couple of years. To be honest, there was little for her sister to be sunny about, Mary conceded to herself.

'What yer lookin' at me like that for?' Kate asked her.

'I was just finkin'.'

'About what?'

'Oh, I dunno. Just thoughts.'

Kate put the ring into the box and handed it back to Mary, her face betraying a wry smile. 'It's better not ter fink too much at times,' she told her. 'I used ter sit fer hours finkin' about where an' when it all went wrong between Will an' me, but I don't any more.'

Mary looked angry. 'Let's face it, Kate, 'e was never any good,' she said sharply. 'Me an' John tried ter warn yer, an' Mum too. She could see frew 'im. You was in love wiv 'im an' nuffing we could say would 'ave made any difference.'

Kate shrugged her shoulders. 'Well, it's over fer good now an' I'm just gonna get on wiv me life. Me an' the kids'll manage wivout 'im. After all, we've bin doin' so fer the past two years.'

'Don't worry, luv, Milldyke Street ain't as bad as it's painted out ter be,' Mary said without believing it. 'I know the people livin' there 'ave got a bad name, but when it comes down to it people are people, wherever they live. I'm sure yer'll make a few friends there, an' the kids too. Yer'll be OK.'

Kate nodded thoughtfully. Milldyke Street was the last place she wanted to live but there was little choice. The rent was only twelve and six a week for an upstairs two-bedroomed flat in Milldyke Buildings, and it was the only accommodation available, apart from furnished rooms which were far too expensive. 'Yeah, we'll be OK, sis,' she said.

'Well, at least yer won't 'ave ter run the gauntlet every day,' Mary joked.

'Yeah, that's true,' Kate replied. 'Fanny was 'er usual charmin' self this mornin' when I came out. I 'eard 'er mumble somefing about good riddance.'

'She 'as room ter talk, the dirty, scruffy ole cow,' Mary said indignantly. 'A bar o' soap wouldn't go amiss on that snuff-caked mug of 'ers.'

The slanting sunlight had moved steadily along the

carpet and Kate reached for her shoes. 'Well, this won't get the baby bathed,' she said sighing.

Mary looked put out. 'Yer've only just got 'ere,' she said quickly. 'I was lookin' forward to a good bit o' gossip.'

Kate relaxed back in her chair. 'All right,' she grinned, 'but I can't stay too long, there's so much ter do still.'

The two women began discussing the local news, and the sun had left the room by the time Kate finally slipped on her shoes. 'I really must go now,' she said anxiously.

Mary took a pound note from her apron pocket and held it out for her younger sister. ''Ere, take this, it'll 'elp yer out,' she told her.

Kate shook her head. 'You ain't got money ter throw away. You keep it.'

'Don't argue, I want yer to 'ave it. Take it.'

Kate reluctantly accepted the note and slipped it into her handbag. 'I'll call round as soon as I get settled,' she said. 'An' fanks, Mary. Fanks fer everyfing.'

'Don't be silly. It's little enough I've bin able ter do.'

'Just bein' there when I need a shoulder ter cry on is more than enough,' Kate replied with a warm smile.

A laden dray lumbered past as she stepped out from Abbey Street into Tower Bridge Road and the van boy perched on top of the beer barrels gave her a saucy whistle. A tram rattled by, and seeing the gap in the traffic Kate hurried across the wide thoroughfare. She had taken that Friday off from her part-time job at the vinegar factory with the intention of getting everything sorted out for the move, but it was after twelve now and she had achieved very little. She would have to get going before the kids came home from school.

Jimmy Flannagan kicked the tennis ball on the half volley

and it flew hard against the playground wall, rebounding to Billy Morris, who missed his kick and fell over grinning widely. The other member of the makeshift team, Stanley Cosgrove, walked away from the wall in disgust. 'I ain't playin' in goal any more,' he moaned. 'You kick the ball too 'ard. I ain't got a chance.'

Billy picked himself up and dusted the seat of his pants. 'Go on then, sod off, Cosgrove,' he said, still grinning at Jimmy.

The two friends watched as the chubby Stanley pocketed the tennis ball and skulked off.

'Come on, let's go an' sit under the shed,' Billy urged. 'I wanna try my knife out.'

They sauntered over and seated themselves on the long wooden bench.

'This is a frowin' knife,' Billy announced as he took the thick penknife from his trouser pocket. 'Look, you watch.'

Jimmy smiled as his friend struggled to pull out the blade. 'That's not a frowin' knife, the 'andle's too 'eavy. Look, I'll show yer,' he said, trying to balance it on his finger. 'Wiv frowin' knives the blade's gotta be 'eavier than the ovver part,' and with a sudden flick he aimed the knife down between them.

It clattered on to the floor and Billy picked it up. 'You can 'ave it if yer like, Jimmy,' he said.

'Nah, you keep it.'

'Go on, take it.'

'Why d'yer wanna give it away?'

'Well, I s'pect yer a bit sad at movin' ter Milldyke an' I thought it'd cheer yer up.'

'Fanks, Billy, but I got a knife already,' Jimmy told him unblushingly. 'I don't bring it ter school though. Yer know what ole Ramsey's like. If 'e finds out yer got a knife on yer 'e'll take it away, an' give yer the cane as well.'

'When I get as big as my dad I'm gonna come back ter this school an' I'm gonna smack old Ramsey right on the chops,' Billy said earnestly.

''E'll be old wiv a long beard by then,' Jimmy replied. 'We could come back an' pull 'is beard though. An' then kick 'im up the arse.'

The two friends laughed loudly at the thought and Jimmy pointed towards Stanley. 'C'mon, let's nick 'is tennis ball off 'im,' he suggested.

The classroom moaner had seen them coming and he hurried off out of harm's way.

'I 'eard that Milldyke Buildin's is a right ole scruffy place ter live,' Jimmy said as he lounged against the school wall.

'They call 'em Milldykers, those people who live there,' Billy told him. 'Tommy Brindley lives in Milldyke Buildin's an' 'e's always gettin' the cane. Ole Ramsey can't stand Milldykers.'

'Well, I'm not tellin' anybody I'm gonna live there,' Jimmy said emphatically.

'Ramsey'll find out.'

''Ow will 'e?'

''Cos yer gotta tell the 'eadmaster when yer change yer address,' Billy explained. ''E's bound ter tell Ramsey.'

'Well, if Ramsey starts usin' the cane on me I'm gonna give 'im one an' run out o' school,' Jimmy growled.

'That won't do yer any good, they'll send the police after yer an' yer'll end up in Borstal.'

'Yeah, but they'll 'ave ter find me first.'

'They will.'

The bell sounded and the two friends sauntered back into the classroom.

'Morris!'

'Yes, sir?'

'Kindly step to the front.'

Billy did as he was bid and was immediately taken by the ear. 'Turn out your pockets, Morris.'

Stanley Cosgrove grinned maliciously as the miserable victim laid his penknife down on the table.

'What is the meaning of this?'

'It's only a penknife, sir.'

'A penknife? You know I don't permit penknives in school,' the thin, hatchet-faced master said loudly.

Jimmy winced involuntarily as Ramsey walked over to the cupboard and produced a cane from inside, swishing it threateningly down by his leg.

'Hold out your hand, Morris.'

The lad took his punishment bravely and fought back angry tears as he walked back to his desk. Jimmy turned to glare at Stanley. 'We'll get you, fatty,' he whispered.

Herbert Ramsey had enjoyed the thrill of the cane in his hand and he was now hungry for more blood. 'Flannagan, step out to the front,' he ordered. 'A caning should be watched in reverence. That means in silence, but you have chosen to disregard my wishes.'

Jimmy walked up to the teacher and was immediately taken by the lobe of his ear. He could feel the sharpness of the master's long thumbnail and he clenched his teeth in pain.

'Hold out your hand, boy.'

'But yer'd finished the canin',' Jimmy protested.

'Don't dare argue with me, boy,' Ramsey snarled. 'I'm not finished until this cane is back in its home. Hold out your hand!'

Like his best friend, Jimmy took his punishment man-fully, and he glowered darkly at the class sneak as he went back to his seat. His hand was stinging and he closed it into a tight fist. Very soon he would be living in Milldyke Buildings and once Ramsey got to know he would be certain to seek him out for punishment at every opportunity. Billy Morris managed an encouraging smile and Jimmy glanced over instinctively to Tommy Brindley, the tousle-haired Milldyker, who sat glum-faced at the back of the class.

The English lesson was completed in silence, with the two friends plotting silently against Stanley Cosgrove.

'Ole Ramsey's a slimy-faced git,' Billy growled as he and Jimmy walked home from school, and then a smile suddenly appeared on his ruddy face. 'D'yer fink 'e *will* 'ave a beard when 'e gets old?'

Chapter Two

Centuries before, when Bermondsey was inhabited by Cluniac monks and peasants who worked the soil, streams and rivulets had crossed the fertile land. The waterways trickled down, converged and flowed into the Thames through woodlands of oak and elm and verdant pastures, and it was not very far from the wide, tidal river that an enterprising gentry farmer instructed a stone mason to build a corn mill on his land. The mill was to have a waterwheel, which caused much puzzlement to the mason, considering that the stream which flowed alongside the site was little more than a trickle for most of the year. The mason worked to the specifications regardless and the landowner was pleased with the construction. He then ordered his serfs to build a dyke nearby, which they made from clay and briarwood. The long ridge served to divert the flow of water from different sources into one full-flowing river, and the power turned the waterwheel.

For many years the corn mill served its purpose, until the advent of the industrial revolution. Tanneries grew up then; the leather artisans stripped the oak trees for their leather-dyeing, and the streams grew dark and filthy. Vast changes brought factories and trade to the river area, and workers' hovels began to cover the pastureland. The milldyke had served its purpose, and in its place an industrialist constructed a block of buildings to house the workers flooding in to the factories and tanneries that had ravaged the once green and pleasant fields. Partly in memoriam, and partly for want of a better name, the tenement block was called Milldyke Buildings.

The young woman who sat squashed between the driver and the furniture porter on that warm Saturday morning had no idea why the ugly Milldyke Buildings should be so called. It merely seemed to her that the name was a hard, ugly one, befitting the slum block that had survived the Blitz and the passage of time. She knew it had been there since 1874 because she had read an article in the local paper referring to the Milldyke Buildings as an eyesore and a slight on the proud and progressive borough of Bermondsey.

'At least we ain't got far ter go,' the driver remarked as he steered the removal van out of Weston Street into Long Lane.

Kate Flannagan nodded in answer, preoccupied with her thoughts. She was leaving some good neighbours behind, as well as the unfriendly ones, and the future was as uncertain as ever. Would she make friends easily at Milldyke Street, she wondered, bearing in mind that gossip soon spreads and there had been a lot of that lately concerning her family affairs.

The van trundled along Long Lane, and as it turned into Abbey Street Kate glanced out of the cab to see if her sister was at her front door. She was not to be seen and the young woman settled back against the hard seat, aware of the strong oily smell coming up from beneath the floorboards. The van rattled over the cobbled road beneath the railway arch and Kate hoped that she had packed the crockery securely, as well as the other few breakable bits and pieces she had accumulated over the years.

They crossed Jamaica Road into Dock Lane and the driver cursed under his breath as he swung the van left into Milldyke Street. A game of football was underway in the turning and it seemed to him that half the children in Bermondsey were taking part. 'They're usin' a bloody tin can as a ball,' he said, sounding his horn irritably as he braked to a stop outside the entrance to C block.

The end of the small cobbled street was shut off by a high brick wall which hid the Dawson sheet-metal works, and it was beneath the sagging glass-topped wall that a battle royal was taking place between the teams of Milldyke Street and Manning Street. The common target was the space between chalked goalposts which seemed to be manned by at least four goalkeepers. The combatants were mainly older children who were more concerned about street pride in winning the match than the arrival of the van, but there were younger members of both street teams who had been frightened off by the ferocity of the encounter and they now clustered around the vehicle.

'Right, you lot, keep out the way or you'll get 'urt,' the driver warned them gruffly as he stepped down on to the pavement.

Milldyke Buildings took up the whole length of the street on the left-hand side, while opposite, white-painted lettering over the factory doors spelled out, 'Blake's Bacon Curers'. That was it: a street with no corner shops and no familiar terraced houses, just a bleak turning with a reputation for housing the dregs of Bermondsey.

The van driver and his helper swung open the rear doors of the vehicle and lowered the tailboard while Kate hurried back to the first block to find the caretaker. Her knock was answered by a tall lean man in his early fifties who squinted at the slip of paper she handed to him. 'I bin expectin' yer,' he told her, scratching at his wiry grey hair. 'There we are, there's two keys. If yer need any assistance yer can knock on the door, long as it's before six that is. I'm off out ternight.'

The street children watched curiously as the few heavy items of furniture were manhandled up to the first floor. A few of them offered their services with the smaller things only to be growled at by the driver. 'I told yer before ter stand clear,' he scolded them. 'Why don't yer go an' play wiv the rest?'

'They're too rough,' a cheeky-faced lad replied. 'I'd 'elp yer fer a tanner.'

The younger man ruffled the lad's red hair and gave him a sympathetic wink. 'We'd let yer 'elp but we'd get inter trouble,' he told him.

'Who with?'

'With the police.'

'We don't get any coppers in our street,' the lad replied, 'only when they come ter nick somebody.'

'Is that a fact?'

'Yeah, they come an' nicked my mum last week.'

'Did they? What for?'

The driver pushed his way past carrying a cardboard box. 'Don't keep 'im talkin', we've got work ter do,' he growled.

The red-haired lad ignored him. 'Me mum walloped the tallyman 'cos 'e give 'er some cheek about not payin'.'

'Never mind,' the porter told him as he took another carton from the tailboard.

'I could mind yer motor fer a joey,' the lad suggested.

The young man handed him a threepenny piece. ''Ere,

make sure yer do a good job,' he said grinning.

Kate had had a little difficulty in getting the key to turn in the lock, and when she eventually walked in and stood in the small room her heart sank. The flat had been given a lick of paint by the caretaker, who was also the handyman, and Mary's husband John had laid the floor covering yesterday evening, but the place seemed much less welcoming than the terraced house she had been forced to leave.

Milldyke Buildings was made up of five four-storeyed blocks, with wooden stairs leading up to two flats on each of the murky landings. Gaslamps lit the timeworn stairways at night and during the day light struggled to shine through the grimy landing windows. Inside Kate's new home at number three, a long passage led into the end room, which overlooked wasteground and the Jamaica Road beyond. Just inside the room and to the right was a tiny scullery that housed the gas stove, and a brown stone sink set under the window. It also housed the toilet. Back along the passageway doors led off to the bedrooms, the larger one looking down into the street and the smaller with a window on to the rusty iron fire escape that was set in a recess at the back of the buildings.

The removal men brought the last of the boxes into the flat and then assembled the beds before they left, and Kate followed them down into the street to check that everything had been cleared from the van. They had been obliging and she handed the driver two half-crowns as a tip. The men seemed anxious to get away, and as she watched the driver back the van out Kate caught sight of a man turning the corner. He was walking quickly with short light steps and he had a shopping bag slung over his arm. Grey flannels flapped against his legs beneath a light tweed jacket and a Paisley scarf was looped flamboyantly around his neck. As he drew level he gave her a friendly smile. 'Are you the new one at number three?' he asked, resting a hand on his hip.

'Yeah, that's right,' Kate replied, returning his smile.

The man put down his shopping bag. 'Well, I'm very pleased ter meet yer,' he said holding out his slender hand. 'I'm Francis Chandler, but everyone calls me Flossy.'

'Kate Flannagan,' the young woman told him, clasping his hand.

The red-haired lad stood a few yards away eyeing the man and he was rewarded with a cold glare.

'Why don't yer run away an' play wi' the ovvers?' Flossy urged him.

'They're too spiteful,' the lad told him.

Flossy looked peeved. 'The kids round 'ere are a bleedin' nuisance,' he moaned to Kate. ''Alf of 'em don't even live in the turnin'.'

'I do,' the young lad said firmly.

'I know you do,' Flossy replied quickly, turning back to Kate. 'That's Charlie, Amy Almond's boy. You'll be meetin' Amy. She lives next door ter you.'

Kate nodded, amused by the way Flossy sucked in his bottom lip as he picked up his shopping bag. 'Well, it's nice ter meet yer,' she told him.

'Likewise, I'm sure,' he replied. 'I must go, I've got so much ter do. I ain't put a broom on the place terday an' me bleedin' curtains need changin'. Gawd knows what people must fink.'

Kate gave him a sympathetic smile, thinking that the state of his curtains would probably be the last thing to concern the people of these buildings. 'Yeah, I've got a lot ter do before me kids arrive,' she said.

'I live at number one in E block. It's the last block,'

Flossy informed her. 'If yer need anyfing don't be frightened ter knock. Us people in the Buildin's should be only too glad to 'elp each ovver out. Nobody else gives a monkey's cuss. D'yer know I bin waitin' nearly a fortnight ter get the bleedin' washer changed on me tap. Drips all the time, it does. It's fair drivin' me mad.'

'Won't the caretaker fix it for yer?' Kate asked him.

'That lazy sod Ferguson won't do anyfing wivout bein' pestered,' he replied. 'I'm fed up wiv askin' 'im, ter tell yer the trufe. I told 'im only yesterday if it ain't fixed by Monday I'm gonna go down the office an' complain. Somefing's gotta be done.'

Kate felt it was time to make her getaway. 'Well, good luck wiv the tap,' she said, turning on her heel.

'It's nice ter meet a kind face,' Flossy said smiling. 'I 'ope yer settle in all right.'

The evening sun had dropped behind the rooftops and the copper sky was taking on a purple hue as Kate sat by the kitchen window. Beyond the wasteground where an engineering works had once stood she could see a tram trundling by in Jamaica Road and people passing to and fro. She heard the rumble of a train over the Abbey Street arch and she sighed dejectedly. She knew that she had to make the best of it, the way things were, but what about the children? Would they be happy here? Things did not look promising. Mary had been caring for the children and when they arrived that afternoon Jimmy had looked a little downcast. Jenny had been eager to see the flat but when she ran back into the kitchen she remonstrated with her mother. 'Yer've put my bed in your room, Mum,' she moaned.

'I 'ad to, luv. There's no room in the ovver bedroom fer

two beds, an' besides, it's not good fer you an' Jimmy ter share a bedroom.'

'Why not, Mum? We did at Weston Street.'

'That was different. There was more room there. Besides, like I said, you're gettin' a big gel now an' us women need our privacy,' Kate told her, running her hand affectionately down Jenny's long dark hair.

Now, as the night closed in, Kate turned from the window. Jenny had gone off to bed and Jimmy was busy emptying the last of the boxes. 'Leave that now,' she told him. 'It's only ornaments.'

Jimmy sat down heavily at the table. 'This is a right dump, Mum,' he said, tracing a line with his finger on the clean white tablecloth.

Kate felt a heaviness in her heart as she sat down facing him. He was a good lad and a credit to her and she loved him dearly, but there were the odd moments when she worried about him. Jimmy took after his father in looks; his hair was fair and his eyes a pale blue, and he had some of his father inside him too: his moodiness, and the occasional flaring temper. Please God, don't let him end up the same way, she prayed.

'I mean, it wouldn't be so bad if we 'ad a little backyard like at Weston Street,' he went on. 'At least I could keep rabbits or make fings out o' wood.'

Kate smiled indulgently. 'But yer never kept rabbits at Weston Street an' yer never made anyfing.'

'Yeah, but I was finkin' about it,' Jimmy replied.

Kate sighed. 'Look, luv, we won't be 'ere fer ever. Yer'll be fifteen in September an' then it's only two more years at school. Yer'll be sure ter get a good job an' earn lots o' money. Jenny'll be older an' I'll be able ter work full time. We'll rent a better place, a place wiv a nice garden in a street that's got trees, somewhere like Bermondsey Square or one o' those nice streets near the park.'

Jimmy's eyes softened as he caught the note of optimism in his mother's voice. 'I'm gonna get a stall in the market, soon as I'm old enough,' he told her. 'I bin finkin' about it. I could 'ave a stall like Cheap Jack. 'E earns a fortune wiv all that stuff 'e sells.'

'I'd sooner yer got a trade,' Kate said quickly.

Jimmy shook his head. 'I couldn't stick workin' as an apprentice on a few coppers a week. I need to earn a lot o' money if we're ever gonna move out of 'ere.'

'We've only just moved in,' Kate replied with a smile. 'Give us a chance ter get fings sorted out first before yer make yer fortune.'

The young lad chuckled and then his face became serious. 'We'll get ter like it 'ere, Mum, so don't worry,' he told her kindly. 'Jenny likes it already, I can tell.'

Kate got up from her chair and went into the scullery to put the kettle on. 'By the way, I met one of our new neighbours terday,' she called out. 'Francis Chandler, 'e said 'is name was. 'E said everyone calls 'im Flossy.'

Jimmy laughed aloud. 'Everyone knows Flossy Chandler. 'E's a nancy boy.'

Kate was frowning as she walked back into the living room. 'I could see that, but 'ow did you get ter know 'im?'

Jimmy was grinning right across his face. 'Flossy plays the pianer at the pub in Long Lane. Me an' Billy Morris saw 'im go in there one night all dressed up.'

'What d'yer mean, all dressed up?'

'Well, 'e 'ad make-up on. Yer know what I mean,' Jimmy chuckled. ''E 'ad powder on 'is face an' 'is eyelashes was blacked. 'E was blinkin' like this.'

Kate couldn't help laughing as she watched her son's

mimicry. 'Well anyway, 'e lives in the end block an' 'e said I should knock if I needed any 'elp,' she told him. 'I thought it was nice of 'im, so I don't want yer takin' the mickey.'

Jimmy's face took on a thoughtful look as he leaned on the table and rested his chin on his cupped hands. 'We'll be called Milldykers now, Mum,' he remarked. 'Ole Ramsey can't stand Milldykers. 'E's always pickin' on Tommy Brindley, just 'cos 'e lives 'ere.'

Kate sat down at the table. 'Now look, Jimmy,' she began. 'Mr Ramsey 'as bin at your school fer donkey's years an' I don't fink fer one minute that 'e'd pick on a boy just because 'e lives in these buildin's. You just be'ave yerself an' there'll be nuffing ter worry about.'

The young lad was not impressed. The cane had become part of life in his class and rarely a day passed without Ramsey taking it out from the cupboard. 'Well, 'e better not try an' cane me fer bein' a Milldyker,' he said spiritedly.

Kate made the tea and prepared two cheese sandwiches, and when they had finished supper Jimmy went off to bed. Kate pulled the flimsy curtains across to shut out the night and then sat down heavily at the table. She was thirty-seven, with no man in her life and two children to support. She was attractive, and her figure was still trim and shapely, if Mary was to be believed. She would have to keep up her appearance whatever happened. Being a Milldyker was not a very nice name to be tagged with, but at least they had a roof over their heads. She would walk proud, knowing that she had not asked for help from anyone. Everything she had around her had been paid for; and she had her two children as well. The future might look bleak, but life had a way of turning cartwheels, she told herself.

Chapter Three

Sunday morning was bright and clear, with the promise of another pleasantly warm day. Children were already out in the street, and as she cleared away the breakfast things Kate could hear laughter and a scraping noise coming from below the kitchen window. She pulled the curtains aside and looked down into the narrow alley that ran behind the length of the buildings to see the red-headed young lad and another boy manhandling a large wooden crate. As she watched, Kate heard a window fly up and a loud voice call out, 'Charlie, get up 'ere this minute. I want yer ter run an errand.'

'Aw later, Mum. We're gettin' firewood ter chop up,' the lad called back.

'I won't tell yer again. Get up 'ere this instant,' came the irate reply.

Kate wondered what her next-door neighbour was like. Flossy Chandler had told her she was called Amy Almond and the intonation in his voice had left her curious to meet the woman. She had very little time to wait, for a few minutes later there was a knock on the door.

'I'm sorry I didn't call yesterday, luv, but I didn't get 'ome till late,' a woman said breezily. 'I'm Amy Almond an' I live next door. I wondered if yer'd settled in OK.'

Kate smiled at the slightly built woman who was wearing a towel fashioned into a turban around her head. 'Yeah, just about,' she replied. 'I'm Kate Flannagan.'

'I 'eard yer front door go so I knew yer was up an' about,' Amy told her.

'It was the kids. They've gone round ter me sister's,' Kate explained.

Amy's green eyes widened slightly. 'I was wonderin' if yer'd like ter come in fer a cuppa?' she said. 'I've always got the kettle on the go. I couldn't survive wivout me tea. By the way, take no notice o' the way I look. I'm tryin' ter do somefing about me 'air. It's a right soddin' mess at the moment.'

Kate followed her neighbour next door, down the dark passage into the living room and saw Charlie studying a slip of paper. He glanced up and gave her a grin.

'I've wrote it all down,' Amy told him. 'Don't ferget the winkles, an' make sure yer bring 'em straight back. Yer lost 'alf of 'em last Sunday lettin' the bag get all soggy.'

Charlie nodded and stood staring at Kate until his mother gently shoved him towards the door. 'That boy'll be the death o' me,' she sighed loudly. ''E seems ter be in a bloody world of 'is own 'alf the time. Anyway, sit yerself down.'

Kate took a chair and looked about the room as Amy went into the scullery. The wallpaper was grimy and torn here and there, and the table was bare, the planking showing signs of damage. A few pictures hung on the walls and the floor covering was cracked and split in places. The coconut mat beneath her feet was frayed, and the kitchen cabinet looked as though it had seen better days.

'Yer on yer own then, you an' the kids,' Amy called out.

Kate frowned. 'Yeah, me 'usband's away,' she replied.

'Me sister Nell lives in Weston Street. You most likely

know 'er,' Amy went on. 'She told me you was gonna move in 'ere.'

'Nell Carter?'

'Yeah, that's right.'

'So yer know the story then,' Kate said.

Amy came back into the room carrying two mugs of tea. 'Yeah, I 'eard all about yer trouble,' she said lightly as she set the mugs down on the table. 'Will Flannagan's pretty well known round 'ere.'

'Too well known,' Kate said quickly.

'It's 'ard bein' on yer own wiv kids ter fend for,' Amy remarked. 'My ole man's at sea. 'E's in the merchant navy. I get ter see 'im from time ter time, but even when 'e is 'ome 'e's out on the piss most o' the time. I do early mornin' office-cleanin' in Tooley Street. The money comes in 'andy an' Charlie's a good lad. 'E looks after 'imself when I'm not 'ome.'

'I met Francis Chandler yesterday,' Kate told her.

Amy chuckled. 'Flossy's as bent as a nine-bob note but 'e's 'armless enough. Makes a pianer talk, 'e does. 'E plays at the Woolpack in Dock'ead at weekends. I'll take yer down there one night if yer like. I usually go out at the weekend. Sittin' in this bloody 'ole on Saturday nights would drive me right round the twist.'

Kate sipped her tea. 'I've not 'ad much chance ter go out lately an' I wouldn't leave the kids on their own anyway,' she replied firmly.

'Mrs Burton's eldest comes up ter mind our Charlie when I go out,' Amy told her. 'Not that Charlie needs any nursemaidin'. I 'ave ter leave 'im ter fend fer 'imself on week mornin's, but I wouldn't do it at the weekends. It wouldn't be fair.'

'What school does Charlie go to?' Kate asked her.

'Fair Street. What about yours?'

'Webb Street.'

'I wish my Charlie went ter Webb Street,' Amy said sighing. ''E's got in wiv a rough crowd at Fair Street.'

'I fink Webb Street's just as bad,' Kate told her. 'I was talkin' ter my Jimmy last night an' 'e seems ter fink 'is teacher's got a down on the kids from these buildin's.'

Amy smiled cynically. 'Everyone's got a down on us Milldykers, luv. We might just as well walk around wiv a bleedin' placard round our necks.'

'I didn't wanna move in 'ere but I 'ad no choice,' Kate replied.

Amy Almond put her empty mug down on the table and pressed a hand to her head to see if her turban was still in place. 'I've got used to it now, but given the chance I'd be out of 'ere termorrer,' she said positively. 'Believe me, there's some right scruffs live in these buildin's, but there's some real nice people too. You take Mrs Burton. She's one o' the best an' always willin' to 'elp anybody. 'Er eldest, Rene, who looks after my Charlie, is a lovely gel, an' so polite.'

'What's the caretaker like?' Kate asked her.

'Ole Jack Ferguson's a bit of a lazy sod,' Amy told her. ''E'll only do what needs ter be done an' then it takes 'im ages. 'E's not married though I've seen a woman go in there now an' then, but most o' the time 'e's in that place on 'is own. 'E's a miserable git, but ter be fair it can't be much of a job bein' the caretaker of a place like this. 'E's at everybody's beck an' call. I s'pose 'e must get fed up wiv it at times.'

'Flossy Chandler was tellin' me 'e's bin waitin' ages fer a new tap washer,' Kate said grinning. ''E said 'e was gonna go round the office on Monday if it wasn't done by then.'

'Fat lot o' good that'll do 'im,' Amy snorted. 'They're a right dopey lot in that office, an' they're only managin' the buildin's fer the owner. 'E's a bigwig so I 'eard. Anyway the lease is up in five years' time, so I've bin told, an' Gawd knows what'll 'appen then.'

'P'raps the Borough Council'll take 'em over,' Kate suggested.

'I wouldn't old out too much 'ope, luv,' Amy warned her. 'I've bin goin' ter meetin's fer a couple o' years now about gettin' the Council ter condemn the buildin's but they keep comin' up wiv excuses. Nah, I'm afraid it's a case of 'ere we are an' 'ere we stay.'

Kate glanced towards the window and then looked back at Amy with a smile on her face. 'When I woke up this mornin' I promised meself that I was gonna stay cheerful,' she said blithely.

'Well, don't let anyfing I've said upset yer, luv,' Amy replied quickly. 'Take my advice though. Get out once in a while. Yer still got yer looks an' it does a gel good ter see the fellers eyein' 'er up an' down. By the way, I got a feller. It's common knowledge round 'ere anyway. Fred works over the road in the bacon curer's. Lovely man 'e is. 'Is marriage is on the rocks an' if you ever see 'is ole woman yer'll understand why. Bloody dragon she is. She's got no kids an' she treats 'im like a doormat. "Fred do this, Fred do that," an' if 'e's not jumpin' ter do 'er biddin' she goes orf alarmin'. Me an' Fred go out now an' then, when 'e can make some excuse ter get away from 'er, which ain't very often, I might add. 'E stayed all night once. Told 'er 'e got caught up in the fog. 'E lives over in Shoreditch, yer see. I told my Charlie that Fred was 'is uncle but I dunno if 'e believed me. Still, yer do what yer gotta do. After all life can be a bitch at times.'

Kate was smiling widely at the varying expressions on Amy's face. The woman was talking to her as though they were old friends and it cheered her. 'What about yer 'usband?' she asked.

Amy waved her concern away with a sweep of her hand. 'Like I said, Bert's 'alf pissed most o' the time when 'e's between ships, an' I've warned Charlie not ter dare mention anyfing about Uncle Fred. I told 'im that 'is dad would belt me fer allowin' anyone in, uncle or not, while 'e wasn't 'ere. Nah, Bert won't find out.'

At that moment Charlie came into the flat carrying a brown paper bag. 'I told the lady on the stall ter put two bags round the winkles,' he said proudly.

'Did yer get the ovver fings?' Amy asked him.

'Yeah, but Mrs Bromfield said the bill's mountin' up an' yer'd better call in ter settle up next week,' he said in a serious voice.

Amy started to unpack the few groceries. 'Where's me mixed spice?' she asked the lad.

'Mrs Blake said she was out o' spice,' Charlie replied casually.

'Well then, don't yer go gettin' on at me about the bread puddin',' Amy told him firmly. 'I can't make it wivout the mixed spice.'

'I got some yer can 'ave,' Kate told her, feeling it was time she left.

'That's kind of yer, luv. Charlie loves 'is bread puddin'. I usually give 'im a big chunk ter take ter school. It fills 'im up. They want some fillin' up these kids of ours, don't they?'

Kate found the spice and handed it over at the door, not wanting to get involved in another long chat that day. Amy seemed to be a very easy person to get on with and it was gratifying to know there was a friendly neighbour next door, but enough was enough and there would no doubt be plenty of other occasions to learn more about the ebullient woman.

Len Copeland had been in his late twenties when the war broke out and he immediately volunteered to serve his country. In 1940 he found himself in France as a member of the British Expeditionary Force, serving as a gunner in the Royal Artillery. Being a rather enterprising young man, he found a way of subsidising his scanty army pay by going into the wine business. He discovered quite early on that by adding a touch of methylated spirit to a bottle of red wine the troubles of the world could easily be forgotten, for a few hours at least. One day Len dubiously acquired a whole barrel of red wine into which he poured two pints of meths, and he was able to sell the fortified claret to his comrades as '1920 Reserve'. One glass was tasty and two heady, but three glasses of the stuff was electrifying, and many a lonely, bored and homesick soldier forgot the misery and worries of life at the front by drowning three glasses or more of the gutrot in one sitting.

Gunner Copeland's little enterprise was wound up all too soon when the German army made their push through Belgium and into France. The remnants of the British Army were trapped at Dunkirk and it was there that Len's army days came to an abrupt end. He was shipped back home with a bullet still lodged in his thigh and it was only a surgeon's skill that saved the leg.

Len Copeland had done his bit for king and country and now decided it was time to do a bit for himself. There were shortages of all kinds and he soon found ways of making life a little more comfortable for many people by 'supplementation'. Len could lay his hands on most things and soon earned the name of Spiv Copeland. He wore smart suits, spectacular kipper ties and real leather shoes, grew a moustache to rival Errol Flynn's and drove around in a verdant-green 1935 Wolseley saloon.

On Sunday morning Spiv Copeland pulled up in Milldyke Street and was immediately surrounded by children. Unperturbed he climbed from his saloon and spotted Charlie Almond. 'The usual deal, Chas,' he said with a grin, 'an' don't let anyone stand on the runnin' board. It's a bit rickety.'

Charlie quickly pocketed the shilling piece and leaned against the front mudguard. 'Are yer gonna be long, Spiv?' he asked.

''Alf an hour at the most,' Copeland told him, aware that after an hour Charlie would charge two shillings. 'Is yer mum in?'

Charlie nodded and Spiv reached into the back of the car and took out a small brown-paper parcel from the rear seat. Amy would be pleased, he thought as he hurried into C block and climbed the creaking wooden stairs two at a time.

Kate had decided that the front bedroom windows were in need of a good clean and she set about the chore with a vengeance. It seemed that there were years of grime on the large panes of glass and it took her two attempts with soapy water and a wash leather to get them up to her standard. It was as she was polishing the last of the windows that she saw the car pull up. Cars in Bermondsey backstreets were not a common sight and she was intrigued to see who it belonged to. The man looked handsome and he was smartly dressed, in a loud sort of way, she thought. The nonchalant roll of his shoulders and his general manner held her attention and she watched him talking to Charlie Almond. The man then came into the block and she heard his hurried footsteps on the stairs. His knock next door was answered with a loud laugh and Kate heard the door shut with a bang.

The windows finished, Kate decided to start peeling the potatoes for lunch, and as she worked at the scullery sink she could hear occasional laughter coming from next door. Things seemed to go quiet suddenly and after a while she heard Amy's front door open and close, followed by the heavy tread on the stairs. Kate's curiosity had been aroused and she hurried into the front bedroom and furtively peered down into the street. The man was standing by his smart car talking to Charlie, and she saw him ruffle the lad's hair before climbing in behind the wheel. The vehicle swung away from the kerb and stopped with its front wheel up on the pavement opposite and then careered back and drove forward again, this time clipping the pavement with its nearside wheel. It stopped sharply and Kate saw the man lean out and blow a kiss upwards before speeding off. Looking down from the first floor the young woman could have been forgiven for thinking the kiss was meant for her, but she knew better. Amy would be hanging out the window taking her plaudit, no doubt, and Kate experienced a tinge of envy. Her next-door neighbour was full of surprises, it seemed.

Chapter Four

Kate hurried from the Buildings on Monday morning, hoping that she had allowed herself enough time to get to work by nine o'clock. The management of Pearson's vinegar factory in Long Lane were sticklers for punctuality, and after being allowed time off to organise her move Kate felt that it was important she wasn't late clocking in. Bob Marsh the foreman would be hovering by the card rack and at precisely seven minutes past nine he would remove all the unstamped time cards and take them to his office. All latecomers would then be compelled to report to him and make their excuses. If Marsh was in a good mood he would sign the card and permit the agitated worker to begin the day without stoppage. If, however, he was suffering from one of his vinegar moods, as the workers described them, he would dip his pen into the red ink and insert the appropriate time to the nearest quarter of an hour. Being seven minutes late at Pearson's meant that a quarter of an hour's wages were lost.

Besides wanting to be fair to the management, Kate was in no mood to lose any wages. Money was already tight enough and the three pounds seven shillings and sixpence she earned for a nine till three week barely paid the bills. However hard it was to manage, though, she was happy in the knowledge that at least it was money that was earned and not begged from the Public Assistance.

As she crossed Jamaica Road and walked quickly along Abbey Street, Kate thought about her two children. Jimmy could be trusted with the responsibility of locking up and escorting Jenny to school, as well as bringing her home now that the journey was longer. She had thought about changing schools, but there had been enough disruption in her children's lives without adding to it.

Bob Marsh was standing in his usual spot as the young woman entered the factory and she could see that he was obviously in one of his vinegar moods. His piggy eyes darted towards the clock and he ran a podgy hand over his shiny bald head. It was two minutes past the hour and Kate imagined that he was willing the minutes to tick away faster. In exactly five minutes' time he would descend on the card rack like a vulture.

'Did yer get moved all right then?' the foreman asked her flatly as she inserted her card into the machine.

Kate nodded in reply. He obviously wasn't interested in her domestic affairs; it was merely his way of reminding her how grateful she should be that Pearson's had been good enough to allow her the time off. The fact that she had not been paid for the day off would not count in Bob Marsh's reckoning. He had been with Pearson's since leaving school and it seemed to be his whole life: he found it hard to comprehend that others did not feel the same.

'Watcher, Kate,' Daisy Wells said cheerfully as the young woman walked into the changing room. 'Did yer get every-fing sorted out?'

'Yeah, we're all settled in,' Kate replied without enthu-siasm.

Daisy smiled sympathetically. She was a chubby woman

in her forties with a happy-go-lucky disposition, and one of the reasons Kate survived the mundane grind of working on the bottling machine was her effervescent company. Daisy worked alongside her and they had become good friends.

'My bloody corns are playin' me up,' Daisy remarked as she struggled into her clogs. 'These poxy fings don't 'elp matters none.'

Kate smiled as she reached into her locker and took out her heavy clogs and green overall. 'Ole Marsh is in one of 'is moods,' she remarked. 'I fink 'e was expectin' me ter fank 'im personally fer givin' me the time off.'

'Poxy ole git,' Daisy growled. 'Can you imagine what it must be like fer 'is ole woman? I bet 'e rabbits off nonstop round the dinner table about who was late that mornin' an' who's in the puddin' club. I wouldn't mind bettin' that 'e's goin' on about Pearson's when 'e's actually doin' it – if 'e ever does. Ter be honest I don't fink 'e's got a shag left in 'im.'

Kate tutted in mock horror as she slipped into the clogs. 'Daisy, yer gettin' worse,' she said.

The chubby woman stood up and winced. 'I'll 'ave ter get some corn plasters. I'm in agony.'

Kate put on her overall and took Daisy by the arm. 'C'mon, luv, or we'll be late,' she said quickly.

Pearson's brewed their own vinegar in large vats situated in a yard at the back of the factory, and pipework carried the malted vinegar to the machines. The working area was cold in winter and always wet underfoot. The machine operators had to keep the slotted metal belts supplied with sterilised bottles, which were filled and capped automatically. Further along the belt women were employed in fitting plastic cap covers that shrank on drying and then the finished article was packed in cardboard containers and stacked ready for removal to the distribution area. The whole process was carried out in a noisy atmosphere and conversation was very difficult. Daisy managed it however, with animated expressions and gestures, and her eyes spoke volumes.

The machinery started up at exactly ten minutes past nine, and by the time the two friends had donned their rubber aprons that were kept by the machines the din had grown up around them. Beside them a belt ran at right angles to the bottling machine and soon it was clogged with rattling bottles from the steriliser. A deft stacking movement was required to keep the machine supplied and the two women worked in unison. They would often glance at each other as they slipped the bottles into the slotted belt and Daisy would be sure to make some remark.

''Ow's the divorce comin'?' Daisy shouted above the clamour with exaggerated lip movements.

'The papers'll be ready fer signin' soon,' Kate shouted back, though Daisy had developed into a very good lip-reader.

'That's good. Yer'll be fancy free then.'

Kate nodded. 'Well, free at least.'

'Yer wanna get yerself a nice feller,' Daisy went on. 'Someone wiv lots o' dosh. Besides, if yer go too long wivout it yer'll dry up like a prune.'

'I ain't lookin' ter get married again,' Kate told her.

'Who's talkin' about marriage?' Daisy shouted.

The noise increased as the machinery began to reach maximum speed and for a few minutes even Daisy found it impossible to communicate. The women worked rhythmically, turning from the hip to pick up the bottles; a repetitive movement only relieved when there was a jam-up on the belt or when the filling machine acted up. Both were left to their own thoughts and secret anxieties, and Kate remembered when her sister Mary had got on to her about being so independent. She had made it clear that in her opinion Kate was being silly in not going to the Public Assistance for help: with a husband in prison and two children to care for she should qualify. Kate knew though that it was something she could not face. There would be a means test and endless questions. Could she not get full-time work? Were there any valuables to sell and had she any savings put away? She had thought about going full time now that the children were older, and it would be nice to get away from the wet, noisy vinegar factory with its constant acidic smell that stung her eyes and made her feel nauseous. Daisy had told her early on that she would soon get used to it, but she never had.

The morning was passing very slowly and monotonously, but at eleven thirty a pipe sprang a leak. Bob Marsh was galvanised into action and the women smiled slyly at his animated attempts to stave off disaster as Pearson's prime malt vinegar flowed along the stone floor and down into the drains. As he hurried by in a fluster Daisy jerked her thumb towards him.

'Ter see that silly ole bastard performin' yer'd fink it was 'is money goin' down the drain,' she growled.

The foreman was now in a heated discussion with the engineer, who looked as though he would have loved to use the monkey wrench he was holding on Bob Marsh's polished head.

'Just look at the silly ole sod,' Daisy was going on. 'Don't it make yer sick.'

Kate rested against the bottle belt and folded her arms over her rubber apron. 'I bin finkin' about goin' full time,' she remarked.

Daisy looked surprised. 'What, 'ere?'

'Nah, I'd try an' get in Peek's, or maybe Crosse an' Blackwell's,' Kate replied. 'I gotta do somefing. The kids are growin' out o' their clothes an' Jimmy's only shoes are right down at 'eel.'

Daisy knew of her friend's feelings about seeking help from the Assistance Board and she refrained from mentioning it. 'Yer could 'ave a word wiv ole Marsh. There might be somefing doin' 'ere,' she suggested.

Kate shook her head. 'I did mention it to 'im last week an' all 'e said was that 'e might be able ter fit me in wiv a double shift when there was somebody off sick,' she replied with a shrug of her shoulders.

'That wouldn't be no good to yer,' Daisy said quickly. 'The evenin' shift don't start till six o'clock, time the pipes are cleaned out an' the machinery oiled up. They don't get away till ten.'

'I told 'im I couldn't manage it,' Kate said. 'I couldn't leave the kids on their own that long.'

Bob Marsh came hurrying back along the gangway looking very agitated. 'Get ready ter start in five minutes,' he told them.

'Did yer lose much?' Daisy asked him, hoping to agitate him still further.

'Over fifty gallons must 'ave gone down the drain, maybe even more,' he fretted. 'Gawd knows what Mr Farrow's gonna say when 'e finds out.'

'Oh dear,' Daisy said with feigned concern, giving Kate a secret wink. 'That's a lot o' money.'

'It is, an' there was no excuse fer it,' Marsh said with a look of disgust on his podgy face. 'It's just bad maintenance. I could do the job better meself.'

'I bet you could,' Daisy said with a respectful expression

on her face. 'It's what I've always said. There's no excuse fer bad workmanship. Us women did maintenance work durin' the war an' we kept fings movin'.'

The foreman hurried off without comment. It was bad enough having an incompetent engineer on the payroll without resorting to women. Whatever next? he thought with a shudder.

The part-time workers at Pearson's got a three-quarter of an hour break which they took in a room furnished with long tables and benches. The women sat together, eating their own sandwiches and drinking insipid tea from thick mugs, compliments of the firm. They were much the same, women with young children who were glad of the suitable hours but who had to suffer the unfavourable working conditions with none of the perks enjoyed by the full-time workers, mainly packers and labellers. There was no time to visit the firm's canteen during their breaks and they had no representation. Disputes were usually resolved by the aggrieved worker leaving the company, and on the whole the part-timers suffered in silence, supervised and watched over by the hateful Bob Marsh.

Daisy unwrapped her sandwiches and offered one to Kate. 'It's brawn,' she said.

Kate shook her head. 'No fanks, Dais, I got cheese,' she replied.

'I thought yer said yer like brawn?'

'Yeah, I do but . . .'

'But yer too stuck up ter take one.'

'No, I'm not.'

'Yes, you are. Go on – take one, I got plenty,' Daisy insisted with a disarming smile.

Kate sighed and reluctantly took a thick crusty sandwich. 'I was gonna get some brawn but there was a bit o' cheese left in the cupboard so I thought I'd better use it up,' she said.

Daisy knew very well that her friend only ever brought cheese sandwiches to work and was aware of the reason. Cheese went further than brawn and it lasted longer. 'Nice, ain't it?' she said grinning.

Kate nodded and tried to smile with her mouth full. The tea lady stood at the counter hands on hips. 'Any more tea wanted before I leave?' she called out.

A few women went up with their empty mugs and Daisy pulled a face. 'Some o' them silly mares would drink anyfing. One cup o' this bloody splosh is enough fer me,' she moaned. 'I fink the ole cow's tryin' ter poison us.'

Kate smiled as she rolled up her food wrapping. 'I've met a couple o' me new neighbours,' she remarked, and went on to tell Daisy about Flossy Chandler and the bubbling Amy Almond. Her friend listened with amusement.

'You should take this Amy up on 'er offer of a night out,' Daisy suggested. 'Yer might get lucky.'

Kate clasped her hands together on the table and for a few seconds she stared down at her thumbnails. 'I 'ad ter do it, Dais,' she said, looking up into her friend's eyes. 'I 'ad ter tell 'im it was over.'

'Well, there was nuffing else yer could do, was there?' Daisy replied. ''E was playin' around wiv ovver women, 'ardly ever seein' the kids. What sort of a marriage is that? An' now 'e's bin banged away fer seven years. What yer s'posed ter do, keep the bed warm for 'im?'

'I've no doubt there'll be those that fink I should 'ave waited fer 'im, give 'im anuvver chance,' Kate said.

'Well, sod 'em. You gotta live wiv it, not them,' Daisy stressed. 'Anyway 'e wanted a divorce as well. What yer worryin' about it for?'

'I'm not worried,' Kate hastened to assure her. 'It's just – I dunno, I sometimes wonder if I've done right by the kids. 'E did come ter see 'em sometimes. Not very often, but 'e did come.'

'Well, 'e can 'ardly come ter see 'em now, can 'e?' Daisy reminded her. 'But when 'e gets out 'e can still see 'em. Besides, yer might meet a nice young man who'll be like a farver ter the kids. Look at my Alec. Four kids 'e took on when that no-good bleeder o' mine pissed orf. Those little sods adore 'im. They call 'im Dad, an' I gotta tell yer it really tickles 'im. Nah, don't you worry. The right feller's gonna come along one day an' yer'll be glad yer free, mark my words.'

Bob Marsh was making his usual noises and the women hurried back to their machines. Daisy gave him a wicked glance as she passed by and then looked at Kate, her large blue eyes flashing. 'The day I leave this job I'm gonna take great delight in givin' 'im a good old-fashioned ear'ole bashin',' she said, 'an' if 'e gets saucy I'll kick 'im right up the cods.'

The June afternoon was pleasantly warm as Kate hurried home, her mind centred on what still had to be done in the flat. It wouldn't look so bad once it was all sorted out, she thought without any real conviction.

Chapter Five

The front bedroom smelled musty and Kate lifted the bottom window to let in what little air there was. She leaned on the sill and glanced down into the street below to see a man locking up the bacon curer's. Amy Almond was talking to him and she guessed that the man was Fred. A little way along the pavement she saw Jenny turning a skipping-rope with another girl, and nearby Jimmy sat at the kerbside talking to Amy's son Charlie. At least they had made friends, she thought. Children seemed to have the ability to adapt more easily than adults. Jenny was giggling as a girl stepped into the twisting rope and got tangled up, and Jimmy appeared to be holding court with Charlie and some more boys who had ambled up.

Amy was hurrying back across the road, and when she looked up and saw Kate at the window she made a funny gesture before entering the block. Kate guessed that her neighbour wanted to speak to her so she pulled down the sash and went to her front door, opening it just as Amy reached the landing.

'Did yer see me talkin' ter that feller?' Amy asked breathlessly. 'That was Fred.'

'I wasn't nosin',' Kate was at pains to assure her. 'I was seein' if the children were all right.'

'Course yer wasn't,' Amy said grinning. 'Got a minute? I got somefing for yer.'

Kate was intrigued as her neighbour let herself into her flat, emerging a few seconds later carrying a small cardboard box.

'I wanna show yer these,' she said mysteriously.

Kate led the way along the passage to her living room and Amy sat down at the table. 'Let's 'ave a look at yer legs,' she said.

'Do what?' Kate replied.

'You 'eard me, turn round.'

Kate turned with a puzzled frown and looked over her shoulder to see Amy nodding appreciatively.

'Nice calves. They'll look a treat on you.'

Kate sat down and watched her tear open the box. 'What yer got there?' she asked her.

Amy took out a handful of flat packets and threw them down on the table. 'Take yer pick. I fink yer'll find your size there,' she said grinning.

Kate saw that they were seamless silk stockings and shook her head. 'I couldn't afford ter buy them,' she said quickly.

'Who's askin' yer ter buy 'em?' Amy replied. 'I want yer ter pick a pair out. It's a welcomin' gift.'

'I couldn't,' Kate said. 'They're too expensive.'

'Yer mean too expensive ter wear, or too expensive ter give away?' Amy queried with raised eyebrows.

'Ter give away.'

'Cobblers. I got loads o' these ter knock out. I won't miss one pair,' Amy assured her. 'Now do as yer told an' pick a pair out.'

Kate selected a pair and looked up to see Amy still grinning, showing her prominent white teeth. 'These are really lovely. Fanks very much,' she said smiling back. 'I'll be scared ter wear 'em in case they get laddered.'

'There's more where they come from,' Amy said with a sweep of her hand. 'Spiv Copeland brought 'em yesterday. 'E gets 'old of all sorts o' fings. I usually knock stuff out fer 'im an' earn a few bob meself.'

Kate stood up and put the stockings into the sideboard drawer. 'Would you like a cuppa?' she asked. 'It's the least I can do. I'm really grateful.'

'I thought yer'd never ask,' Amy said. ''Ere, d'yer like me 'air?'

Kate nodded. 'Yeah, it looks very nice,' she told her, although she really thought it looked a mess. Amy had obviously used a chestnut dye on her natural ginger hair and it had taken very patchily. Her thick locks had been cut short and set around her ears with a front fringe partially covering her forehead.

'I did it meself, cut an' perm. Not bad, eh?' Amy said, touching it gently. 'I could do yours if yer like.'

Kate was horrified. 'Me sister usually does mine,' she said quickly as she went into the scullery.

'Well, if yer ever get stuck yer know where ter come,' Amy told her as she put the packets of stockings back into the box.

The warm evening sky was a blaze of colour at sunset, and in the kitchen at number three C block, Milldyke Buildings, Amy was in full flow as she sipped her tea. 'There's Mrs Burton below you at number one an' next door to 'er at number two is Albert an' Ada Thomas. They've lived 'ere years. They're both gettin' on now an' they don't go out much. Now on the landin' above us is the Dennises. Jack Dennis works on the docks an' Muriel works at the Council offices. They've got two married daughters. They're both a bit stuck up, if you was to ask me.'

Kate sipped her tea, trying desperately to keep up with all the names Amy was throwing at her. 'Who's stuck up, them or their daughters?' she asked.

'The daughters,' Amy told her. 'One lives in Sidcup an' the ovver at Greenwich. I s'pose they fink they're a bit above us Bermon'sey people. Mind you, Jack an' Muriel are a real nice couple. Old Barney Schofield lives next door ter them. I'll tell yer about 'im later. Now on the top floor there's the Sandfords. They're above you. Joe Sandford does night work at the sausage factory an' Stella works at the pie shop in Tower Bridge Road. She's a big blonde gel. They ain't bin married long an' they ain't got no kids yet. Next to the Sandfords is Ernie Walker. 'E's a funny ole bloke who's always sittin' by the winder. I fink 'e must know just about everyfing that goes on in this street. As a matter o' fact 'e's bin on 'is own since before the war. 'E must be knockin' on seventy-five if 'e's a day. Mind you though, 'e seems ter manage them stairs OK, considerin' 'is age.'

Kate felt that she had been given about as much information on the neighbours as she could absorb at one time and she attempted to change the conversation. 'I noticed a nice car in the turnin' yesterday. Did that belong ter the feller yer mentioned?' she asked.

'Yeah, that was Spiv Copeland's,' Amy replied. 'Spiv's real name is Len, but everyone calls 'im Spiv. 'E took me fer a ride in that car of 'is once. Nuffing 'ookey you understand. Me an' Spiv do business tergevver. 'Ere, I could introduce yer to 'im if yer like. 'E's loaded.'

Kate shook her head quickly. 'No offence meant, Amy, but I'm not ready fer a new feller just yet,' she told her.

'I understand, luv,' Amy replied. 'Yer'll know when yer ready. In the meantime you just get Will Flannagan right out o' yer system. It don't pay ter dwell on the past, it's over an' done wiv. Anyway that's enough preachin' from me. I bet yer fink I'm an interferin' ole cow, but us women 'ave got ter stick tergevver. After all, it's all right fer the blokes. They can go out an' get pissed an' chat the gels up whenever the mood takes 'em. We can't, or we'll get called all the dirty whores goin'. That's 'ow they labelled ole Annie Griffiths. That poor cow didn't deserve what 'appened to 'er.'

'Who's Annie Griffiths?' Kate asked.

'Was,' Amy corrected her. 'She used ter live in the far-end block, block E. Annie liked a drink. She used ter stagger 'ome well pissed every Saturday an' Sunday night. She lived on 'er own. Couldn't 'ave bin no more than fifty, though she looked older. I s'pose it was the drink that done it. She always 'ad that red bloated look about 'er. They said she was always on the muvver's ruin. Drunk it like water. Bloody shame it was.'

'What 'appened?' Kate asked impatiently.

'She was strangled one night comin' 'ome from the Woolpack,' Amy said plainly. 'It 'appened just round the corner. They found 'er on the edge o' that bombsite by Jamaica Road. Can't be much more than six months ago when it 'appened. It was just before ole Ferguson took over as caretaker an' 'e's bin 'ere six months, accordin' ter Mrs Burton. The police kept comin' back ter talk ter the ovver caretaker. In fact people were startin' ter wonder; I fink that's why ole Dan Adams left the job. People can be so wicked at times. Poor ole Dan wouldn't 'urt a fly. Very obligin' too, not like that lazy git Ferguson.'

'I remember readin' about it now,' Kate told her. 'Wasn't

she strangled wiv a bootlace?'

Amy nodded. 'They never got the bloke who done it,' she went on. 'It makes yer go cold when yer fink about it. 'E could still be walkin' around out there. They say it must 'ave bin someone who knew 'er. Annie Griffiths never got in company; she wasn't one ter stand chattin'. Mind yer, she was well known in the Woolpack. It could 'ave bin one o' the regulars who strangled 'er, but I can't see it. I remember it said in the papers that Annie was well liked at the pub. Everyone there was shocked.'

'I s'pose it could 'ave bin one o' those religious maniacs,' Kate suggested.

Amy shrugged her shoulders. 'Yeah, it might well 'ave bin,' she replied. 'Annie could let rip at times. She used ter swear like a docker, 'specially when she was pissed.'

Kate reached for the empty teacups. 'Would yer like anuvver?' she asked.

Amy shook her head and then stood up. 'I'd better get goin', luv,' she said. 'Spiv's bringin' me round some jumpers later an' I wanna tidy the place up a bit before 'e arrives. At the moment it looks like a bloody shit tip.'

'Well, fanks very much fer the stockin's,' Kate said smiling.

'Don't mention it,' Amy told her.

As soon as she had left Kate took the stockings out of the drawer and admired the softness and the sheer quality as she gently pressed them between her thumb and forefinger. It was a very long time since she had been given anything so nice, she thought.

Jimmy Flannagan had been taken on a tour of the immediate area by Charlie Almond and now they were back in the street.

'I'll 'ave ter go in soon,' Jimmy told him.

'Yeah, me too,' Charlie sighed.

Jimmy sat down at the kerbside and retied his shoelace. 'Our school stinks,' he said, suddenly remembering the change-of-address letter he had handed in that morning.

'Yeah, so does mine,' Charlie sneered. 'Some o' the kids call me a Milldyker. My muvver said these buildin's 'ave got a bad name an' a lot o' people don't like us just 'cos we live 'ere.'

'Yeah, it's the same at Webb Street,' Jimmy replied. 'Our teacher's a nasty ole git an' 'e's always canin' us. I'm gonna get caned fer sure as soon as ole Ramsey finds out I'm a Milldyker.'

''E can't cane yer just 'cos yer live 'ere,' Charlie said incredulously. 'That's not right.'

'Nah, but 'e'll find some ovver excuse ter give us the cane,' Jimmy told him. 'I tell yer what though. If I keep gettin' whacked I'm gonna 'op the wag.'

'They'll send the school-board man round if yer do.'

'They won't find me 'cos I'll be fousands o' miles away.'

'Where would yer go?'

'India, or maybe China.'

'Cor.'

'Yeah, I'd get on board one o' those ships in the docks an' 'ide away till it sails, an' then I'd go an' see the captain. They let yer work till yer get ter the ovver end.'

'I wouldn't fancy goin' on one o' them Chinkie ships,' Charlie said fearfully. 'They might cut yer froat an' toss yer overboard. No one'd ever know about it an' yer muvver'd be lookin' everywhere for yer.'

'I might even go up ter Scotland,' Jimmy said as he picked away at the worn sole of his shoe.

'That's nearly as far as China.'

'Charlie!' a loud voice called out.

'It's me mum. I gotta go in,' the young lad said.

'Yeah, me too,' Jimmy told him.

They climbed the stairs to the first landing and Charlie turned to his friend. 'We could go ter China tergevver,' he suggested. 'They wouldn't dare kill both of us.'

'I shouldn't fink so,' Jimmy agreed. 'See yer termorrer evenin', Charlie.'

'See yer, Jimmy.'

Jenny was already tucked up in bed and as Jimmy sipped his cocoa and munched on a Marie biscuit his mind was still dwelling on faraway places. 'Mum, 'ow far's China?' he asked her.

'It's in the Far East,' Kate told him, frowning.

'Is it a fousand miles away?'

'Much more. Why d'you ask?'

'Me an' Charlie might go there.'

'You're too young ter go that far. Wait till yer firteen,' Kate said with affection as she ruffled his fair hair.

Less than a mile away in Abbey Street Kate's sister Mary Woodley sat darning a sock. Her husband John sat facing her, his head drooping.

'Why don't yer turn in,' Mary suggested.

John sat upright in his comfortable armchair and rubbed a large hand over his face. 'Yeah, I fink I will,' he yawned. 'It's bin a busy day.'

Mary put down the darning and made to get out of her chair but John leaned forward and put his hand on her knee. 'Stay there an' I'll make the tea,' he told her.

The two sat sipping the hot sweet tea and Mary looked up at him. 'I'm worried about our Kate,' she said. 'I told 'er she could 'ave Mum's ring ter pawn when she came round on Friday but she wouldn't take it.'

'I can understand that,' John replied. 'She'd never be able ter redeem it. Those pawnbrokers sell unredeemed stuff after a while.'

'There was no ovver way I could 'elp 'er, luv, an' she does need 'elp.'

'What about that money in the jug? We won't be needin' it fer a while,' John reminded her.

'That's our 'oliday money. I couldn't offer 'er that, it wouldn't be fair on you after the way yer've scrimped an' scraped ter save it,' Mary told him.

'I can make it up next month when the fruit ships start comin' in,' John replied. 'We always do well wiv the bonuses.'

Mary smiled warmly. 'It's a nice gesture, luv, but you know our Kate. She won't take money from anyone an' she'd know where it came from.'

John shrugged his shoulders. 'Whatever made 'er get 'iked up wiv that toe-rag in the first place?' he growled. 'We all knew what 'e was like. Why couldn't she see frew 'im? All the signs were there.'

Mary gave a deep sigh and slowly shook her head. 'She was in love wiv 'im, John, it was as simple as that,' she said quietly. 'She was young an' impressionable, an' Will was always flashin' 'is money about. 'E showed 'er a good time at the beginnin' an' it was all so excitin'. She wouldn't 'ave a word said against 'im, even when she was beginnin' ter discover what 'e was really like. Put it down ter pride. Yer know our Kate well enough.'

John nodded as he rested his hand on Mary's shoulder. 'I'd better make us anuvver cuppa,' he said.

Chapter Six

As the balmy June days drifted by, Kate Flannagan was beginning to feel more relaxed in her new surroundings. She was becoming acquainted with some of the neighbours and found Amy Almond to be a mine of information. The children too seemed to have settled in quite nicely and had made friends, and Jimmy in particular appeared to be less worried about the stigma of being called a Milldyker. That was because he had not yet been caned again, though it crossed Jimmy's mind on a few occasions that maybe his teacher had not yet discovered there were now two Milldykers in the class. However, he managed to stay out of trouble by working extra hard to improve his class position.

The main worry Kate had was that her son had become very chummy with Charlie Almond, who seemed to be very streetwise. From what Jimmy had told her it seemed that Charlie was a leader and the rest of the Milldyke lads looked up to him. That in itself was no bad thing, Kate realised, but Amy Almond had let it drop that her son had already had a few brushes with the police. It was nothing serious, Amy had been at pains to point out, but nevertheless Kate was concerned.

On a bright Saturday morning a very serious conversation was going on at the kerbside in Milldyke Street, and had Kate been privy to the plot she would have been truly concerned.

'It's dead easy ter get in there,' Charlie was saying. 'We can shin up the drainpipe at the side an' nobody'll see us from the Buildin's 'cos the fanlight's on the ovver side o' the slopin' roof. They keep the fanlight open all the time 'cos o' lettin' the smoke out, so it'll be a cinch ter get in.'

''Ow d'yer know they leave the fanlight open?' Jimmy asked him.

Charlie glanced briefly up at the Buildings as though expecting his mother to be listening from her window. 'There's a bloke who works there called Fred Logan,' he told him. ''E's pretty friendly wiv me muvver an' I 'eard 'im tellin' 'er one night. Yer see what 'appens is, they 'ang the greenbacks up ter be smoked an' they're left like it all night.'

'What's greenbacks?' Jimmy asked.

'They're sides o' bacon what gets delivered from the docks,' Charlie went on. 'You've seen 'em. Those slimy 'alves o' pigs what the men carry in wiv sacks wrapped round 'em. Anyway they 'ang 'em up on 'ooks over these red-'ot coals an' then they sprinkle oak chippin's over the coal an' all the smoke cooks the bacon.'

Jimmy was very impressed with his friend's knowledge of the bacon-curing business and was eager to learn more. 'What 'appens next?' he asked.

'Well, when they're smoked the sides o' bacon go all brown an' stiff, then they get delivered ter the shops,' Charlie explained.

Jimmy stared down into the dry drain grating for a few moments then he looked up at his friend. 'I ain't scared o' climbin' in the factory,' he said, 'but what about after we nick the side o' bacon? Won't they miss it?'

'Nah, they've got loads o' bacon 'angin' up, an' there's tons more layin' around,' Charlie told him. 'I know 'cos I've bin in there wiv Fred loads o' times.'

'What do we do wiv the bacon when we nick it?'

'We'll sell it ter Spiv Copeland.'

'Would 'e buy it?'

'Yeah, Spiv buys anyfing.'

'Where do we 'ide it till we sell it?'

'On the roof.'

Jimmy seemed satisfied with the answers and he nodded. 'When do we do it?' he asked.

'Termorrer mornin',' Charlie said positively, then he smiled. 'C'mon, we gotta get ourselves a rope.'

Jimmy got up from the kerbside and followed Charlie along the turning. 'Where we goin'?' he asked quickly.

'Round the washin'-lines.'

'Somebody might see us.'

'Nah, they won't.'

At the end of the buildings a narrow alleyway led along to the communal dustbins and beyond them a doorway led into a gravel area dotted with iron posts. Here and there washing-lines were stretched between them and Charlie selected one. 'This looks the best o' the lot,' he remarked. 'We'll need one that won't snap.'

Jimmy looked up anxiously at the windows as Charlie shinned up a post to remove the rope and he winced as one of the windows flew up.

'Oi you! What yer doin'?'

'Just playin', missus,' Charlie called back as he slid down to the ground.

'Well, piss orf an' play somewhere else,' the irate woman shouted down at him.

The two lads ambled off with Charlie mumbling under

his breath, and as they walked out of the alleyway they almost collided with Flossy Chandler who was carrying an overflowing dustbin.

'What you up to, Charlie Almond?' he asked quickly. 'I 'ope you ain't bin playin' round them bins. You'll catch scarlet fever playin' on that rubbish.'

'We wouldn't play round the dustbins,' Charlie told him indignantly. 'We ain't that stupid.'

Flossy had put the heavy bin down to massage his fingers and he gave Charlie a hurt look. 'Don't you be so saucy,' he said quickly. 'Any more of it an' I'll go an' see yer muvver.'

'She ain't in.'

'Out wiv the boyfriend is she?'

'I dunno.'

'Well, just you mind yer manners,' Flossy told him as he picked up the dustbin.

'Stupid ole poof,' Charlie growled as Flossy hurried into the alley.

Jimmy took a kick at a flattened tin can and sent it spinning along the street. ''Ere, I know where we can get a rope,' he said suddenly. 'They've got the road up down Shad Thames. I saw it yesterday. There's a rope stretched round this big 'ole.'

'C'mon then, let's go,' Charlie said enthusiastically.

Jenny Flannagan was waiting her turn to jump under a thrashing skipping-rope that was being turned by two bigger girls. 'Don't ferget you're ter take me ter the pie shop fer our dinner,' she called out.

'It's too early yet,' Jimmy called back. 'I won't be long anyway.'

The two lads hurried along Dock Lane to Shad Thames, a narrow cobbled lane that housed Butler's Wharf and the spice warehouses.

'It's much too big,' Charlie remarked as he studied the rope. 'We'll need ter cut some off it.'

Jimmy realised that his schoolfriend Billy Morris had been right when he said that everyone should have a penknife. ''Ow we gonna cut it?' he asked.

Charlie was not about to be beaten. 'Let's go an' find a milk bottle,' he replied.

One hour later Charlie and Jimmy walked into Milldyke Street looking pleased with themselves. They had safely hidden a good length of rope on the bombsite in Dock Lane, and when they saw smoke drifting up over the bacon-curing factory Charlie Almond smiled slyly. 'There'll be plenty ter pick from,' he remarked.

When Kate hurried into Milldyke Street later that morning carrying a laden shopping bag she spotted Amy talking to Elsie Burton at the entrance to the block. Elsie was a big woman with a disarming smile and a fat friendly face. Her husband Michael was a lighterman with a ruddy face and a likeable disposition, and Kate wondered how such a nice respectable couple as the Burtons came to be living in Milldyke Buildings.

'Elsie's told me 'er gel wouldn't mind lookin' after 'em ternight,' Amy said as Kate drew level.

'Nah, course not,' the big woman said with a smile.

Kate put down her shopping bag and looked a little uncomfortable as she rubbed her sore hands together. 'I'm not up to it, Amy. Really I'm not,' she told her.

'It's bloody nonsense. Course you're up to it,' Amy replied. 'It's just what yer need, a good Saturday night out. Yer know the kids'll be OK wiv Rene. Besides, it'll give yer a chance ter meet my Fred. Yer'll like 'im, 'e's good company. Spiv Copeland's a good laugh too an' yer don't 'ave ter worry, it's only a foursome's night out. Yer've no need ter write anyfing into it.'

'Yeah, I understand, but I'd sooner not. Maybe some ovver time,' Kate told her.

Amy shrugged her shoulders. 'Well, if yer change yer mind let us know.'

Elsie Burton looked along the street and then nudged Amy. 'Briscoe's just gone in,' she said.

Amy pulled a face. 'That's all we want,' she sighed, turning to Kate. ''As Briscoe bin in ter see you yet?'

'Who's Briscoe?' Kate asked her frowning.

'Ted Briscoe's the agent fer the Buildin's,' Amy told her. 'Didn't yer see 'im when yer got yer flat?'

Kate shook her head. 'When I went ter the office I saw a Mr Brown. 'E was a nice ole bloke.'

'Well, that's more than can be said fer that slimy git,' Amy growled as she nodded her head towards the first block.

Elsie Burton shuddered and folded her arms over her ample bosom. 'That bloke fair gives me the creeps,' she said. 'It's 'is eyes, an' the way 'e's got o' lookin' right frew yer.'

'I know what yer mean,' Amy replied. 'My Charlie said Briscoe reminds 'im of Bela Lugosi. Mind you, 'e does look like 'im a bit, what wiv that black 'air all smarmed down over 'is collar. Ter be honest I feel like takin' a pair o' scissors to it.'

'Sounds like someone I'd sooner not meet,' Kate said smiling.

'Yer'll meet 'im right enough,' Amy told her. ''E comes round the Buildin's every month an' always on a Saturday. It's about the only time 'e can catch most people in. 'E checks the rent accounts wiv ole Jack Ferguson an' then 'e wants ter see everybody's rent books. 'E makes sure that people are takin' their turn cleanin' the stairs too. All in all 'e's a nasty job o' work.'

Elsie nodded in agreement. 'What about that Mrs Irons who 'ad a bad back? She missed 'er turn an' the neighbours got the 'uff so they left 'em too. Anyway Briscoe kicked up merry 'ell when 'e called round one Saturday an' saw the state o' the stairs. Poor ole Mrs Irons ended up gettin' notice ter quit an' it was only Ferguson who got 'im ter change 'is mind.'

'Sounds a nice character,' Kate remarked.

'Yer'll find out soon enough,' Amy warned her. 'Briscoe's a dirty ole goat an' 'e likes a bit o' young stuff.'

'Well, I won't invite 'im in,' Kate said disgustedly.

'Yer'll 'ave no choice,' Elsie told her. ''E 'as the right ter go in an' see that people are keepin' the flats up ter scratch. It's in the tenancy agreement so there's little anyone can do about it.'

Kate picked up her shopping bag. 'I'd better go an' tidy up then,' she said with a grin.

Amy watched her go into the block then she turned to Elsie Burton. 'It's a bloody shame,' she said shaking her head. 'A nice-lookin' woman like 'er goin' ter pot over that ole man of 'ers. 'E was never any good an' now she's left on 'er own wiv two kids. Bloody shame.'

'From what yer told me she's well rid of 'im,' Elsie remarked.

'Yeah, that's true,' Amy replied, 'but it ain't right fer a young woman like 'er ter be on 'er own.'

'Well, it's 'er life an' she's gotta do what she finks is best, fer 'er an' the kids, so there's no sense in tryin' to interfere,' Elsie warned her.

At number one A block Ted Briscoe pushed back the tattered ledger and reached for his fountain pen. 'I'll need ter talk ter Mrs Sattersley about that cat of 'ers an' I'll 'ave ter go an' see the new arrival at number three C block,' he announced.

Jack Ferguson nodded and watched while Briscoe signed the ledger. 'By the way, is that business wiv Annie Griffiths sorted out yet?' he asked.

Briscoe shook his head. 'All 'er stuff's still in the ware'ouse,' he replied. 'The police 'ave bin in lookin' at it once or twice but they don't seem too interested any more. Trouble is, we can't dispose of it while there's a chance of a relative claimin' it. I wouldn't mind but it's only a few sticks o' furniture an' some bits an' pieces. If I 'ad my way I'd chuck the lot on the fire.'

Jack Ferguson stretched in his chair. 'D'yer want me ter come round wiv yer?' he asked.

'Nah, I can manage,' Briscoe told him. 'I 'ear that the new tenant's a bit of all right. I fink it's time ter make 'er acquaintance.'

The caretaker hid his distaste as he eyed the leering agent. One day Briscoe was going to step over the mark, and he for one would be glad to see the back of him.

Chapter Seven

The Saturday visit to the pie shop in Dockhead was a treat for the Flannagans and Jimmy was licking his lips in anticipation as he bundled Jenny into a vacant seat.

'Well, young man?'

'Pie an' mash an' double liquor twice,' Jimmy ordered as he placed a two-shilling piece down on the counter.

The buxom woman rubbed her hands down her white apron and lifted the lid of a copper container, and the young lad watched expectantly while she scooped a large portion of mashed potatoes on to the plates and added a hot pie before dipping a large ladle into the parsley gravy.

'Double liquor,' Jimmy reminded her.

'I 'eard yer the first time,' she said with a grin. 'Now don't spill it all over the floor.'

Jimmy carefully carried the plates over to the bench seat and set them down on the marble surface.

'Where's the knives an' forks?' Jenny asked impatiently.

'All right, give us a chance,' he replied, hurrying over to the counter once more.

The two children tucked into the meal and when Jimmy had scraped his plate clean he sat back to wait until Jenny was finished. She was taking her time and he began to get impatient. 'Are yer gonna be much longer, Jen?' he asked her. 'I got fings ter do.'

'Mum said yer mustn't rush yer food or yer'll get ulcers,' his sister reminded him curtly.

'Well, you won't get ulcers that's fer sure,' Jimmy told her with a sigh.

Jenny would not be hurried and Jimmy sat thinking about the coming adventure. From what he had seen in the grocery shop rashers of bacon were not cheap, and a whole side of bacon would cut up into a lot of rashers. Charlie had said that Spiv Copeland would buy the side of bacon from them and the money they got would buy quite a lot of things. They would have to be careful though. Maybe he could say they had found the money on the bombsite. Yes, that was it. He would have to have a word with Charlie to get their stories right.

'I'm ready now,' Jenny announced.

Jimmy took her hand as they hurried across the main road.

'Slow down, Jimmy, I can't walk as fast as you,' she grumbled.

'I told yer I got fings ter do,' he replied as he slowed his pace.

'Jimmy, d'yer fink Mum's very un'appy?' she asked suddenly.

'Over Dad, yer mean?'

'Yeah.'

'Nah, I don't fink so. Our dad was never 'ome – well not much anyway.'

'I can't 'ardly remember what 'e looks like,' Jenny said frowning.

They walked into Milldyke Street and Jenny spotted her friends. Jimmy watched as she skipped over to them, thinking about what she had said. He could remember his father very well and how he had tried to please him by showing how grown-up he was. He remembered the times he had waited up for his father to come home at night and pleaded with his mother for a few more minutes when it had become late and she hustled him off to bed. Dad had never seemed to be around much, and whenever he had shown up there were always people with him. Other dads went to watch their sons play football and took them to see the ships along the river but his dad never had. Now he was locked away in prison for seven years. Jimmy wondered with an empty feeling inside whether like Jenny he would soon forget what his father looked like.

The sound of a window being raised and a loud voice calling out made him look up anxiously.

'Charlie! Charlie Almond!'

Jimmy saw Charlie's mother leaning out of her window but he could see no sign of the wanted lad.

'Jimmy, 'ave you seen my Charlie?' Amy called down to him.

'No, Mrs Almond.'

'If yer do see 'im tell 'im I'm gonna give 'im what for,' she said. 'I sent 'im on an errand ages ago an' 'e ain't come back.'

Jimmy gritted his teeth in dismay. He didn't want the adventure they had planned being spoilt by Charlie's mother keeping him in as punishment: he realised he had better search him out while there was still time.

Kate looked down into the turning and saw Jenny playing happily with her friends, but there was no sign of Jimmy. He would no doubt be off somewhere with Charlie Almond, she thought as she went back down the long dark passage to the living room and looked around. The room was tidy enough and the new net curtains helped to brighten it up a bit. There was nothing to worry about, she assured herself, but listening to her neighbours earlier had given her a feeling of apprehension nevertheless.

The rat-tat on the front door startled her and when she hurried along the passage and opened it she found herself face to face with a tall, slightly stooping man whose greasy black hair was combed back from his forehead, accentuating his receding hairline. He smiled briefly showing yellowing teeth, then his face set in a serious expression.

'Mrs Flannagan? I'm Ted Briscoe, the agent fer Harris Estates,' he announced. 'Can I come in?'

Kate nodded and stood back, catching a smell of stale sweat as Briscoe stepped into the passage.

'I see the caretaker's done the room up,' he remarked as he walked into the living room. 'Everyfing all right?'

'Yeah, I'm satisfied, Mr Briscoe,' Kate told him, pulling up a chair for him.

The agent sat down and loosened his coat to expose a double-breasted waistcoat. His eyes appraised her and Kate felt uncomfortable. 'Yer'll be wantin' ter see the rent book,' she anticipated.

He was staring at her as she went to the sideboard and she could feel his eyes on her back. 'There we are,' she said, laying the book down in front of him.

Briscoe picked it up and studied the entries for a few moments then he flipped it back down on to the table. 'That's fine,' he said. 'I understand from Mr Brown that your 'usband's not livin' 'ere.'

''E's away,' Kate said quickly.

'Umm, shame that,' Briscoe replied, his eyes coming up

68

slowly to meet hers. 'It can't be easy. What wiv two kids ter look after, I mean.'

'I manage,' Kate said, looking away from the uncomfortable gaze. 'I've got a job.'

'Where d'yer work, Mrs Flannagan?'

'Pearson's.'

He frowned quizzically.

'The vinegar factory.'

'Oh, I see. In the office?'

'No, in the factory.'

Briscoe shook his head slowly. 'Well, I wouldn't 'ave thought it.'

'I beg yer pardon?'

'Yer don't strike me as bein' a factory gel,' the agent said, looking her up and down. 'I mean ter say, an attractive young woman like you should be workin' in some office.'

'There's nuffing wrong wiv workin' in a factory, Mr Briscoe,' Kate replied sharply. 'It's honest work an' the hours suit.'

'No offence meant,' he was quick to tell her. 'It's just that I thought . . .'

'No offence taken,' Kate cut him short.

Briscoe stood up and buttoned up his coat, giving her a crooked smile. 'Well, I've some more tenants ter see this mornin',' he told her. 'Now if there's anyfing worryin' yer – wiv the flat I mean – feel free ter come an' see me. I'm in the office most days. Yer'll find I'm not the ogre I'm painted out ter be. Not that you strike me as a woman who'd listen ter such talk.'

Kate nodded, anxious to see the back of him, and when she had seen him out she stood for a few moments in the dark passageway with her mind racing. Amy and Elsie were right. The man gave the impression of being a nasty character and she could see now why Amy called him a slimy git. His eyes had virtually undressed her and that leer of his had been intimidating.

Kate walked into the living room and sat down at the table, still feeling unsettled. Briscoe no doubt had her down as a woman on her own and unsure of herself and probably fancied his chances. Well, he was the last person in the world she could possibly fancy.

Charlie came out of the block with a sheepish grin on his round face. 'I got a good tellin'-off but she's let me out,' he told Jimmy.

They spotted two boys kicking a tennis ball against the factory wall and hurried along to join in but they were stopped in their tracks by a loud voice. 'Charlie Almond, can yer run an errand for me?'

The lad looked up at the first-floor window of D block and pulled a face. 'Aw not now, we're just gonna play football, Mrs Johnson,' he called out.

'I can't get out meself 'cos o' me legs,' Mrs Johnson told him. 'I wouldn't trouble yer if I could. I'll give yer a tanner.'

'Oh all right,' Charlie sighed, going into the block with Jimmy at his heels.

'Now there's the note,' she told him as the two boys stood in the living room. 'I want a quarter o' margarine, two ounces o' cheese an' one egg. 'Ere's me ration book an' don't lose it. Make sure yer don't crack that egg neiver. After yer got 'em I want yer ter call in at the oilshop. Get me two flypapers an' a tin o' Zeebo. Ask the man if 'e can let yer 'ave a black-lead brush, mine's worn out. Oh yeah, an' while I fink of it, I want yer ter tell yer muvver ter call in fer 'er dress I took up. Now can yer remember all that?'

While Meg Johnson was briefing his friend, Jimmy took the opportunity of looking around the room. There was a tattered coconut mat spread over the bare floorboards and ashes littered the small grate. On the table he noticed a tin of goat's milk with dead flies stuck around the rim and a plate with bits of food dried hard on it. The place smelled bad, and the wallpaper was hanging down in places. On the sideboard a glass bell-jar covered what looked like a stuffed squirrel climbing a branch, and next to it there was a black-framed photograph of a group of people dressed in white overalls.

'Yeah, I can remember, Mrs Johnson,' Charlie sighed. 'C'mon, Jimmy, let's get goin'.'

Meg Johnson gave Jimmy a curious look. ''Ave you just moved in 'ere?' she asked.

The lad nodded. 'My mum's Mrs Flannagan,' he told her.

'Well, tell yer muvver if there's any sewin' or mendin' she wants done ter come an' see us,' she said ushering them out of the room.

'Bloody ole witch,' Charlie growled as they hurried along the street. 'I'd tell 'er ter piss orf an' get 'er own shoppin' but me mum said I 'ave ter run 'er errands if she wants me to. She's a bit funny in the 'ead an' me mum feels sorry for 'er.'

'Did you see that fing under the glass?' Jimmy asked him. 'It looked like a real squirrel.'

'Nah, it's a dummy one 'cos I asked 'er once,' Charlie replied.

'Didn't it stink in there?' Jimmy remarked as they turned towards Dockhead.

Charlie's face broke into a wide grin. 'I 'eard me mum tell Fred Logan that it always smells like pissy drawers in ole Muvver Johnson's flat.'

'I thought it was that squirrel I could smell,' Jimmy said grinning back at him.

The mention of Fred Logan's name reminded Jimmy of what had been planned for the following morning. 'I 'ope no one's found that rope we stashed on the bombsite,' he remarked.

'Nah, it's safe enough,' Charlie replied. 'Can you climb a rope?'

'Yeah, course I can.'

'We'll earn a few bob on that bacon,' Charlie told him. 'I'm gonna buy a proper cricket bat wiv my money.'

'I'm gonna buy a pair o' football boots wiv mine,' Jimmy declared.

The queue at the grocery shop moved up slowly, and while they were waiting impatiently, Flossy Chandler came up with a small canvas bag hanging from his arm. ''Ello boys, runnin' errands?' he asked.

'Mrs Johnson,' Charlie replied curtly.

'Oi you! This is the back o' the queue,' a woman called out.

'This boy's minded me place,' Flossy told her sharply as he patted Jimmy on the head.

'Get at the back o' the queue, Pansy Potter,' another woman called out loudly.

Flossy looked hurt as he shuffled back to the rear. 'It makes yer sick,' he hissed.

The shopping errand completed and the message about the dress passed on, Charlie and his best friend sat in the kerbside to discuss important matters. Along the turning young children bounced in and out of a chalked hopscotch bed, while a group of young lads tossed coins against the factory wall. Up in number three D block, Meg Johnson hung her flypapers up, scraped the dead flies from the tin of goat's milk and proceeded to clean the ashes from the grate. Once she interrupted her chores to go along the passage to the front door and reassure herself that the bolts were on. What had happened to Annie Griffiths could quite easily happen to her, a woman alone, she reminded herself.

Amy Almond took out her curlers and set about brushing out her red hair. The dye she used had proved to be a disaster but she persevered. Fred wasn't the sort to make any disparaging remarks anyway. Nice man, really, and good to young Charlie. Shame about that dragon of a wife he suffered. Never mind, it was going to be a good night out, and it was great news about the old bag going away with her cronies for the weekend. Fred would be able to experience a warm, loving bed for a change.

''Ello, gel, anyfing wrong?' she asked when she answered a knock at the door.

Kate smiled. 'Nah, it's just that I've bin finkin'. Is the offer still on?'

'About comin' out ternight? Course it is,' Amy told her.

'I want ter get out ternight, Amy.'

'I should fink so too.'

'What about Rene?'

'I'll go an' see 'er now. We'll give 'er two bob each. Can yer spare two bob?'

Kate nodded. 'Instead o' my two comin' in your place why don't your Charlie stay wiv us. 'E could sleep wiv Jimmy. There's plenty o' room.'

It was getting better and better, Amy thought, grinning at Kate. Charlie was not the sort of lad to give his mother problems and he usually slept soundly, but nevertheless it was not right to flaunt her affair with Fred in front of the lad when it could be avoided.

'That's a good idea,' she said. 'Charlie's a good boy, 'e won't be no trouble.'

Kate hoped that she was doing the right thing as she went to her wardrobe and stared at her meagre array of clothes. The black dress that Mary had given her was still serviceable but it might be too suggestive, she thought, what with that low neckline. The grey costume might do, although it was more suited to winter. The summer dress was pretty, though it would need a good pressing. That, with her olive green jacket, would be the thing, she decided. She would have to do something about her hair too. Lucky it was short and easy to manage. A quick wash and set with the curling-tongs would do.

'Is that you, Jimmy?'

'Yeah. I just come up fer a drink o' water. Can Charlie 'ave one too?'

Kate smiled to herself. 'There's some lemonade in the kitchen cabinet,' she told him.

Their thirst slaked, the lads made ready to leave. ''Ere, Mum, 'ow much is the bacon ration?' Jimmy asked.

'Three ounces a week. Why?'

'Just askin'. Is it dear?'

'Dear enough.'

The boys exchanged secret glances and Jimmy nodded. 'We bin runnin' errands,' he told her.

'Who for?'

'Mrs Johnson in D block,' Charlie piped in.

'Oh?'

'Mrs Johnson said ter tell yer if yer got any clothes ter mend she'll do it for yer,' Jimmy added.

'That's werf rememberin'. Now off out, you two, an' Jimmy, keep yer eye on Jenny. Don't let 'er go out the street, is that understood?'

In the quietness of the afternoon Kate Flannagan set about doing her hair, her mind on the coming evening. She would have to be careful in the way she presented herself. Spiv Copeland might be a nice bloke and not one to take advantage, as Amy had said, but he was a man, and any single man – and some married men too come to that – could be expected to push their luck if given the chance. She would play it very carefully, not letting him think she was looking for someone. Maybe she should hint to him that she had a feller. No, Amy would know differently. Make Spiv Copeland aware that she was still carrying a torch for her husband, perhaps? It wouldn't work. God! What was she getting herself into?

Chapter Eight

'I'll kill the little bleeder, so 'elp me,' Amy growled as she stepped out quickly beside Kate and set off towards Dock-head police station.

'I could 'ave died when I saw that copper at the door,' Kate told her.

'I couldn't get anyfing out of 'im 'cept that the two kids were bein' 'eld at the station,' Amy went on.

'I 'ope it's nuffing bad,' Kate sighed, her stomach churning. 'My Jimmy's never bin in trouble before.'

Amy resented the implication. 'My Charlie's not an angel, but 'e's not a bad boy,' she said. 'All right, 'e's a bit of a mad 'un at times, but I can't believe 'e's done anyfing really bad.'

'Well, we'll soon find out,' Kate replied as the two of them hurried up the steps of the police station.

'If you'll take a seat I'll make inquiries,' the desk sergeant told them.

Amy and Kate sat down on the long wooden bench, silently immersed in their own anxieties, until a stocky young man in a grey suit appeared from a back office and spoke with the sergeant for a few seconds.

'Mrs Almond and Mrs Flannagan?' he asked as he came over to them. 'I'm Detective Sergeant Cassidy. If you'll follow me, please.'

The women walked into the back office and sat down in the chairs provided, staring anxiously at the detective as he made himself comfortable behind his desk.

'Jimmy and Charlie were both seen on the roof of Blake's Bacon Curers in Milldyke Street,' he announced. 'They were spotted by a man exercising his dog on the bombsite. It appears they were trying to prise open the fanlight and the man stopped a patrolling officer who subsequently arrested the lads for attempted breaking and entering.'

'I'll slaughter 'im when I get my 'ands on 'im,' Amy said, gritting her teeth.

The detective allowed himself a smile and Kate noticed his white teeth.

'I've interviewed both lads and their excuse was that they were searching for a ball they had kicked up on to the roof,' he told the women. 'Of course that doesn't tie in with the fact that they were seen trying to force open the fanlight. When I asked them about it they both said they were curious to see the bacon being cooked and they had no intention of breaking in. I've given them a good talking to and I think that should suffice. However, I have to say that should either of them get into any trouble whatsoever in the future then their little adventure will certainly count against them.'

'We're really grateful, ain't we, Kate?' Amy said quickly. 'Can we take 'em 'ome?'

The detective nodded. 'If you'll wait outside I'll get them brought up,' he said with a disarming smile.

As soon as Amy laid eyes on the sorry-looking Charlie she gave him the sharp end of her tongue. 'Didn't I warn yer, yer little sod,' she ranted. 'Didn't I tell yer about keepin' out o' trouble? I might just as well talk ter that brick wall fer all the good it does. There's me tryin' ter keep us respectable an' you go an' let me down. Yer've gone too far this time, Charlie, an' yer gonna pay fer it. In the first place there's gonna be no more pocket money, an' . . .'

Kate had gone to Jimmy and pulled him to one side. 'Just wait there,' she said with an angry look in her dark eyes, then she turned to the sergeant. 'Could I see the detective again, just fer a few minutes, please?' she asked.

Detective Sergeant Cassidy was busily shuffling some papers at the rear of the outer office and he looked over to her. 'It's all right, sergeant,' he said.

Kate was shown into his office and she stood in front of the desk. 'I didn't get the chance ter really fank yer fer not chargin' the two boys,' she told him.

He motioned her into the chair. 'Look, Mrs . . .'

'Mrs Flannagan.'

'I know the area you live in, Mrs Flannagan,' he began. 'Milldyke Street has long been a bone of contention as far as the police are concerned. Those buildings should have been pulled down long ago, and for the people living there it must be a nightmare. There's a stigma attached to the place and it would be very easy for us to label everybody living in the street with the same tag. We're not that stupid though, whatever people would have you believe. We understand some of the problems and the reasons for people being housed there, and we tend to take that into consideration. Bringing a juvenile before the courts is bad enough, but when it's made known that the offender lives in Milldyke Buildings the chances are that the lad could well be sent to a detention centre. Borstal isn't a very nice place, Mrs Flannagan, and it might be a good idea if you'd remind your son of that fact.'

Kate was staring into the detective's pale blue eyes as he

spoke, intrigued by his easy manner and his somewhat cultured voice. 'I will, fer sure,' she said in reply.

Cassidy ran his fingers through his thick fair hair and sighed as he glanced down at the paperwork in front of him. 'I should be at church,' he said jokingly.

Kate stood up, returning his friendly smile. 'So should I,' she replied.

Jimmy was waiting for a tirade but Kate took him by the arm without a word as they walked out of the police station. Up ahead Charlie was still on the receiving end of a terrible tongue-lashing. 'If yer Uncle Fred finds out yer tried ter break in there 'e'll go mad,' Amy was going on. 'Whatever possessed yer ter do such a fing? If it wasn't fer that nice detective you could be goin' ter Borstal.'

Jimmy walked beside Kate feeling grateful that at least he was not being told off publicly. Charlie had got it wrong when he reckoned that the fanlight was always left open. Not at weekends it wasn't. Saying that they were fetching their ball from the roof was quick thinking on his part though, and the bit about wanting to see the bacon cooking. Good job the man who spotted them hadn't seen the rope or he would have told the copper about that too. It was still up on the roof, hidden by the stone balustrade, and as far as Jimmy was concerned it could stay there.

Kate had been ready to give her son a severe dressing down too but after listening to what the detective had to say she thought better of it. A good quiet talk would be more sensible, she decided.

Jenny looked wide-eyed as she saw her mother and brother walk into the turning. 'What did yer do?' she asked breathlessly.

'It's OK, luv, you go back an' play, an' don't go wanderin' out o' the turnin',' Kate told her.

Jimmy sat at the table looking very sorry for himself as Kate faced him.

'I remember yer tellin' me once that yer've never lied ter me, so I don't want yer ter start now,' she said in a quiet voice. 'I want the trufe. Did you an' Charlie try ter break into the factory?'

Jimmy nodded as he stared at the floor. 'We was gonna nick a side o' bacon, Mum,' he said quietly.

'So that's why you was askin' me those questions yesterday,' she replied. 'An' where did yer fink yer was gonna sell it?'

'Spiv Copeland.'

'Did you talk about this ter Spiv Copeland?' Kate pressed.

Jimmy shook his head. 'Charlie reckoned Spiv would buy it. 'E buys anyfing.'

'Didn't it worry yer that stealin's wrong, that you could get caught an' be sent ter Borstal?' Kate said sharply.

Jimmy looked up slowly, his blue eyes full of remorse. 'We didn't fink they'd miss one side o' bacon, an' we didn't fink it was anyfing really bad, like stealin' from 'ouses, Mum,' he said in a subdued voice.

'All stealin's wrong, whoever it's from,' she replied. 'The fact that we 'ave ter live in this street, in these Buildin's, doesn't mean ter say that we can be'ave any differently from when we lived in Weston Street. I want us to 'old our 'eads up 'igh an' know that we still 'ave some pride despite all that's 'appened ter this family. Do you understand that?'

The lad nodded slowly, his eyes fixed on his mother's. 'Don't worry, Mum, I'd never do anyfing like that again,' he answered. 'The policeman told me an' Charlie all about Borstal. We was really scared in case we got sent there.'

'The detective told me 'e was gonna give yer both one

more chance,' Kate told him, 'an' ter be honest I fink you're both very lucky. Don't turn out like yer farver, Jimmy, whatever yer do. It'll only bring us all trouble an' grief.'

'Do I 'ave ter stay in?' he asked sheepishly.

Kate felt a wave of emotion run through her as she saw the look in her son's eyes. She wanted so much for him, but with a father in prison and being forced to live in the most notorious part of Bermondsey there seemed little chance of her hopes being fulfilled. The lad was coming up to thirteen and in just over two short years he would be out at work. Would he go the way of so many slogging away in some factory and struggling to support a family? Worse still, would he come to reject a life of toil and hardship and go the way of his father?

'No, yer can go out,' she told him.

Jimmy's face lit up and he scampered out of the room, feeling that he had been let off very lightly. Kate watched him go and sighed sadly. He was a good boy and she had to shake off her feeling of dread for his future. People did rise out of the straits life had consigned them to. She had seen it happen to people she had known, and Jimmy had the ability, if only he was given the chance. Maybe the lenient attitude of Sergeant Cassidy would one day come to be rewarded in full. She prayed to God it would be.

Milldyke was quiet on that balmy Sunday afternoon. The toffee-apple man had come and gone, the younger children were at Sunday school, and even the inevitable game of tin-can football was suspended. The street was all but deserted, except for two young lads sitting side by side in the kerb discussing their good fortune.

'It was my fault,' Charlie conceded. 'I should'a known they don't do smokin' at weekends.'

'It don't matter,' Jimmy told him. 'At least we didn't get charged. That copper scared the life out o' me when 'e went on about Borstal. Fancy 'avin' ter go there.'

''E told me they beat yer up there,' Charlie replied. ''E said that everyone 'as ter wear short trousers, even the older boys.'

'What about that rope we left up on the roof?' Jimmy asked him.

'It'll just 'ave ter stop there,' Charlie said quickly. 'Nobody'll know it belongs to us.'

Jimmy nodded. 'I expected my mum ter keep me in fer ever,' he said with a grin.

Charlie chuckled. 'I got me pocket money stopped fer four weeks, but me muvver said she wouldn't keep me in. She's always goin' on about me gettin' under 'er feet, an' besides, she wants me out o' the 'ouse when Spiv Copeland comes round, an' when me Uncle Fred's there. 'E's not me uncle really. I fink she only told me that so I wouldn't ask too many questions. Fred Logan's me muvver's boyfriend an' she 'as ter be careful 'cos o' me dad findin' out.'

'D'yer like yer dad?' Jimmy asked him.

Charlie shrugged his shoulders. ''E's all right, I s'pose, but I don't see much of 'im, 'im bein' a sailor.'

'It must be really good bein' a sailor,' Jimmy remarked. 'Fancy goin' to all them places like China an' America. Does yer dad bring yer 'ome presents from abroad?'

Charlie shook his head. 'Nah, 'e's a stoker. Stokers don't get much money. That's what 'e told me mum anyway, but she don't believe 'im. I 'eard 'er tellin' Fred the only fing me dad ever brought 'ome was a dose o' clap.'

'What's clap?'

'It's what yer get when yer go wiv dirty women.'

'What, like gettin' fleas?'

'Sort of.'

'Is Spiv Copeland one o' yer mum's boyfriends?' Jimmy asked.

'Nah, 'e just brings fings fer 'er ter sell for 'im,' Charlie explained. 'Spiv's comin' round this afternoon. 'E might let us sit in 'is car if we ask 'im.'

The two lads waited by the kerbside and Charlie stared over at the locked bacon factory, his mind dwelling on what might have been, had that man not spotted them, and that fanlight been left open.

'There 'e is,' Jimmy said suddenly as the smart car turned into Milldyke Street and purred to a halt at the kerb.

'Can I mind yer motor?' Charlie asked quickly as Spiv got out.

'I dunno, it seems pretty quiet this afternoon,' Spiv remarked.

'The kids from Abbey Street are comin' round fer a stone fight later,' Charlie replied. 'Yer might get yer winders broke if I don't keep me eye on it.'

Spiv grinned as he fished into his trouser pocket. ''Ere's a tanner,' he said.

'Can me an' Jimmy sit in it?'

'As long as yer don't touch anyfing.'

'Jimmy'll 'elp me mind it,' Charlie said expectantly.

'Well, I s'pose I'd better pay 'im too,' Spiv replied, his grin widening.

Kate heard heavy footsteps on the stairs and then Spiv Copeland's voice as Amy opened the door to him and she smiled to herself. It had been a pleasant enough Saturday night out, she thought, and the young man was good company, but she had begun to feel a little put out by Amy's attempts at matchmaking. They had gone to the Woolpack in Dockhead and listened to Flossy Chandler's piano playing. Spiv had had them laughing at his endeavours to stay one step ahead of the law and Fred too had been in good form. He was a dapper man with a quick wit who seemed to be very much taken by Amy, but the night had been spoiled somewhat by Amy constantly trying to pair her and Spiv off. Spiv had noticed it and apologised for her, and Kate had been quick to let him see that she was not man-hunting. There had been no ringing bells or leaping heart on her part but she sensed that Spiv was interested in her. He was a smartly dressed, good-looking man with broad shoulders and a confident air about him. He talked easily and had treated her very courteously, hinting that it might be good to meet again without having Amy around acting as some fairy godmother. Kate had smiled and not committed herself, feeling that it was much too early to let herself become involved with another man, though Amy would be certain to think otherwise.

Spiv had called to deliver a dozen black silk negligees and a second consignment of silk stockings, much to Amy's delight. The first consignment had been eagerly gobbled up and she had done quite well out of the transactions. However, Amy had a few bones to pick with Spiv, and he had barely recovered from her diatribe about her son's criminal activities when he was forced to defend his manhood.

'You surprised me last night, Spiv,' she began. 'There was me puttin' meself out ter get you two all nice an' cosy an' yer didn't seem interested. That gel's all on 'er own an' I can tell yer fer sure she ain't got a feller. You should 'ave got in there.'

Spiv knew that it was useless to argue with her and he made an attempt at pacification. 'Yer did a good job, I 'ave ter say,' he replied, 'but it struck me that I should play it nice an' steady. She's a very attractive woman an' I'd like ter see 'er some more, but it don't always do ter go like a bull in a china shop, Amy.'

'Well, tell me, 'ave yer made a date?' Amy asked.

'I did suggest that we might get tergevver fer anuvver night out soon,' he replied nonchalantly.

'Bloody 'ell, Spiv, yer disappoint me,' she said quickly. 'What wiv your track record wiv women you should 'ave bin well away.'

The young man sat up in his chair, feeling slightly irritated. 'Now listen, gel, I know what I'm doin',' he said frowning. 'In the first place I twigged from the start that she ain't easy. The woman's got a lot o' pride, it stood out a mile. Yes, I am interested, an' yes, I wanna see 'er again, but like I said, I'll do it my way.'

Amy seemed somewhat mollified. 'P'raps you're right,' she replied nodding. 'Kate's goin' frew a divorce an' I can understand 'er bein' careful, but don't let it put yer off.'

'No, it won't,' he told her testily. 'Now what about those dresses? Can yer take two dozen?'

Chapter Nine

At number six C block Barney Schofield was preparing to take a stroll, and he used a stiff brush one more time on his highly polished boots and then took a brush to his coat before daring to venture out. A good turn-out was essential, he maintained. Smartness was discipline and there were all too many signs of the lack of it these days, he thought.

At fifty-two, Barney Schofield had felt that he was still young enough to serve his country, though the powers that be deemed otherwise when he strode proudly into the recruiting office to offer his services. He had realised that he was too old to serve at the front, but he had the benefit of twenty-five years' experience in the colours, including service in the First World War in which he won the Distinguished Service Medal and rose to the rank of sergeant major. He could be usefully employed in training, or in organising the Home Guard, he considered, but the recruiting officer had declined his offer. 'Go 'ome an' put yer feet up, Dad, yer've done your bit,' he was told.

Now, at fifty-eight and having spent the war years as a fire-watcher, Barney was aggrieved. He had never married, and when the house he lodged in was destroyed by a bomb during the Blitz he had been forced to seek alternative lodgings. The flat in Milldyke Buildings was supposed to have been a temporary accommodation, so the housing officer at the town hall had promised him, but there he went and there he had stayed.

Not only was he aggrieved at the treatment meted out to him, a long-serving soldier with a gallantry medal to boot, Barney Schofield was also disgusted by the lack of moral fibre in the civilian population hereabouts. He himself was a military man through and through, and although he was now receiving an army pension, to his mind in many ways he was still on active service. In the army men had discipline and walked with pride. Their billets were spotless and even the coal bunkers were whitewashed. The troops always had to be well turned out, which was more than could be said for the people around here. If the stairs and landings were scrubbed once a week it was a miracle, and how half the tenants could see out of their filthy windows was a mystery.

Barney Schofield reflected on the sad decline of the civilian population as he left the flat for his evening stroll. He usually walked over Tower Bridge and through Tower Gardens to look with a feeling of reassurance at the guards on duty at the Tower and the Beefeaters, immaculate in their navy and red uniforms. There he could drink in the atmosphere and once again dream of his army days, when he had stood rigidly to attention with his pacing stick tucked under his arm, defying anyone to step on his barrack square without specific leave to do so. 'Only two people have the right to walk on my square without permission,' he had often screamed out to a raw recruit, 'me an' Jesus Christ!' Now he walked the streets and saw the rabble kicking tin cans about, with socks round their ankles and boots that were sorely in need of a tin of blacking, and sometimes he had to restrain himself from ordering them to the guardhouse on the spot.

'Evenin', Mr Schofield,' Joe Sandford called out as he hurried down the stairs behind him, off for his night shift at the sausage factory.

Barney stepped aside to let him pass. Another poor blighter caught up in the general decline of standards, he thought. Sandford won't be out of the street five minutes before that long-haired excuse for a man comes calling on his wife. He had heard it and seen it with his own eyes. But that was for them to sort out.

'Evenin', Mr Schofield,' Flossy said with a smile as he flounced into the turning.

'Ye gods,' Schofield mumbled to himself after giving the man a cursory nod. 'Why doesn't he put on a skirt and high heels and be done with it.'

'Evenin', Mr Schofield,' he heard again as he was walking along Dock Street.

'Evenin', Mr Dennis,' Barney replied. At least his next-door neighbour was upright and smartly turned out. Could have made a good army man, he conceded.

The ex-sergeant major strolled on and turned left on to Tower Bridge Road, his eyes fixed ahead, his pace equivalent to the regimental march of the First Battalion West Sussex Regiment. He whistled the tune, indulging himself in reverie, until he saw a shambling figure coming towards him. The man looked drunk, and if there was one thing Barney Schofield could not abide it was drunkenness.

'Got the time on yer, mate?' the man asked in a slurred voice as he drew level.

'A quarter ter seven,' Barney barked out.

'You ain't got a couple o' coppers fer a cup o' tea, 'ave yer, mate?' he asked.

'Tea?' the military man queried. 'What yer doin', collectin' fer a pint?'

The drunkard realised that he had accosted the wrong man and he made to shuffle off without comment.

'There's a few coppers, now be on yer way,' Barney told him in his most crisp manner.

The man raised his cap and hurried off, stopping a few yards along the road to take another glance at the old soldier. 'The poor bastard's shell-shocked, I shouldn't be surprised,' he told himself as he set off for the first pub he could find.

Barney afforded himself a smile at his benefaction. Discipline had to be maintained, but could be tempered with a little compassion here and there, he felt.

The evening wore on, with a sky full of promise for the morning. A slight breeze stirred the dust in the gullyways, bringing Ernie Walker back to his window. From his top-floor flat Ernie could look down on the street and the goings-on. As he had admitted to his neighbour Amy Almond, it was something he was adept at. 'There's nuffing much misses my eye,' he had told her more than once. There's that man Chandler going out to the pub, he thought. Stella Sandford's boyfriend will be along soon. Here he comes, right on time. Strange to see the two boys out after what they got up to this morning. Being marched away by a policeman probably hadn't figured in their plans, and it was a wonder they had not been kept in as punishment. Still it was not for him to speculate. Here comes Mrs Johnson. Always in a hurry, always with a worried look on her face. She had never been the same since poor old Mrs Griffiths was murdered. It seemed to him as though she fully expected to be the next victim. Strange they never caught the man who killed the old bird, Ernie mused. Perhaps Mrs Johnson knew more than she ever let on.

The wireless crackled and faded and Ernie cursed. 'It's that bloody accumulator,' he growled aloud. 'Bloody fing don't seem ter last more than a few days.' It wasn't as though he was always using the wireless.

Mindful that talking to oneself could be construed as a sign of ageing, Ernie promptly shut up. At seventy-five he was entitled to his little idiosyncrasies, it was true, but he must avoid having these conversations with himself.

The knock on his front door made him start a little and he puffed his way down the passage.

'There's yer Nosegay an' there's yer pipe-cleaners,' Stella told him. 'Anyfing yer want me ter bring yer in termorrer?'

'Nah, I'm OK fanks, luv,' he replied. 'I might get out fer a few hours termorrer. Judgin' by the sky it looks like it'll be anuvver nice day.'

Stella Sandford went back into her flat and Ernie smiled to himself. She was a nice young woman, despite her carryings-on. What she got up to was no concern of his, though he had to spare a thought for her husband Joe. There he was hard at work all night at the sausage factory while that young fellow of Stella's was keeping the bed warm.

Ernie resumed his seat at the open window. It would be a quiet spell until the pubs turned out, he thought. Time for a pipeful of baccy and a glass of stout.

Kate always enjoyed the late evenings when the children had gone off to bed and the wireless played softly. There was time to get things sorted out and then sit quietly with a cup of tea. It was the time of day to meditate and hope for better times, in whatever form they came. It would be nice to meet a man who could make her happy, and have a better job that she could enjoy doing. It would be very nice to see the children into good jobs with the chance to make something of themselves. She sat quietly sipping her tea, and for a brief moment or two she found herself thinking about Will. It was over between them and the bitterness she had felt was fading away along with the past she had left behind. He had preferred another woman, and perhaps she was sitting at home this very moment missing him badly. Probably not, but in any case Will was paying for what he had done, and at least he had not offered any objection to her divorcing him. She was now in a position to get on with her life and do the best she could for Jimmy and Jenny. She could get out more, as Amy had told her to.

Kate finished her tea and went to look at the black dress she had decided against wearing the previous evening. It needed shortening slightly and maybe a matching piece sewn into the revealing neckline. Jimmy had told her about Mrs Johnson in D block. She might be able to do the job.

'Jimmy, are you asleep?' she whispered as she peeped into his bedroom.

'Nah, I bin readin',' he told her.

'I'm just poppin' along ter see Mrs Johnson about alterin' me dress,' she told him. 'I won't be long.'

Meg Johnson lived on the first floor in D block, and when Kate knocked on her front door she had to wait until the woman had satisfied herself that it was safe to open it.

'Who's there?'

'It's Mrs Flannagan from C block.'

'Mrs Flannagan?'

'Yeah, I believe yer spoke ter my boy Jimmy yesterday.'

'Jimmy?'

'Jimmy was wiv Charlie Almond. They run an errand for yer.'

'Yeah, I remember.' Still the door remained closed.

'Mrs Johnson, I've got a dress fer you to alter. Can yer do it?'

'Just a minute.'

Kate heard the bolts being drawn and then the door opened slowly.

Meg Johnson looked relieved. 'I've seen yer about, Mrs Flannagan,' she told her. 'Yer'd better come in, I don't like leavin' this door open too long. Yer never know who's prowlin' about.'

Kate saw the frightened look in the woman's eyes and quickly stepped into the passage.

'Let me take a look,' Meg said as they walked into the kitchen.

'It's about two inches too long an' I want a piece put in the neckline,' Kate explained as she let the dress hang down in front of her.

'I could take it up all right,' Meg replied, 'but the panel's a bit awkward, unless yer got a spare bit o' material.'

'I was finkin' of a white lace insert maybe.'

Meg did not look too enthusiastic. 'Ter be honest I think it'd spoil it,' she said. 'Yer could use a bit o' black lace. Yer might get it at the market in Tower Bridge Road. That stall outside the baker's shop sells lots o' remnants.'

Kate nodded. 'That's a good idea. I'll try there.'

'In the meantime I could do the takin' up,' Meg offered.

'I'd be much obliged,' Kate said smiling.

Meg Johnson brought over a large sewing box and laid it on the table. 'Slip yer dress on an' I'll pin it,' she told her.

Kate felt a little embarrassed about taking off her skirt and blouse in front of a stranger but Meg was busy delving into the sewing box for the tins of pins and she did not look up until Kate had the dress on.

'Yeah, I can see. Yer'll need at least two inches taken up, but ter tell yer the trufe that neckline looks very nice,' Meg remarked.

Kate smiled shyly. 'Yer don't fink it's too revealin'?'

'Gawd luv yer no,' Meg said chuckling. 'If I was your age an' 'ad your figure I'd wear it as it is.'

Kate stared down at her cleavage. 'I dunno really,' she hesitated.

Meg looked her up and down for a few moments. 'I tell yer what,' she said. 'If yer get a piece o' material I'll just pin it in an' then yer can make up yer mind one way or anuvver.'

'Could yer?'

'No trouble at all.'

Kate let her eyes stray around the grimy living room while Meg adjusted the hemline of the dress, her glasses perched on the end of her large nose. She was short and plump, with a round pale face and large brown eyes, and her short mousy hair was parted in the middle and gathered into a hairnet. The apron she had on was spotless, and as she worked away with the pins Kate noticed that her hands were small with the fingernails cut very short. She was humming nervously, pins clamped between her lips.

'That seems about right,' she said after a while.

Kate eased off the dress while Meg put the sewing box back in the corner of the room.

'Would yer care fer a cuppa? I don't usually get any callers on Sunday evenin's,' she said, restlessly brushing her hands down her apron.

'I can't stop,' Kate replied. 'I left the kids in bed.'

'I'd just made a pot when yer knocked,' Meg told her.

'All right then, if it's ready,' Kate relented as she saw her look of disappointment.

Meg smiled quickly and took herself off to the scullery.

''Ave yer settled in all right?' she asked as she brought in the tea.

'Just about,' Kate told her.

'I wish ter Gawd I could move out of 'ere,' she sighed. 'I'd be gone termorrer.'

'I agree it's not the best place ter live,' Kate replied.

Meg Johnson's eyes narrowed over her cup. 'I s'pose yer've 'eard about what 'appened to Annie Griffiths?' she queried.

'Yeah, I did.'

'Terrible that. A woman on 'er own.'

Kate saw the frightened look in Meg's eyes and attempted to change the subject. 'My two seem to 'ave made friends 'ere,' she said quickly.

Meg put her cup down on the table. 'I got Jack Ferguson ter put me two new locks on after what 'appened ter poor Mrs Griffiths,' she went on.

'Did yer know 'er very well?' Kate asked.

Meg nodded. 'She liked a drink, did Annie, but she was no trouble. She used ter come 'ome the worse fer wear sometimes but she never interfered wiv anyone. The poor cow's gone an' whoever done it is still walkin' the streets. It fair makes yer shiver. Who's gonna be next, I keep askin' meself.'

'I shouldn't distress yerself too much,' Kate told her kindly. 'It was more than six months ago. The man who done it could be long gone.'

''E's not finished,' Meg said in a tone of voice that sent a shiver up Kate's spine. 'I met Annie in the street a few days before she was murdered an' she said somefing very strange. It was somefing about a ghost from the ovver side. She'd seen it. Mind you, Annie was always readin' them 'oroscopes an' lookin' at tea-leaves. I didn't take a lot o' notice at the time 'cos she was drunk, but it makes yer fink. I 'ad nightmares about it fer weeks after.'

Kate tried to ease Meg's fears by laughing aloud. 'Ghosts don't strangle people, luv.'

'Well, I got them bolts on anyway. It's a comfort,' she sighed.

'I must get back in case the kids wake up,' Kate said as she stood up.

Meg got up to see her out and she reached out her hand to adjust the framed photograph on her sideboard. 'A very strange business,' she said almost to herself.

Kate felt the need to get out of the grimy flat and she gulped in large breaths of air as she hurried back to C block.

Chapter Ten

Jimmy Flannagan had seen very little of the other Milldyker in his class outside of school and he soon learned the reason why. Tommy Brindley's widowed mother had been taken into a sanatorium with T.B. and Tommy had gone to live with his grandmother in Walworth. For a few weeks the lad had travelled back and forth from her house, but now a place had been found for him at a local school.

'I'm leavin' on Friday,' he announced to Jimmy and Billy Morris as they waited in the playground for the morning bell to sound.

'Sorry ter see yer leave,' Jimmy told him.

'Yeah, me too,' Billy said.

'At least I won't be gettin' the cane any more,' Tommy grinned.

'Ole Ramsey's gonna be lookin' fer somebody else ter take it out on,' Billy remarked. 'Yer wanna be careful, Jimmy, it could be you.'

'If 'e starts pickin' on me I'm gonna go an' see the 'eadmaster,' Jimmy said firmly.

''E won't do anyfing,' Tommy said with disgust. 'I went ter see 'im once about Ramsey pickin' on me an' 'e told me not ter be such a baby. I fink 'e's scared of 'im.'

Jimmy had been feeling confident of staying out of

trouble, but when they were back in the classroom he was not so sure.

'Wonders will never cease,' Herbert Ramsey growled as he gave out the marked arithmetic test papers. 'Ten out of ten for Flannagan and nine out of ten for Brindley and Cosgrove, but as for the rest of you guttersnipes, the results are atrocious.' He walked slowly between the desks, his hands clasped behind him. 'I hope you'll stay out of trouble in your new school, Brindley, but I doubt it very much,' he said harshly, his small eyes widening malevolently. 'Nine out of ten is a very good mark for you, but I have to wonder. Just you bear in mind that if I find out you've been cheating, Brindley, I'll make sure you get a caning you won't forget. Is that understood?'

The young lad nodded, wishing it was Friday, and Ramsey leaned over him. 'Don't just sit there nodding, boy. Do you understand?'

'Yes, sir.'

The class set to work, copying from the blackboard the history of the Plantagenet kings, and while they huddled over their notebooks Herbert Ramsey slid open his desk drawer to begin the last chapter of *Maidens in Chains*. He kept the banned novel inside the drawer so that he could hide it quickly should another teacher, or indeed the headmaster, enter the classroom. Ramsey found the novel extremely titillating and he was eager to obtain the next title on the list, having already sent off a large stamped addressed envelope and a postal order for one shilling and sixpence. Wouldn't he have loved to change places with the plantation overseer in that sunny southern state. There would be no whip as far as he was concerned though. The cane would be a much more effective punishment when inflicted on the bare bottoms of the slacking slaves.

The master looked around furtively at the lowered heads of his pupils and then began the last chapter. The overseer looked handsome in his high leather boots, into which he had casually tucked his light cotton trousers. He wore an open-necked shirt and a red bandanna loosely gathered round his thick neck. His chiselled face was tanned beneath his straw hat and his white even teeth flashed as he saw the beautiful Hanna come towards him. She swayed in that provocative way of hers, her winding hips a mute, succulent promise of pleasures to come. He had spared her the punishment she thoroughly deserved and now she was coming to him, her eyes lowered in servitude, her natural movement sending shivers of pleasure through his six-foot-six frame. There was a debt to be paid, down in the tall cane grass near the water's edge, and as Hanna drew near he licked his full lips at the smell of her musky fragrance. The time had come and . . .

'Just brought in the revised class list, Mr Ramsey,' the headmaster said, placing the papers down on the desk. 'I say, are you feeling all right? You look a bit hot under the collar. Not going down with anything, I hope.'

Ramsey had been just about to go down into the warm grass with the beautiful slave when Charles Goodright barged in, and the shock had caused large beads of perspiration to break out on his forehead. What was more he had shut one of his thumbs in the drawer. 'Just . . . just the weather I think, headmaster,' he stammered.

With his bruised thumb stuck in his mouth Ramsey went quickly through the list Goodright had brought in. He immediately noticed that the boy replacing Brindley was named Friar and lived in Crimscott Street. Well, that was a relief, he thought to himself. At least from next Monday there would be an absence of Milldykers in his class. Wait a minute, what was this? A change of address? Good God! Was he ever to be free of those infernal slum dwellers? Would he ever be allowed to forget that day?

Kate stepped out from the vinegar factory and screwed up her eyes against the bright sunlight that bounced up from the granite pavement. She had seen an advertisement in last week's *South London Press* that said women were wanted at Wheatley's new plant which was opening soon in Dockhead, and she was eager to get an interview. The notice had announced that it was a forty-hour week with pleasant working conditions and the women could expect to earn good bonuses. It sounded too good to be true. It would mean more money and would be right on her doorstep. Of course, it was full time, but the children were old enough now to manage till she got home in the evening.

The car pulled in to the kerb suddenly and the driver called out to her. 'Can I give yer a lift?'

Kate peered into the car and smiled as she saw Spiv Copeland. 'As a matter o' fact, I'm on me way ter Wheatley's at Dock'ead,' she told him. 'I'm goin' fer a job.'

'Say no more,' Spiv replied with a grin as he leaned over to unlock the nearside door. 'I'll 'ave yer there in two shakes.'

Kate climbed in and nestled back against the leather seat as Spiv pulled away from the kerb. 'It's a new factory openin' soon,' she explained to him. 'It's gotta be better than bottlin' vinegar.'

'Well, I 'ope yer lucky,' he told her, shifting the gear lever forward.

Kate gave him a sideways glance and noticed the firm jawline and his fair wavy hair blowing in the breeze from the open window. He was certainly handsome, with a ready smile which seemed to reflect the free-and-easy approach to life she had seen in him last Saturday evening. It was obvious that he was prospering too. What was it about him that failed to arouse her? Most women of her age would have been pleased with the attention he was paying her. Maybe she had been on her own too long. Perhaps what Daisy had said was true and she was in danger of becoming a grizzled prune before her time. No, that was nonsense. She still felt the singing in her loins at times, and her dreams were not always innocent. It was just something about him that made her feel uneasy, unsure of herself. It could well have something to do with his lifestyle, she realised. Perhaps hard experience was warning her off.

'It was a good night on Saturday,' Spiv said without taking his eyes off the road. 'I enjoyed it. Did you?'

'Yes, I did,' she said smiling.

They crossed the Tower Bridge Road and carried on along Abbey Street, Spiv Copeland sitting relaxed behind the wheel, one arm resting on the door frame. 'Maybe we could do it again this Saturday,' he suggested.

'I dunno. I don't like leavin' the kids,' she replied, biting on her lip.

''Ere, I'll tell yer what. Why don't you an' the kids come fer a spin on Saturday,' he said enthusiastically. 'We could go down ter Kent. I got plenty o' petrol.'

The idea suddenly seemed attractive. 'I'd like that, an' I'm sure the kids would too,' she told him.

'Right then,' Spiv said grinning widely. 'I'll meet yer on the corner o' Milldyke Street about ten o'clock. 'Ow's that sound?'

'That'll be fine,' Kate replied as they pulled into the kerbside.

'Good luck wiv the interview,' the young man called out as he pulled away.

For far too long the tenants of E block had been forced to put up with the nuisance of the communal dustbins that were situated under their windows. The disturbance caused by the noise of bins being emptied at all hours and loud clangs as the galvanised lids on the large receptacles were dropped back into place was bad enough in cold weather, and during the summer months the situation was virtually unbearable. Worse than the noise was the fetid smell, with plagues of flies and bluebottles invading the flats should a window be left open. Consequently, the people of E block in particular were forced to keep their windows tightly shut and resign themselves to sweltering in the heat.

The long-suffering tenants gathered in Liz Fogan's flat on the second floor that Monday evening and she spelled it out in no uncertain way. 'If nuffing's done soon we're gonna 'ave an epidemic on our 'ands. It stands ter reason, what wiv all them flies an' bluebottles.'

'I always use those flypapers,' old Mrs Champion butted in.

Maud Sattersley from number two nodded her head vigorously. 'I get mine from the oilshop in Dock'ead. Those ones Cheap Jack sells ain't no good whatsoever.'

'Now look 'ere, we ain't come 'ere ter talk about bloody flypapers,' Liz said angrily. 'We're 'ere ter get somefing done.'

'Too bloody true,' Flossy Chandler said quickly. 'I get the brunt of it on the ground floor. I'm frightened ter leave me curtains open, the way they all look in me winder. D'you know that silly ole cow Emmy Drew stares in every time she empties 'er bin. "Seen enough?" I shouted out one day.'

Liz Fogan hid a smile. 'Now look, you lot,' she continued, 'I ain't prepared ter stand fer it any longer. Somefing's gotta be done an' quick. I vote we get up a petition an' get everybody in the Buildin's ter sign it, then we take it round the Council.'

'Good idea, Liz,' Flossy told her enthusiastically. 'I'm wiv yer.'

'I dunno,' Maud Sattersley said anxiously. 'Look at the trouble I got in wiv ole Briscoe about me cat shittin' on the stairs. 'E gave me a right mouthful of abuse.'

Ada Champion had been the complaining tenant on that occasion and she gave her neighbour a withering glance. 'Yer gotta admit it did stink the place out,' she said sharply. 'I trod it all in me flat. Ruined me best mat it did.'

'Fer Chrissake, don't let's get sidetracked,' Liz resumed. 'An' as fer Briscoe, 'e can like it or lump it. We got rights, same as anybody else.'

'We don't 'ave ter let Briscoe know what we're doin',' Flossy said. 'As long as no one goes openin' their mouth.'

'I'm prepared ter go round wiv a petition,' Liz told the gathering. 'Who's gonna come round wiv me?'

'I'd be only too glad,' Flossy replied, 'but I don't get on wiv some of 'em.'

'I ain't interested in whevver I'm liked or not,' Liz said sharply. 'All I'm concerned about is gettin' some action taken.'

'I'd go round wiv yer if it wasn't fer me back,' Mrs Irons told her. 'It's bin givin' me gyp this last couple o' weeks.'

'I wondered why yer didn't do the stairs last week,' Ada Champion remarked, looking at Mrs Elmley for support.

Sadie Elmley lived on the top floor and as a rule she had

little to say to anyone, but on this occasion she was fired up enough to respond to her neighbour. 'It's bad enough puttin' up wiv flies an' bluebottles wivout 'avin' dirty stairs,' she said to the surprise of all present.

Mrs Irons eyed Sadie with a piercing stare. 'I do 'em when I can,' she growled. 'You wait till you get somefing wrong wiv yer. P'raps yer'll understand then.'

'Now look, gels, it ain't doin' no good bickerin',' Liz told them with unusual restraint. 'We've all got ter stick ter-gevver over this. Now, is anybody gonna come round wiv me or do I 'ave ter do it on me own?'

'I'll come round wiv yer,' Ada volunteered.

'Oh all right, I'll 'elp yer,' Flossy said, 'but not on Friday. I'm playin' at the pub on Friday.'

The gathering of malcontents was interrupted by a knock on the door and Liz opened it to admit Mary Enright from number eight. She was carrying a shoebox under her arm and looked smug as she nodded to all present. 'I'm sorry I'm late,' she declared. 'It was our Mick. 'E's off wiv 'is back. I've 'ad ter strap 'im up wiv me stays again. It's the only way 'e can get any ease.'

'Why don't yer try that Wintergreen ointment?' Mrs Champion suggested. 'That's all I use when my Sid complains of 'is back.'

Mrs Enright sat down and placed the shoebox under her chair, still smiling mysteriously. 'Well, what's bin decided?' she asked expectantly.

'We're gonna get a petition up,' Ada Champion informed her.

'Those bins attract all sorts o' vermin,' Mary Enright said pointedly.

Liz Fogan was eager to get back on track. 'When we've got all the names on the petition we'll ignore the estate office,' she told them. 'We'll go directly ter the Council. We'll insist on seein' the doctor of 'ealth, or the mayor if need be.'

'Good fer you,' Mary Enright said in a loud voice. 'We'll certainly make 'em take notice.'

Mrs Champion glanced at Mrs Irons. ''Ere, what's that I can smell?' she asked quickly.

'Don't look at me like that, it ain't me,' Freda Irons said sharply.

'I can smell it too,' Maud Sattersley cut in.

'Well, that's a relief,' Mary said, reaching under her chair. 'Now fer your information it's this box what smells. As a matter o' fact I got this little specimen orf the bombsite. I've 'ad it 'angin' on me fire escape fer a few days now an' I fink it's just about ready fer inspection.'

Ada peered into the shoebox as Mary gently lifted the lid and she suddenly recoiled in horror. 'Oh my good Gawd! It's a bloody rat!'

'Nice size, ain't it?' Mary said grinning. 'We'll take this round the council when we 'and in the petition. I'll tell 'em it climbed up me drainpipe an' got in me scullery winder an' my Mick killed it wiv the broom. That'll make 'em sit up.'

Liz looked at the shoebox with disgust. 'Do us a favour, Mary. Take that out, will yer? No! Not the rat, yer silly cow! Take the box out.'

Mary looked unconcerned as she tucked the cardboard box under her arm. 'I'll put it behind the bins,' she told them.

As soon as she had left Ada Champion had to have her say. 'If she finks I'm gonna walk round that Council wiv 'er she's got anuvver fink comin',' she growled. 'That smell's made me feel fair ill.'

'Silly bloody mare,' Freda Irons fumed. 'It's enough ter start a plague.'

Flossy Chandler was looking particularly distressed. 'Seein' that rat made me go all of a shiver,' he wailed. 'She'll be the death o' me, that woman.'

'Now don't upset yourself,' Liz said, not without compassion. 'She only meant well.'

'So did 'Itler,' Flossy moaned.

'When yer gonna take the petition round?' Maud Sattersley asked Liz.

'We'll start termorrer evenin',' Liz replied. 'There's no sense in waitin' any longer.'

'We'll 'ave ter be careful ole Ferguson don't get ter know,' Freda reminded them. ''E's bound ter tell Briscoe.'

'We'll warn everybody ter keep their mouths shut,' Liz said. 'Right then. Who's fer a cuppa?'

'I fink I need a stiff drink,' Flossy groaned.

'You make do wiv tea,' Maud chided him. 'P'raps Liz'll give yer one of 'er nice tea fingers.'

'I couldn't eat anyfing the way I feel,' Flossy went on. 'I intended givin' me flat a good goin' over, but now I'll need to 'ave a lie down.'

The meeting finally broke up, and as soon as she could Freda Irons went along to see Jack Ferguson. 'It's not that I disagree wiv what they're gonna do,' she told him, 'but I fink you should know after what yer did fer me when Mr Briscoe was gonna give me notice ter quit.'

'Look, I'm not interested in their petition,' the caretaker growled. 'It's no skin off my nose.'

'I just thought yer should know, that's all,' Freda said, looking a little downcast.

'Well, I ain't runnin' round ter tell Briscoe, if that's what yer mean,' he replied testily. ''E'll get ter know soon enough.'

Freda Irons went back to her flat in a worried frame of mind. She would be compelled to add her name to the petition and Briscoe had already warned her about her future conduct. What if he took it out on her? Perhaps she should have a word with Liz Fogan. If they all stood by her it would be all right. Briscoe couldn't evict them all – or could he? She'd better do the stairs this week, just in case. Better not give her neighbours any more reason to complain.

Chapter Eleven

Kate had been pleasantly surprised at the Wheatley interview and she was looking forward to starting work there next Monday. The week had dragged on, and now on Friday afternoon she felt uplifted. She was looking forward to the Saturday out with the children and her only nagging worry was Jimmy's unusual quietness. It was quite unlike him. Normally he was a cheerful and animated boy but for the past week he had seemed strangely subdued. It might have something to do with the episode at the police station, she thought, but then again it might be something else. Was he being bullied at school? No, he was quite able to take care of himself. Perhaps he was sickening for something. Whatever it was she would have to get to the bottom of it. The day out would no doubt restore him; the chance to get into the country and breathe some fresh air would do them all good.

'I'm really gonna miss yer,' Daisy Wells said sadly as they toiled at the bottling machine. 'I bet they'll get some miserable ole cow ter take yer place, probably someone who don't say a word all day long. I was only sayin' ter my Alex last night, "I'm gonna miss Kate," I told 'im. I was tellin' 'im about yer new job an' 'e said I should try an' get a job there as well. I would too, if it wasn't fer the hours.'

Bob Marsh the foreman was hovering in the background and he decided to make his presence felt. 'I 'ope all this chattin' ain't the reason why there's gaps in the bottle line,' he said. 'If there's spaces it tends ter cause problems wiv the machinery.'

'It ain't our fault, it's the cases,' Daisy replied sharply. 'A lot o' the bottles are broken an' we've gotta sort the broken glass out. There's a lot cracked too. Yer wouldn't want us ter put cracked bottles on the belt, would yer?'

'All right, all right,' he growled. 'It was a bad batch. The next lot are OK.'

Daisy pulled a face at him as he skulked away. 'Bloody ole goat,' she hissed. 'I don't s'pose 'e's gettin' any, that's why 'e's so cantankerous.'

Kate smiled. 'I 'ope yer'll call round now an' then. Yer know where I live.'

'Yeah, I'll do that, no fear,' Daisy replied with a grin. ''Old tight, 'e's back again.'

The foreman came up and stood watching them hard at work for a few minutes and then sauntered off, making a mental note to keep his eye on Daisy Wells. She was far too talkative, he thought. Well, she was going to be very disappointed with her new workmate. Mrs Canfield was stone deaf but a good worker. Her decision to go part time had solved a problem for him and he chuckled to himself as he made his way to the office.

On Friday morning Herbert Ramsey was in a foul mood, and the last straw came just before lunch when he settled down to a few pages of his latest novel, *Lust in the Sun*, only to find that the book was missing from his desk drawer. It was Brindley who had taken it, there was no doubt, he seethed. At morning break the little guttersnipe had been slow to leave the classroom. It would be just like him to try to get his own back for the canings now that he was leaving the school.

When the class resumed for the afternoon session Ramsey was ready. 'I have the sad duty to tell you that we have a thief in the class,' he said in a voice full of menace. 'A special textbook has been taken from my desk drawer and I have a good idea who the culprit is. Now I'm going to leave the room for ten minutes and when I return I expect the book to have been put back. I don't want to have to use the cane more than is necessary but I can assure you that if all else fails I will not hesitate to cane you one by one until the thief is exposed. Do I make myself clear?'

The shocked silence only served to make Ramsey even more irate. 'Well then?'

'Yes, sir,' the class chorused.

As soon as he had left Stanley Cosgrove turned to Tommy Brindley. 'I ain't gonna get the cane fer you,' he whined. 'I bet you took it.'

'Oh no I didn't,' Tommy said quickly. 'Why pick on me, it could 'ave bin you.'

'You're the one always gettin' the cane,' Stanley went on.

'Shut yer noise, fatty,' Billy Morris said sharply.

'Well, I ain't gonna get the cane over 'im,' the plump lad grumbled.

'I tell yer what, I ain't gonna be caned on me last day, that's fer sure,' Tommy said with spirit.

'What yer gonna do about it when Ramsey comes back, refuse ter go up an' get it?' Stanley sneered.

'Yeah, that's right,' Tommy told him in a calm voice.

The door flew open and Ramsey strode purposefully to his desk. 'Right then. I see the book has not been returned,' he announced in a threatening voice.

The whole class held their breath as he went to the corner cupboard and took out the cane.

'Brindley took it, sir,' the terrified Stanley Cosgrove blurted out.

'Oh, and why do you suspect Brindley?' Ramsey asked him.

''E was 'angin' round the classroom at break,' the fat boy replied.

'Brindley, come out here,' Ramsey ordered.

'It wasn't me, sir,' the unfortunate lad protested.

'Get out here! Now!'

Brindley stood up slowly. 'I'm not gonna be caned fer somefing I didn't do,' he said firmly.

Ramsey brought the cane down on his desk with a frightening noise. 'Get out here, boy!' he screamed.

Tommy Brindley walked to the front of the class, tears of anger welling in his eyes. 'I didn't take yer book,' he gulped.

'It wasn't 'im, sir,' Jimmy cut in. ''E was wiv me all the time.'

'Shut up, you little rat,' Ramsey shouted. 'One Milldyker sticking up for another, it's only as I would expect. Hold out your hand, Brindley.'

As Tommy hesitated his wrist was grabbed by the master but he pulled free. 'I'm not gonna be caned,' he said hoarsely.

Ramsey moved towards him, a white film of saliva on his lips, and suddenly Tommy Brindley jumped at him and pushed him backwards with his outstretched hands. Ramsey fell to the floor in a heap and as he staggered to his feet Brindley dashed from the room. The terrorised children sat numb with shock as the master chased out after him, then Billy Morris turned to Stanley Cosgrove. 'When we go 'ome I'm gonna wait fer you, Cosgrove,' he snarled. 'I'm gonna smash you up.'

'Yeah, an' I'm gonna 'elp 'im,' Jimmy growled at the tearful sneak. 'We're gonna do yer proper, fatty.'

'I'll tell the teacher,' Stanley whined.

'You can tell who yer like,' Jimmy sneered. 'See if I care.'

Ramsey had hurried to the headmaster's study and Charles Goodright sighed with foreboding. 'This is a bad thing, Ramsey,' he remarked. 'Assault on a teacher is unheard of. I'll have to inform the police. You'll be required to make a statement.'

Ramsey felt confident that the pupils in his class would be sensible enough to respond to his promptings and he nodded. 'I understand,' he replied.

Word spread like wildfire as the school turned out that afternoon. Other classes gathered in the playground as Billy Morris sought out Cosgrove. The frightened fat boy tried to slip down the far stairs but Jimmy was lying in ambush. 'Billy Morris is waitin' fer you, you little squealer,' he snarled as he manhandled him from the building.

In the centre of the tightly packed circle Billy raised his clenched fists and looked menacingly at his opponent. 'C'mon then, Cosgrove. Put 'em up,' he shouted.

'I ain't gonna fight you,' Cosgrove moaned.

Billy jabbed him in the chest with a fist. 'C'mon, sneak, put 'em up,' he ordered.

The plump lad half-heartedly raised his hands and immediately took a straight-arm jab on the nose. Blood started to run down his face and he whimpered as he tried to defend himself. Billy was looking confident as he hit Cosgrove once more but the circle had broken and the children backed off as the headmaster stepped into the makeshift arena. 'That'll be enough of this!' he shouted. 'I want you all to go home this minute. I want the playground emptied in five minutes,' he told them sharply.

Stanley Cosgrove took the opportunity to run off and Billy Morris took his coat back from Jimmy with a grin. 'I'll get 'im termorrer,' he vowed.

The two lads walked along Tower Bridge Road together until they came to the junction with Grange Road. 'I'll see yer on Monday,' Billy said with a cheeky grin.

Halfway along Abbey Street Jimmy saw Tommy Brindley standing outside a sweetshop. 'I expect Ramsey sent fer the police,' he said fearfully as Jimmy came up to him.

'Yeah, I expect so,' Jimmy replied. 'Are yer all right?'

Tommy's face was tearstained but he forced a smile. 'I couldn't let 'im cane me any more, not when it wasn't me who took 'is stupid book,' he said with a quiver in his voice.

'What yer gonna do now?' Jimmy asked him with concern.

'I'm gonna run away ter sea,' Tommy told him. 'I can be a cabin boy. I'll tell 'em I'm fifteen.'

'What about yer grandmuvver?' Jimmy asked.

'I can't go 'ome to 'er, the coppers'll be waitin' there. I'll write to 'er when I get ter some foreign place,' he replied.

'You could come 'ome wiv me till yer get on a ship,' Jimmy told him with a smile. 'My muvver won't mind, not when I tell 'er all about what 'appened.'

Tommy looked desperate. 'Wouldn't she mind really?'

'Nah, course not. C'mon.'

Detective Sergeant Cassidy sipped his strong black coffee and pulled a face. 'This tastes like varnish,' he growled at the young detective constable. 'How did it go?'

D. C. Harris looked across the desk at Pat Cassidy. 'I

spoke first to Charles Goodright, the headmaster, and he seemed to feel that the incident had been blown up out of all proportion. To be honest I don't think the master concerned is very high in his esteem. It seems the lad, Tommy Brindley, has been caned on quite a few occasions and this time he refused to take it.'

Cassidy smiled. 'Oh he did, did he? That's unusual.'

Tom Harris consulted his notebook. 'The form master, Herbert Ramsey, apparently had a textbook stolen from his desk during the morning break and he suspected Brindley. He stated that when he confronted him Brindley pushed him roughly on to the floor and ran from the class.'

'Was Ramsey hurt?'

'Not really, though he seemed to be making a lot of it. Sprained back, shook up and shaking.'

'What was your impression?' Cassidy asked him.

'A nasty character,' Harris replied. 'He reminded me of a teacher at my school. Cane happy. Used it for every little misdemeanour.'

'What about Brindley? Did you manage to find out why he had been caned before?'

'The usual things. Lack of attention. Poor work. You name it.'

'Well, I think it'll keep till Monday,' Cassidy said, sipping his coffee. 'What's the lad's address?'

'Number five, Orchard Row, Walworth.'

'Walworth? That's a long way from Webb Street School,' Cassidy remarked.

'Brindley's staying with his grandmother,' Harris replied. 'Apparently his mother's got T.B. and is in a sanatorium. As a matter of fact the headmaster told me that it was the lad's last day at the school. A place has been found for him in Walworth.'

'We'll need to contact Carter Street police station,' Cassidy said, draining the coffee cup. 'They might be able to send an officer round to check if Brindley's returned home.'

Harris looked a little uncertain. 'Do you want me to follow this up, sarge?' he asked.

Cassidy rubbed the tips of his fingers over his forehead. 'I think it'll be better to wait until we hear from Carter Street,' he sighed. 'Just leave it with me for the time being. After all it was nothing more than a minor disturbance at a school. Frankly, Harris, my main concern is for the lad, not the master. Brindley could have run off somewhere. In that case we'll have the grandmother reporting him missing.'

As soon as Harris had left the office Cassidy leaned back in his chair and closed his eyes. It had been a hectic week and he was due for a few days off. Perhaps it would be nice to go and visit Karen's mother, he thought. She was ailing and still grieving for her only daughter and grandchild. Maybe he could fit in a day at the coast. Brighton or Hastings would be pleasant. Karen had loved Hastings. It would get him out of the house anyway. Staying there alone was getting to him more than ever. Maybe he should ask for a transfer to some other division. It would have to be far enough away to escape the daily reminders that tightened his throat and started up the dull ache in his chest.

Charles Goodright made his way up the long flight of steps to London Bridge Station carrying his briefcase and wearing the type of tweed hat preferred by the English country gentleman. The four fifty-five would get him home in time to catch Florence before she left for her infernal bridge party. He dearly wanted to talk to her, try to make her aware of the problems involved in being headmaster of a school in working-class London. He had tried so often in the past, but to no avail. It always seemed that Florence was mocking him with that condescending smile of hers whenever he broached the subject. She was financially independent of him and totally immersed in the busy social calendar of Tinsley Green. All else was of little interest. 'Of course, Charles.' 'Yes, I understand, Charles.' Then he was forced to watch the irritating last-minute preening before she left for some idiotic social event. What if he came home one evening and told her he had contracted V.D.? 'Yes, I understand, Charles.' Quite likely, he sighed sadly.

The train pulled out of the station and gathered speed. He had time on his hands to finish the crossword. It would save having to look at his fellow travellers crammed in the carriage. It would be nice to sit back and follow the adventures of Mark Holbury, he thought smiling to himself, but he dared not. The novel remained concealed in his briefcase and he would have to wait until Florence left for her bridge party before he discovered how the hero fared in his quest to seduce the hitherto unobtainable dusky maiden in *Lust in the Sun*.

Chapter Twelve

Kate looked at the desk sergeant anxiously. 'Will 'e be in termorrer?' she asked.

'No, 'e's off fer a few days,' the officer told her. 'What exactly is the problem?'

Kate thought hard for a few moments. The detective sergeant had been very nice when she last had reason to go to the police station and he seemed to be very understanding, but she couldn't be sure of a similar reaction from some other policeman. 'It's all right, I'll come back in a few days,' she replied.

The evening sun was dripping down behind the rooftops and shadows were lengthening as Kate Flannagan stepped out of the station and stood on the steps pondering. It couldn't wait for a few days. She had a runaway at her home and people would be concerned. The police would be looking for the lad and his grandmother would be very worried that he hadn't come home from school that afternoon. What should she do? There was only one thing for it really. The police had to be told. As she turned to go back into the station she spotted Sergeant Cassidy a few yards along the street talking with an elderly man.

Kate took in a deep breath and hurried down the steps as the two men shook hands. She might get short shrift from the officer but she had to try. A young lad was very distressed and needed her help.

''Ello, sergeant,' she said nervously as she reached him.

Pat Cassidy turned, and for a moment he looked puzzled. Then he smiled. 'It's Mrs . . .'

'Flannagan.'

'That's right. And how's the boy? Keeping out of trouble, I hope.'

Kate nodded, feeling at a loss as to how she should begin. 'I called in the station an' they said yer'd just left,' she told him. 'I was really anxious ter see yer.'

Cassidy smiled, and Kate could feel her face flushing. 'I'm sorry, I . . . I just needed ter . . .' she faltered.

'Take it easy,' he said, his smile widening. 'What exactly is the problem?'

'I've got a runaway stayin' wiv me an' I don't know what ter do about it,' she said quickly.

'And you came to the station to report it,' he prompted.

'Yes.'

'And did you?'

'No, I didn't.'

'Why not?'

'I wanted ter talk ter you about it.'

'Wouldn't another officer have done?'

'Not really. I mean I expect so, but it's not a simple matter.'

Cassidy looked bemused. 'Tell me, Mrs Flannagan. Who exactly is this runaway?'

'A young boy who's in Jimmy's class at school.'

Cassidy nodded sagely. 'Don't tell me, it's Tommy Brindley.'

'Yes.'

'We've been involved,' he told her.

Kate sighed deeply. 'I'm worried about the lad,' she said, fixing him with her eyes.

'Look, I was just off home but there's no immediate rush. Would you like a coffee?' he asked. 'There's a nice little cafe in Jamaica Road and we can talk there. That's if you can spare the time?'

'I can, I was just 'opin' you could,' she replied with a smile.

Kate could see the traffic rumbling by and a constant stream of homeward-bound workers as they sat facing each other in a window seat. She watched as he sipped his coffee and noticed the look of satisfaction on his handsome face. 'This is good,' he remarked. 'Much better than that rubbish we get at the station.'

Kate had preferred tea, and as she stirred a spoonful of sugar into her cup she prepared herself. It had been difficult getting Tommy Brindley to see the sense in her reporting his whereabouts to the police, but after a lot of gentle persuasion he had come round. 'Trust me,' were her parting words as she left the flat.

Pat Cassidy listened without comment until Kate had finished and then he studied the grounds of the coffee for a few moments. 'It seems to me there are still a few questions need answering,' he remarked.

''E swears 'e never took the book,' Kate said quickly.

'Well, his refusing the cane would back that up,' Cassidy replied. 'But he could have taken the book as a last chance to get his own back for all the canings he'd received.'

'I believe the lad,' Kate said firmly. 'My Jimmy told me that the teacher was always pickin' on Tommy just because 'e lived in Milldyke Buildin's. Jimmy said that just before 'e left school terday 'is teacher called 'im back an' warned 'im not ter become like the rest o' the filth in Milldyke

Buildin's or 'e'd find himself in serious trouble.'

'Well, that could be natural concern for a pupil who's gone to live in a not-very-desirable location,' Cassidy suggested.

'Well, it didn't come over that way ter Jimmy, nor ter me fer that matter,' Kate replied angrily. ''Erbert Ramsey's a nasty, vindictive man wiv a down on the kids from Milldyke. My Jimmy's tryin' really 'ard to improve at school an' his marks show it, 'cos I've seen 'em. There was no need ter threaten the boy in the way 'e did. I would 'ave thought some encouragement would 'ave bin more appropriate. An' what about Tommy Brindley? The poor little sod's got a muvver in a sanatorium an' 'ad ter travel from Walworth every day, only ter be caned at every excuse. Then on 'is last day at the school 'e's branded a thief. Tell me, sergeant, wouldn't you be tempted ter run away if it was you?'

Pat Cassidy had been watching the young woman with intrigue as she went on, and he smiled disarmingly. 'I probably would,' he replied. 'The problem we have is that Brindley assaulted the teacher in the process. If the teacher wishes to press charges Tommy Brindley could end up in Borstal.'

'Because 'e comes from Milldyke Buildings,' Kate said for him.

'Exactly.'

'It's not fair.'

'There's a lot not fair in this life,' Cassidy remarked, and he seemed suddenly to stop himself.

Kate noticed the clouding in his eyes. 'Are you married, sergeant?' she asked him.

'Do I look married?' he countered.

She shrugged her shoulders. 'I dunno. Maybe you do.'

'Can I get you another tea?' he asked.

Kate nodded, eager to learn more.

As he went over to the counter she watched him. He was well built, maybe a little under six foot, with broad shoulders and a thick neck. His fair hair was slightly unkempt and hung down to his shirt collar. There was something about him that intrigued her: the look in his eye she had seen, and his reluctance to answer her question. Was he married? Maybe he was separated and did not want to talk about it. He would be somewhere in his mid-thirties, maybe even forty, she guessed.

'We'll need to get the boy back with his grandmother,' he said as he passed the tea over to her. 'I'll phone the police station in Walworth and get them to send an officer round to her to explain the situation.'

'Could you tell 'em that Tommy'll go 'ome termorrer?' she asked.

Cassidy nodded. 'Tell me,' he said, 'are you on your own?'

'Does it show?' she asked with a smile.

'Well, you've not mentioned a husband, and when you came in to see me about Jimmy there was no mention of his father taking the belt to him.'

'My 'usband's doing seven years fer robbery,' she told him.

'Will Flannagan. I should have made the connection,' he replied.

'I'm in the process o' getting divorced.'

'It must be hard on the lad.'

'I've got a girl o' nine too,' Kate told him. 'Jenny doesn't remember much about 'er farver. 'E was two-timin' fer years an' 'e was never 'ome much. Jimmy remembers 'im though.'

'I'm sorry,' Cassidy said quietly. 'I had a daughter too. She would have been going on eight now.'

'I'm very sorry,' Kate replied, noticing the faraway look in his eyes.

'I was at the station on night duty when the word came through,' he went on. 'Parish Street had been destroyed by a high explosive. There was nothing left of it. It was hours later when Karen was pulled from the rubble. She was holding Sarah in her arms. They were both dead.' He took a deep breath. 'Two months later I volunteered for the army. I went into the special investigation branch. It was mainly routine work but there was a section concerned with investigating war crimes and tracking down war criminals. That's what I was involved with. I could have stayed on after the war as there was still a lot of work to be done in that area, but I'd had enough. I just wanted to get back to being a normal policeman.'

'Do yer regret it?' Kate asked.

'No, I love the work – well, most of the time. We have our moments, just like everyone else,' he said with a grin.

Kate was leaning on the table with her chin cupped in her hands and he felt encouraged to go on. 'There's a certain satisfaction in the job,' he said. 'It's worthwhile, and necessary. Take right now. A pretty young woman comes to see me and she's obviously very worried. We talk, and I reassure her that it's nothing that can't be solved, or at least I hope I do. Then she sits very quietly and lets me gabble on.'

'I'm very interested,' she was quick to tell him.

'Why?'

'Because you seem different ter what I imagined coppers . . . I mean policemen ter be.'

'Different in what way?'

'Well, you seemed to understand what it's like livin' in those buildin's. What it's like ter be tainted wi' the stigma. You was also willin' ter give my Jimmy anuvver chance. Milldyker. It's an ugly word, isn't it?'

'The buildings stand on the site of a milldyke,' he told her. 'Apparently the dyke was built to divert the path of the stream towards a flour mill. You see, I've studied my local history.'

'I bet it was a much prettier place at that time than it is now,' she replied.

'Mm, I should think so,' he said. 'Those buildings should have been pulled down years ago.'

Kate sipped her tea. 'I'll make sure that Tommy goes 'ome termorrer,' she told him.

Pat Cassidy nodded. 'I'll go and see the headmaster and the teacher concerned on Monday,' he replied. 'With a bit of luck we might be able to persuade them not to press charges. After all, Webb Street School has a good name and I'm sure they won't relish bad publicity.'

'You're a good man, sergeant,' Kate said smiling.

'Pat will do fine,' he told her.

'Patrick?'

'Yeah, there's some Irish on my mother's side,' he laughed.

'Well, Patrick, I must be off,' she said. 'I don't wanna leave the kids on their own too long. By the way I 'aven't told yer my name. It's Kate. As in Katherine.'

'Well, it's been nice meeting you, Kate. Maybe our paths will cross again in the not-too-distant future. For the best reasons, I hasten to add.'

Kate felt the strong grip of his large hand and she smiled. 'Fanks again, fer everyfing,' she said.

The young woman walked home feeling elated. Pat

125

Cassidy had made her feel good inside. The way he looked at her when she was talking and the way he listened with interest made her feel confident. His sad grey eyes and handsome face touched something in her, and it had been hard to tear herself away from his company.

Chapter Thirteen

Spiv Copeland looked surprised as he pulled up at the corner of Milldyke Street and saw that there were three children standing with Kate. 'I thought yer said you only 'ad two kids,' he remarked with a smile as he got out of the car.

Kate looked at him with a sheepish grin. 'This is Tommy, Jimmy's school friend,' she replied. 'Tommy stayed wiv us last night. There's bin a little upset. Would it be possible ter drop 'im off 'ome first? It's at Walworth.'

'Yeah, sure,' he told her. 'Right then, kids, in yer get.'

The three children squeezed into the rear seat and Kate climbed in beside Spiv. 'Tommy'll show yer the way,' she said.

As they drove along to the Bricklayer's Arms and then over the junction into New Kent Road, Kate explained in a low voice what had happened the previous day and occasionally Copeland shook his head in sympathy.

'I don't see it comin' ter much,' he commented when she had finished.

'I 'ope not,' Kate sighed.

At the Elephant and Castle Spiv steered the car into Walworth Road and Tommy leaned forward in his seat. 'It's the fifth turnin' on the left,' he said.

A grey-haired old lady answered Kate's knock, her rheumy eyes peering out of wire-framed glasses. 'It's always the same wiv kids o' terday,' she moaned. 'No consideration whatsoever. Worried sick I've bin. An' after the copper knocked at me door last night I 'ad a bad turn. I expected the worst when I saw 'im standin' there. I'm too old ter be faced wiv all this worry. I'll be glad when 'is muvver comes 'ome. Gawd knows when that's likely ter be. She could be in there fer anuvver six months fer all I know. I don't fink I can cope that long.'

While the old lady was whining on to Kate, Spiv tried to engage the children's interest. 'Yeah, I was in the war,' he replied to Tommy's question. 'I won a medal too fer capturin' twenty Germans. I marched 'em all in to the camp at bayonet point an' that same day I captured a German tank.'

'Cor! Did yer get a medal fer that as well?' Tommy asked him.

'Nah, they can't keep givin' medals out,' Spiv said with a serious face. 'Anyway the tank was empty at the time. The crew was sittin' at the roadside 'avin' their tea an' I crept up an' climbed inter the tank wivout bein' spotted. Yer should 'ave seen the Germans' faces when I started it up an' roared away. "Kommen Sie back mit der tank," the officer called out but I was already tearin' down the country lane full pelt, an' I never stopped till I reached our lines.'

'Cor!'

Jimmy had got to know Spiv well enough to realise that anything he said should be taken with a large pinch of salt. Last week Spiv had told him and Charlie a far-fetched story about parachuting behind enemy lines on a secret mission.

Kate came back to the car looking a little concerned. 'OK, Tommy, out yer get,' she told him.

Spiv noticed the sad look in the lad's eyes and he winked at Kate. 'Would the ole gel let 'im come wiv us?' he asked quietly.

Kate's face lit up in a grateful smile. 'I'll go an' see,' she said quickly. 'Wait 'ere fer a minute, Tommy.'

Inside an hour the metropolis had been left behind and green fields spread out on either side of the wide road. There was little traffic that Saturday morning and in the back of the car the three youngsters chatted away happily.

'It was a nice gesture,' Kate told Spiv as he changed down a gear to climb Wrotham Hill.

'What was?'

'Lettin' Tommy come wiv us.'

'No worry.'

She looked ahead, idly watching the endless white line that stretched out in front of them in the centre of the road, and after a few minutes' silence she glanced back at Spiv. 'Did Amy tell yer about the little episode last Sunday?' she asked.

'About the side o' bacon?'

'Yeah.'

'Charlie seemed ter fink I was gonna buy it off 'im,' Spiv replied without taking his eyes off the road. 'I 'ad ter tell 'im in no uncertain terms that I don't buy stolen gear, an' certainly not from children. Well, it's partly true,' he grinned.

'A half trufe.'

He nodded, briefly casting his eyes towards her. 'I 'ave ter do what I do best, Kate,' he said in a resigned voice. 'The way I operate no one gets 'urt an' people get what they couldn't get ovverwise. Supply an' demand, yer might say.'

A few miles past Maidstone they stopped at a pub, and

when the children had gulped down lemonade and then run on to the village green to play Spiv reached out across the wooden table and rested his hand on Kate's. 'I'm glad yer agreed ter come out terday,' he said quietly.

She let her hand rest under his and looked up at the ivy-covered walls, then over to where the children were playing before matching his intent gaze. 'It makes a very nice change fer them,' she replied.

'An' what about you?'

'Yeah, me too.'

'I'd like ter get ter know yer better, Kate,' he said.

She slid her hand from beneath his and took up her drink. 'I like yer company, Spiv, but I need time ter sort me life out,' she told him. 'I can't afford any complications, not just yet. Since Will got caught it's bin a tryin' time fer me, an' fer the children as well, an' I've gotta see to it that they don't suffer. It's not easy fer them wivout a farver, not that they ever saw much of 'im at the best o' times, but people tend ter talk an' they can be cruel at times. Children pick fings up very quickly an' I've 'ad to answer a lot o' difficult questions already.'

'I understand,' he replied, 'but I'd like ter be around when yer feel the need ter move on wiv yer life. I'm a patient man, Kate.'

'I believe you are, Spiv,' she said smiling.

'Everyone calls me Spiv,' he told her. 'I'd prefer you ter call me Len.'

They gathered the children together and left the pub, driving along country lanes into the very heart of Kent. Orchards spread out around them and Spiv took pleasure in pointing out the ripening hops and red-brick drying kilns. After a while he swung the car into a narrow lane and then pulled up in a gravelled lay-by beside a rolling field. 'This is where I used ter come when I was a kid,' he said. 'Me an' a few pals used ter cycle all the way. We always took 'ome a load o' bluebells an' sometimes a few tiddlers in a jam jar. There's a stream at the ovver end o' the field.'

'Cor! Could we go fishin'?' Jenny asked.

'We've got no rods, but yer'll be able ter see the fish,' Spiv told her.

They got out of the car and climbed over a stile into the field, walking along a narrow track in the hot sun. Spiv carried a rolled rug and a wicker basket which he had taken from the boot of the car and he whistled merrily as he led the way. After a while the field dipped down into a dell and at the bottom they could see the stream flowing swiftly.

'See those trees,' Spiv said pointing. 'That's our base, OK?'

Kate smiled at his exuberance and let go of Jenny's hand. 'Don't go gettin' lost,' she called out as the three children ran off towards the copse.

'It's all right, there's a wire fence just frew the trees. They can't wander off,' Spiv reassured her.

It was very quiet, with the soft sound of the babbling brook drifting up to where they were reclining on the rug Spiv had set down under a large mossy oak tree. Far off in the distance a tractor engine coughed and spluttered and occasionally sounds of the children's happy excited voices rang out, and Kate lay back contentedly, her head cushioned on her clasped hands. 'This is sheer paradise,' she sighed, her eyes almost closed.

Spiv Copeland lay beside her, his feet resting on the wicker basket as he stared up at the gently swaying branches above them. 'This place 'asn't changed since I was a kid,' he told her. 'It was our own little piece of 'eaven. It seems so far away from the grimy backstreets an' smokin' chimneys.'

'Millions o' miles,' Kate mumbled.

He turned to face her, studying her face as he propped himself up on his elbow. ''As anyone ever told yer 'ow beautiful you are?' he said in a quiet voice.

'Many times,' she replied, a cheeky grin appearing on her face.

'Well, I'm tellin' yer now,' he whispered.

She turned her head slightly as he moved his face closer, and before she could resist his lips had reached hers. The touch was soft and gentle and she moulded her mouth to his, enjoying the kiss. His hand strayed to her midriff and moved up very gently, his palm opening to cup her breast. She knew she should push him away, but the kiss was sweet and his hand was gentle. How long had it been since a man had kissed her? How long since her desire had been stirred?

He moved his head back to look at her and she saw the fire burning in his deep blue eyes. Danger lurked there, she knew, but for the moment time was standing still, and for the first time in a very long while Kate Flannagan felt excitement growing, a delightful tingling in her loins. In these endless seconds she could savour his kisses and enjoy his gentle hands on her warm body and she started to tremble as she felt his breathing coming faster. He was touching her knee, and then very slowly he stroked his fingers up beneath her summer dress. His hand felt rough on her bare thigh and she struggled to regain control of her spinning senses. This was not an awakening of youth, the sweet temptation of a young virgin with a heart full of love and a head full of dreams. This was pure and unadulterated lust, the potent animal need for fulfilment, and in that instant of realisation the magical thread was broken.

'No. Please,' she gasped, clamping her hand on his arm.

'I love yer, Kate,' he gulped, his body pressing down over her.

'Len. No,' she said firmly as she wriggled clear and sat up. 'I shouldn't 'ave let yer kiss me. It was wrong.'

He turned and sat forward, awkwardly brushing his hands through his dark wavy hair. 'I meant it, Kate. I do love yer,' he said quietly.

She could see the children coming over the rise of the field and she looked at him frowning. 'You 'ardly know me,' she replied.

'It makes no difference,' he told her. 'There's no special time span where love's concerned.'

'I know, but we're all different, Len,' she said softly. 'I've told yer I'm not ready fer a commitment. I like yer, I like yer a lot. Yer a very nice man an' fun ter be wiv, but . . .'

'But yer don't love me.'

She looked down at her clenched hands as the children drew near. 'I don't know 'ow I feel. I'm all confused. You got me confused.'

He did not say anything for a moment, then he seemed to regain his composure and he gave her an embarrassed smile. ''Ere are the kids,' he said. 'We'd better get the food out.'

They sat beneath the large oak, shaded from the warm sun while they ate cheese sandwiches and slices of sweet currant cake. They quenched their thirst from a large bottle of orangeade, and with the irrepressible vitality of unbridled youth the children were off once more to seek out the mysteries and wonders of the countryside. Len sat quietly drawing on a cigarette, his gaze fixed on the copse where the children were playing. 'I nearly got married once,' he said after a while.

'What 'appened?'

'It was just before the war. She was nineteen an' I was in my late twenties,' Spiv went on. 'We'd got engaged an' planned ter get married the followin' year, but the war came an' Angela decided it'd be better ter wait. I was a bit impulsive, an' we 'ad a few words. After one bitter row I joined up. I was wounded at Dunkirk an' that was me army days over. When I came out of 'ospital I went ter see 'er, only ter find that she'd gone sweet on some sailor boy.'

'I'm sorry,' Kate said.

'I'm not,' Spiv grinned. 'I've seen 'er lately. Fifteen stone at least, wiv four kids an' a tongue that could strip wallpaper from twenty feet away. Nah, I was the lucky one.'

'I married Will when I was nineteen,' Kate told him. 'I was young an' impressionable, an' 'e was a Jack-the-lad. They all tried ter warn me off, me sister an' me friends, but no, I wouldn't listen. I was smitten.'

'I knew Will Flannagan,' Spiv replied. 'It was on the cards 'e'd end up the way 'e 'as. Did 'e ever knock yer about?'

Kate looked horrified. 'Knock me about?' she echoed. 'I might 'ave bin young an' stupid, but not that stupid. If 'e'd 'ave raised 'is 'and ter me I'd 'ave left 'im there an' then.'

'Yeah, I believe yer would 'ave,' Spiv said smiling. 'There's a lot o' fire bottled up inside of yer, Kate, I can tell.'

The sun was starting to dip down in the summer sky and the children had returned. Jenny looked tired with the effort of trying to keep up with the two boys and both Jimmy and

Tommy were grubby from climbing trees and rolling around in the lush grass.

'We'll walk along by the stream an' then cut back frew the trees ter the car,' Spiv said as he gathered up the rug and basket.

The cool clear water tumbled over stones and eddied around bullrushes by the bank as they walked along to the copse, where the channel veered away. It was becoming cooler now. Overhead clouds were gathering, and up ahead a rabbit stopped on the well-worn path and watched their approach, only to dart into the tall grass as Jenny spotted it.

'It's bin a lovely day,' Kate sighed, looking at Spiv.

'I've enjoyed it too,' he replied. 'Really I 'ave. I just want yer ter know that I don't regret what 'appened. I couldn't resist kissin' yer.'

'I enjoyed it too, Len, but I didn't want fings ter get out of 'and. They so easily could 'ave done.'

They walked through the trees and on to the main footpath, and soon they were in the car once more, the wooded, empty countryside rushing away behind them and giving way at last to urban grey. Up ahead the working heart of the capital loomed oppressively; large factories, emptied of their sweating, tired workforce for the weekend, still issued dirty strands of sulphur smoke from their dampened coke furnaces, like brooding monsters squatting on the land.

The diversion to Walworth was tinged with sadness as Jimmy said goodbye to his school chum and Tommy Brindley shyly thanked them all for his unexpected day out before leaving to face the grumblings and recriminations of his worn-out old grandmother. Then they drove along to Bermondsey, with the quaysides deserted and the tall cranes resting, and only the wash of the eddying river flowing out to sea and the squawk of seagulls diving down for morsels in the sour mud disturbing the melancholy stillness.

A tired family stepped out of the car on the corner of Milldyke Street and went into the grimy buildings that dominated the small turning, after first waving goodbye to Spiv Copeland as he drove away. Tired heads touched cool pillows and sleep came in a moment, but in the darkening kitchen Kate sat deep in thought. Her life could move on and the emptiness be filled so easily, if she wanted, but hard experience in the past had left scars that she was still learning to live with.

Chapter Fourteen

Amy Almond was an early riser, even after a hectic Saturday night out, and on Sunday morning she knocked on Kate's door as soon as she heard signs of life. Amy was not one to beat about the bush, and as usual she came straight to the point. 'Well? 'Ow did it go?' she asked with big eyes.

Kate still had her dressing gown on and she stood back to let her neighbour in, yawning widely as she followed the nosy woman along the passage to the kitchen. 'It was a lovely day. The kids really enjoyed it,' she told her. 'Len . . . Spiv took Jimmy's schoolfriend too.'

'So it's Len now,' Amy said quickly, a sly smile forming on her small lean face.

'I don't like callin' 'im Spiv,' Kate replied, yawning again as she sat down at the table.

Amy had already made herself comfortable in a chair. ''E's used to it,' she remarked. 'Everybody calls 'im Spiv. Anyway, did you enjoy the day out? I've bin dyin' ter know 'ow you an' 'im got on. I was gonna pop in last night when yer got 'ome but I guessed yer'd be tired. Besides, me an' Fred went out early. We went up town.'

Kate realised that Amy was expecting a blow by blow account and she stood up to tighten the cord of her dressing gown. 'There's some tea in the pot,' she said. 'Fancy a cup?'

'Make it a strong one, gel,' Amy requested. 'I got a bit of an 'angover after last night. We did knock a few back. Fred was a bit upset when 'e called round. 'Im an' the dragon 'ave 'ad a bust-up. She's started accusin' 'im of playin' around wiv ovver women. As if 'e would.'

Kate brought the tea in and sat down facing her. 'I'll 'ave ter call in on Mrs Johnson this mornin',' she said. 'She's takin' up a dress o' mine. I should 'ave gone ter see 'er yesterday but it slipped me mind.'

'Well, there were ovver fings ter fink about,' Amy replied with a smile. 'I mean ter say, it ain't everybody who gets taken out fer the day in a nice car by a smart feller.'

'Amy, I don't know what's goin' frew that mind of yours but I can assure yer it was just an innocent trip,' Kate countered. 'Nuffing untoward 'appened.'

'Nah, I know yer just went fer the kids' sake,' Amy mocked. 'I bet yer liked 'is company though.'

'Course I did. Len's a nice bloke, but there's no romance in the wind,' Kate replied, sipping her tea.

'You could do a lot worse. Spiv likes yer. 'E likes yer a lot,' Amy persisted.

Kate shrugged her shoulders and sought to change the subject. 'Did yer find out 'ow the petition went?' she asked.

'Everyone in this block signed it wiv the exception of ole Schofield,' Amy told her. 'Even old Ernie Walker signed it.'

'Why didn't Schofield put 'is name on the list?' Kate asked.

''Cos 'e's a nutcase, that's why,' Amy replied. 'Liz Fogan told me that 'e gave 'er an' Flossy Chandler a good ear'ole bashin'. 'E told Flossy 'e was a disgrace an' told Liz she was doin' it all wrong. 'E reckons they should 'ave appointed a spokesman ter front the Council. Did you ever 'ear anyfing so stupid? Still, I s'pose that's the way they do fings in the army, an' I'm sure Schofield still finks 'e's in uniform. Silly ole git.'

'Well, it takes all sorts,' Kate remarked dismissively.

'Those councillors'll soon realise that on Monday,' Amy said grinning. 'Mary Enright's got a nice little surprise in store for 'em. Accordin' ter Liz, she's got a dead rat in a cardboard box an' she's gonna take it round the Council on Monday when they 'and the petition in. The bloody fing's stinkin' to 'igh 'eaven already an' Mary's got it stored on 'er fire escape. I'm sure she's 'alfway round the twist. By the way, while I fink of it: did you 'ear about the rumpus on Friday night?'

'No.'

'Joe Sandford 'ad a set-to out the front.'

'Who wiv?'

'Chalkey James.'

'Who's Chalkey James?'

'Why, 'im from the market,' Amy went on. ''E's got the veg stall next ter Cheap Jack. 'E's bin knockin' Stella Sandford off fer ages while Joe's on night work. Anyway on Friday night Joe came over queer at work an' they sent 'im 'ome. 'E caught Stella an' Chalkey in bed tergevver an' 'e went stark ravin' mad. 'E gave 'er a black eye an' dragged Chalkey out o' the flat by 'is 'air ter give 'im what for. Ernie Walker saw it all from 'is winder. 'E told me if Jack Dennis 'adn't pulled Joe off Chalkey 'e would 'ave killed the dirty bleeder.'

Kate refilled the teacups and listened to Amy gossiping on about the neighbours. It seemed that the woman knew something about everyone who lived in the Buildings.

'That Meg Johnson's a strange woman,' Amy went on.

'She gets my Charlie ter run errands for 'er. Never bin the same since Annie Griffiths got strangled. I'm sure she finks she's gonna be next on the list.'

'She's a very nervous woman,' Kate remarked.

'I fink she's a bit touched if you ask me,' Amy said with a knowing look. 'She used ter live wiv a seaman over in Long Lane. 'E was separated from 'is wife. Nice bloke by all accounts. Scottish feller, from Glasgow. The poor sod got killed on the convoys. Went down wiv the ship in forty-one. That's when Meg Johnson moved in 'ere. The war was on an' they let the flats ter people on their own at that time. They wouldn't do it now though. I remember just after ole Annie got murdered, Meg Johnson played merry 'ell wiv ole Ferguson ter put new bolts on 'er front door. She wouldn't go out the flat at all fer months after, an' she used to love 'er drink. Used ter come 'ome sloshed all the time till Annie copped it. She goes out now, but she's always 'ome before it gets dark. Very strange woman that one.'

One hour later Amy left and Kate breathed a huge sigh of relief. Names had been bandied about and private lives laid bare by the incorrigible woman, and now time was getting on and there was the dinner to get. The place needed tidying up too and Kate had to remember to collect her dress, sew those buttons on Jenny's dress and try to make some inroads on the ironing which was piling up. She should pop round to see her sister Mary too, she told herself. She would be pleased to hear about the new job. Mary was always going on to her about finding some better work.

At midday Barney Schofield left the Buildings for South-wark Park. It was more than two miles away, he estimated, but nothing when compared with those long route marches in the blazing sun. At the end of those exhausting treks there was only short relief, a quick swig from the water bottle, and then the agony of blistered feet on the journey back. Today, the two miles would culminate in a seat at the front of the bandstand while the East Surrey's military band performed. Good band that, he reflected. Smart presentation too. No need to walk back either. The tram was a better proposition, he thought. Must remember to have a word with Briscoe though. Maybe he would call in at the estate office tomorrow morning. It would be up to Briscoe to nip the unrest in the bud. No need to read the riot act. A few well-chosen words would be enough. Might as well have a word too about the disgraceful behaviour in the street on Friday night. Tenants had responsibilities. Brawling and drunken carryings-on should not have to be tolerated. In the army there was always the threat of the glasshouse to ensure order. In Milldyke Street it seemed that anarchy was reigning.

Ernie Walker had decided to take the air and pop in the Woolpack for a lunchtime drink that Sunday. He put on his collar and tie and then went to close the window before leaving. Down below he could see the children busy at play and Amy Almond talking to Liz Fogan. Along the turning Flossy Chandler was in earnest conversation with Mrs Irons and he spotted Joe Sandford talking to the caretaker. Ernie sat down. There was time yet, he decided. Joe was no doubt talking about the fight on Friday night. Good scrap that. Maybe Jack Dennis should have let them get on with it. Chalkey was overdue for a good hiding, the way he was carrying on with Stella. Silly girl. Joe was a good provider and hard-working. What did some of these women expect? Chalkey was no oil painting anyway. Whatever Stella saw in him was a mystery to Ernie. The man wasn't fit to lick

Joe's boots. Hello, who's this coming in the turning? Strange face. Never seen him before. He's going in the end block. Maybe one of Flossy's fancy friends come to pay him a visit.

An hour later Ernie was still sitting in the window surveying the world below. The toffee-apple man had been and the ice-cream vendor too. Strange the old rag-and-bone man hadn't been round this morning. He was always calling in the street. Perhaps he was ill. Always something to see, Ernie thought. Who's this scruffy old gent?

A shuffling figure came into the street wearing a long overcoat despite the warm weather. He carried a cap in his hand and when he reached C block he stepped into the roadway and laid the cap down at his feet. Taking a long breath he started to sing in a deep voice, or rather uttered an unconnected series of notes, the words little more than grunts and groans. Occasionally the old man looked up at the windows and then lowered his head to continue his performance. Pennies clanked down and the children chased after them, dutifully taking them to the old man and dropping them into his greasy cap. Another group of children sat in the kerbside behind him, out of reach of the copper offerings as they mimicked him cheekily.

Ernie Walker watched the scene, estimating that at least one and fourpence had been tossed down to the singer, which would almost be enough to buy a couple of pints. He willed the old man to leave so that he himself could go to the pub, but the man was in no hurry it seemed. At last the recital ended and the children followed the old boy from the turning, at a discreet distance. Ernie decided that there was little more to see and little to miss now, and as he got up to close the window he saw the stranger coming from the end block. He appeared to be in a hurry and as he reached the corner of the turning he looked back once before disappearing from view.

Meg Johnson took a long time as usual to answer Kate's knock late on Sunday afternoon. 'Who's there?' she asked.

'It's me, Kate Flannagan.'

The bolts were slid back and Meg stood aside to let Kate in. 'I expected yer yesterday,' she said.

'I was out yesterday, Meg,' Kate told her. 'I 'ope I ain't inconvenienced yer.'

'Nah, I was just 'avin' a nap an' the knock made me jump,' she replied. 'Never mind, I'm glad yer called. I wanted to 'ave a word wiv yer.'

'About the dress?'

'Nah, it's about that petition we all signed.'

'Oh?'

'I'm worried, Kate,' Meg told her. 'S'posin' they give us notice ter quit. Where could I go? I'd 'ave ter find some furnished accommodation. A woman on 'er own couldn't get a flat the way fings are these days.'

'Look, there's no need ter worry, believe me,' Kate said positively. 'It's more than they dare do, give us notice ter quit. As long as we all sign an' all stick tergevver they've gotta do somefing about those dustbins. They're a disgrace. We can smell 'em in our block, so what d'yer fink it must be like fer those people livin' over 'em.'

'As long as yer fink it's all right,' Meg said, pinching her chin anxiously as she sat down at the table.

Kate stood in the middle of the kitchen studying her neighbour closely. 'Are you all right?' she asked her. 'You look worried.'

'Yeah, I'm all right. Now where did I put that dress?'

Kate sat down while Meg rummaged in the corner. The

143

room looked a mess and there were newspapers strewn around everywhere. She was beginning to regret ever asking the woman to alter her dress, but when Meg came over holding it up she could see that it had been taken up expertly. 'That looks just right,' she remarked. 'Was that your trade?'

'Goodness me, no,' Meg said smiling. 'I never 'ad a proper trade but I've always liked sewin' an' dressmakin'. It's a sort of 'obby I picked up. I used to earn quite a bit o' money at one time doin' alterations an' repairs. I wouldn't 'ave the patience ter do big jobs now, although me eyes are still good. Yer need good eyes fer dressmakin'. My Alec used ter marvel at the way I sewed. 'E used ter be sure I'd ruin my eyes wiv the work I did.'

Kate feigned ignorance. 'Your 'usband?'

Meg smiled and shook her head. 'We couldn't get married. Alec was spliced already an' 'e couldn't get a divorce. She was Catholic, yer see. It didn't matter, we were 'appy. Alec was in the merchant navy. 'E was a very good man, Gawd rest 'is soul. 'E went down wiv 'is ship in the Atlantic.'

'I'm terribly sorry,' Kate said sympathetically.

'That's me when I worked over Poplar,' Meg said, pointing to a framed photograph as she dabbed at her eyes.

Kate gazed at the group of white-overalled women and an old man who stood to one side with a large grin on his face, and as she was about to ask her more about the picture Meg reached out and touched her arm. 'I'm sorry. I never asked yer if yer wanted a cuppa,' she said quickly.

Kate had been trying to ignore the strong musty smell since she came in and she shook her head. 'It's all right, Meg, I gotta get back. There's so much I gotta do. 'Ow much do I owe yer?'

''Alf a crown,' Meg replied.

'Well, if I find anyfing else needs alterin' I'll know where

144

ter come,' Kate said getting up.

'I'll put that in a bag for yer,' Meg said.

'No, it's not necessary,' Kate replied. 'I'm only goin' next door.'

Meg followed Kate along the dark passage and before drawing the bolts once more she called the young woman back. 'Don't you start goin' out after dark,' she warned her. 'This area's not safe, not after what 'appened ter poor Mrs Griffiths.'

'You shouldn't upset yerself too much, Meg,' Kate told her, touching her arm kindly. 'You're quite safe 'ere.'

'These bolts are a comfort,' Meg replied. 'I got ole Ferguson ter put 'em on for me. Whoever it was killed old Annie Griffiths could be after me next.'

'Don't be silly,' Kate said smiling at her.

'You don't know the 'alf of it, me gel,' Meg replied as she drew the bolts. Kate heard the door being secured as she hurried down from the first floor and out into the cool evening air. The woman was obsessed, she sighed. What had she meant about her not knowing the half of it? Living alone must be affecting her mind.

Flossy Chandler rushed along Milldyke Street feeling very nervous. The man who had called on him that afternoon with the message was insistent that he should be on time. Flossy had not taken kindly to the fat, cigar-smoking little man squeezing his knee as they talked the other day, though, nor to having his cheek tweaked. What did they take him for? He wasn't that easy. Anyway he had had to suffer the indignities in order to get his big chance. It was an opportunity that he simply couldn't miss, and should it all go well Flossy Chandler would become something more than just a figure of fun.

Chapter Fifteen

Thomas Wheatley's new pie factory in Dockhead was only a few minutes' walk from Milldyke Street and when Kate arrived there at ten minutes to eight on Monday morning she found a crowd of young women standing by the entrance chatting together nervously.

'As long as it's not as noisy as the tin basher's I don't mind,' a buxom woman said to her young companion who was wearing thick-lensed glasses and seemed a little nervous.

'I was at the bottle washer's in St Thomas's Street,' she replied. 'I 'ad ter get out o' there before I got crippled up wiv arthritis. We was standin' in water all the time an' those rubber boots was playin' me feet up somefing terrible.'

Kate smiled to herself, sympathising through her own experiences.

'Where did you work, luv?' the big woman asked her.

'Pearson's in Long Lane,' Kate told her.

'What, the vinegar factory? What a dump that is,' the woman said pulling a face. 'I worked there fer a time, till I upset the foreman. I told 'im ter stick the job up 'is arse an' I went ter Dawson's the tin basher's. Drove me round the bloody twist it did. Talk about noise. I come 'ome every

147

night wiv me 'ead poundin'. My ole man was beginnin' ter fink I'd gone off 'im.'

A tall reedy-looking woman came out of the factory carrying a clipboard under her arm. 'If you'll all follow me, ladies,' she said officiously.

After a quick tour of the factory the women were assigned their jobs. Kate was put to work alongside the big friendly woman and the nervous one with the thick glasses. A thin woman with dyed blonde hair made up a foursome and she looked uninterested as the tall thin supervisor explained what was required. 'You'll be packing ready-wrapped pork pies into these cardboard boxes and sealing them for transportation,' she began. 'Two dozen packets to a box and this is the way they're to be packed.'

The blonde raised her eyes to the ceiling as the woman repeated the packing demonstration. 'Yeah, we've got it, luv,' she said sighing.

The supervisor gave her a hard look. 'I'll be back later to see how you're getting on,' she announced.

'Silly prat,' the blonde growled. 'Does she fink we're all stupid or somefing?'

The buxom woman chuckled. 'We'd better get ter know each ovver. I'm Bet Groves,' she said.

'I'm Milly Tate,' the nervous one added, blinking behind her thick glasses.

Kate introduced herself and the blonde gave her a searching look. 'Did you used ter live in Weston Street?' she asked.

Kate nodded, sensing what the next question would be.

'Are you Will Flannagan's wife?'

'Yeah, that's right,' Kate replied, not wanting to let her know about the pending divorce.

'My Gary knocked around wiv your Will,' the woman told her.

'What's your name then?' Bet cut in.

'Norma Prentiss,' she replied, puffing as she got into a mix-up with the packing.

The supervisor came up at that moment and gave Norma a stern look. 'It's quite easy if you just pay attention,' she told her. 'No, not like that. The other way round.'

Kate was glad of the interruption. She would have to be careful about letting Norma Prentiss know too much, she thought.

The first day at Wheatley's seemed to pass quickly and Kate felt quite content as she made her way home that evening. Bet Groves seemed nice and friendly, with a good sense of humour. Milly Tate was a very timid young woman but it was apparent that Bet had already taken her under her wing, protecting her from Norma's barbed comments by skilfully manipulating the conversation. As for the work itself, it was clean and much less noisy than the vinegar factory.

Monday morning had started very early for Charles Goodright. He had caught the early train and arrived at school before the rest of the staff. His first task was to replace *Lust in the Sun* in Ramsey's desk, then he made himself a coffee while he pondered over the forthcoming police visit that morning. He smiled slyly as he pictured the look on Ramsey's face when he arrived a little later and opened his desk. Now that the missing 'textbook' had been returned there would be little mileage in pursuing a case against Thomas Brindley.

At ten o'clock Detective Sergeant Cassidy was shown into the headmaster's study.

'I'll get my secretary to fetch the master concerned,' Goodright said as he motioned the policeman into a chair.

'I'd rather have a brief chat with you first,' Cassidy replied. 'Can you tell me a little about Herbert Ramsey? His attitude towards his class, his teaching record. Does he favour the cane? Is he very strict?'

The headmaster leaned back in his chair and sighed. 'I'd like to be able to tell you that Herbert Ramsey has a good rapport with his class, but I'm sorry to say that's not the case,' he began. 'Ramsey's been at this school for over ten years now and to be perfectly honest I think it's time he made a move. Don't get me wrong, there's nothing amiss with his teaching. On the contrary he's a first-rate teacher, academically speaking, but he does tend to overdo the discipline. As headmaster I am responsible for signing every teacher's punishment book and I do find that Ramsey rules with the rod.'

'What about Brindley? Has he been caned very often recently?' Cassidy asked.

Goodright sighed again. 'Too much, I'm afraid.'

'And did you not query it?'

'Yes, I did,' Goodright replied, 'but Ramsey told me that the boy had been getting out of control. He seemed to feel that where the lad lived had something to do with it.'

'Milldyke Buildings?'

'Yes.'

'Is Ramsey a local man?'

'No, he lives in Sutton.'

'Does he know Bermondsey well?'

'The immediate area, I would say.'

Pat Cassidy leaned back and clasped his hands together in his lap. 'I think I'd better have a chat with him now,' he said.

When Herbert Ramsey walked into the headmaster's study he looked a little uncomfortable. 'Morning, Mr Goodright,' he said, giving Cassidy a quick look.

'This is Detective Sergeant Cassidy from Dockhead police,' Goodright informed him.

Ramsey gave the officer a weak smile then turned to the headmaster. 'I think I should tell you first that my textbook has been returned,' he said. 'I found it in my desk drawer this morning.'

'Oh?'

'Whoever took it must have arrived early and replaced it before assembly,' Ramsey explained.

'Then we just have the assault business to think about,' Goodright replied. 'By the way, I hope you're feeling well after the weekend rest.'

Ramsey seethed inside at the inference. Goodright was more concerned about the good name of the school than the welfare of his staff. He had always placed them second. As for the novel, he wouldn't be surprised if Goodright had borrowed it himself. 'I'm feeling a little stiff,' he answered.

'I have to ask you if you still wish to press charges against the boy,' Cassidy cut in.

Ramsey glanced quickly at the headmaster before replying, and seeing no expression of support he shrugged his shoulders. 'I don't wish to put the good name of the school in jeopardy, but I do think that as teachers we should be prepared to stamp out the sort of violence I was subjected to,' he asserted. 'Brindley's violent outburst on Friday was nothing more than I would expect from the likes of him.'

'Would you like to enlarge on that, Mr Ramsey?' Cassidy pressed him.

'Brindley lives in Milldyke Buildings, sergeant, and I'm sure you don't need me to tell you about that place,' the teacher responded. 'In the ten years I've been at this school I must have had a dozen or so pupils from Milldyke Buildings, and I found that without exception they were bad-mannered, unruly and academically poor. What's more I've found them to be very disruptive. It seems that the rest of the pupils tend to look up to them for some unfathomable reason.'

'So you would like us to charge the lad?' Cassidy asked him.

'I should think very carefully, Ramsey,' the headmaster said with a frown. 'At last week's headmasters' conference the anti-corporal punishment lobby made considerable gains, and questions will be asked in court as to your personal interpretation of class discipline and the measures you have applied in that direction. Of course I will have to submit the punishment book for scrutiny, and in my opinion certain magistrates might well take the view that you have been too severe with the cane during the past few months.'

'Do you share that opinion?' Ramsey asked quickly, his forehead creasing. 'You've never questioned my methods.'

'My opinion doesn't matter. It will be of no relevance in court,' Goodright replied. 'The magistrate will make his or her own judgement.'

Pat Cassidy sat up straight in his chair. 'Does the name Duggan mean anything to you, Mr Ramsey?' he asked.

The master paled noticeably. 'I . . . er . . . I don't recall the name,' he faltered.

'Let me refresh your memory,' Cassidy said. 'Two years ago you had reason to go to Milldyke Buildings to see a Mrs Duggan about her son's conduct. From information we gleaned it seemed that Mr Duggan came home from work rather the worse for drink and resented your presence there. I understand he assaulted you. Was that so?'

'I know nothing of this,' Goodright remarked with a frown.

'It's a long time ago,' Ramsey replied, his shoulders sagging. 'Mrs Duggan came to see me after the School Board inspector called on her about her son's poor attendance record. You'll have his report on file. My follow-up was voluntary and out of school hours so I didn't see the need to submit an official report. At the time Mrs Duggan was also concerned about her son's unruly behaviour and she asked me to make sure that he was properly disciplined in class. I made arrangements to visit her at home for a further discussion, but unfortunately it was misinterpreted by Mr Duggan, who I might add was well known for his violent behaviour when in drink. I was asked to leave and Mr Duggan followed me from the buildings shouting abuse. I was not badly assaulted. In fact I was merely shoved as Mr Duggan attempted to force me out of the street.'

Pat Cassidy nodded. 'I mentioned this to highlight the difficulties you might encounter should you decide to proceed with a prosecution,' he began. 'You see, Mr Ramsey, pupil violence directed at a teacher is almost unheard of and the local press will be interested in reporting the event. When the people of Milldyke Buildings get to read about it they'll be reminded of your visit to their street, and you have to consider that they too might have misinterpreted your visit. Their sympathies will quite likely be for the Brindley boy, considering that his family are neighbours and Mrs Brindley is very ill. It would only need one of them to talk to the newspapers. So I suggest you give it some very serious thought before making any decision.'

Herbert Ramsey had already made up his mind to drop the whole thing before he left the headmaster's study, and after he had closed the door behind him Charles Goodright gave the policeman a confident smile. 'That was very well handled, if I might say so,' he remarked.

Back in his classroom Ramsey sat thinking about what the policeman had said. To his credit he had been discreet. The true account was something better forgotten. Bella Duggan had been very generous with her favours and he had only just made himself presentable when that drunken docker husband of hers barged in. Being dragged from the flat and along the street by his hair was bad enough, but to have it done in full view of most of the Milldyke scum who were sitting in their windows laughing and shouting obscenities was worse than anything he could ever have imagined, and it still caused him nightmares.

Francis Chandler worked by day at Moreland's, a gents' outfitter's in the Old Kent Road. On Friday and Saturday evenings he played the piano at local pubs and had become a firm favourite with the clientele. Flossy's effeminate ways left him vulnerable to certain nasty elements known to frequent pubs in Bermondsey, but he felt safe at the Woolpack and at the Horse and Groom in Long Lane. Customers there were largely rivermen and they ensured that no one took advantage of their talented ivory-tickler. Often they would invite him round to parties at weekends and Flossy was happy to oblige. He enjoyed the bawdy banter of the tough dockers and the sympathy he received from the womenfolk. He could always be sure of a friendly ear too when he was feeling low and in need of advice, and he could always get a pair of curtains run up or cushions re-covered to enhance his flat. All in all Flossy Chandler was happy with his lot, but deep down inside he sometimes wondered whether or not he was making the most of his musical talents. Although he usually played by ear he could read music, and his repertoire was extensive.

The young man's comfortable life had been shaken up one Saturday evening when Bernie Gilchrist visited the Woolpack after getting a tip-off about Flossy's piano playing. The fat, cigar-smoking impresario had plans to produce a talent night at the Trocette cinema and already he had signed up a juggler, two singers and an impressionist, as well as a dancing troupe, and he felt that a pianist would give the show a good balance.

Bernie Gilchrist knew that he could fill the cinema by promoting local talent competitions and then be on hand to sign up the winners, who would appear under contract at selected talent competitions throughout the country. He was shrewd enough to realise that the whole entertainment industry was going through dramatic changes and he wanted to be in on the ground floor.

On Saturday evening Bernie listened to Flossy Chandler as he played the pub customers' favourite melodies and was very impressed. After an arranged meeting Flossy was signed up to appear at the Trocette cinema in two weeks' time.

'I was really shocked,' the young man said to Liz Fogan as they stood chatting outside E block. 'Just fancy, me up on the stage in front of all you lot. I'll just die, I know I will.'

'What d'yer mean, in front of all us lot?' Liz teased him. 'Who ses we're gonna come?'

'Well, I'm bankin' on yer support,' he retorted sharply. 'I got a chance o' winnin', so Mr Gilchrist reckons. I could be a big star one day an' you'll be able to say that yer knew me once.'

'Countin' yer chickens, ain't yer?' Liz replied.

'Mr Gilchrist gave me some tickets ter sell. They're only 'alf a crown,' Flossy told her. 'I've saved two for yer.'

'Never mind about the tickets, what about the meetin' wiv the Council?' Liz reminded him.

'When is it?' he asked.

'This Thursday afternoon,' she told him.

'Yer mean I gotta waste me 'alf day goin' to a bleedin' Council meetin'?' Flossy groaned. 'I was intendin' givin' me place a good goin' frew. Those mats o' mine need takin' out the yard an' givin' a good shakin' an' I was gonna turn me cupboards out. I don't get much chance ovver times.'

'Well, it'll just 'ave ter keep,' Liz said firmly. 'Freda can't come, nor can Mrs Champion. That only leaves me an' you, Mary Enright an' Sadie Elmley.'

'Mary ain't bringin' that poxy rat, is she?' Flossy asked, looking horrified. 'It'll be stinkin' to 'igh 'eaven by then.'

'You know Mary. She won't be put off,' Liz said smiling.

'I can't come wiv yer on Thursday,' Flossy wailed. 'I couldn't face it if she took that rat out of the box. I'd die, I know I would.'

'Right then. No meetin', no support, so put that in yer pipe an' smoke it,' Liz told him sharply. 'An' yer can put them tickets where a monkey puts 'is nuts.'

'All right, all right, you win,' the young man sighed, pouting. 'But don't let Mary Enright anywhere near me, I'm tellin' yer.'

Liz Fogan smiled to herself as she watched him hurry off along the turning. It had been hard work getting everyone in the Buildings to sign the petition, and then there had been the wrangling to get a firm commitment from the councillors. Now though it seemed that some progress might be made and Liz went into the block to see Mary Enright. Flossy was right, she thought. That rat would be too much to contend with, even for the hard-nosed councillors on the housing committee.

Chapter Sixteen

The Harris estate office was situated by the river, tucked between two grimy wharves. The building had once been occupied by a cordwainer who drank his profits away, and when he was no longer able to pay the rent on the property Harris Estates repossessed and moved in themselves. The upper floor had been turned into offices and the ground floor was used for storage. In the far corner, behind the bags of plaster, lead piping and timber, stood the bits and pieces of furniture and bric-a-brac that had belonged to Annie Griffiths. They had been taken there after the police had finished going through them for clues to Annie's murder.

Harris Estates had held on to her personal effects for more than seven months now, and as no one had come forward to claim them they contacted the local branch of the Salvation Army to have them taken away. The Salvationists were always on the lookout for furniture and ornaments, the latter to be sold off to raise funds while the main items of furniture were distributed to the needy.

Ted Briscoe was glad to be getting rid of the stuff, but he had had his eye on two oriental vases with gold figuring and he felt that charity began at home. Why allow the Salvation Army to sell them off when he could dispose of them himself? True, they were both chipped at the rim and scratched in places, but they looked very old and were no doubt worth a few bob. He would have to be careful though. Harris Estates were particular about doing things by the book and the whole of the contents of Annie Griffiths's flat had been itemised. Mr Brown the estate manager would have sent a copy off to the Salvation Army and they would sign on receipt of the items.

Late on Monday afternoon a van pulled up outside the estate office and Briscoe was waiting. The driver and his assistant soon loaded the furniture on to the van and Briscoe fished into his pocket for the tip. Mr Brown always allowed five shillings for a tip but to Ted Briscoe's way of thinking it was excessive. Half-a-crown was plenty, considering that the men were getting a wage anyway. 'There we are,' he said, passing a half-crown over. 'The only items you ain't got are the two broken ornaments. They've gone in the dustbin.'

The driver did not seem interested as he signed the list. As far as he was concerned the storeman in Spa Road never bothered to check incoming items. It was all rubbish anyway. Any decent sticks of furniture would be dropped off at the second-hand shop and the profit shared.

That evening Ted Briscoe took the vases to a shop in Greenwich and discovered that they were nineteenth-century ceramics, of a kind that had been commonly imported after Japan opened up to the West. As the shopowner explained, in pristine condition they would have fetched quite a considerable sum, but being chipped and scratched as they were he could only pay five shillings for each. Anyway it hadn't been a bad day, Ted thought. He'd pocketed half the tip and now he'd got a ten-shilling note for the vases. The silly old cow should have taken more care of them, he mumbled to himself as he left the shop.

★ ★ ★

Kate cleared away the tea things and set about the washing-up. Jenny helped her mother with the drying while Jimmy got on with his homework. Ramsey had been unusually quiet that afternoon and the tasks set for completion by next morning didn't seem too hard by his standards.

Kate was looking forward to a quiet evening after her first day at Wheatley's and the knock on the front door made her sigh irritably. That would be Amy Almond, she guessed. She did seem to pick the most inconvenient times to call, and when she got chatting it was hard to get rid of her.

'I hope I'm not calling at an awkward time,' Pat Cassidy said smiling.

Kate was a little taken aback but she returned his smile. 'Of course not. Come in.'

Jimmy looked up with concern as the policeman walked into the living room but Pat reassured him with a large wink. 'Homework?' he asked.

The lad nodded and Kate put her hand on his shoulder. 'Jimmy, can yer do that in yer bedroom?' she asked him.

The detective smiled at Jenny who had come from the scullery still holding the tea towel. 'So this is Jenny,' he said amiably.

The young girl looked at him curiously and Kate took the cloth from her. 'You go in there wiv Jimmy, luv,' she told her. 'An' don't you torment 'im while 'e's busy.'

'I was just on my way home,' Cassidy told her as soon as they were alone. 'I thought you might like to know that Ramsey's decided to drop the charge against the Brindley lad. I got a call from the headmaster this afternoon.'

'I'm so glad,' Kate replied. 'Won't you take a seat fer a minute? I'm sorry I've got no coffee but I can make yer a cup o' tea.'

Pat could see that she was a little uneasy and he held up his hand as he sat down at the table. 'To be honest I've drunk more than enough coffee today. Tea would be fine,' he said, smiling disarmingly.

Kate went into the scullery and looked back into the room. 'D'you take sugar?'

'Two please.'

She lit the gas under the tin kettle and reached for the tea caddy. 'I was just wonderin' if you 'ad anyfing ter do wiv Ramsey's decision,' she remarked.

'I just spelled out the difficulties involved,' Pat said, smiling to himself. 'I think the headmaster twisted his arm a little. The good name of the school and all that.'

'Of course,' Kate replied with a slight intonation. 'You take your job very seriously, don't yer?'

'I do my best,' he answered, tracing a line along the white tablecloth with his forefinger. 'I'm thinking about a transfer.'

Kate felt a sudden twinge of regret. 'I'd be sorry ter see yer leave this area,' she said impulsively.

'Oh?'

'Yes, I would,' she said, gaining courage. 'Not all policemen are as sympathetic as you, not in my experience.'

'I grew up in Bermondsey,' he told her. 'I know some of the problems, and this particular street has certainly posed a few for us.'

'I s'pose a bad name tends ter stick,' Kate replied as she took the boiling kettle from the gas. 'Ter be honest, I dreaded movin' in 'ere but there were no ovver choices open ter me. The rent 'ere's cheap in comparison, an' they don't ask too many questions.'

Pat Cassidy sat back in his chair and wearily rolled his stiff neck, brushing his hand over his thick fair hair. Kate noticed as she came in carrying the filled teapot. 'You look tired,' she remarked.

Pat sat up straight and smiled. 'Being a policeman is like most jobs,' he sighed. 'We get good days and bad days. Today was a bad day, until I got that phone call from the school. To be perfectly honest, I think Ramsey brought the attack on himself by his attitude. It seems that to his way of thinking the cane is the answer to everything.'

Kate poured the tea. 'You were sayin' yer might get a transfer. Where to?'

'Oh, I don't know, really. Somewhere out of London. Essex maybe, or down in Sussex. Somewhere away from the reminders, the ghosts.'

'Do we ever leave 'em be'ind, or do we take 'em wiv us, wherever we go?' Kate asked, her eyes meeting his.

Pat smiled and shrugged his broad shoulders. 'It's a good question,' he replied.

Kate handed him his tea and saw the signs of fatigue etched in his handsome face. 'The two boys 'ave bin very well be'aved since that Sunday,' she told him.

He grinned. 'I got into the same sort of trouble when I was their age. My punishment was a clip round the ear, and another from my father when the policeman took me home.'

Kate sipped her tea, glancing at him over the cup. 'Do yer live far?' she asked.

'Catford. I've got a furnished flat.'

'Is it nice?'

'It's functional.'

'Is there anyone special?' Kate asked, feeling her face redden a little.

He shook his head. 'I'd be poor company at the present time, and a bad investment for any young woman, what with the working hours and the sort of job I do.'

Kate put down her cup and rested her arms on the table. 'I don't believe that,' she said smiling. 'Fings can be good, whatever the job, provided the relationship's right. In my case the long hours I spent alone were anxious ones. I never knew what Will was gettin' up to an' I was ferever fearin' the knock on the door. The kids must 'ave felt it too. Jimmy at least.'

Pat Cassidy's eyes came up to meet hers. 'Are you coping?' he asked quietly.

She nodded. 'I've come ter terms wiv it. The kids are growin' up an' I've just got a full-time job at Wheatley's. Jimmy'll be thirteen this September. Anuvver two years an' 'e'll be startin' work.'

'That's good,' he replied, putting his empty cup back in the saucer. 'Well, I'd better be getting off home, I suppose.'

'I could rustle you up somefing,' she suggested.

Pat shook his head. 'Right now I need a stiff drink and then I'll settle for a good night's sleep. Thanks very much for the offer though.'

'It's the least I could do,' she replied, giving him a shy smile.

The tired policeman left the Buildings and walked quickly towards London Bridge Station. The evening rush was over, and the Tooley Street wharves were draped in shadows. A tram rumbled past and a few late workers hurried by. Pat's immediate thoughts centred on a quiet half hour in the pub opposite the station before catching the train to Catford Bridge. What had really prompted him to go and see Kate Flannagan? he asked himself. Was it to reassure her about her son's schoolfriend, or was it to see her again? She had stirred his suppressed feelings that evening in the coffee house to such a degree that he had not been able to get her out of his mind. She had reminded him of Karen in looks and colouring. She had Karen's eyes too, large and expressive, but there was a depth, a mysterious side to her that contrasted with Karen's outgoing nature.

When the late train pulled out of London Bridge Pat Cassidy rested his head back against the seat and closed his eyes. Tiredness was weighing down on him but he knew that he could not let go or he would wake up in Brighton. Work had been his crutch and the double shifts an excuse to avoid the loneliness of his dingy flat in Catford. The chief superintendent had been concerned at first and then insistent. 'Either you ease up or I'll book you in for a medical,' he had warned. 'Take some leave, there's plenty due.'

The train trundled along and the rhythmic clatter of the wheels served to magnify his fatigue. He saw the young woman clearly in his mind and she was smiling prettily behind his stinging eyelids. As much as he tried to hang on, sleep finally overtook him and her features faded. Another face appeared, misty at first but growing in clarity. It was gaunt to the point of being skeletal, and the lips were blue and edged with a white crusty film. The man was wearing a striped uniform and a skull cap and he raised a bony hand. 'Over there in the hut,' he croaked. 'With the sick ones.'

The officer drew his service revolver as he crossed the muddy compound, and when he entered the hut he had to fight back an almost overpowering nausea at the fetid stench. Two rows of bodies lay under thin blankets, and at the end of the row he found him. He looked well nourished, with tell-tale strands of blonde showing faintly against the dyed hair. The patient did not resist as he was pulled roughly on to his feet and subjected to a body search but his cold arrogance was only too apparent as he stared down at the dying. The emaciated man who had located him was waiting outside and more had gathered. They made no attempt to exact their revenge but stared hollow-eyed, pointing their fingers as the manacled captor who had dared to hide amongst the sick and dying was brought out. Everyone was nodding, and the tormentor's shoulders sagged. There was no escape. His creed was different, hostile, but he understood. An eye for an eye.

The officer dragged him roughly away, round to the rear of the hut, and there in the mud and filth of the concentration camp he forced the guard to kneel. What was the alternative? the officer thought. A trial, in a clean, sterile courtroom, far removed from the unspeakable horror of the death camp. The chance to argue, to object, to protest. What chance had he given the prisoners under his control? What chance had his ilk given Karen and tiny Sarah?

The prisoner turned his head to glare up at the officer, and with a cynical smile he bowed to the mud. Better here and now, he thought. A bullet rather than a rope. It was clean and sudden. The soldier's way.

There were no last words, no last cigarette. Time was short and the starving and dying needed tending. The officer pointed his revolver at the back of his captive's head and squeezed the trigger.

The inmates heard the shot and made room for him to pass, their faces destined to be etched in his mind until the day he died. The jeep was waiting and the young corporal gave him a white-faced attempt at a smile as he clicked in the gear. Another death camp had been found and help had to be co-ordinated swiftly. Tears formed in the young soldier's eyes at what he had witnessed but Lieutenant Patrick Cassidy of the Army Special Investigation Branch was dry-eyed and devoid of remorse.

Doors slamming shut woke him with a start and he just had time to clamber down on to the platform before the train pulled out of Catford Bridge Station. It had happened again, he thought, and this time in more detail. Maybe the superintendent was right. Maybe he should get himself checked out and take some leave.

Twilight in the suburban street made the trees seem darker, like twisted bodies reaching hopelessly up to the sky, and Cassidy shuddered as he put his key in the lock. Please God let there be something left in the bottle, he prayed.

Chapter Seventeen

As Kate left for work on Thursday morning she ran into Liz Fogan who was coming home from her early-morning cleaning job.

'Wish us luck this afternoon, luv,' Liz said, pulling a face.

'Yeah, I 'ope it goes well,' Kate told her. 'Did yer manage ter get enough signatures?'

'Everyone signed, except that ole bastard Schofield,' Liz replied. 'Mind you, it's nuffing more than I'd expect from that silly old git. Anyway we'll do our best, an' Mary Enright's got a nice surprise for 'em.'

'Yeah, Amy told me,' Kate laughed.

Liz rested her hand on Kate's arm. 'Flossy Chandler's comin' wiv us too,' she said with a quick raising of her eyes. 'I got a feelin' it's gonna be quite an afternoon, what wiv one fing an' anuvver. By the way, 'ave yer seen anyfing o' Flossy lately?' Kate shook her head. ''E's entered fer a talent contest. Apparently it's at the Trocette on Saturday week,' Liz went on. ''E's floggin' tickets fer it. Oh well, I must get 'ome. I got a lot ter do before that meetin'.'

Kate hurried along Dock Lane feeling cheerful. Her new job was proving to be much more congenial than the vinegar factory and Bet Groves's bawdy sense of humour helped to make the time pass quickly. The children had settled into their new surroundings nicely and Jimmy appeared to be working hard at school, if the way he tackled his homework was anything to go by. The neighbours seemed a friendly lot on the whole, though they were very diverse. Ernie Walker always had a few words to say when she passed him on the stairs, and even Barney Schofield had passed the time of day.

The morning was bright and sunny and Kate could smell the river as she neared the factory. Pat Cassidy's visit on Monday evening had been a pleasant surprise and had given her plenty to think about. Was he genuinely interested in her or had his visit been solely out of duty?

The day began as usual with the clatter of machines and buzz of conversation in the large airy factory. The only thing different this morning was that Norma Prentiss had been replaced by another young woman who seemed to know Bet Groves very well.

'The flash cow seemed a bit dopey ter me,' Bet remarked to her workmates. 'I mean ter say, it don't take much ter learn 'ow ter put pies in boxes, but she was makin' 'ard work of it. I know that supervisor's a bit of a dragon, but give 'er 'er due, she was soon on to 'er. Anyway we're better off wivout Norma. Yer can't expect to earn a bonus wiv somebody like that on the bench.'

The new worker smiled slyly at Bet. 'Yer dead right, gel,' she told her.

Kate caught the look between the two and guessed that Bet had had something to do with Norma Prentiss being taken off the bench. It was just as well. She had been very nosy about Will's affairs and Kate had suspected from her attitude and her snide remarks that the blonde could have been one of his fancy women.

The morning passed quickly and when the factory whistle sounded at midday Kate prepared to hurry home for a cup of tea and a sandwich.

'It's a glorious day, why don't yer come wiv us?' Bet suggested. 'We're goin' in the church gardens an' we've got enough sandwiches ter share.'

Bet's friend Lucy Halliday linked her arm through Kate's in a friendly gesture. 'Yeah, c'mon, it'll be nice.'

Kate was persuaded and she spent a pleasant lunch hour in the quiet flower-filled gardens of St James's Churchyard. The women chatted away around her and there was time to think: of Len Copeland, who had unexpectedly rekindled her dormant sexuality and reminded her that she was still desirable, and Pat Cassidy, the policeman with a kind streak and a friendly nature who had constantly filled her thoughts since the first time she met him.

Bet's gravel voice broke through her reverie. 'C'mon, gels, look at the time.'

The big black clockface in the church tower showed ten minutes to one o'clock and there were many more pies to pack.

Liz Fogan stood outside E block waiting for Maud Sattersley to join them and she turned to Flossy in exasperation. 'Go an' see if that scatty mare's ready,' she growled at him. 'We mustn't be late.'

Finally the women and the young man left the turning, with Liz Fogan leading the way. Flossy walked beside her, dressed in his smart grey suit with a silk scarf tied at the neck. Behind them came the widowed Maud Sattersley, her grey hair neatly waved, her slight frame shrouded by a loose cotton dress and thick brown cardigan. Freda Irons had linked arms with her and she looked spruce in a light summer coat with her dark hair pulled into a bun at the nape of her neck. Feeling guilty for telling the caretaker about the petition, Freda had decided to be brave; after all, she wouldn't be alone. They were all in it together.

Plump-faced Ada Champion and the worried-looking Sadie Elmley were at the rear, both wearing their Sunday-best coats. Their leader was pleased with the turnout. At first every one of them had made excuses not to go to the meeting, but with some gentle persuasion and a few well-chosen words that made them all feel guilty they had responded to the call to arms.

'I 'ope that mad cow Mary don't turn up wiv that box of 'ers,' Ada said sharply.

'If she does I'm off,' Flossy declared adamantly. 'I'd die a death, really I would. I wouldn't know where ter put me face.'

'Don't worry, I told 'er the meetin' wasn't fixed yet,' Liz reassured them.

'She'll be upset when she finds out,' Ada replied.

'Look, don't worry,' Liz said. 'She's at work all day. When I see 'er I'll just say that a man come round from the Council an' told us the meetin' was fixed fer terday. She won't be any the wiser.'

They walked determinedly along Abbey Street and into Spa Road. Ahead they could see the Council offices and Flossy sighed nervously. 'I 'ope they don't start shoutin' at us,' he remarked. 'Shoutin' gives me an 'eadache.'

'Anyfing gives you an 'eadache,' Ada muttered.

'I can't 'elp it, I'm just sensitive,' Flossy replied with a blinding look at the elderly woman.

'Oh Gawd blimey! Look who's standin' on the steps,' Freda moaned.

There in front of them was the indomitable Mary Enright

with the cardboard box tucked under her arm and a wide smile on her round flat face.

'C'mon, gels, we don't wanna be late,' she said as the party reached her.

'We only just found out about the meetin',' Liz told her, looking guilty.

'Don't give me that,' Mary replied a little indignantly. 'I know yer didn't want me 'ere, but the caretaker told me when the meetin' was, so 'ere I am.'

'Who told 'im?' Liz said frowning.

Freda tried to hide her embarrassment. 'Gawd knows,' she said.

The campaigners walked up the steps and just inside the main hall they were intercepted by a Council attendant. 'Yes, ladies?' he queried.

'Go an' tell that bloody lot we're 'ere, young man, an' quick about it,' Ada Champion commanded him.

The attendant smiled indulgently. 'An' what bloody lot are yer referrin' to, madam?' he asked her.

Liz intervened. 'We're the Milldyke representatives,' she told him in her best voice. 'We've got a meetin' wiv the 'ousin' committee at two forty-five.'

The group were shown up the main staircase and they were all out of breath by the time they reached the main Council chamber.

'I know why this meetin' was fixed fer upstairs,' Ada gasped. 'They reckoned we'd all be speechless by the time we got 'ere.'

'Well, they thought right,' Freda replied, fighting for breath.

Mary Enright was standing next to the attendant as he waited for them all to compose themselves and he suddenly gave her a hard look. 'What you got in that box?' he asked.

'None o' your business,' Mary told him sharply.

The attendant moved away from her quickly and addressed the party as a whole. 'The meetin's arranged in the side committee room off the main chamber. Now, if you'll all be patient I'll go an' see if the members are convened.'

'Never mind about that,' Ada said. 'Just see if they're ready.'

Finally the Milldyke petitioners were shown through the main chamber into the oak-panelled side room. Facing them behind a long polished table were the committee members, all looking very business-like.

'If you'll kindly be seated, folks,' Councillor Bradley said with a friendly smile.

The delegation from Milldyke Buildings took their seats in the front row facing the committee and Bradley quickly opened the proceedings. 'I'm Joe Bradley, chairman of the housing committee, and this is Councillor Tom Smythe,' he said pointing to his right. Then turning to his left he added, 'And this is councillor Alma Gordon and Councillor Bill Kelly.'

Liz Fogan was in no mood to go through the niceties of introducing her group; instead she made her name known and nodded towards the papers in front of Joe Bradley. 'That petition yer got there was signed by all the tenants in Milldyke Buildin's, bar one, so yer gotta listen,' she began.

Bradley hid a smile. 'One omission. There's always one,' he replied.

''E would 'ave signed too if 'e wasn't such a silly ole git,' Ada Champion cut in.

Liz Fogan leaned forward in her chair. 'Yer know what our complaint is, so what d'yer intend doin' about it, or are yer gonna sit back an' let some plague break out before yer respond?'

Bradley sighed deeply and studied the papers on the table for a few seconds. 'Up until May we collected the rubbish once a week,' he reminded them, 'but being aware of the problems we now collect twice a week as you know. We've also issued instructions about proper disinfection after the dustcart calls. I don't see what more we can do.'

'Are the tenants of Milldyke aware that there are forty tenancies in the Buildings?' Alma Gordon remarked, looking over her gold-rimmed glasses at the petitioners.

'We can count, luv,' Ada said sourly.

'Ada, be quiet,' Liz admonished her. 'Let me do the talkin'.'

'Who's stoppin' yer?'

'Right then.'

Alma Gordon was sniffing the air and Tom Smythe pulled a face at the chairman.

'What's the matter wiv 'er? She looks like one o' the Bisto kids,' Freda hissed at Liz.

Bradley whispered something to Tom Smythe who got up and opened another window.

'Tell 'im about the vermin what breeds round them bins,' Sadie prompted her leader.

Liz took a deep breath. 'We've 'ad our own meetin's about those bins an' there was certain proposals come up,' she said, looking from one to another. 'Firstly there should be a proper brick-built place ter put the rubbish. Secondly there should be new bins that can be wheeled out ter the dustcarts; an' most important of all there should be a compulsory purchase order put on the buildin's.'

'Tell 'im about the vermin,' Sadie Elmley said in a louder voice.

'We've started ter get rats an' mice in our places,' Liz said, looking along the committee for effect.

'The disinfectant powder we use is in fact a rat poison,' Bradley replied.

'Well, 'ow come we get rats?' Liz asked him.

'You mean to tell me you've actually found rats in the flats?' Alma Gordon asked as she fished into her handbag for a handkerchief.

Mary Enright stood up slowly and made for the table, holding the cardboard box out in front of her. The committee stared in growing horror, realising now where the bad smell was coming from.

'What have you got there?' Alma Gordon said shrilly.

Mary placed the box down in front of her. 'Go on, open it,' she dared her.

'Mary! Mary!' Liz shouted. 'Come an' sit down.'

'Why should I?' she said defiantly. ''Ere's the proof. Why shouldn't they see it?'

Bradley pulled the box towards him as Alma Gordon recoiled, and his face took on a sickly pallor as he peeped inside. 'Good God, woman! You'll start a plague. Take it away. Get it out of the room,' he exclaimed.

'Oh no, you don't,' Mary said sharply. 'That's my rat an' it's goin' back on my fire escape as proof.'

'The woman's mad, totally mad,' Alma Gordon said hysterically.

Mary Enright snatched the box back and tucked it under her arm as she walked back to her seat. Flossy had been fearing the worst and he backed up against the door where he had already positioned himself.

Bradley was trying to restore order. 'Come and sit down, young man,' he pleaded. 'Now please listen. That smell is overpowering and it'll be impossible to make any progress until the cause is removed. Now please let's see sense.'

Mary got up and gave the committee a haughty look. 'This box is not goin' out o' my possession till the doctor of 'ealth's seen it,' she declared firmly, and with that she made for the door. Flossy screamed out in panic and backed away from her.

'I feel faint,' he gasped as he sat back down in his seat.

'Would you like some water?' Tom Smythe said kindly.

'I know what 'e does want,' Ada growled.

Bradley held up his hands for order. 'Now to get back to business,' he resumed. 'The proposal to build a brick rubbish store was considered at our last meeting, but after we discussed it with the building department their architect reported back that there wasn't enough room to make it practicable. As to the mobile bins, that would also be impracticable due to lack of space. Believe me, we have gone into this very thoroughly already.'

'What about gettin' the 'ole bloody lot pulled down?' Ada cut in.

Bradley glanced quickly at Smythe for support. 'I'm afraid that we can't do anything until the lease expires,' he told them.

'When's that?' Liz asked him.

'In five years' time.'

'Yer mean we gotta put up wiv this fer anuvver five years?' she said incredulously.

'I'm afraid so.'

'Why can't yer put one o' them there compulsory orders on the place?' Ada butted in quickly.

'Believe me, we'd be more than glad to, but we have to be guided by central government,' Bradley explained. 'There's only a limited amount of money available and so much rebuilding to do after the war. Even if we were empowered to take over the buildings we wouldn't be able to rehouse you all. You'd be going from one slum to another.'

'So yer do agree that Milldyke Buildings is a slum,' Liz pressed him.

'Of course. How could I argue?'

'Well then, what yer gonna do about our bins?' Ada growled.

'Shut up, Ada, fer Gawd sake,' Liz implored her, turning back to the committee. 'So that petition was a waste o' time then,' she said despondently.

Bradley shook his head slowly. 'No, Mrs Fogan, it wasn't,' he replied quietly. 'Like you and your neighbours we too are concerned about living standards and the well-being of the people of this borough. We were voted into office on that very same mandate. What we can do is take another look at the Buildings and your rubbish problem. Let's see if we can put our heads together to try to alleviate the suffering this particular problem is causing. I promise you all that very soon we'll be inspecting the site and we'll be accompanied by the borough architect himself.'

'That's very kind of you,' Flossy replied spontaneously.

Liz nodded. 'That sounds fair,' she added.

'Tom, can you see about laying on some tea for these kind people?' Bradley asked him.

'Certainly,' Smythe replied, looking relieved that the session had not turned into a slanging match.

Ada Champion snorted. 'Bloody fine meetin' this was,' she whispered to Sadie Elmley. 'All we're gettin' out of it is a poxy cup o' tea. Bloody devious bastards. They're all the same. I don't know why I bovver ter vote, I'm sure I don't.'

Sadie remembered Ada telling her once that she never bothered to vote anyway, but as the woman was so fired up she refrained from mentioning it. 'You're right, luv,' she answered.

Mary Enright had left the committee room with her specimen and immediately bumped into the attendant.

''Ow's it goin'?' he asked her.

'Not too bad,' she replied. ''Ere, by the way, can yer put this in the bin?'

The attendant suddenly reeled. He hadn't been sure about the smell before but there was no mistaking now: it was coming from the box. 'What is it?' he asked timorously.

'I shouldn't worry about it, luv, it's only an ole pair o' shoes,' Mary answered smiling.

The man was at a loss as to why she would want to bring an old pair of shoes to a Council meeting but he decided not to challenge her. As he took the box he flinched visibly. 'Good Gawd! It smells like a dead rat,' he wheezed.

'I can't smell anyfing,' Mary replied, glad to be rid of it.

The attendant hurried as fast as he could to the side entrance and dropped the box into the large dustbin, holding his breath most of the way, then he went back to his cubby-hole to take a very welcome drag on a cigarette. Later that evening old Ferdy the tramp would come past on his way to the arches, he thought, and as was his custom he would rummage through the dustbin. He would no doubt find the shoes, but the attendant was willing to wager that even he would shy away from wearing that pair.

Chapter Eighteen

The people from Milldyke Buildings did not fret too much over their spiritual and moral health, but whenever they did give it some thought they concluded that they were no better and no worse than anyone else. There were lapses, they would readily have admitted, but on the whole they were God-fearing, industrious and alive to their neighbours' worries and problems. Had they been present at the diocesan conference earlier in the year, however, they would have been rudely awakened to the fact that, as far as the bishop responsible for their diocese was concerned, Milldyke Street was Sodom and Gomorrah rolled into one. They would have taken comfort in discovering that the bishop was not asking the Lord to send down fire and brimstone upon them, for he had other plans for that particular part of his episcopal territory.

At the conference the spiritual and moral welfare of Dockhead was high on the agenda. As the bishop explained, Father Toomey had done wonders and performed veritable miracles, but he was getting old and deserved a less stressful parish to see out his days in office. It was essential that the good father's post be filled by a much younger man, but one with experience of serving in a working-class parish. The bishop stressed that to appoint a novice to a parish containing such dens of iniquity as Milldyke Street would be like sending a Christian into the Roman arena: he would be eaten alive.

In the warm July sunshine Father O'Shea looked a little the worse for wear as he stood on the corner of Milldyke Street viewing the Buildings with a bleary eye. He was short and stocky and middle-aged, with an unruly mop of ginger hair and a flat round face that was showing the signs of his affair with the bottle. Father O'Shea was known to drink a bottle of Irish whiskey a day, and often his shelter for the night was anywhere except his bed. He preached a fiery sermon and went out into the community as much as he could, but when he entered the pubs to preach the gospel he invariably ended up getting sidetracked by the canny landlords, once they got to know him and his enormous thirst.

On this particular Saturday morning Father O'Shea had just emerged from St Mary's Church, where he had spent the night stretched out on the rear pew. How he had got there was a mystery to him, but he vaguely recalled sitting on the hard bench and discussing with himself whether or not it would be a transgression to bed down by the altar in his inebriated state. It mattered little now, he decided. Here in front of him lived some of his new flock, as yet not aware that they were sorely in need of his spiritual guidance. Where better to start than amongst the children, who were milling around the end wall with a battered tin can at their feet?

'What's the score?' he asked Charlie Almond as he reached the fighting scrum.

'They're winnin' three nil,' Charlie gasped. 'They got more kids than us.'

Father O'Shea smiled. 'Right then, I'll be on your side.'

Ernie Walker was sitting in his usual vantage point and he shook his head in disbelief as he saw the priest take off his coat and join in the game. Father Toomey would have a fit if he could witness this, he thought.

Ada Champion was coming back from the market and she stopped to confer with Amy Almond who was talking to the caretaker. 'That must be the new priest playin' wiv them kids,' she remarked. ''E's as mad as they are.'

Amy was not a Catholic but she had been on good terms with Father Toomey and was sorry to see him leave. 'They said it was gonna be a younger man,' she replied. ''Ave yer met 'im yet?'

Ada was Catholic herself, though she had not been to church for some time. 'It's the first I've seen of 'im, an' lookin' at the way 'e's performin' I dunno as I want to,' she told her.

Jack Ferguson had been waylaid by Amy moaning about her dripping tap and he had no desire to stand chatting. 'Well, I better be off, I got fings ter do,' he growled.

'Miserable git,' Ada muttered as he took himself off.

The priest soon found that playing football with a tin can was not the most enjoyable of pastimes and he made his exit after getting a painful kick on the shin. The Woolpack would be filling up by now, he reckoned, and there were undoubtedly some sinners there in need of spiritual succour and redemption.

Amy and Ada watched him leave the street on the other side and they both nodded a brief salutation. A few minutes later Spiv Copeland drove into the turning and pulled up alongside the two women. 'Amy, I got some swag-lines. Wanna take a look?' he asked her.

Ada looked interested too but Amy nodded towards the block. 'Bring 'em up,' she said.

Charlie Almond seized his chance and, along with Jimmy Flannagan, he stood guard over the car as Spiv carried a large bundle into the buildings.

'Now take a look at these,' Spiv told Amy as soon as they walked into her kitchen. 'These are first-quality cotton nightdresses, suitable fer all occasions.' He took the lid off one of the flat boxes. 'Just look at that stitchin'. Just feel the quality. I'm knockin' 'em out at five bob. You can sell 'em at seven an' a tanner wiv no trouble.'

'Is that the lot?' Amy asked.

'As a matter o' fact I got a few more in the boot,' he told her. 'I was gonna see if Kate wanted a few ter take inter work. She should be able ter knock a few out.'

Amy give him a sly smile. 'Why don't yer pop in an' see 'er,' she suggested.

Kate was busy ironing and she looked surprised as she opened the door to him.

'Thought I'd give yer a look in,' he said smiling. 'I was only next door.'

Kate showed him into the living room. 'Amy told me you were away fer a few days,' she said, offering him a seat.

'Yeah, I bin up ter Bolton on business,' he replied. 'I just got back this mornin'.'

'Was it a good trip?' she asked.

'Yeah, it was as a matter o' fact,' he told her. 'I got some swag-lines up there. That's why I called.'

'Oh, I see.'

Spiv smiled as he met her gaze. 'I'm tellin' a lie. I just wanted ter see yer again. I bin finkin' about yer. Can yer come out fer a drink ternight? Amy an' Fred'll be there as well.'

Kate shook her head. 'Fanks all the same, but I don't fink it's a good idea,' she replied.

'Why not?' he asked. 'It's just a social night out.'

'No really, Len, but fanks fer the offer,' she said with a wan smile.

He reached out and clasped her hand in his. 'Look, you know the way I feel about yer, Kate. Yer gotta give me a chance ter show yer I'm serious. Just say yes. There'll be no strings attached, I promise.'

The young woman pulled her hand away and then sat down facing him at the table. 'Look, Len, I really enjoyed last Saturday, but I let it get a little out of 'and. I like yer very much an' I appreciate the gesture, but I'm really not ready ter get involved wiv anyone just yet. You 'ave to understand it's not you, it's me, the way I feel at the moment.'

'I'm not givin' up easily,' he replied.

Kate sighed, drawing her hand back as he tried to take it again. 'I can't stop yer tryin',' she told him, 'but yer'll be wastin' yer time.'

'Let me worry about that,' he said smiling. 'Spiv Copeland ain't the sort o' bloke ter give up wivout a fight. Anyway, while I'm 'ere, would yer like ter see me latest swag-lines?'

'What's swag-lines?' she asked, looking puzzled.

''Ang on a minute an' I'll show yer,' he said, getting up.

A minute or two later he came back into the kitchen carrying a bundle of the boxed nightdresses. 'Now this is what we call swag-lines,' he explained. 'Look at the quality an' see the way they're packed. They look expensive, but as a matter o' fact they're bankrupt stock that's bin packaged ter pass fer expensive. There's a dozen boxes 'ere an' I'm knockin' 'em out at five bob. You can stick 'alf-a-crown on an' they'll still sell like 'ot cakes. I reckon there's plenty o' yer workmates who'll jump at 'em at that price. All yer 'ave ter say is that it's bent gear bein' knocked off cheap. It works every time.'

'So they're not stolen?'

'Course not, but would it 'ave made any difference?' he asked her.

'I couldn't take the chance o' sellin' dodgy stuff,' she told him firmly. 'Remember I got the kids ter fink of.'

'These nightdresses are kosher. True as I'm sittin' 'ere,' Spiv said holding his hand up to his heart. 'I can let yer 'ave these fer starters an' if yer want any more just let me know.'

Kate nodded. 'OK, I'll see what I can do.'

As he walked out of her flat Spiv turned and laid his hand gently on her arm. 'Just remember what I said, Kate,' he told her quietly. 'I don't give up easily.'

Meg Johnson had managed to get Charlie to run her errands while she strived to tidy her grimy flat. It wasn't too bad during the winter months, she felt, but in the summer, with the bright sun lighting up the kitchen, she could see how neglected it all was. The wallpaper needed replacing and the woodwork was crying out for a good coat of paint. The mat too could do with a good shake and the oilcloth needed a hard scrubbing. There weren't many visitors to worry about, but if she were to get back into doing alterations and repairs people would be calling, and they would be sure to talk.

Meg worked hard all day Saturday and at the end she was pleased with the result. There was nothing she could do about the wallpaper but the paintwork had responded to the soda water and a good rub. The room smelled fresher too and with new flypapers hanging up the tired but happy Meg Johnson felt it was time to relax with a cup of tea.

Kate Flannagan the new tenant in the next block seemed

nice, she thought as she sipped her tea. She was a very attractive woman too and that lad of hers was a credit to her. He always seemed to be with Charlie Almond but he was less cheeky and very well behaved. Goodness knows what she must have thought about the state of the place when she first called in.

The sun was dipping down over the bacon factory and the shadows in the room lengthened as Meg sat back in her fireside chair. Wouldn't it be nice to go out to the Woolpack like she used to before Annie got murdered, she thought. She had made some good friends there and no doubt they would be glad to see her again. What wouldn't she give for a nice milk stout or two. No, she daren't. It was a lonely walk back past those wharves and anyone could jump out on her. Of course she could go the longest way round via the Jamaica Road but even that route wasn't safe with all those foreign seamen coming out of the pubs at closing time. Perhaps it would be all right if she left the pub before it closed, or asked one of the women to see her as far as the turning. It would be nice, and it would help her confidence. Staying in the flat all the time was getting her down.

In C block Stella Sandford was getting ready to go out and she walked into the kitchen wearing her new dress. 'Are yer sure it's not too – you know?' she asked.

Joe shook his head. 'Nah, it's OK, long as yer don't go bendin' down in front of anybody,' he told her grouchily.

Stella went back into the bedroom to take it off. Joe was still smarting over finding her with Chalkey James. Still he had a right to be peeved, she admitted. She had been stupid. Joe was a good provider and until recently easy to live with. The trouble was, he wasn't very romantic in bed: as soon as it was over he would turn over and be snoring in seconds. A woman needs a little more than that, she told herself.

Chalkey was different. He knew how to pleasure a woman and be very loving afterwards. He wouldn't be around any more though, not after the way Joe walloped him. She was surprised Joe had it in him. Anyway things were on the mend; she would do her best not to antagonise him in any way, and be careful to play the dutiful wife for the time being.

'Come on, ain't you ready yet?' Joe called out. 'All the seats'll be gone if we don't get there soon.'

'Just comin', luv,' she called out, gritting her teeth.

Ernie was sitting in his window and he heard the young couple go down the stairs. He leaned out and saw Stella take her husband's arm as they set off along the street. That's a turn-up for the book if ever there was one, he thought: Stella and Joe Sandford like a couple of love birds.

Hold tight, who's this? Well, well, I don't believe it. It must be ages since Mrs Johnson went out at night, and she's looking quite smart too. Surely she hasn't got a fancy man stashed away somewhere. She could look the part still, with a bit of care and attention. He could have been in the frame himself if he were a few years younger.

Amy left the block with Fred Logan, and Flossy Chandler hurried along the street with a distinctive swaying of his hips and shoulders. Jack and Muriel Dennis stepped out of the block a few minutes later for their usual Saturday night at the pub and Ernie remembered how the big docker had pulled Joe Sandford off that long-haired piece of tripe. Others came and went as Ernie Walker kept his watch. It was the usual Saturday night parade. Time for a pipe and a drink, he thought, reaching down for the quart bottle at his feet. Just a moment, why's he off out again? Barney Schofield's evening stroll commenced on the hour and was always concluded within sixty minutes. He had only been back ten minutes and there he was off again. 'Strange. Bloody strange,' Ernie mumbled aloud.

Twilight faded and darkness settled down over the dockland borough, and still Ernie sat at his window. At seventy-five he had much to mull over and tonight he had recalled many old memories, until the brown ale took effect. Now, with the cool night air drifting in through the open window, Ernie Walker was in dreamland.

Chapter Nineteen

Meg Johnson was feeling nervous as she walked towards the Woolpack on Saturday evening, sure that everyone's eyes were on her. She wore her best coat, fawn with a deep collar, and brown shoes that were pinching her feet. Her legs felt shaky and her breath was coming fast, which she put down to not getting enough exercise. At one time she could walk for miles, and often had when Alec was alive. Once they had even strolled right over Westminster Bridge and into St James's Park. That was on a nice summer evening, and the next day Alec went to sea.

As she reached the Woolpack Meg hesitated before pushing open the door of the snug bar. She could hear Flossy tinkling on the keys and raucous laughter coming from inside. What kind of reception would she get? Would any of her old acquaintances still be using the pub? Well, there was only one way to find out, and taking a deep breath she went inside.

The snug bar was tiny by any standards and the two bench seats had been taken. The women sitting there were strangers as far as she could see but one of them immediately recognised her. ''Ello, Meg. Somebody said yer'd moved away.'

'Nah, I'm still at the Buildin's,' Meg replied, staring at

the woman with a puzzled frown.

'What yer 'avin'?'

'It's all right . . . I'll . . .'

'Nah, come on,' the woman said, fishing into her purse and taking out a two-shilling piece. 'I 'ad a double up terday, didn't I, gels?'

The other women occupying the seats chuckled, already sipping their free drinks.

'Fanks, luv. I'll 'ave a stout then,' Meg told her, getting a sudden flash of recognition. 'Mrs Jacobs?'

'Yeah, that's right. Molly Jacobs,' the woman said, giving Meg a toothless smile. 'I thought yer'd remember me. Me an' Annie Griffiths always used the public bar one time, Gawd rest 'er soul.'

Meg took the money and ordered her drink, and while she was doing so Molly turned to the woman sitting next to her. 'Shove up a bit, luv, there's room fer anuvver one 'ere.'

The two elderly women sitting opposite Molly were eyeing Meg up and down. 'Wasn't you a friend of ole Annie's?' one of them asked.

Meg shook her head as she collected her drink and eased herself down beside Molly. 'Nah, we wasn't exactly friends,' she replied, not wanting to say too much, 'but I used ter see 'er in 'ere sometimes. Annie preferred 'er own company.'

'She was a funny woman at times, though I don't like talkin' ill o' the dead,' Molly remarked. 'She was as good as gold when she was sober, but in drink she could be very nasty. Mind yer, I got on wiv 'er all right. I knew 'er, yer see. I remember that last night she was alive. I'll never ferget it. I was in the public wiv ole Mrs Grimes an' Liza Dineford, the one wiv the 'are lip. Anyway Annie come in an' she was already 'alf pissed. I asked 'er if she wanted a drink an' she nearly bit me 'ead off. She couldn't abide Liza, yer see. Well, I thought ter meself, sod yer then an' I left 'er ter get on wiv it. She sat down in the corner all on 'er own an' before long she was arguin' wiv this big woman. Gawd knows what it was all about. Old Smiffy the potman told 'er ter keep 'er voice down an' she nearly walloped 'im.'

'Yeah, that's right,' one of the other women cut in. 'Me an' Gert was sittin' nearby an' she was goin' off ten ter the dozen – an' the language! Well, I've never 'eard a docker say such words.'

'As I was sayin',' Molly went on with a disapproving look at her companion, 'the pub was packed that night, an' the next fing I 'eard was Annie swearin' at the lan'lord. 'E was tryin' ter get 'er out the place. What 'ad 'appened was, accordin' ter Liza Dineford, Annie 'ad insulted this bloke who was sittin' on the next table. 'E'd got up an' walked out sharpish. No one seemed ter get the rights of it but the bloke must 'ave took the 'uff. Anyway they managed ter get Annie out the door an' the next I 'eard was that somebody 'ad strangled 'er on 'er way 'ome. She was found on the bombsite next ter Milldyke Street.'

'The coppers was in 'ere the next mornin' tryin' ter find out who the bloke was,' the woman opposite butted in again.

'Yeah, all right, get on wiv yer drink, Bella,' Molly told her sharply. 'I'm tellin' this story. She's right though. The coppers was in 'ere the next day an' they came back on the night talkin' to all the people 'ere. They was tryin' ter find out who this geezer was that Annie 'ad upset but nobody could tell 'em anyfing. Accordin' ter the lan'lord 'e was a stranger an' 'e wasn't in the place a few minutes before Annie started on at 'im. Mind you, the pub was packed that night an' it all 'appened so quick.'

Meg felt cold fingers of fear running down her spine as she listened. A ghost from the other side had come to haunt her: those were Annie's last words to her, the night before she was killed. Was it the stranger who had waited for her outside, followed her home and strangled the life out of her? Or was it something else, as the poor woman had hinted fearfully?

'Let me get yer a drink,' Bella said to Molly without any enthusiasm.

'No, I'll get this one,' Meg offered, getting up and leaning on the counter.

The woman next to Molly put her empty glass down on the small table at her elbow and folded her arms. 'Tea-leaves an' 'oroscopes. Never could abide people who put too much store by it,' she mumbled.

'What yer talkin' about, Lil?' Molly asked her with a frown.

'Annie Griffiths,' Lil replied. 'She used ter read the tea-leaves, an' yer 'oroscopes. Believed in it, she did. She wanted ter read my fortune once, but I told 'er ter piss orf. As I said to 'er, me luck's out an' you or nobody else is gonna change it. I was a bit 'ard on 'er, I s'pose, but she was goin' on a lot about such fings. As a matter o' fact she showed me this little charm she kept in 'er purse. Said it brought 'er luck. It didn't bring 'er much in the end, did it?'

'Never did catch 'im,' Bella remarked. 'It makes yer wonder. None of us are safe wiv people like that walkin' about the streets.'

Lil was mumbling again. 'Jack the Ripper. Never did catch 'im. They say it was someone who knew yer Royalty.'

'Jack the Ripper killed more than one,' Molly told her. ''E used ter slice 'em up.'

The silent woman decided that the conversation was not right and proper for a Saturday night and she finally intervened. 'Can't we change the subject?' she asked sharply. 'Ain't there bin enough killin' in the war wivout us rakin' over Gawd knows what?'

'Yer dead right, Rita,' Molly replied. 'Let's talk about somefing else.'

''Ere, I got a tip terday from the bookie,' Bella said in support. ' "Chance yer Arm" at Ascot next Friday. I'm gonna put a tanner each way on it.'

'Never take a tip from a bookie,' Molly warned her. 'That's 'ow they make their money, from dud tips.'

With their drinks replenished the women chattered on and Meg began to relax. Now that the conversation was of more pleasant things she was starting to enjoy her night out. The thought of walking home in the dark crossed her mind but she reasoned that one or two of her neighbours would be in the public bar and she could tag along with them at closing time.

It was hotting up in the other bar as the evening wore on and Flossy was playing some favourite old melodies. People were joining in, and their voices carried into the snug bar. Bella, Lil and Rita began to sing along and Molly sat back and smiled, her face flushed with pleasure at the old-time songs. They were singing "Red Sails in the Sunset" and Meg was reminded of the love of her life. He would go sailing no more now. For him the last resting place was the cold North Sea.

'Are you all right, luv?' Molly asked as Meg dabbed at her eyes.

'Yeah, I'm all right. Some songs just make me cry,' she replied with a brave smile.

'C'mon, Bella, gonna get 'em in?' Molly said, and she

nudged Meg as the woman got up. 'There'll be moths flyin' out of 'er purse.'

The landlord's deep voice calling for last orders was followed by Flossy Chandler's rendering of "We'll Meet Again" and then a blur of voices as the pub started to spill out its merry drinkers. Meg got up and buttoned her coat against the night air, wanting to get outside quickly to see if she could spot anyone from the Buildings.

'Well, it was nice seein' yer again,' Molly told her. 'Mind 'ow yer go 'ome.'

Her words were innocently meant but they made Meg feel nervous once more, and with a brief farewell to her drinking friends she stepped out on to the pavement. Her spirits were raised momentarily when she spotted the Dennises. Jack and Muriel were talking to another couple and then to her dismay they all walked off in the opposite direction before she had time to approach them. She stood there for a while but it seemed that everyone else was walking in the general direction of Jamaica Road. Although it was a little longer she could go that way too, but then she would have to pass the bombsite at the far end of Dock Lane. There was nothing for it but to go back the way she had come, Meg decided, and with that she set off, her coat collar pulled up even though the night was balmy.

She hummed nervously to herself as she proceeded along towards the river end of Dock Lane. There were still some people about and she took comfort. Once into the long narrow lane, however, she found herself quite alone. Her footsteps sounded loudly on the pavement and then suddenly she heard another footstep some way behind her. She turned quickly but the lane seemed to be empty, the feeble light from a streetlamp falling on the cobbled roadway and dying away into the thick shadows of the factory doorways.

She increased her pace and again there came a sound behind, faster now, matching her step. Her heart pounded in her chest as the truth hit her. She was being followed.

Jack Ferguson put down his copy of *Shoot-out at Boulder Creek* and stretched leisurely. His passion for Western novels was plain to see from the stack of them on the shelf at his side. They gave him a lot of pleasure, reminding him of his younger days when he too went off in search of adventure. He was halfway through the latest novel and it served to lift him out of his humdrum existence, transporting him to hot dry prairie lands where men drove cattle and drank black coffee by camp fires before settling down to sleep beneath the stars. Cattle towns and lively saloons; ghost towns, where tumbleweed rolled through the deserted dusty mainstreet; and wide flowing rivers, where the cattle and horses drank their fill and the cowpokes washed the dust from their tired bodies: that was the life, he sighed as he went out into the scullery to make a cup of black coffee.

The knock on his door sounded urgent and the caretaker of Milldyke Buildings cursed as he hurried out to answer it. Back to reality, he growled. Burst pipes and faulty tap washers were his daily calling, but at this time of night it would be something else. Some drunken tenant who had lost their key no doubt.

'I've bin follered 'ome! 'E's after me!' Meg cried out as she stumbled into the passageway.

'Take it easy. Who's follered yer?' Jack Ferguson said, taking her arm in an effort to calm her.

'I dunno. 'E was there right be'ind me,' Meg Johnson gasped. 'I could 'ear 'is footsteps follerin' me.'

'Wait 'ere,' Jack told her as he went out to the block entrance.

'Is there anybody there?' she asked in a croaky voice when he came back into the passage.

'Nah, it's all quiet,' he reassured her. 'It must 'ave bin some drunk.'

'No, it wasn't. A drunken bloke don't 'urry along the street,' Meg told him sharply. 'This bloke was walkin' quick, I could 'ear 'is feet.'

'Yer didn't actually see anybody then?' the caretaker asked her.

'No, but I could tell 'e was follerin' me,' Meg replied, beginning to shed tears.

'Look, if yer didn't actually see anyone it ain't anyfing ter worry about,' he said. 'I'll see yer up ter yer flat if it'll make yer feel better.'

'Would yer?'

'Yeah, come on.'

When they reached Meg's first-floor flat the caretaker stood back while she fished into her handbag for her key. 'That's anuvver fing,' she said, looking at him with frightened eyes.

'What d'yer mean?'

'Why, this lock. It's old. Anyone could get in 'ere.'

He watched her turn the key. 'If yer worried get a Yale lock,' he suggested. 'Yer can't pick a Yale lock like yer can a mortise lock.'

'D'yer fink if I asked Ted Briscoe 'e'll let me 'ave one?' Meg asked.

The caretaker shook his head. 'They don't supply Yale locks, but if yer buy one yerself I'll fit it for yer.'

'I'll get one first fing on Monday,' she told him. 'Fanks fer seein' me in.'

As Jack Ferguson stepped out of D block he saw Barney Schofield enter the Buildings and he frowned to himself,

and before he had reached his own block Flossy Chandler
hurried into the turning.

'G'night, Jack,' the pianist said as he drew level.

''Ere, you ain't bin puttin' the fear up ole Muvver
Johnson, 'ave yer?' the caretaker asked him.

'Whatever are you on about?' Flossy said, looking
peeved.

'She just come in ter me scared out of 'er life. Said
somebody was followin' 'er,' Jack told him.

'Well, it wasn't me,' Flossy said with an indignant flick
of his head. 'Mind you, it's a bit scary down Dock Lane
after dark. Anyone could jump out on yer from those deep
doorways.'

'Well, g'night then,' the caretaker mumbled.

Voices down below roused Ernie Walker and he sat up
straight in his chair by the window. He ran a hand over his
face and then looked down to see Flossy and the caretaker
walking away from each other. What was that about somebody being followed? Who were they talking about? he
puzzled.

The evening's activity was not over yet, for just as he
was about to lower the curtain on events in the street below
Ernie saw Joe Sandford turn the corner. The young man
looked very much the worse for drink and as he staggered
along towards the block Stella hurried into the street.

'Joe! Wait a minute!' she yelled out to him.

'What's the use?' he slurred as he reeled round to face
her. 'Yer can't keep yer eyes off the bloody men, can yer?'

Ernie leaned back in his chair, not wanting to be spotted
but eager to see and hear the rest.

'I gotta look, don't I,' she shouted at him. 'What yer want
me ter do, wear a poxy blindfold every time I go out?'

'I saw yer givin' 'im a crafty smile,' Joe said bitterly, loud enough for Ernie to hear clearly. 'Don't fink I didn't notice.'

'There was no 'arm in it,' she retorted angrily.

Joe staggered away as Stella tried to take his arm and he almost fell as he wended his way into the middle of the street. 'My wife can't keep 'er bloody eyes to 'erself!' he shouted up at the windows for everyone to hear.

You can say that again, Ernie thought as he eased his head back into the darkened room.

'Joe. Get in the block! Joe, can you 'ear me?' Stella called out to him. 'Get in 'ere, yer makin' a spectacle o' yerself.'

'A spectacle, is it?' he replied loudly, staggering as he tried to stay on his feet. 'My wife mucks about be'ind me back, but not content wi' that she's got the nerve to eye up the fellers in front o' me face. What d'yer fink about that then?'

'Joe! Get in 'ere at once!'

'When I'm good an' ready.'

'Well, sod yer then. Stay out there all night fer all I care.'

'An' sod you too.'

Suddenly the drunk lost his footing and tumbled backwards, banging his head against the hard cobbles. He lay on his back, his legs and arms moving in imitation of the dying spasms of an upturned beetle until Stella rushed over and helped him on to his feet once more.

'Yer've cut yer bloody 'ead open,' she said in horror.

'I can't feel it,' he answered frowning.

'No, but yer will in the mornin'. Now get inside before I get really mad,' she told him firmly.

'Night everybody,' he called out with a swing of his arm which almost toppled him again.

Ernie heard unsteady footsteps on the stairs and then hushed voices.

'I never did.'

'Oh yes, yer did.'

'I was only lookin' over at Mrs Ford.'

'Well, yer could've fooled me.'

'Get indoors, Joe, before I get really cross.'

'I ain't got the poxy key. Where'd I put it?'

'I got it, now get indoors.'

The Sandfords' front door slammed shut and Ernie afforded himself a smile. 'They say true love never runs smooth,' he said aloud to himself. 'That marriage's like a bloody fairground ride.'

Chapter Twenty

The new week started with a rush and an air of expectancy for a few of the Milldykers. Amy Almond and her friend Elsie Burton hurried off to their early-morning cleaning job with carrier bags full of Spiv Copeland's swag-lines. Neither Amy nor Elsie knew just how many nightdresses they would sell that morning, but they worked on different floors of the large office building and were hopeful of doing a good trade. It would mean hanging around after they finished cleaning at eight thirty to catch the staff who came to work at nine o'clock but they expected it would be worth it. Amy also had a few friends in Dockhead that she could drop in on, and then there was the woman in the pie shop who usually bought just about everything on offer.

Meg Johnson went out early and bought a Yale lock at the ironmonger's, and at nine sharp she was knocking on Jack Ferguson's front door.

'I said I'd fix it but yer can't expect me ter do it straight away,' he moaned. 'I got ole Muvver Champion's winder sash ter mend an' Sadie Elmley's after a new tap washer. I can't do everyfing at once.'

'What's more important, a new tap washer or a safety lock?' Meg went off at him. 'She gets 'er drip fixed an' I get murdered in me bed.'

'All right, all right, don't go on about it,' the caretaker groaned. 'I'll try an' manage ter put it on this afternoon.'

Meg went away satisfied and immediately came face to face with Flossy Chandler who gave her a wide grin. 'Just the person,' he said, pulling out a large envelope from his coat pocket. ''Ow many d'yer want, luv?'

''Ow many o' what?' Meg asked him sharply.

'Tickets fer the talent night,' Flossy told her. 'They're only 'alf-a-crown each.'

'What talent night?'

'Mine, luv. I'm gonna be a big star one day.'

'What the bloody 'ell yer talkin' about?'

'Didn't yer friends tell yer?' he queried. 'I bin floggin' meself ter death puttin' the word about but it seems I bin wastin' me time.'

'Yeah, I did 'ear somefing,' Meg sighed. 'Give us one then.'

'Ain't yer got a friend ter take?' Flossy asked her.

'No, I ain't, an' if I did she'd 'ave ter buy 'er own,' she said curtly.

'Sorry I mentioned it,' the young man muttered petulantly as he peeled off a ticket from the large pack.

'It's all right fer you, I got follered 'ome from the Woolpack last night,' Meg informed him.

'Yeah, so I 'eard,' he replied folding his arms. 'That silly git Ferguson 'ad the cheek to ask if it was me. Gawd 'elp us, I live in fear meself.'

'I'm gettin' 'im ter fit me a new lock,' Meg went on. 'That one o' mine wouldn't keep a pussy out.'

'Well, I wish yer luck,' Flossy said with a smile. 'I waited long enough fer my new tap washer.'

Kate Flannagan started the day well, and by lunchtime she

had sold the last of the nightdresses and taken orders for a dozen more. Declining the offer of lunch in the gardens with her bench team she hurried home to see Amy about ordering some more.

'Bloody 'ell, Spiv's gonna be pleased,' Amy remarked. 'I got an order fer two dozen an' I dunno about Elsie yet.'

'Well, I better not stop,' Kate said getting up.

'Sit yerself down,' Amy told her. 'I'll do yer a sandwich an' a cuppa. I got somefing important ter tell yer anyway.'

Kate had to wait until her neighbour had made cheese sandwiches and a pot of tea before she got the mysterious news.

'Keep it ter yerself,' Amy said as she reached for a sandwich. 'Fred's left 'is ole woman.'

Kate looked inquiringly at Amy. ''Ow will it affect you?' she asked.

'It's a bit tricky really,' her friend replied with a screwed-up expression on her small face. 'Yer see, Fred didn't actually walk out on 'er.'

'No?'

'No, she chucked 'im out.'

'Oh, I see.'

Amy washed a mouthful of sandwich down with her tea before elaborating. 'We've bin seen tergevver. When Fred went 'ome on Saturday night 'e got a right old earful from 'er. Somebody 'ad told 'er about me an' she frew 'is supper at 'im. Saveloy an' pease puddin' all down 'is best suit. Yer can imagine! Fred accused 'er o' carryin' on as well, one fing led to anuvver an' she told 'im I was welcome to 'im.'

'So what 'appens now?' Kate asked.

'Well, 'e can't move in 'ere,' Amy replied quickly. 'Carryin' on is one fing but livin' tergevver is a different kettle o' fish. What about when my ole man comes 'ome?

Mind you, I do believe 'e'd climb in bed between the two of us an' not notice.'

'What'll 'e do then, get a furnished flat?'

'Gawd knows.'

Kate finished her tea and was about to move but Amy quickly refilled her cup. 'Drink that first,' she urged her, 'yer got time.'

Knowing it was useless to argue Kate acquiesced, and Amy went on in her inimitable fashion. 'Me an' Fred are like that,' she said, crossing her fingers in front of her, 'but the way that ole bitch 'is 'as bin actin' lately 'as caused us a few problems. The poor sod don't know whevver 'e's comin' or goin'. She cut 'is best shirt up the ovver night, an' then she accused 'im of keepin' 'er short o' money. It ain't as if I take anyfing from 'im. Every time we go out I go 'alves. Anyway yer don't wanna sit 'ere listenin' to all my troubles, luv. 'Ow's the job comin'?'

'It's fine. I like it,' Kate told her. 'The kids manage quite well. Jimmy's a sensible lad an' 'e's old enough now ter look after Jenny till I get 'ome at night.'

''Ere, 'as Flossy flogged yer any tickets yet?' Amy asked.

'No, I 'aven't seen anyfing of 'im,' Kate replied.

'Don't worry – you will,' Amy laughed. 'Flossy's sure 'e's gonna win. I got a couple off 'im fer me an' Charlie. I was askin' 'im if it was 'alf price fer kids an' 'e said all kids over ten 'ave ter pay full price. Bloody swindle that is.'

Kate thanked her for the tea and sandwiches and made a swift exit after realising that her talkative neighbour had made her late. She quickened her pace along Dock Lane, only to be accosted by the hopeful virtuoso.

'Just the woman I bin wantin' ter see,' Flossy said grinning.

'Look, I can't stop, I'm late gettin' back ter work,' Kate told him as she hurried past.

''Ow many d'yer want?' he called out.

Kate raised three fingers, which brought a satisfied smile to the young man's face. The way things were going it would be a sell-out, he thought. According to Bernie Gilchrist he would walk it, and then there would probably be a spot on radio and a contract to appear on the music hall circuit. One day people would come to visit the Buildings just to see where the great Francis Chandler once lived. Ah well, it was nice to dream, he told himself. Better ask the caretaker if he wanted a ticket, and then there were the men at the bacon curer's. Fred Logan seemed to think they would be interested. Mustn't forget the market people, and maybe ask Ted Briscoe too. No, better not ask him. He would be more likely to applaud the opposition out of sheer cussedness.

Herbert Ramsey's cold narrow eyes appraised his class as they copied the historical information from the blackboard. They had been very studious and uncharacteristically well behaved of late and the cane had not seen the light of day for a whole week. Ramsey could not recall a similar period of quiet and he was feeling a little put out. In his desk, in place of the erotica, lay a copy of the headmasters' conference report and Goodright had had the gall to underline one pertinent paragraph. It made depressing reading, he thought. What were things coming to when teachers were criticised for using the cane to instil discipline? Was a teacher expected to go down on hands and knees and plead for order? Well, they could count him out. As soon as one of the little guttersnipes in his class stepped out of line he would produce the cane and exact a swift and judicious punishment. It was the only way, whatever people like Goodright thought. The man was getting past it. Too soft by half. If he had not put his oar in, the Brindley boy would be in Borstal by now.

Quietness reigned, but when Ramsey looked up again and saw Jimmy Flannagan staring into space he suddenly felt provoked. A cheeky reply and the boy would be for it, he growled to himself. 'Have you nothing to do, Flannagan?' he barked out.

'I've finished, sir.'

'Well, check it,' he told him curtly.

'Yes, sir.'

'Morris. What are you grinning at?'

'I wasn't grinnin', sir. I got a toofache.'

'Are you making fun of me, Morris?'

'No, sir. Definitely not, sir.'

Ramsey lowered his head. How depressing it all was, he sighed. With the class busy at work, and time on his hands he could have been engrossed in the latest novel from the pen of Martin Mantine. *Slave Woman* looked a tasty read but he dared not bring it to school now that his secret was out. At the moment the book was safely concealed in his garden shed and it would have to stay there until the weekend. At least the shed was one place his good lady never entered. Spiders terrified her.

Charles Goodright had no such problems. He had noted down the complete list of titles inscribed at the back of *Lust in the Sun*, and had already sent off the required postal order and was eagerly awaiting his copy of *Slave Woman* which was to be delivered to the school in a plain brown envelope marked 'Confidential'.

Flossy Chandler had taken the Monday morning off from

his job at Moreland's to sell his tickets on the understanding that he would make up the time. Unbeknown to him, however, the owner Benjamin Moreland had happened to make a rare appearance at the Old Kent Road branch of his rapidly growing business empire. He was duly briefed on Flossy's absence and puzzled by the white suit hanging on one of the racks. As far as he was concerned white suits were the last thing anyone would be expected to buy in this particular neck of the woods and the suit was taking up valuable space. The manager Ken Swales could throw no light on the mystery, other than to say that the new stock of off-the-peg suits had arrived late the previous Saturday evening and Francis Chandler had displayed them before leaving.

When Flossy walked in the store that afternoon Ken Swales was waiting for him. 'What's that white suit doin' there?' he asked quickly.

'I put it on the order manifest last Monday,' Flossy replied casually.

'You never told me about no white suit. Who ordered it anyway?'

'I know, an' I'm sorry, but you were very busy last Saturday evenin' when I unpacked the stuff,' Flossy told him with a disarming smile.

'The big boss 'imself paid us a visit this mornin' an' 'e was askin' questions I couldn't answer,' the manager said irately. 'I looked a proper fool. Moreland was goin' on about wastin' store space on suits that wouldn't sell.'

'Well, that one will,' Flossy said smiling craftily.

'Oh, an' what makes yer so sure?'

'Snake-eye Monzarelli, that's why.'

'Yer mean ter tell me Snake-eye's bin in 'ere! When?'

'Last Monday mornin'. While you was at the dentist's.'

'Why didn't yer tell me when I got back?'

'I didn't 'ave the 'eart to,' Flossy said, trying to look concerned. 'When I saw 'ow swollen yer face was I felt I just couldn't trouble yer wiv trifles.'

'Trifles?' the manager gasped. 'Snake-eye Monzarelli, the biggest crook south o' the river, comes in our shop an' yer don't tell me. I just 'ope 'e wasn't casin' the place.'

'No, as a matter o' fact 'e was quite nice,' Flossy went on. ''E pulled up outside in this big car an' I said ter meself, 'old tight, who's this? Yer could 'ave knocked me down wiv a feavver when I saw Snake-eye get out an' walk over. Surely 'e's not comin' in 'ere, I ses ter meself. Bloody 'ell 'e is. Anyway I gave 'im a big smile an' 'e was very polite. Nice as pie in fact.'

'An' 'e actually ordered a white suit?' Swales said incredulously.

Flossy nodded. 'I told 'im very nicely that we don't stock white suits but I could order one if 'e allowed me ter take 'is measurements. I can tell yer now, my 'ands were really shakin', 'specially when I did 'is inside leg. Apparently the man's openin' up a new gamblin' club over the river next week an' 'e wanted somefing special ter wear fer the occasion.'

'Christ! I 'ope 'e's satisfied wiv it,' Swales gulped. 'When's 'e due ter pick it up?'

'This Saturday afternoon,' Flossy told him casually.

'Well, it's down ter you if 'e don't like it,' the manager said firmly. 'I can see 'im turnin' the shop over. I fink I'll take the day off.'

'Please yerself,' Flossy replied with a shake of his head.

Ken Swales went into the back room with a decidedly worried frown on his face and phoned Benjamin Moreland, but when he re-emerged he was smiling.

'Everyfing all right?' Flossy asked with a hint of sarcasm.

'I just bin talkin' ter Ben Moreland about the suit an' 'e told me ter say well done,' Swales reported. ''E reckons that if Snake-eye likes the suit 'e'll most likely give us 'is custom.'

'Fingers crossed then.'

The manager busied himself about the shop but after a while he came back over to Flossy looking a little worried. 'I'm still wonderin' why yer didn't tell me about Monzarelli comin' in,' he remarked.

Flossy put on a hurt look. 'Mr Swales, when I first started 'ere yer told me ter take decisions, do the orderin' an' 'elp take some of the load off yer shoulders. All right I should 'ave told yer about the suit, but yer gotta remember yer was under the weavver last week an' I knew yer'd be worried, so I decided not to. That's not a crime, surely?'

'No, it's not, Flossy, an' yer right,' Swales said sighing deeply. 'I would 'ave bin worried. I bloody well still am.'

'Well, there's no need,' the young man told him. 'Now why don't yer put yer feet up fer a spell while it's quiet?'

Ken Swales had employed quite a few salesmen in his time, but none had ever volunteered to hold the fort while he put his feet up and he nodded appreciatively. 'That's nice of yer,' he said.

Flossy gave him a big smile. 'By the way, Mr Swales, can I sell me tickets ter the customers?' he asked.

'As long as yer don't go upsettin' anybody,' Swales told him.

''Eaven ferbid,' Flossy said holding a hand up to his flat chest.

As soon as Swales disappeared into the back room his willing assistant took out his tape measure and ran it over the smart white suit. Well, at least the measurements were right, he sighed thankfully.

Chapter Twenty-One

Detective Sergeant Cassidy had always prided himself on being ready and fit for duty, regardless of his drinking habits. The tragedy of losing his family had been very hard to bear at times, but he had never let it interfere with his work, and he considered his backlog of cases to be no greater than that of any other officer in the division. As far as the booze was concerned, he only drank at home during the evening and was always recovered enough to get to the station on time. It was therefore a shock to sit there and hear his superintendent criticising him.

'The case is over seven months old, Pat. Then there's that robbery at the wharf last month. OK, your overall record is good, but I have to take stick from the gold-braid lot. You know the score: they want results. What do I tell them in my reports? Believe me I can write "No further progress" blindfolded. You've got a good team working with you and there's no lack of commitment on their part. What's the problem?'

'Just a minute, sir, you said commitment on *their* part. Does that mean you consider it's a lack of commitment from me that's holding things up?'

'No, I didn't mean that, sergeant,' the superintendent replied hastily. 'It's just that the hours you put in here are not in keeping with the results I expect.'

Pat Cassidy glanced down at his clenched hands for a few moments and when his eyes came up there was a steely look in them. 'Can I speak freely?' he asked.

'Go ahead.

'We both know that every division has its share of unsolved cases,' he began, 'and every now and then one division is targeted for the big stick by the top brass. I'm sorry for the problems it causes you but we're not miracle workers. We can't produce results out of a hat, as well you know.'

'That's right, but go on.'

'I've got a gut feeling that you want me to put in for a transfer because you feel that I've burned myself out as far as this division goes,' the sergeant said, gazing intently at his superior. 'I need a straight answer.'

Superintendent Tom Cox pursed his lips and joined the tips of his fingers as he chose his words carefully. 'Pat, how long have we known each other?' he asked.

The other's silence prompted him to continue. 'Long enough to cut the bullshit, so I'm giving you a straight answer as you've a right to expect. You're perfectly right on both counts. Yes, I want you to submit a transfer request and yes, I do feel that you're burned out here. A new area out of central London would be the best tonic you could ask for. Get away from the ghosts, son. Who knows, with new surroundings, new friends and acquaintances – maybe then you'll be able to have a life outside of police work.'

Pat laughed bitterly. 'I thought we decided to put our cards down on the table,' he replied. 'You forgot to mention the booze.'

Tom Cox shook his head slowly. 'Now you listen to me,' he said sharply. 'I'm quite aware that you like a drink. Who could blame you: OK so perhaps you lean on it a little heavier than most of us here, but that's not my immediate concern. Your mental attitude is. Rest assured, if I was worried about your boozing habits I wouldn't wait for a transfer request to be put on my desk. I'd have you out of here like a shot.'

Pat Cassidy leaned back in his chair digesting his superior's words, and his eyes narrowed slightly. 'I need another six months, sir,' he stated calmly. 'Things are beginning to happen and I need that amount of time. If you're not completely satisfied in six months I'll put in the request. I promise.'

Tom Cox nodded slowly. 'All right, sergeant. I feel you've earned it from your overall performance over the years. Now get out of here before I change my mind.'

As Pat reached the door he turned to nod his thanks and caught a humorous glint in the superintendent's eye.

'Have you met someone?' Tom Cox asked.

'Could be,' Pat replied.

Meg Johnson waited all day for Jack Ferguson to arrive and by teatime she was in a state of nervous agitation. 'Charlie. Charlie Almond, come up 'ere a minute,' she called down into the street.

The young lad was sitting in the kerb with Jimmy Flannagan and he gritted his teeth in irritation. 'Don't look up there,' he growled. 'The silly ole cow's always wantin' somefing.'

Jimmy giggled and lowered his head. 'Make out we're deaf,' he said.

'You, Charlie. I know yer can 'ear me. I want yer.'

'It's no good, she'll keep callin' till I find out what she wants,' Charlie sighed in resignation.

'You, Charlie! I know yer can 'ear me.'

'What d'yer want, Mrs Johnson?'

'I can't shout down. Come up.'

As usual Jimmy followed his friend up the stairs to Meg's flat, but to their surprise no shopping list was produced.

'Charlie, I want yer ter go along an' knock on the caretaker's door an' tell 'im Mrs Johnson still ain't 'ad 'er lock changed,' the old woman told him. 'Can yer remember that? I'd go meself but 'e might be in one o' the flats an' come 'ere while I'm out.'

Charlie frowned at Meg's explanation but nodded anyway. 'Yeah, OK,' he replied.

'I don't like knockin' at Ferguson's,' Charlie remarked as they hurried along to the first block. ''E's a miserable ole sod.'

'P'raps 'e ain't in,' Jimmy suggested with a grin.

'Ole Muvver Johnson's gonna be mad if 'e ain't,' Charlie said as they stepped into A block. 'When she gets mad she screams out. Once I went fer an errand an' got the change wrong an' she really started goin'. I run out an' me muvver went ter see 'er. I wouldn't mind but it was only tuppence.'

Their knock went unanswered and the two boys looked at each other grinning widely.

'She's gonna do 'er nut,' Charlie said.

Jimmy reached up and knocked once more but still there was no answer. 'I'll wait downstairs while yer tell 'er,' he told his friend as they walked out of the block.

'Nah, come up wiv me,' Charlie asked him.

Meg Johnson was at her window as the boys came along. 'Ain't 'e in?' she shouted down.

'We knocked twice, Mrs Johnson,' Charlie called up.

Her head disappeared inside and then the window came

crashing down loudly, and the two boys breathed a sigh of relief as they took up their positions at the kerbside.

''Ere, 'as your mum got a chopper?' Charlie asked after a spell of silence.

'I dunno. I don't fink so,' Jimmy replied.

'My muvver's 'id our chopper an' we're gonna need one when the summer 'olidays start,' Charlie went on. 'I know a place where they've got a lot o' boxes. It's a factory down by the river an' they let yer take 'em away fer nuffing. We can chop a lot o' wood up an' sell it in the Buildin's.'

'I'll ask me mum if she's got one,' Jimmy volunteered.

'I bet she won't let yer lend it. My muvver's frightened I'll chop me fingers off,' Charlie growled.

'I got one an' sixpence in me tin,' Jimmy remarked. ''Ow much you got?'

'Two an' tenpence, I fink,' Charlie replied.

'That makes four an' fourpence,' Jimmy calculated. 'I bet we could buy a chopper fer four an' fourpence.'

'C'mon, let's get our money an' see if the shop's still open,' Charlie said, getting up quickly.

The shopkeeper at the ironmonger's spread his hands out on the linoleum-covered counter and looked down at the two young lads. 'Choppers come at all prices,' he told them. 'It all depends on what yer want it for. I mean yer can buy one ter chop down trees, an' then there's the long-'andled chopper fer woodwork, an' there's one 'specially fer choppin' up firewood. That one comes a bit cheaper.'

'That's the one we want,' Charlie said quickly.

'I thought it might be,' the shopkeeper said grinning. ''Ere, do yer parents know yer after buyin' a chopper?'

'Yeah, course they do,' Charlie replied.

''Ow much is it?' Jimmy cut in.

'Well, the cheapest one we do is four bob,' the shop-keeper told him. 'Then the next one is seven an' a tanner.'

'We'll take the cheapest one,' Charlie said, putting a handful of money down on the counter.

Their acquisition suitably wrapped in brown paper, the two lads made their way back to Milldyke Street with Charlie looking rather thoughtful. 'I bin finkin',' he said. 'We can't very well take this indoors. Our muvvers'll be sure ter find it.'

'Let's 'ide it on the bombsite,' Jimmy suggested.

'Good idea.'

'Come on then, let's go.'

'Where've you two bin?' Amy Almond called down as the lads marched into the turning. 'I've 'ad yer dinner ready fer ages. You're in fer it too, Jimmy Flannagan. Yer muvver's bin callin' out as well.'

As they hurried up the creaking wooden stairs to the first floor Charlie had a few parting words. 'If we make a lot o' dosh on the firewood we can buy that seven an' a tanner chopper. I bet that'll really chop up good.'

As the evening wore on Meg Johnson was becoming more and more agitated. It seemed that the caretaker wasn't coming and it was very bad of him, she fumed. After all, he knew how frightened she was. It wouldn't have hurt him to at least come and tell her that he hadn't got the time to fix the new lock that day and would call tomorrow. At least then she would have felt a little better. As it was, she might as well not have bought the bloody thing.

In the sideboard Meg kept a bottle of port for medicinal purposes and she found it beneficial whenever she had a stomach upset or when she was feeling particularly low. It had been a Christmas present from Mrs Smedley next door and there was still more than half of it left. Maybe a tot would help steady her nerves, she conjectured.

After she had taken two tots Meg was feeling a little more relaxed, though she was still seething about the caretaker, and she stared at the bottle on her table. It should go back in the sideboard or she might be tempted to have another, she thought. No, just one more won't hurt, then back it goes.

The warm feeling inside her was pleasant and soothing and Meg began to ponder. Mrs Smedley always went up to the pub in Jamaica Road for her pint of each in a jug and it would be nice if she could fetch her back a pint of milk stout. The beer would help to make her sleep soundly and milk stout was like a tonic. After all they recommended it to pregnant women.

The widow Rene Smedley was a creature of habit and at eight o'clock exactly that evening, she put on her coat and hat and reached for the chipped enamel jug. Meg Johnson was waiting by her front door and as soon as she heard the latch sound she called out, 'Is that you, Rene?'

'Yeah, who'd yer fink it was?'

Meg opened her door. 'I wonder if yer'd be so kind as ter fetch me a pint o' milk stout, Rene,' she asked sweetly. 'I'm feelin' a little under the weavver.'

'If that's the case I'd get a quart,' Rene replied with a smile.

'Why not? There we are. I'm much obliged.'

Rene Smedley took the money and gave her neighbour a searching look. 'You do look a bit peaky,' she remarked. 'Never mind, a good drop o' tiddly'll soon put yer right.'

Fortified with yet another tot of port Meg was feeling decidedly better. In fact she even hummed to herself while she awaited her neighbour's return.

★ ★ ★

Kate sat in the kitchen calculating. One dozen nightdresses had brought her in thirty shillings and there was a further thirty shillings to be earned, providing Len Copeland could manage another dozen. Maybe she could get that dress material for Jenny. The children were short of clothes, and with the school holidays only a week away it could pose a problem. Bet Groves at work had told her that she always made her daughters' dresses herself with the help of a pattern. There should be enough to buy Jimmy a strong pair of shoes and trousers as well.

Kate looked up at the clock and saw that it was nearing nine thirty. It might be an idea to have a word with Meg Johnson, she thought. She would be able to offer her some advice.

The young woman hurried along to D block and as she reached the first landing and knocked on Meg's front door Rene Smedley came out of her flat.

'I was just about ter see if she was all right,' she said with concern. 'She's on the turps an' I just 'eard a bang like she's fallen over or somefing.'

Kate hammered loudly on the door but there was no answer. 'I wonder if the caretaker's got a spare key,' she said.

'It wouldn't make any difference,' Rene reminded her. 'Meg keeps the door bolted.'

Kate looked at the woman anxiously. 'If she's fallen over she could be bleedin' ter death fer all we know.'

'Try again,' Rene told her. 'If there's still no answer Ferguson'll 'ave ter smash the door down.'

Kate banged on the door once more and then suddenly they heard Meg's voice. She was singing to herself. It seemed as though she was having trouble with the bolts, and when the door finally opened the old woman swayed alarmingly in the opening.

'Are you all right?' Rene asked quickly. 'I thought yer'd fell over an' 'urt yourself.'

'We was just gonna fetch the caretaker ter break the door down,' Kate added.

Meg stepped back, holding on to the wall for support. 'Come on in, luv,' she said in a slurred voice. 'You too, Rene. I'm 'avin' a little drink.'

'I'll see yer termorrer, gel,' Rene told her, pulling a face at Kate as she went back into her flat.

Meg weaved a very unsteady path along the passage into the living room and sat down at the table with a big sigh. 'It's all right, luv. I've . . . I've sorted it out,' she said with difficulty. 'It's safe now. Ole Nick's mindin' it.'

Kate stood over her looking perplexed. 'Meg, yer need ter get ter bed,' she said firmly.

'Sit yerself . . . sit yerself down an' 'ave a nice milk stout,' Meg replied with a sweep of her arm. 'There's no need ter worry, it's quite safe now.'

'Meg, yer not makin' any sense,' Kate told her.

'Better the devil yer know,' she replied, tapping her forefinger against the side of her nose.

Kate went into the scullery to see if there was any coffee in the place but had to settle for tea, and by the time she had made a strong brew Meg's head was buried in her chest and she was snoring loudly.

Chapter Twenty-Two

The following day during her lunch hour, Kate hurried along to the market and bought two and a half yards of gingham material as well as matching cottons and buttons. She also bought a pattern recommended by the woman on the stall. Bet Groves looked at it that afternoon at tea break and nodded in approval. 'It's an easy one,' she told her. 'If yer get any trouble bring it in an' I'll 'elp yer wiv it.'

Kate smiled to herself as she imagined the pattern being laid out on the bench with the hawk-faced supervisor hovering in the background, and decided that it would be a better idea to consult Meg Johnson.

The machine was spilling pies by the hundreds and the women were kept busy. They worked as a team and were quickly becoming expert at packing and sealing.

'We should be on a good bonus this week,' Milly Tate remarked.

'There'll be trouble if we ain't,' Bet growled.

The busy afternoon passed quickly and as Kate hurried home that evening she felt she ought to pop in and see Meg as soon as tea was over. Last night she had managed to get her sufficiently roused to drink the strong tea and had then helped her on to the bed fully clothed, pulling a quilt over her. It was strange the things she had said, Kate thought. Most likely she wouldn't remember a word of it.

The dustbin action committee were told by Liz Fogan that she had received a letter from Councillor Bradley in which he said that the borough architect was coming round on Wednesday afternoon, along with an official from the sanitation department. Bradley said that he would be joining them too and asked her to be there as well.

'Let 'em try an' stop me,' Liz declared to her team with passion.

'I reckon they're finkin' o' buildin' one o' them there incinerations,' Sadie Elmley offered.

'Incinerators,' Ada corrected her.

'Well whatever.'

Liz shook her head. 'You all 'eard Bradley say there was no room round the back fer any buildin' work. Nah, I reckon they're gonna measure us up fer new bins.'

'That won't get rid o' the stink,' Ada replied irritably.

'It'll 'elp,' Freda Irons cut in. 'At least the lids'll fit better. Those two we've got there now are just about fallin' ter pieces.'

'What they gonna do about the rats? That's what I'd like ter know,' Mary Enright remarked.

'They'll put rat poison down like they said,' Liz Fogan replied.

'As long as we don't 'ave someone stickin' 'em all in shoe boxes,' Ada Champion said curtly, with a wicked look in Mary's direction.

'You can take the piss, Ada, but if I 'adn't showed 'em that rat we'd be waitin' ferever ter get some action,' Mary told her forcefully.

Liz Fogan raised her hands up for attention. 'Now listen,

gels,' she addressed them. 'We've got the bleeders worried, an' at this stage o' the proceedin's I don't wanna let 'em off the 'ook. So no bickerin' in front of 'em, an' no gettin' sidetracked.'

'Nuffing'll satisfy me apart from the Council smackin' an order on the Buildin's,' Ada declared. 'The places should 'ave bin done away wiv years ago.'

'We all feel the same way, Ada luv, but it ain't possible,' Liz said quietly. 'Whatever way yer look at it there ain't no money available. We just gotta sit it out till the lease expires an' see what 'appens then.'

'Yeah, fer five bloody years,' Ada snorted. 'I'll be in me box by then.'

'Nah, yer won't,' Mary cut in. 'Yer'll still be makin' a bleedin' nuisance o' yerself.'

Ada looked down her glasses in a haughty fashion. ''Ark at 'er. Anyone'd fink I was a troublemaker.'

''Ere, changin' the subject,' the elderly Maud Sattersley piped in. 'Are we gonna buy any o' those poxy tickets orf o' Flossy?'

'I'm not,' Ada said firmly.

'No, nor me,' Sadie said in support. 'What about you, Liz?'

'Well, you lot can do as yer like, but me an' Ted'll be goin',' their leader informed them. 'The way I see it, these buildin's 'ave got a bad name an' we're all seen as a load o' rubbish. We know different an' we've got our pride. Now there's Flossy, Gawd luv 'im, wavin' the flag fer us an' people sayin' sod 'im, let 'im get on wiv it. Well, I ain't. Me an' my Ted'll be there cheerin' for 'im, an' I'm prayin' 'e wins the contest. It'll show 'em all that we ain't the dirty, scruffy, ignorant lot they make us out ter be.'

'Yer dead right, Liz,' Mary told her. 'Count me in.'

Ada Champion felt a little ashamed as she looked around at her friends. 'It ain't that I don't wanna go an' support 'im,' she said grudgingly. 'It's the bloody drag, what wiv me legs, an' me back.'

'That's no excuse. We can get the tram,' Mary answered. 'It'll be a right laugh if we all go tergevver.'

'Yeah, and we can pop in the 'Orseshoe fer a drink afterwards,' Liz said smiling.

'Right then. Order me two tickets fer me an' Sid,' Ada replied.

'Count me in too,' Sadie said. 'I'll 'ave one.'

The meeting got back to order and when it finally broke up Liz was feeling a little happier.

Later that evening Kate went to see Meg Johnson and found her nursing a sore head. 'I thought I'd better look in on yer, Meg,' the young woman told her. 'You were really off yer trolley last night.'

'Yeah, an' I feel like gettin' pissed ternight too,' Meg growled. 'That lazy bleeder still ain't fixed me new lock on.'

''Ave yer bin ter see 'im again?' Kate asked her.

'Yeah, an' 'e said 'e'd do it as soon as 'e got time,' Meg replied. ''E told me 'e's bin busy puttin' a new ceilin' in Mrs Brindley's flat 'cos they reckon she won't be comin' back an' they're gonna re-let it.'

'The poor woman must be worse,' Kate said sighing. 'I feel sorry fer young Tommy. It can't be very nice fer 'im, livin' wiv 'is ole granny. I met 'er when I took the boy back 'ome after 'e stayed the night wiv us. She seemed very grumpy.'

'Did you ever meet Mrs Brindley?' Meg asked her.

'No, I never.'

'Strange woman. Mind you it might 'ave bin 'er illness, but she never stopped ter chat to anybody. Always kept 'erself to 'erself. 'Er place was always clean an' tidy, so Mrs 'Aliday told me. She used to pop in there.'

'Was Mrs Brindley on 'er own?' Kate inquired.

'Yeah, 'er 'usband Albert got killed in the Far East,' Meg told her. 'I never met 'im, but they say 'e was a very nice man.'

'Is Tommy the only child?'

'Yeah. Lovely boy to 'is mum. Couldn't do enough for 'er.'

'It must 'ave bin 'ard fer the poor little sod,' Kate remarked sadly.

Meg reached for the teapot. ''And yer cup over,' she said.

The first cup had been stewed and lukewarm and Kate shook her head. 'No, I'm OK, fanks.'

Meg filled her own cup then added two heaped spoonfuls of sugar. 'Last night was a blur,' she sighed. 'I 'ope I didn't go on too much.'

Kate chuckled. 'You were no trouble, but yer was ramblin' a bit.'

Meg seemed worried. 'What did I say?'

'Well, ter be honest I couldn't make 'ead or tail of it,' the younger woman replied. 'Somefing about it bein' all right now 'cos the devil was mindin' it for yer.'

'What else did I say?' Meg asked quickly, looking concerned.

'Nuffing that made any sense.'

'It must 'ave bin playin' on me mind,' she said, pinching her chin.

Kate could see consternation written all over the woman's face. 'Is there anyfing yer wanna tell me, Meg?' she asked quietly.

Meg Johnson sipped her tea with a thoughtful, preoccupied expression, then she put down her cup and folded her arms on the table. 'It's bin worryin' me sick,' she said.

'What 'as?' Kate asked.

Meg stared down at the table for a few moments then she looked up, her eyes troubled. 'Do yer remember me tellin' yer that I bumped into Annie Griffiths a few days before she was murdered, an' what she said?'

Kate nodded. 'About some ghost bein' after 'er?'

It was Meg's turn to nod. 'Well, that wasn't the last time I saw 'er,' she went on. 'I bumped into 'er the night before she met 'er end, an' this mustn't go outside these four walls. I was comin' back from the Woolpack on Friday night an' I saw Annie comin' terwards me. She was unsteady on 'er feet an' I guessed she'd 'ad a skinful. I waited for 'er on the corner o' the street an' when she come up ter me I could see she was well sozzled. She told me she'd bin up the Farriers Arms. That's the little pub in Jamaica Road. She sometimes used it instead o' the Woolpack. Anyway I walked in the turnin' wiv 'er an' we stopped outside this block. Annie was goin' on about what she was gonna do when she saw 'im again, an' somefing about gettin' 'im good ter rights, but she wasn't makin' a lot o' sense. It was like she was ramblin', an' then when I offered ter see 'er as far as 'er block she got shirty. Very independent, she was. Well, I stood there while she fumbled wiv 'er purse fer the keys an' then she went ter step in my block. That's 'ow drunk she was.'

Kate was listening intently and saw the sad look on Meg's face as she paused to recall the evening properly. 'Go on, Meg,' she urged her.

'I stood outside this block while Annie staggered off along the turnin' an' then when I saw 'er go in the end block I just 'appened ter look down at the step an' I saw somefing shinin' on the pavement,' Meg related. 'It was wrapped in a bit o' paper what 'ad come undone. It was a little brass charm, like what they advertise in the papers ter bring yer good luck, an' that's when I realised that Annie must 'ave dropped it out of 'er purse. It 'ad ter be 'ers. Anyway, I picked it up, paper an' all, an' then I noticed that the paper was a cuttin' from some newspaper, a picture o' some men standin' tergevver. I wrapped the charm up in it again wiv the intention o' givin' it back to Annie the next day. I did go an' knock in the afternoon but there was no answer, an' that turned out ter be the last chance. That night she was murdered.'

'So yer still got the charm an' the newspaper cuttin',' Kate said.

'The first fing I did after I 'eard about Annie was ter chuck that charm away. I kept the bit o' paper though, 'cos I 'ad it in me mind that it could've bin tied up wiv what she said about gettin' 'im good ter rights.'

'So one o' those men in that photo could 'ave bin the killer,' Kate said, her eyes widening. 'Did yer tell the police about it?'

Meg shook her head vigorously. 'When the coppers come round ter talk to us all the next day I stayed dumb. I never even told 'em I knew Annie very well.'

'But why?'

''Cos I could've bin next if the murderer found out I'd bin rabbitin' ter the police, that's why,' Meg told her emphatically.

'But 'ow would 'e 'ave found out?' Kate asked her.

'The newspapers, that's 'ow,' she replied. 'They get ter find out fings an' then they'd 'ave bin pesterin' me fer a story. I weighed it all up in me mind. I might 'ave bin wrong, but I just couldn't say anyfing. I thought they'd catch 'im soon anyway, but they never did.'

'It's not too late, Meg,' the young woman urged her. 'Go an' see 'em. Show 'em the newspaper cuttin'. I'll come wiv yer if yer like.'

Meg Johnson shook her head jerkily. 'Don't ask me, gel. I just can't.'

Things started to come together in Kate's mind. 'So what yer was sayin' about the devil mindin' it concerned the bit o' paper, the picture o' those men?' she prompted.

'That's right,' Meg replied. 'I kept it in me bedroom, under me spare blankets in the cupboard, but after I got follered the ovver night I got ter finkin'. That door-lock o' mine ain't too strong. S'posin' someone broke in 'ere an' ransacked the place while I was out shoppin' or somefing. They could quite easily find the cuttin'.'

'Yeah, but unless it was the killer 'imself it wouldn't mean anyfing to 'im, would it?' Kate pointed out.

'Yeah, but say it was 'im, an' 'e was lookin' ter see if I 'ad anyfing on 'im, what wiv me talkin' to Annie an' all,' Meg explained. 'That bit o' paper could cost me me life. That's why I found a very good place to 'ide it. 'E won't find it where I've put it.'

Kate looked quizzically at the older woman, her forehead creasing in a frown. 'Meg, if yer've no intention o' showin' it ter the police why didn't yer just put it in the fire?' she asked quickly.

'As a matter o' fact I did fink about it, often,' she replied, 'but somefing told me I shouldn't. I dunno what it was. Maybe it might serve some purpose, some day. I dunno.'

'Well, as yer said, it's in a safe place now. What wiv the devil lookin' after it,' Kate said jokingly, in an effort to ease the tension she could see etched on Meg's face.

It did not succeed. Meg looked at her with pain in her

eyes. 'It's quite possible that bit o' paper won't never see the light o' day, not while I'm alive,' she told her, 'but as fer destroyin' it, I just can't bring meself ter do it.'

Kate nodded acquiescently and shrugged her shoulders. 'You know best,' she said sighing. 'Changin' the subject, I 'aven't 'ad a chance yet ter tell yer about the nice bit o' material I got fer Jenny's dress. I got a pattern too. Now what I wanna know is . . .'

Herbert Ramsey sat back in the packed carriage of the four twenty from London Bridge and stared out at the large food factory as the train gathered speed. He had spent a lot of years at Webb Street School and he had never felt so frustrated as when the headmaster used the classroom incident as an excuse to criticise him, and in front of the policeman too. Goodright and the detective had ganged up together and browbeaten him. A pupil attacks his teacher in front of the whole class and is allowed to get away with it scot-free. What was the world coming to? A load of namby-pamby people in positions of power and influence, that's what. In a few years' time the cane would be outlawed, if the latest report from the headmasters' conference was anything to go by.

The train clattered on, the rhythm of iron wheels on steel lines constant and mesmerising, hammering out the message: away with the cane. Away with the cane. The humiliated master's fingers drummed the slogan on the side of the briefcase held on his lap and he was hard put not to tap his feet in time. Away with the cane. Away with the cane. The sudden switch in tempo as the train crossed over tracks brought Ramsey out of his peculiar trance and he blinked hard. Mustn't let this get to me, he told himself. Perhaps he should do as Warren Curbishey had suggested and write to the public schools. Yes, that was the answer. After all, he was well qualified, and a strict disciplinarian into the bargain. No banning of the cane for them, to their credit. They saw the practicality of it all: the well-chastised pupils, attentive and servile whilst within the hallowed walls of Eton, Harrow, Charterhouse and Rugby, but going forth to become roaring lions in the City, the far corners of the British Empire and on the bloody battlefields of countless wars.

'I usually do a cable pattern,' the large woman sitting next to Ramsey confided to her friend. 'The woollies tend to be much harder-wearing with cable stitch.'

'You'll have to show me,' the friend replied. 'I'm all fingers and thumbs. I can just about manage plain and purl.'

'Yes, of course I will. You should see the jumper I knitted for Mary's boy Johnny. It really turned out well. Johnny didn't seem too keen until he tried it on, then he wanted to go to bed in it, would you believe? Certainly got a mind of his own, that one.'

Ramsey had the almost uncontrollable urge to stand up and bang the two women's heads together. Good God! Was this to be his lot for the next ten years? Kowtowing to disruptive little guttersnipes all day and then having to listen to mindless balderdash like this. If he was not careful one evening he would snap and end up under the train, not in it.

When he finally stepped out on to the platform Herbert Ramsey had made up his mind: first his resignation, then one last foray through the backstreets of Bermondsey to purge his inner being before going on to pastures new and worthy of him.

Chapter Twenty-Three

On Wednesday afternoon as promised, the Council officials came along to Milldyke Street equipped with a tape measure, a clipboard and a tatty-looking plan of the buildings, which the architect spread out on top of one of the bins. Councillor Bradley stood back a pace or two while the men conferred and he soon found himself being prodded by Ada Champion. 'What they doin'?' she asked loud enough for the men to hear.

'Checking things,' she was told.

'I shouldn't 'ave thought it needed much checkin',' she snorted. 'Anybody wiv 'alf a brain could see what's needed.'

'It's a matter of space,' Bradley whispered.

The elderly woman nodded reluctantly. 'I 'ope they ain't gonna be too long,' she growled. 'I got better fings ter do than stand round this poxy place.'

'Shut up, Ada,' Liz Fogan told her sharply. 'We want fings done so give 'em a chance.'

Words were exchanged between the architect and the engineer and then they turned to Bradley. 'The new bins are slightly deeper but they'll fit in all right,' the architect told him.

Liz heard the comment and she stared at the official. 'Are

yer sure there's no room fer a brick-built place fer the bins?'
she asked him. 'It'll keep the rats away.'

The official shook his head. 'We've looked at it, but it's
not possible,' he replied. 'At least with the new bins and a
twice-weekly pick-up your problems should be solved.'

'It's still an antiquated bloody system,' Ada growled.
'People in them new Council buildin's put their bins out
twice a week an' the rubbish is tipped straight in the
dustcart. Wiv us we gotta carry the bins round 'ere an' it all
'as ter be shovelled up an' carried out ter the road.'

'We're quite aware of that, love, but the dustcart can't
drive up this alley like it can into the new buildings,'
Bradley pointed out.

'Well, if we still get rats I'm gonna be bringin' 'em round
ter the Council, never mind about Mary Enright,' Ada told
him firmly.

More measurements were taken, heads were scratched
and finally the tatty plan was folded up neatly. 'Well, we're
about finished here,' the architect announced.

'I wish we were,' Ada said, giving him a hard look.
'What wouldn't I give fer a nice ground-floor flat in one o'
yer new buildin's.'

'Never mind, one day yer might get yer wish, Ada,' Liz
said sympathetically.

'Yeah, an' one day pigs'll fly.'

Kate had been feeling guilty because she had not visited her
sister and family for some time, and she made plans to take
the children along that Saturday. Her good intentions were
overturned, however, when Amy called with a message on
Wednesday evening. 'I saw Spiv Copeland terday,' she said.
''E's got some more o' them nightdresses an' 'e wants you
ter go wiv 'im ter pick 'em up.'

'When?' Kate asked, looking suspicious.

'Saturday afternoon.'

'I was gonna take the kids round ter see me sister on Saturday,' she protested.

'Can't yer take 'em Saturday mornin'?' Amy queried.

'It's too awkward, what wiv the shoppin'.'

'Well, it's up ter you what yer do, but I thought yer wanted some more,' Amy replied, looking a little peeved.

'Why do I 'ave ter go wiv 'im?' Kate asked.

''Cos o' the colours I expect.'

''E could just get some of each.'

'Yeah, but a woman's got a better idea about colours.'

'Is that Spiv's excuse or yours?' Kate said grinning.

Amy feigned hurt. 'It wasn't my idea, luv, but I 'ave ter say Spiv's got a fing about yer. I s'pose 'e'd just like yer company. 'Ere, I tell yer what. Why don't yer get 'im ter drop the kids off at yer sister's on the way, an' then 'e could take yer back there afterwards?'

Kate felt that Amy was still trying hard at matchmaking but she had to agree it sounded a good idea under the circumstances. 'Yeah, I s'pose that wouldn't 'urt,' she replied.

Amy's face lit up. 'There we are, problem solved,' she said with a big grin.

When Stella Sandford first approached Ernie Walker about buying a ticket in support of Flossy Chandler he was adamant. 'I ain't gonna sit listenin' ter that bleedin' pansy poncin' about on the pianer,' he told her plainly.

'So yer'd sooner sit in that winder all night.'

'It's a sight better than sittin' in that flea-pit.'

'Ernie, yer gettin' miserable in yer old age.'

'Oh no, I'm not.'

'Oh yes, you are.'

The elderly man tried not to smile. 'I got me beer an' pipe. Why should I wanna go ter some tuppenny-'a'penny talent night?'

'I dunno, you tell me,' Stella persisted, her large blue eyes mocking him. 'I should 'ave thought a feller like yerself would appreciate music. Besides, yer'd be supportin' a neighbour.'

'Well, I'll fink about it.'

'Don't be too long makin' yer mind up,' she warned him. 'Nearly all the tickets are gone. Liz Fogan told me they're sellin' like 'ot cakes.'

'Oh all right. Anyfing fer a quiet life,' Ernie groaned.

'Right, then I'll get yer one, if there's any left,' Stella said with a smile. 'An' as a special favour you can come wiv me an' Joe.'

'Yeah, long as you two don't get argufyin' again.'

'What, me an' my Joe argue? 'Eaven ferbid!'

Ken Swales felt anxious every time he caught sight of the white suit hanging up in the corner of the shop, and for the umpteenth time that week he checked with his assistant. 'Flossy, what time did yer say Snake-eye was callin' fer that suit?'

'Late Saturday afternoon,' the young man said without batting an eyelid.

''Ow late?'

'Gawd knows.'

'Well, 'e'd better be 'ere before six.'

'I told 'im what time we close,' Flossy sighed.

'I've no intention o' stayin' open till 'e makes a show,' Swales said irritably. 'I'm goin' out on Saturday night.'

Flossy cast a quick covetous eye over the suit. 'Don't

worry. I won't mind waitin',' he replied. 'After all, it is my sale. Anyway, if yer goin' out on Saturday night why don't yer leave early. I can manage.'

'P'raps I will, if yer don't mind.'

'Course I don't,' Flossy said with a big smile.

Barney Schofield was not particularly pleased with the current mood of his neighbours. They appeared to be very mutinous of late and the petition business served to bear him out. In the army it would be seen as outright mutiny, for which they could be shot, the Fogan woman at least. As it was she was free to incite rebellion without restraint, but that didn't mean that she should be allowed to get away scot-free. Someone had to read the riot act.

The opportunity arose when Barney saw the Bermondsey Boadicea coming towards him as he stepped out of the block on Wednesday evening.

''Ello, Mr Schofield. What a lovely evenin',' Liz said pleasantly as she drew level.

'Evenin', Mrs Fogan,' he replied, remembering the simple courtesies.

'Would yer care ter buy a ticket fer the talent show on Saturday night?' she asked him.

Schofield frowned. What new plot was this, he wondered. Heinous insurrection no doubt. 'Talent show?' he queried.

'Ain't you 'eard about it, Mr Schofield?' Liz asked with raised eyebrows. 'It's at the Trocette an' Flossy Chandler's entered. We're all supportin' 'im. The tickets are only a couple o' bob.'

Barney breathed easier. The army were adept at putting on shows for the troops and it was always seen as a real morale booster. Better to have the woman concentrating her mind on that sort of activity rather than preaching anarchy. 'Saturday night, yer say,' he said in an officious manner. 'Might try ter come, but can't promise though.'

Liz gave him another of her best smiles. 'Flossy asked me to 'elp 'im sell the tickets,' she explained. 'I fink it's nice that one of our own can get up on the stage an' show everybody that we ain't useless an' stupid just because we live in Milldyke Street.'

'Good point,' Schofield said quickly. 'I remember well a postin' ter Durham. Way back in twenty-six. Morale was rock bottom. The men were rebellious and the camp itself 'ad a very bad name with the civilian population. Changed in no time at all.'

'So yer'll buy one? Would yer want one fer a lady friend?'

Schofield coughed nervously. 'Just one please,' he replied curtly.

Liz handed him a ticket. 'Mrs Drew who lives next door ter the caretaker bought one only a few minutes ago,' she told him. 'She was a bit concerned about not 'avin' anyone ter go wiv so I said she could come wiv us. P'raps you'd like to escort 'er?'

Barney Schofield felt that he had been manoeuvred into a corner. To refuse would seem ungentlemanly, but to agree might make it look as though he was available, God forbid. 'Well, I . . . er . . .'

'There's no need ter make yer mind up now,' Liz told him. 'Mrs Drew would be pleased if yer did decide to escort 'er. She was only sayin' the ovver day what a smart feller yer was. I told 'er you was a sergeant major once an' she said it showed by the way yer carried yerself.'

Barney Schofield continued on his evening stroll with an added spring in his step. Maybe things were not as bad as they had seemed, he thought. At least the woman was rallying the troops. As for Mrs Drew, he hardly knew her but felt that she was presentable enough. At least as presentable as some of the army wives he had been compelled to escort to military functions at various times. Had he known of the inquisitive Mrs Drew's true feelings towards him, however, he might well have donned camouflage and gone to ground.

Meg Johnson was very relieved when Jack Ferguson knocked on her door late on Wednesday afternoon. 'I thought yer was never gonna do it,' she moaned.

'I told yer I'd fix it soon as I could,' the caretaker grumbled. 'I got me 'ands full, what wiv one fing an' anuvver.'

'Well, if yer make a start I'll put the kettle on,' Meg told him.

While the banging went on Meg made the tea, and as soon as the noise stopped she hurried along the passage to see the lock being screwed into place. 'Are yer sure that's strong enough?' she asked him.

Ferguson gave her a look of contempt. 'If I've put it on it's strong enough,' he growled.

'Well, I'll pour the tea out then,' Meg replied. 'Come in soon as yer ready.'

A few minutes later the caretaker sat sipping his tea, thinking that she must have made it with gravy powder. He looked around the dingy kitchen and pulled a face. 'I s'pose Briscoe'll be gettin' me ter paper this place next,' he grumbled. 'It's bad ventilation, that's the trouble.'

'Well, I can't 'ave the winders open wiv that bloody smell comin' up from the bins,' Meg complained. 'Ted Briscoe needs ter get somefing done about them.'

Ferguson snorted. ''E wants an easy life. 'E ain't gonna go makin' trouble wiv the Council. Anyway it's Council business.'

Meg got up and went to the sideboard, moving the framed picture to one side while she turned out the contents of a vase. 'Now, 'ow much do I owe yer?' she asked.

'A couple o' bob'll do,' he replied.

'There's 'alf-a-crown,' she said, handing it to him. 'What about me keys?'

The caretaker took one of the two keys from the ring. 'I'll need ter keep one. It's the rules,' he said.

Meg was about to ask him whether he was going to the talent-night contest but he hauled himself out of the chair. 'I gotta fix a drippin' sink,' he said gruffly. 'Fanks fer the tea.'

The timorous woman followed him along the passage, and as soon as he had gone she clicked up the catch and then slid the bolts. At least the door don't rattle now, she thought, and that new lock looks sturdy enough.

Across the street at the bacon factory Fred Logan humped in the last of the greenbacks and stood while two of his workmates took it from his shoulder and hitched it on to a large hook hanging from the rafters. Fred helped the men slide the full consignment along the runners until all the fleshy, greasy sides of best Danish bacon were in place, while another worker made himself busy raking the hot coals. A further liberal sprinkling of oak chippings over the coals completed the operation and the men sat down to one side watching as a pungent smoke drifted up around the meat.

''Ow's yer love life, Fred?' one of his workmates remarked with a sickly grin.

''As 'e bin tellin' yer about it?' Fred asked him, giving the fire raker a dark glance.

Dan Collet nodded. 'I was askin' Percy if 'e knew what was troublin' yer an' 'e told us all about it,' he replied.

Fred looked down at his feet for a few moments. 'I'm in a proper quandary,' he sighed. 'I can't do right fer doin' wrong it seems.'

'Why, what's the problem? I thought yer got it made movin' in wiv Amy,' the second man queried.

'That's the problem, Bert,' Fred told him. 'I ain't exactly moved in wiv 'er. I just spend the odd night there.'

'Yeah, but now your ole woman's kicked yer out I thought yer was livin' wiv Amy.'

'Nah, I bin kippin' at the 'ostel in Tooley Street most nights,' Fred replied. 'It's OK an' the beds are clean, but it ain't the same as snugglin' up to a woman at night.'

'Well, you should know,' Bert said grinning at Dan Collet. 'You 'ad two ter pick from.'

'Not any more I don't,' Fred growled. 'After me ole woman kicked me out Amy got a bit nervous about our arrangement. I fink she thought I was after movin' in on a permanent basis. Trouble is, Amy's ole man's due 'ome any time now an' I've bin given the elbow.'

'Yer mean she's called the 'ole fing off?'

'Nah, it's just a bit complicated.'

'Well, if it's yer oats yer worried about yer can always do it on the bombsite,' Dan told him. 'That's what ole Percy does wiv that ugly mare 'e's got 'iked up wiv.'

The coal raker ambled over and sat down wearily alongside the others. 'I'm takin' Maria ter the talent night,' he announced without any apparent enthusiasm.

'Me an' Amy are goin',' Fred replied. 'What about you two?'

Dan and Bert both nodded. 'We'll be there,' they chorused.

The greenbacks were beginning to turn a smoky colour as the men changed out of their grease-stained overalls, and Fred wore a miserable expression as he made his way to the cafe in Tooley Street, before another cold, lonely bed at the hostel.

Chapter Twenty-Four

Having dropped Jimmy and Jenny off at her sister's house in Abbey Street Kate sat back against the soft cushioned seat while Spiv Copeland steered the car out into Tower Bridge Road. He was looking a little flamboyant, she thought, with his navy-blue blazer, grey trousers and white shirt opened at the neck to reveal a tightly knotted Paisley scarf. Gone was his loud tie, loose-fitting pinstripe suit and crepe-soled shoes, and she could only think that it was for a special reason.

As they drove over Tower Bridge Spiv turned to her and gave her a wide grin. 'These receivers I do business wiv are all ex-servicemen, an' the boss 'imself was a major in the Grenadier Guards,' he explained. 'As far as they're concerned I'm regular army, invalided out o' the tank corps wiv the rank of company sergeant major. Hence the get-up. Ter be honest I feel like a prize prat, if yer'll pardon the expression, but it does pay ter play up to 'em. I'm gettin' quite a bit o' business by lettin' 'em fink I'm one o' them.'

Kate grinned back at him. 'I fink yer look very smart,' she remarked.

'Yeah, but could yer see me walkin' in the Woolpack dressed like this?' he replied. 'I'd never live it down.'

'Shouldn't you be wearin' one o' those regimental badges

241

on yer top pocket?' Kate queried.

'Nah, there's a limit to 'ow far even I would go,' he said chuckling.

Once over the bridge they turned into Whitechapel Road and took a left into a narrow backstreet.

'I'm gonna tell 'em you're my chief rep an' yer've come to observe,' Spiv told her as he stopped the car outside a grimy-looking warehouse. 'Don't worry, just relax.'

Kate stared wide-eyed at the goods displayed inside and she felt a little ridiculous as Spiv introduced her to a tall man sporting a large handlebar moustache.

'Well, I hope you'll be impressed by our range,' the military man said, giving her a charming smile.

Spiv squeezed her arm and jerked his head slightly. 'Take a look round, Mrs Flannagan, while I have a chat with the major,' he said, his eyes sparkling mischievously.

Kate spent an intriguing time walking along the wide aisles staring at the variety of goods on sale. There were pots and pans, cutlery and chinaware, clothes, footwear and women's coats, all coded and priced. She spotted the nightdresses that were very similar in design to the ones Spiv had brought back from Bolton, and saw that they, too, came in various colours and shades, and she felt a little sad when she remembered that all the goods on show had come from businesses that had failed.

Other buyers were making notes as they inspected the stock and Kate afforded herself a wry smile. They looked like predators, gloating over a stolen feast, and she wanted to get out into the fresh air. This was not for her. Buying and selling was a hard business that required toughness and shrewdness. Her very limited experience selling the night-dresses had made her feel guilty of exploiting her work-mates, even though they were pleased with their acquisitions at such a reasonable price.

Spiv Copeland returned looking very pleased with himself. 'I've got a gross of every colour except mauve,' he announced.

Kate stood back while a warehouse man brought the goods out to Spiv's car and helped him load them into the boot and on to the back seat. Her advice had not been sought and she felt a little put out. He was only out to impress her.

'I know a nice pub, an' then we can go ter Tubby Isaac's,' Spiv said as he opened the passenger door for her.

'I should be getting back,' she said.

'There's plenty o' time. It's only one o'clock,' he replied dismissively.

Kate sat in silence as Spiv drove the car out of the backstreets and pulled up a short distance along Whitechapel Road. The small pub was packed and she found herself tucked into a corner beside two excited businessmen who were chattering away in loud voices. She could see her escort pushing his way to the front of the bar and she felt uncomfortable as the two buyers began to pay her some attention. Spiv was soon back with the drinks and as she sipped her small shandy Kate was aware of the pungent smell of stale tobacco smoke hanging in the air. Spiv looked totally at ease as he took a large gulp from his pint of ale and he gave her a smile. ''Ave yer ever bin ter Tubby Isaac's?' he asked.

'No, but I've 'eard about 'im,' she replied.

'Yer can't get better jellied eels or whelks anywhere,' he told her.

Kate's dubious expression made him chuckle. 'Yer mean ter tell me yer've never tried jellied eels? What about whelks?'

She shook her head, feeling a little defensive. 'I like cockles wiv lots o' vinegar though,' she said quickly.

Spiv slapped his hand down on the table. 'Right then. Cockles it'll be,' he declared enthusiastically. 'Yer won't get better than Tubby's cockles. They're fresh daily from Leigh-on-Sea. That's where the best cockles come from.'

They left the pub and walked the few yards to the seafood stall on the corner of Brick Lane. A large man in a straw hat and striped apron wearing a huge grin on his ruddy face was busy serving customers, and Spiv had to wait some time before his turn came. After the drink Kate felt a little unsure about eating shellfish but when Spiv handed her the small plate and sprinkled the large cockles with a liberal amount of spiced vinegar and pepper she found that they tasted delicious.

Spiv was studying her closely. 'I always call 'ere whenever I'm over this side o' the water,' he remarked.

Kate averted her eyes as she finished the cockles, feeling sure that he was going to suggest another visit somewhere. 'I can't leave the kids fer too long,' she said weakly.

Spiv took her arm as they left the stall. 'Look, why don't we drive frew the tunnel an' stop off at Southwark Park?' he said with a glint in his eye. 'We could stroll frew the flower gardens. It'll be nice an' quiet.'

'I don't fink it's a good idea, Len,' she replied. 'It's bin nice this mornin' so let's leave it at that, shall we?'

They reached the car and set off towards Tower Bridge. Spiv pushed the gearstick forward and glanced in her direction. 'I'm not givin' up, Kate,' he told her firmly. 'You know the way I feel about yer.'

As the car accelerated over the centre span she looked up at the walkway high above them and sighed deeply. 'I can't manufacture feelin's, Len,' she answered in a quiet voice. 'I really like yer, an' yer good fun ter be wiv, but . . .'

'But it's not enough,' he finished for her.

'Not fer me. I'm sorry.'

'I sensed somefing different when we were down in Kent,' he replied, looking straight ahead. 'I thought you were on the verge o' lettin' yer feelin's go, wantin' me ter go on.'

'I was grateful to yer fer the day out an' fer makin' young Tommy Brindley's day an' I s'pose I overreacted,' Kate explained. 'I didn't wanna push you away, but I could only go so far. It could 'ave got out of 'and if we'd 'ave carried on.'

Spiv drove slowly along the Tower Bridge Road and pulled up at the traffic lights, a quiet seriousness in his deep-set blue eyes as he looked at her. 'I want us ter go on seein' each ovver, Kate,' he said almost entreatingly. 'Then one day I'm gonna succeed in breakin' down that brick wall yer've built around yerself. I can give yer love an' make yer feel good. I'm a patient man, I can wait fer you ter love me. It could 'appen. Love doesn't always strike like a flash o' lightnin', not fer many of us. Love can grow slowly an' blossom like a flower openin' ter the sun. Sometimes that can be the best sort.'

Kate gave him a warm smile. 'D'yer know somefing, Len? Under that flash exterior there's somefing poetical lurkin'. I'm impressed.'

'Impressed enough ter come out wiv me ternight?' he asked.

'I can't,' she replied. 'It's the talent night.'

'Yer could give it a miss.'

'I can't, I'm takin' the kids.'

They moved off and Spiv Copeland swung the car into Abbey Street. 'By the way, is that the way yer see me?' he asked. 'A flash 'Arry?'

'No, of course not, but yer don't lack confidence.'

Spiv grinned, his thick fair hair moving in the draught from the open side window. 'I may come over as bein' a bit flash, it goes wiv the business I'm in, but I don't work at it,' he remarked. 'I wouldn't take advantage of yer, Kate. I want yer like mad, but as I said, I can wait.'

They reached the row of terraced houses and the car squealed to a stop.

'I've enjoyed it,' Kate told him with a smile as she prepared to get out.

He leant towards her and kissed her briefly on the cheek. 'Just remember what I said, Kate. I could make yer 'appy,' he said in a low voice.

The curtains in the parlour moved as Kate walked to the house and Mary opened the door quickly, eyeing the car as it pulled away. 'Well, well,' she said grinning. 'Just fancy, our Kate ridin' around in fancy motors. What's 'e like?'

'Give us a chance ter get in, sis,' Kate replied with a demure smile.

Mary hugged her. 'Yer lookin' very well.'

'So are you. Are yer puttin' on weight?'

'Yeah, but I'm not pregnant, if that's what yer finkin',' Mary said reprovingly.

John Woodley got up as Kate walked into the parlour and gave her a friendly peck on the cheek. 'So 'ow's my favourite sister-in-law?' he asked.

Kate sat down with a sigh. 'Where's the kids?' she asked.

'They're all up the park,' Mary said, then she glanced at John. 'I bet the kettle'll be boilin' its guts out.'

John raised his hands in a defensive gesture. 'All right, I'll make the tea,' he told her, taking himself off to the scullery.

'C'mon then. What's 'is name? What's 'e like? Are you

an' 'im goin' tergevver?' Mary gushed.

Kate kicked off her shoes and began to massage the sole of her foot. 'In the first place we're not courtin',' she said calmly. ''Is name's Len Copeland an' 'e's a friend of a friend. We were just on a bit o' business.'

'It's gettin' more an' more mysterious by the second,' Mary replied with raised eyebrows.

Kate went on to explain about the swag-lines and Mary gave her a cheeky grin. 'I could do wiv one o' those nightdresses in black,' she cut in. 'John loves ter see me in black underwear.'

'I'll save yer one,' Kate said smiling. 'Anyfing ter keep you two close.'

'Me an' John are fine, luv,' Mary told her. 'I just wish there was some nice feller in your life. Ain't there any chance wiv you an' this Copeland bloke?'

Kate shook her head. 'Len's a very good-lookin' feller an' 'e's nice ter be wiv, but 'e's not my sort, sis. 'E doesn't ring any bells wiv me.'

'Is 'e interested?'

'Yeah, I fink so.'

'Yer fink so. Don't yer know?'

'Yeah, 'e wants me ter go out wiv 'im.'

'Well, why the bloody 'ell don't yer?' Mary growled. 'Just 'ave a good time an' who knows what might develop.'

John came back into the room carrying a laden tea-tray. 'Is that woman o' mine tryin' ter play Cupid?' he asked.

'Not so's yer'd notice,' Kate grinned.

'Did I tell yer I'd applied ter be a tally clerk?' he remarked.

'Yeah, yer did.'

'Well, I've bin accepted.'

'That's lovely. Congratulations.'

''E'll 'ave a job ter get frew that door if 'is 'ead gets any bigger,' Mary laughed.

'It's not just yer average bloke who could do the job,' John said winking at Kate. 'Anyway it'll be more secure than 'avin' ter line up fer work.'

Mary looked up at the clock on the mantelshelf. 'Fancy a trip down the market before they close?' she asked.

Kate nodded. 'What about the kids though?'

Mary turned to her husband. 'John, if the tribe comes in could yer get 'em all a drink an' cut 'em a slice each o' that Dundee cake?'

He bowed mockingly. 'Any ovver wish, your majesty?'

'Piss orf,' she replied with a comical look at her sister.

They left the house and walked quickly towards the Tower Bridge Road market. 'Do you believe in love at first sight?' Kate asked as they crossed the main thoroughfare.

'That's a funny question to ask,' Mary replied.

'Well, do yer?'

'I dunno. I s'pose it does 'appen ter some people.'

'What about wiv you an' John?'

'I couldn't stand the sight of 'im at first.'

'Why was that?'

''E was too cock-sure of 'imself, but after a while . . .'

''E sort o' grew on yer.'

'Yeah, that's right.'

'An' now yer love 'im.'

'Like crazy.'

'This love at first sight fing: is it love, or just passion?' Kate asked her.

'What d'yer mean?'

'You remember when I first met Will?' Kate went on. 'It was at that dance an' I couldn't keep my eyes off 'im. I wouldn't say I was smitten wiv love but I was intrigued by 'im. It was a few nights later, after our second date, when I felt that I was fallin' in love wiv 'im. Yer couldn't really call that love at first sight.'

'So come on, tell me.'

'Tell yer what?'

'Tell me about the feller who 'as rung yer bell.'

'Oh I dunno, it sounds silly,' Kate said dismissively.

'I'm listenin'.'

'This feller's a detective.'

'A copper?'

'Yeah, I only met 'im a few weeks ago an' I keep finkin' about 'im. I'm really 'opin' we'll meet up again.'

''Ow did yer meet in the first place?'

Kate explained to her sister about Jimmy and Charlie Almond's episode on the factory roof and when she had finished Mary shook her head sadly. 'That's what comes o' livin' in Milldyke Street,' she sighed. 'Anyway it's nice ter know there are some decent coppers about. Not many would 'ave given the boys anuvver chance.'

''E is different, an' 'e cares.'

'I take it 'e's married.'

''E lost 'is wife an' baby durin' the Blitz,' Kate told her.

All around them the din of the marketplace and the sellers' cries went unheeded as the two sisters chattered together. Kate sounded buoyant and Mary felt cheered by her sister's disclosures.

'So you intend ter see 'im again?' she asked as they walked back to Abbey Street empty-handed.

'Yeah, I do. Don't ask me when, but it'll 'appen, I just feel it,' Kate said with conviction.

Chapter Twenty-Five

On Saturday evening Flossy Chandler's neighbours left Milldyke Street in force, watched by the surly-looking caretaker who lounged in the block entrance with his arms folded over his grubby shirt. Why they should be so keen to support the bloody pansy was beyond him, he thought. Well, they could get on with it as far as he was concerned. He had other things to do.

'Nice evenin'',' Liz Fogan remarked to him as she passed by holding on to Ada Champion's arm.

The caretaker nodded in reply and then went inside before someone stopped to remind him about another maintenance job outstanding.

Freda Irons, Sadie Elmley and Mary Enright were in close formation beside their campaign leader and some distance behind them came the grey-haired Maud Sattersley holding on to Emmy Drew. The elderly Maud was rather poor-sighted and glad of someone to latch on to, even if it meant having to listen to Emmy Drew's tales of woe.

Mick Enright, Ted Fogan and Sid Champion had gone on ahead, not wishing to listen to womanly chat and more importantly wanting to get a quick pint at the Horseshoe next to the Trocette cinema.

'I was shocked when Liz asked me if I'd mind 'im

escortin' me ternight,' Emmy was going on. ' "No bloody
fear," I told 'er. "Let 'im find somebody else." I mean ter
say, what would people fink, seein' me wiv me arm stuck
frew 'is? Besides, the man's an ignorant git. It's 'ardly a
word yer get out of 'im the best o' times.'

'I know, luv, but never mind, don't let it get yer down,'
Maud replied. 'Liz was only finkin' o' you.'

'I dunno so much,' Emmy moaned. 'It makes yer fink.'

Other people from Milldyke Buildings were spilling out
at intervals and from his vantage point above the street
Ernie Walker surveyed the scene with interest. 'Look at 'er,'
he said chuckling to Stella who had just called in to see if
he was ready. 'She's done up like a bleedin' dog's dinner.'

'Who is?'

'Why, that Mrs Willmot. An' look at 'er. First time I've
seen 'er lookin' anywhere near the mark.'

Stella was craning her neck to see. 'Who yer on about
now?' she asked.

'Why, ole Muvver Stevens, the bagwash woman. I've
never seen 'er out wivout that scruffy ole coat an' that
'orrible greasy 'at.'

'Ernie, yer gettin' ter be a nosy ole sod,' Stella told him
with a smile. 'Now come on, shut that winder an' let's get
goin'. My Joe's gonna get all shirty if we don't 'urry up.
'E's bin ready fer over an hour.'

More people were emerging from the buildings and as
Ernie Walker took one last look he shook his head in
disbelief. 'I never knew Flossy 'ad so many friends,' he
remarked.

'Well, we live an' learn,' Stella replied quickly. 'Now
will you shut that bleedin' winder or we're gonna be late
gettin' there.'

'The Trocette's a flea-bitten bloody place to 'ave a talent

contest,' the old man muttered as he finally slammed the sash down. 'The poxy seats are 'ard an' it's not very clean in there.'

Joe Sandford was standing by his front door as Stella and Ernie came out of the old man's flat. 'C'mon, Ernie, or we'll be late,' he grumbled.

'Now don't you start. I've 'ad enough o' your ole woman 'urryin' me up,' Ernie growled back.

Amy Almond left the buildings along with Kate and their children, Jenny holding on to her mother's arm and the two boys walking a few paces behind. 'It might 'ave sounded a bit 'ard, but it 'ad ter be said,' Amy was telling her next-door neighbour. 'Don't get me wrong, Fred's a really nice bloke, but like all fellers 'e don't fink. All I know is my ole man's expected 'ome in a few days' time. 'E could walk in termorrer fer all I know. I would be in shit creek if 'e come in an' found Fred in me bed. "No Fred, yer'll 'ave ter make some ovver arrangements," I told 'im.'

'So what's 'e doin'?' Kate asked her.

'As far as I know 'e's kippin' down in that men's 'ostel in Tooley Street,' Amy replied. 'I told 'im it's only a temporary arrangement but 'e wasn't too 'appy about it.'

'Will 'e be there ternight?' Kate asked her.

'I 'ope so. 'E said 'e'll be goin' wiv 'is mates from work,' Amy replied.

Barney Schofield had polished his brown boots and flattened his wiry grey hair down with brilliantine before leaving his flat. It was just as well his escorting duty had been cancelled, he thought. Better to slip in the damned place unnoticed. He could stand at the back maybe and effect a quick withdrawal after it was all over.

Jack and Muriel Dennis were amongst the last to leave, along with Elsie Burton and her four children, and finally

Meg Johnson stepped out into the turning with Rene Smedley, her next-door neighbour.

'I 'ope 'e does well,' Meg remarked.

''E should do wiv the support 'e's got,' Rene replied. 'I should fink 'alf o' Bermon'sey'll be there ternight.'

The contestants were already assembled in the wings on one side of the stage and Flossy looked very nervous as he twiddled his fingers. 'Frightened?' he replied to a juggler who lounged against the wall, 'I'm bloody shittin' meself.'

'Relax when yer go on an' just do yer best,' the man told him. 'They ain't gonna eat yer.'

Flossy could not stop worrying as he waited. The crowd might not be about to eat him, but his manager probably would on Monday morning when he found out about Snake-eye Monzarelli's suit.

Bernie Gilchrist was there, dressed in dinner suit and bow tie and puffing on a large cigar. He stopped to talk to a pretty young woman in a spangled dress which was daringly low at the front and she giggled at something he said.

'Lecherous ole bastard,' a dapper-looking man dressed like a costermonger remarked to Flossy.

'Yer don't 'ave ter tell me, luv,' Flossy replied. 'What you doin'?'

'Spoons.'

'I'm playin' the pianer.'

'She's doin' a bit of opera by all accounts,' the spoon man told him.

Bernie Gilchrist felt happy as he joked with the young woman. He had successfully negotiated with the manager of the run-down cinema to put on his talent-night show between film performances. *Lives of a Bengal Lancer* and *Bowery Boys* was not a programme that would be expected to pack the crowds in, and the manager was only too glad to recoup a bit more money by hiring out the place to the up-and-coming impresario.

'Right then,' Bernie called out to the waiting performers. 'Buck Wilson, you're first on. Now in two minutes I'm goin' on stage to introduce the show an' when I call yer name out be ready. Give it all yer got an' we'll all be rootin' for yer.'

High up in the grimy cinema the manager sat looking out from the projection room and he grunted appreciatively. It was many years since he had seen the place filled up, and he was on a percentage too.

'Makes a nice change ter see the seats full,' the projectionist remarked. 'Last time I saw it so packed was when we showed Charlie Chaplin in *The Goldrush*, just before the war broke out if I remember rightly.'

Bernie Gilchrist appeared on stage to polite applause and announced with elegant aplomb that his show comprised the finest talent this side of the water, adding that the contestants would be judged by none other than Vic Golding and Susanna Greenbaum from the notable theatrical agency, London Productions. He then went on to introduce the accompanying pianist, Nan Grierly, and with a grand sweep of his arm he called for the first artiste. 'Ladies and gentlemen, give a big hand to Buck Wilson, the spoon man!'

'Spoon man?' Ada said in a loud voice.

''E's playin' the spoons,' Liz told her in a whisper.

'Speak up, I can't 'ear yer,' Ada moaned.

The dapper performer beamed widely as he dashed to the centre of the stage and proceeded to click the two spoons between his legs, around his neck and up his arm to the tune of 'Goodbye Dolly'. Some of the audience started to clap in time, which was not to Ada's liking. 'Bloody rubbish,' she growled. 'I've seen better in the pub.'

The applause was led by Buck's supporters and Bernie hurried on stage once more to introduce a tap-dancing trio.

'At least they're better than the first act,' Sadie said to Mary as the threesome pranced about the stage.

The applause was slightly more enthusiastic and then the juggler appeared. He started well but suddenly dropped one of his clubs.

'Want some glue?' a loud voice called out.

'Shut yer poxy noise,' another voice rejoined.

'Who you talkin' to?'

'You, that's who.'

'I'll come over there an' smash yer ugly face in.'

'You an' whose army?'

'I won't need no 'elp.'

'C'mon then.'

The juggler had had enough and he skulked off the stage while a couple of cinema attendants tried to get the two women to sit down.

'What a palaver,' Ada remarked. 'The poor sod didn't 'ave a chance wiv them two scatty mares leadin' off like that.'

A comedian was next on and most of his gags were received in silence until someone intervened. 'Where d'yer get them poxy jokes, out o' Christmas crackers?'

The comic gave the heckler a wicked look and then appealed to the rest of the audience. 'I've seen a tram drive in a tunnel smaller than that geezer's norf an' souf.'

'An' I've 'eard better jokes from my eight-year-old.'

'So yer got kids as well. It's a wonder yer mouf was still long enough, or did someone 'ave it in for yer?'

'Don't you come the old soldier wiv me, pal.'

'Well then, shut yer trap.'

Barney Schofield had heard enough. 'Quiet in the ranks!' he bawled out from the back of the auditorium.

'An' you can shut yer noise too,' the disillusioned comic shouted back before storming off stage.

'I've never bin so disgusted in my life,' Ada growled. 'Any more o' this an' I'm orf 'ome, Flossy or not.'

Amy Almond had been trying to spot Fred Logan and she suddenly saw him sitting a few rows behind her and waved out to him. 'I feel mean about 'im 'avin' ter stay at that 'ostel, but what could I do?' she sighed to Kate.

The children had started giggling and Kate hushed them up as Bernie Gilchrist stomped back on stage. 'I feel I've gotta say this,' he began, shaking his head slowly. 'In all my years in the profession I don't think I've ever witnessed scenes like those of tonight. We can close the show right away if you're not satisfied, but I tell you this. If you leave now you'll miss a treat. Judy Garland, Shirley Temple and Deanna Durbin all rolled into one. Now are you all ready?' The response was little more than a murmur and Bernie appealed to them once more. 'I said are you ready?'

This time the response was loud and clear and the impresario smiled thankfully. 'Now I want you to give a big hand to Marion Masters.'

The young woman walked on to the stage looking very nervous and she smiled sweetly at the audience and then the pianist, who smiled back encouragingly as she began to play an introduction to 'One Fine Day'.

The strong, clear voice was like the pure call of a nightingale and the audience was stunned to silence. Effortless and eloquent the young woman's mellifluous singing charmed the hearts of everyone present, and as she worked towards the end of her performance the crystal tones were penetrating the very limits of the rambling cinema. Even as the last note died away people were applauding. Ada dabbed at her eyes and her friends around her looked dewy-eyed themselves. Kate and Amy joined the rest of the audience in unashamed adulation, and even Ernie Walker was moved to swallow hard.

'I don't give much fer Flossy's chances now,' Sadie whispered to Mary Enright as the applause went on.

The hopeful pianist stood in the wings waiting to make his appearance and he wholeheartedly joined in with the clapping. When order returned and he was introduced he glanced off stage and gestured with his hand in a show of magnanimity. He bowed low and then walked to the piano, and seating himself with a flourish he proceeded to play a medley of well-loved tunes, spiced with his own brand of link phrases, all the while smiling at the audience, willing them to like him. A few people joined in and it encouraged Flossy to greater heights, but in his heart he knew that at the very best he could only come second to the pretty young songbird.

'That's a smart suit 'e's got on,' Sadie remarked.

'I fink it's an ole one bin whitewashed,' Mary joked.

'Must 'ave cost 'im a few bob,' Liz whispered.

'What yer mumblin' about?' Ada growled at her.

'The suit. D'yer like the suit?' Liz asked her.

'I fink 'e looks like a bleedin' decorator,' Ada replied.

When he had finished his performance loud applause rang out and Flossy took another bow.

The judging was a formality, and when the young singer walked on to the stage to receive an envelope containing ten pounds, cheering and loud clapping filled the auditorium. Flossy then went up to receive the second prize of five pounds and he bowed solemnly to the audience yet again.

Backstage there were some harsh words spoken, however.

'I wouldn't be seen dead in this bloody dump again,' the comedian growled.

'I felt like whackin' that loud-mouf git over the barnet wiv me club,' the juggler told him.

'This place is a right shit-'ole,' the spoon man remarked. 'It could do wiv a good scrubbin' out an' decoratin'.'

Bernie meanwhile was fluttering around the young singer like an overweight moth and he was lavish with his praises. 'You'll be singing on the wireless soon, mark my words,' he gushed. 'Now I want you to meet me tomorrow and I'll draw up a contract. That way I can get the very best for you.'

Flossy sat down feeling drained. He had managed to keep the white suit from getting marked but that was only half of the operation, he reminded himself. The suit had to be back on the rack at Moreland's first thing Monday morning, which shouldn't prove too difficult as Ken Swales invariably arrived a few minutes after the shop was opened. The main problem would be convincing the manager that Snake-eye had changed his mind when he came into the shop at closing time on Saturday, after Swales had left for the weekend.

'Hard luck, Flossy,' Bernie said, giving the worried pianist a sympathetic slap on the back. 'Never mind, I'll try and get you some decent engagements, soon as the dust settles.'

Flossy hurried from the Trocette and took a diversionary route home, not wanting to meet up with his supporters and eager to get the suit off before something happened to it. He had no need to worry since his loyal followers had other ideas, crowding out to join their husbands in the pub next door. Later, having slaked their thirst, they all praised the young singer unstintingly and commiserated with each other about Flossy Chandler as they waited for a tram home.

Barney Schofield had left the Trocette sharply, and he too walked the long way home. After witnessing the outrageous scenes of disorder and then being privileged to hear the beautiful voice that had penetrated even his gruff heart, the ex-sergeant major was feeling rather strange. It was as though his whole regulated existence had once again been thrown into turmoil, and as he stepped along briskly his heavy military tread sounded loudly on the paving stones.

Chapter Twenty-Six

Sunday morning began as it always did in Milldyke Street, with the children out early and the old rag-and-bone man pushing his squeaking barrow along the cobbles and then squatting on one of the arms to smoke his pipe. The young girls danced in and out of twirling skipping-ropes and jumped between the rude chalkmarks of hopscotch squares while boys kicked battered tin cans at the wall or ran along the kerbside in pursuit of coloured glass marbles. An ordinary, uneventful Sunday morning, until Sid Champion succeeded in setting the scullery alight while trying to reclaim his underpants from a line Ada had fixed up over the gas-stove. The item of clothing fell on to the lighted gas-jet and immediately set a towel on fire. The flames reached the ceiling in no time at all, and the panic-stricken Sid called out for Ada as he tried to reach the sink.

'What the bloody 'ell!' Ada screamed out, accidentally throwing the stewed remains from the teapot over him as she tried to dowse the flames. Luckily the tea was cold and Sid dashed along the passage to grab his old coat, his hair spattered with tea-leaves. The coat was thrown over the gas-stove which put out the burning underpants and towel, but the flames had attacked the adjacent toilet doorframe which had several thick coats of oil paint covering it.

Mary Enright and Sadie Elmley were in the process of emptying their dustbins and they caught sight of the black smoke pouring from the Champions' scullery window.

'Oh dear,' Mary sighed. 'It looks like Ada burnt the rashers.'

'It looks more like she's left the toast under the grill,' Sadie remarked.

Ada had managed to get to the sink and with the aid of a large saucepan she finally doused the fire. 'You dopey, good-fer-nuffing, ugly-lookin' git,' she ranted. 'See what yer done? Me scullery's ruined. After all the time I spent paintin' that bloody woodwork.'

'It's your bloody fault,' Sid shouted back at her. ''Ow many times 'ave I gotta tell yer about airin' fings over the gas. It's bloody dangerous.'

'It wouldn't be dangerous if yer showed a bit o' sense. Course that's askin' too much wiv you, yer great big fat lummox,' Ada screamed.

''Ow was I s'posed ter get me clean pants down from up there?' Sid growled.

'The same way I do, wiv the broom 'andle, after yer've turned the bloody gas out,' Ada growled back.

'Well, 'ow the 'ell was I s'posed ter know yer used a broom 'andle,' Sid went on.

'I'll 'ave ter go an' see that lazy git Ferguson now,' his irate wife groaned.

'What for?'

'So 'e can sort it out,' she told him. 'We can't leave it like that. If Ted Briscoe sees it in that state we're in trouble. 'E could put it down ter negligence an' 'ave us out.'

'It was an accident, pure an' simple. Surely Briscoe wouldn't give us notice ter quit over a little accident like that,' Sid said, looking worried.

'You don't know Briscoe. The fornicatin' git takes pleasure in doin' such fings,' Ada replied forcefully. 'Look at the way 'e nearly put poor Freda Irons out on the street.'

'Look don't worry, luv, I'll . . .'

'Don't you "luv" me, you stupid ole goat.'

'Now calm down,' Sid pleaded. 'I was only gonna say that I'll borrer Mick Enright's scraper an' paintbrushes. I can 'ave the job done in no time at all.'

'Oh no you don't,' Ada told him firmly. 'I remember the last time yer done a bit o' paintin'. Six months it took ter dry out. Yer put it on like treacle.'

'That's 'cos I didn't 'ave any turps ter thin it down wiv,' Sid replied.

In the yard the two women stood looking up at the Champions' window.

'Whatever it was they've put it out,' Mary remarked.

'It could 'ave caught the 'ole Buildin's alight,' Sadie replied with a worried frown. 'The place is like a poxy tinderbox.'

Mary gave her an evil grin which made the nervous Sadie go cold. The Enright woman was game for anything and setting fire to the Buildings was not beyond her, she fretted.

A short while later Ada went to see the caretaker, which did not make her feel any better. 'Can't do that. Not till Briscoe gives me the OK,' he replied, shaking his head. 'Repaintin' that scullery's gonna take two days at least. There's the ole paint ter scrape off first an' then yer'll need an undercoat. I can't just get paint when I like. It's gotta go frew the channels.'

'What about if I treat yer?'

'Sorry, I'd like to 'elp yer out, but me 'ands are tied. Rules is rules.'

Ada returned to the flat and gave her beleaguered

husband another roasting. 'See, I told yer what'd 'appen. Briscoe's gotta see the damage first. Now p'raps yer'll be more careful when yer try ter do fings. Yer so bloody clumsy. Look at that tap washer yer tried ter change when Ferguson was off sick. Drowned the bloody place out an' ruined 'er underneath's new wallpaper in the bargain. Honestly, Sid, yer like a walkin' time bomb. Now go an' get the winkles an' shrimps, an' see if yer can make a balls-up wiv that.'

Kate Flannagan cleared the breakfast things from the table after Jimmy and Jenny had gone out to play and then tidied up quickly. The day looked like being another scorcher, she thought. Maybe she could find time this afternoon to have a go at that dress pattern, providing she could get the ironing out of the way. The problem was, Amy usually called on Sunday mornings and that would be an hour wasted.

Kate sighed as she set about the washing-up. Perhaps she was being unfair. Amy Almond had been the first person to befriend her and she owed her a lot. For instance, there were the items of swag Amy had put her way. The nightdresses had sold very well, allowing her to buy a few things she would otherwise not have managed. Moving into the street had given her the chance to make other new friends too. The cocky Len Copeland had been instrumental in helping her find herself again, and then there was Pat Cassidy. Until she had met him the thought of forming another relationship with a man was far from her mind, but now she found herself constantly thinking about him. He was a kind, generous-spirited man who had stirred her feelings and made her feel a real woman once more. He had put no pressure on her; in fact he had not really tried to encourage her, but there was certainly something about him that excited her and she could not help but feel optimistic about the future.

Up above the street Ernie Walker watched the comings and goings as usual, his alert mind tuned in to his next-door neighbours' problems. Joe and Stella Sandford had made ground in their attempts to heal their rocky marriage, but it seemed there was still a long way to go. Only last night he had heard raised voices after they had all returned from the talent show and it sounded like the cause of the verbal fracas was the interest a young buck had shown in Stella. As always she had denied any complicity but Joe would have none of it. There was only one thing for it as far as Ernie was concerned, and he would be only too glad to state his views when the chance arose.

Before noon Ted Briscoe made his entrance, and after consulting with the caretaker he went off to see Ada Champion. 'I'll need ter take a look at the damage,' he said curtly.

Sid was feeling guilty for putting Ada through it and he decided to play his part in defusing the tension. 'Come in, Mr Briscoe,' he said pleasantly. 'Ada's got the kettle boilin'. Would yer like a couple o' slices o' toast wiv yer tea?'

Briscoe shook his head as he walked along the dark passageway. 'Just tea'll do,' he said without thanks.

'Very sorry ter be a nuisance, but it was a pure accident, Mr Briscoe.'

The agent took a brief look at the damage and shook his head. 'Yer really must be more careful,' he growled. 'These places need a lot of upkeep an' the costs are risin' all the time.'

'I offered ter do it meself, but the good woman don't

trust me,' Sid replied with a rueful grin.

Briscoe sat down at the table and ran his hand through his untidy, thick dark hair. 'Where is the good woman?' he asked sarcastically.

'She's gone down the lane ter buy 'erself a tonic off the medicine stall,' Sid told him. 'The fire's shook all 'er nerves up.'

'It would do,' Briscoe remarked.

'Sure yer wouldn't like anyfing else wiv yer tea?' Sid asked him.

'I'm sure.'

'Well, if yer'll bear wiv me fer a few seconds I'll pour it out.'

The agent lounged back in his chair and looked around. The room seemed to be well kept and everything looked in place. No sense in making too much out of it, he thought. Ferguson could fix the scullery in one day and then get back to renovating the Brindley flat ready for the new tenant. He must go and see the Faircloughs though. They would have to be made to realise that keeping rabbits in hutches on the fire escape was against regulations. Last time it was their banging late at night which had to be addressed. Now it seemed they were into farming. Whatever next?

Sid Champion reappeared in the living room looking a little uneasy after putting a light under the kettle. 'I'm sorry about the tea, Mr Briscoe, but the tea canister got upset this mornin' as I tried ter put the fire out. I'll just see if we've got any more in the cabinet.'

The agent watched with distaste as Sid rummaged through the kitchen cabinet and then he puffed loudly. 'Never mind. Leave it. I'll get a cup o' tea at the Faircloughs',' he said irritably.

'I shouldn't 'ave a cup there,' Sid warned him. 'They

gave my Ada a cup o' tea once an' it made 'er feel ill fer a
week. 'Ere, I found some coffee.'

'That'll do,' Briscoe sighed.

'One sugar or two?'

'Four.'

'A sweet toof, eh?'

'Not so's yer'd notice.'

Sid scooped a heaped teaspoon of powder into the cup
and added the boiling water. It did not seem very black so
he added another spoonful and then the milk and sugar.
'There we are,' he announced.

Ted Briscoe had been on his own ever since his wife
walked out on him before the war, and although he had
managed to persuade the occasional woman friend to stay
the night not one of them had been able to make decent
coffee. It was always either too weak or too strong, but this
was something again. This coffee tasted like nothing he had
ever tasted in his whole life. After two gulps he put the cup
down. 'I can't finish this,' he growled. 'It tastes like gravy.'

'I'm sorry but it must 'ave gone stale,' Sid told him
apologetically. 'Me and my missus don't drink a lot o'
coffee, yer see.'

Briscoe got up to leave with a surly look on his flat pasty
face. 'I'll clear fings wiv Ferguson,' he said brusquely as he
walked out of the room.

Ada looked down from Liz Fogan's window and smiled
back into the room. 'The ugly bastard's just left,' she said.

''E's s'posed ter be checkin' all our rent books soon. I
'ope it ain't this mornin',' Liz remarked.

When she got back to her flat Ada gave Sid a searching
look. 'Well?'

'It's all right, 'e's gonna clear it wiv the caretaker,' he
told her.

'Wonders'll never cease. Did yer make 'im a cup o' tea?'

'Nah, I couldn't.'

'Why not?'

''Cos the tea caddy got spilled when I was puttin' the fire out.'

'When who was puttin' the fire out?'

'All right, when you was puttin' it out.'

'So yer never give 'im a drink. It's a wonder we got a result.'

'Oh, I gave 'im a drink. I made 'im a cup o' coffee.'

'But we ain't got no coffee.'

'Oh yes, we 'ave.'

'Where?'

''Ere, in the coffee tin. Look.'

'Oh my good Gawd!' Ada exclaimed. 'That's where I keep my Bisto!'

'I wondered why 'e didn't finish it,' Sid said grinning.

The afternoon sun was hot and the street folk enjoyed the tranquil sabbath. Children sat in the shade making their plans, now that the school holidays were upon them. Grown-ups took the opportunity to have a nap or listen to the wireless, and after Charlie had told her that he and Jimmy Flannagan were going to the open-air swimming pool in Southwark Park, Amy Almond went to bed with Fred Logan.

Kate first made sure that Jenny had not wandered from the street before setting out her dress pattern. It was the first time she had attempted to make a dress from a pattern but she had been assured by Bet Groves at work that it was simplicity itself. The cutting-out would be easy, she thought. The cutting lines were clearly marked, as were the tacking marks, but then she suddenly hit a snag. The jargon used in the instructions was alien to her and what should have been a simple task proved otherwise. For a while Kate pored over the plans and then finally she gave up. Bet Groves would sort it out for her on Monday, she told herself.

The hot sun reflected from the granite chippings in the pavement and the street children sat in the shade of the bacon-curing factory. Folk slept on and others tuned in to the Home Service for the afternoon transmission of theatre organ music direct from the Gaumont, Leicester Square. Kate sat quietly sipping her tea when suddenly she had an idea. Why didn't she pop along to see if Meg Johnson could unravel the puzzle?

After the usual wait Kate heard Meg's voice, and when she had announced herself the door opened.

'It's quite simple when yer get used to it,' Meg told her. 'What yer do is this. See this selvedge?'

'Where?'

'Along 'ere.'

'Yeah.'

'That's where yer pin the front piece.'

'Oh, I see. I was lookin' at it upside down.'

'No, yer was lookin' at it inside out.'

Kate was still not sure but as Meg helped her pin the pieces together it all became crystal clear. 'I'm very much obliged, Meg,' she said gratefully. 'I could never 'ave managed it wivout your 'elp.'

Meg Johnson gave her an indulgent smile. 'When yer've tacked it all tergevver bring it back an' I'll take a look before yer start sewin' it,' she offered.

'It won't be till ternight.'

'It's all right, I never go ter bed early.'

Once back in her flat Kate set to work, interrupted by

Jenny who came in with a friend for a drink, and then by Jimmy and Charlie who had been thrown out of the swimming pool by the attendant for 'bombing'.

'Can't you two ever keep out o' trouble fer more than five minutes?' she scolded them. 'Anyway, what's bombin'?'

'It's divin' in on people,' Charlie explained.

'That could be dangerous.'

'Nah, not the way we do it,' Jimmy told her.

'Well, why did they chuck yer both out then?'

''Cos the attendant's a miserable ole sod,' Charlie said with a hurt look on his cheeky face.

'Well, get yerselves a drink then go out an' play. I've got fings ter do,' she told them.

Trying to finish the tacking proved too lengthy a task before tea and it was late evening by the time Kate finally finished it. At nine o'clock Jenny was settled in bed and the young woman looked into Jimmy's room to find him happily engrossed in a tattered copy of *The Man On All Fours*. 'Where d'yer get that?' she asked.

'Charlie gave it ter me. 'E said it was really scary.'

'An' is it?'

'Yeah.'

'I'm just gonna pop along ter see Meg Johnson fer five minutes,' she said. 'Don't go 'avin' nightmares.'

Jimmy gave her a smile and buried his head in the novel once more.

The night was cool and the moon was riding high in the sky as Kate hurried along to the next block. When she turned on to the landing from the dark stairway she saw that the front door of Meg's flat was ajar and fingers of dread gripped at the young woman's stomach as she gingerly eased it open. 'Meg, are yer there?' she called through. 'Meg! It's Kate.'

Along the passage she could see the light of the moon shining down into the living room which was otherwise unlit. 'Meg, it's me, Kate.'

Holding her breath the young woman tiptoed along the dark passageway and as she reached the kitchen she was suddenly rooted to the spot. There in front of her, sitting in a chair with her arms hanging by her sides was Meg Johnson; her face purple and bloated, her lifeless, bulging eyes wide open. Tied so tightly round her neck as to be almost invisible between the fleshy folds was what appeared to be a black bootlace.

Chapter Twenty-Seven

Pat Cassidy sat back against the hard seat as the train neared Paddington, his eyes fixed once more on the grimy factories and tenement blocks, tiny backstreets and main thorough-fares which were all too familiar to him. He was back to his roots: back to where sad memories rose up and almost choked him when he was least expecting it; back to where his profession took him down in amongst the darkest realities of life, which sapped his energies more and more with a terrifying, inexorable certainty. Behind him he had left the serene and beautiful countryside of Wiltshire and the village of West Blaydon, where the lanes threaded through pasture lands of verdant green and corn yellow and snaked past whitewashed thatch-roof cottages and ancient lichen-covered churches. There the smallholding stood, with its stone farmhouse clinging to the sloping field that led down to a wide valley and the still water of Blaydon Mere. Beyond the tranquil green lake the land rose gently up to a ridge, where thin pines lined up against the skyline like ageless guardians of the soil, and where wicked steel traps were set and dead, pellet-ridden rooks were pinned out in crucifixion to deter their living fellows.

The policeman had enjoyed the brief stay with his younger sister and her husband. Gilda and Norman Knight were proper countryfolk: she an adopted daughter from the smoky streets of the city, and her spouse a son of pure farming stock who had tilled the land with horse-pulled ploughshares and cut the dry grass with roughly honed scythes and sickles before the advent of the motorised tractor and the new hay-baling machines. It was a strange coupling but a successful one. Norman had met and fallen in love with the young Gilda when he first saw her at a village dance. She was with friends, down from London on a working holiday, and he was on vacation during his final year at Oxford where he was studying for his law degree. Within one year Gilda Cassidy became Mrs Knight and she was happy.

The war came and Norman, recently qualified as a solicitor, went off to fight, seeing action in the North Atlantic as a sub-lieutenant on a destroyer. Gilda waited, her time spent helping to organise fêtes and church bazaars to raise money for the war effort, before she became a nurse at the local military hospital.

When the war ended Norman Knight joined the local law firm Hoseason and Willets as a junior partner and with his tidy inheritance he bought a smallholding known as Blaydon Mere Farm, where Gilda kept pigs and a small dairy herd and struggled to find the time to cultivate the arable land, helped by Norman at weekends and holidays.

It was to Blaydon Mere Farm that Pat Cassidy had come for a long weekend. His younger sister was delighted to see him but shocked by his city pallor and his lean frame, and there and then she vowed to coax him to Blaydon whenever possible. In the meantime she made a point of serving him huge portions of food and persuading him to go with Norman up to the ridge to view the breathtaking landscape beyond. The fresh air had already put some colour back into the young city man's cheeks and a fresh bounce in his step, and the disgustingly large platefuls of bacon and eggs, fried bread, and tomatoes fresh from the farm's vegetable patch had already padded his ribs, Gilda swore.

'You must come back, Patrick, and often,' she pleaded as she kissed her brother farewell.

'Yes, you must, and maybe you'll give us a hand with the low meadow,' Norman joked.

Now the smoke-laden air was once again in Pat's nostrils and the nervous, darting eyes of the city dwellers surrounded him as he walked out from the station into the wide and busy thoroughfare. One hour later he had crossed the metropolis and was letting himself into his Catford flat. He had already eaten on the train and now fought the urge to bring out the bottle of whisky. Gilda had obviously been shocked by the way he looked when he arrived at the farm and he felt it would be a kind of betrayal to resume his punishing drinking habits so soon after.

He washed, shaved and made himself a strong coffee, promising himself that he would finish reading the evening paper before he went to sleep, but his eyes were soon drooping and the last thing he concentrated his mind on before sleep claimed him was the dark and beautiful woman from Milldyke Buildings. He was hoping to see her in his dreams but his sleep was leaden and he awoke next morning with a heavy head.

Chief Superintendent Ray Baxter had been obliged to reorganise the local C.I.D. to deal with the murder at Milldyke Buildings and already teams were out taking statements from everyone within the close vicinity. He was waiting eagerly for the first briefing session set for that lunchtime, and he paused to finish his lukewarm coffee before studying the report prepared by the squad investigating the warehouse robbery in Dockhead the previous month.

The phone rang and Baxter growled in annoyance as he picked up the receiver. 'Speaking. Right. Send him in right away.'

Pat Cassidy came into the office, having been updated on events since his departure to Wiltshire last Wednesday evening, and he was noticeably shocked. 'How's . . .?' he started.

'Your chief super's doing well,' the officer in charge informed him. 'It's nothing serious, I'm glad to say. Strictly a case of overwork, so the doctors say. He collapsed last Friday morning, as you may have heard already. I'm only here on a temporary basis. Take a seat, Cassidy.'

'About the murder in Milldyke Buildings, sir . . .'

'First things first,' Baxter said quickly. 'How was Wiltshire?'

'Very beautiful at this time of year,' Pat replied with a puzzled frown.

'I got to see your super and I've been thoroughly briefed,' Baxter said with a smile. 'He speaks very highly of your achievements. He tells me that it's mainly due to your hard work that we can now send our report on the warehouse robbery to the D.P.P. for action. Well done! As for the present, I want you to organise and head a squad with responsibility for countering dock pilferage, especially around the Tooley Street area. There's been far too much of it lately and the port employers feel it's getting out of hand.'

'I beg your pardon, sir, but what about the Milldyke case?' Cassidy said quickly. 'I was directly involved in investigating the other murder in the Milldyke Street area eight months ago, and I've been told that there are similarities.'

'So there are, sergeant, but they needn't concern you. There's other work for you to get your teeth into.'

'But it doesn't make sense to me that I should be excluded,' Pat replied angrily. 'I know more about the details of that first killing than any other detective in this division. Surely I'd be more use to you investigating the latest murder than pissing around in Tooley Street chasing shanks of ham and tins of peaches.'

Superintendent Baxter afforded himself a smile. 'As I said earlier, I've been well primed about you, and frankly such insubordination is nothing more than I expected. Get your team sorted out, Cassidy, and let me see some developments soon. As I said, those dock workers are starting to get above themselves and they need to be sat on.'

Pat Cassidy sat still in his chair, fighting to control his rapidly rising temper, and Baxter grew furious. 'Well, see to it, man,' he ordered.

Cassidy stood his ground. 'If I can't persuade you to change your mind, sir, then I'm reporting sick, and it's valid. I'm carrying a piece of shrapnel around in my back and it's giving me pain. And while I'm away I shall be putting in a request for transfer, stating amongst the reasons an incompatibility with the new divisional head.'

Baxter's face went livid and he choked back an angry tirade. 'You're even more stubborn than I was led to believe,' he growled.

Pat Cassidy leaned forward in his chair. 'I beg your pardon, sir, but I've already heard enough information on the latest killing to convince me that the two are linked. As I just said, I believe I have a head start over any other detective here, and for me not to be given the investigation could only smack of personalities.'

'Don't adopt that high-handed tone with me, Cassidy!' Baxter exploded. 'Any more of it and you'll go on report.'

'I'm sorry if I've stepped out of line, sir, but I'm not one to bow and scrape in front of my superior only to curse him to hell behind his back. What you see is what you get and in saying that I don't consider I'm being disrespectful. On the contrary, I'm a committed policeman with a good record, and if you find it necessary to put me on report then I'll be obliged to challenge it in every way possible.'

'Get out of here, Cassidy,' Baxter scowled. 'I'll decide what I do in my own time.'

After he had left the superintendent's office the angry sergeant sought out the detective who was heading the murder investigation, only to discover that he was still out on the streets.

'If you'd care to wait in the canteen I'll be happy to send D.S. Murphy along to see you as soon as he gets here,' the desk sergeant offered.

'No, I need some fresh air,' Pat told him. 'I can be found in the Woolpack. Saloon bar, sergeant.'

Less than half an hour later Detective Sergeant Bill Murphy walked into the pub and spotted Cassidy sitting in a far corner. 'I've just been called into the super's office,' he remarked, his eyes narrowing. 'It seems there's been a change of plan. I'm to head an anti-pilfering team.'

'At Tooley Street?' Pat queried, trying to hide a smile.

'You're a bastard, Cassidy,' Murphy snarled. 'This murder case was going to be good for me.'

'Why? You're not a rookie looking for pats on the back, are you?' Pat said sarcastically.

'Don't get flash with me,' the irate officer growled.

Pat Cassidy raised his hands in a friendly gesture. 'Look, Bill. You've heard the talk. I'm all but washed up here,' he said quietly. 'I've been walking a thin line for ages and this new super's been primed. I can't afford to slip any further down in the mire. I need this case more than you do. Remember I know this area, and I know all about the last killing. It'll be a time-saving exercise with me taking over. Let me owe you a favour. By the way, what're you drinking?'

'Same as you, I guess.'

'You won't like this. It's ginger ale.'

'Pull the other one. It's got bells on.'

'I'm serious. I'm off the hard stuff, pal.'

Murphy shook his head and grinned. 'I really believe you bloody well are.'

'True as I'm sitting here. Get yerself whatever.'

Murphy picked up the ten-shilling note Pat had thrown down on the table and sauntered over to the counter. 'Is that really ginger ale he's drinking?' he asked the barman.

The saloon bar was beginning to fill up and Pat glanced at his wrist watch as Sergeant Murphy came back clutching a gin and tonic. 'Look, I'd better get back, Bill,' he said, 'our new super'll be going spare if I'm not on hand. By the way, who was it discovered the body?'

'You'll be going to the de-briefing,' Murphy replied.

'I was just curious.'

'It was a young woman who lives in the next block. Kate Flannagan.'

Cassidy sucked in his breath quickly. 'I know her.'

'You do?'

'I met her when her boy got into a scrape a few weeks ago,' Pat told him.

'Well, you'd better be getting back or they'll be sending out the scouts and that wouldn't do, would it?' Murphy said archly before taking a sip from his glass.

Pat got up and held out his hand. 'Thanks for not being too aggrieved,' he said smiling. 'Good luck with the Tooley Street business.'

Murphy took his hand and then scowled. 'Get out of here, Pat. I don't go a lot on people who drink ginger ale.'

Meg Johnson's murder had had a devastating effect on the people of Milldyke Buildings and when Flossy Chandler went to work on Monday morning he was still feeling physically sick. People were out in the street, standing silently in small groups as the body was taken away. The police had asked him questions. Had he seen anything unusual? Had there been any strange person or persons hanging around the area? Did he know of anyone with a grudge against Meg Johnson?

Flossy remembered shaking like a leaf then, and he did not feel much better now. He opened up the shop and put the white suit back on the rack before boiling the kettle. Swales was going to raise the roof when he saw that suit, he sighed.

Ten minutes later the manager breezed into the shop. 'Mornin', Francis,' he said cheerily. 'Well, 'ow did it go? Did yer win?'

The young salesman eased himself between Swales and the suit rack. 'I got second prize, Ken,' he replied.

'Well, that wasn't too bad. 'Ere, what's the matter wiv you? Yer look very peaky this mornin'.'

'There was a murder in our buildin's last night,' Flossy told him.

'Good Gawd. Who was it?'

'This nice ole lady got strangled.'

'Good Gawd.'

'I've not bin able ter stop shakin'.'

'Do they know who done it?'

Flossy shook his head. 'I 'ope they catch 'im soon or we could all be murdered in our beds.'

'I wouldn't go gettin' yerself all screwed up,' Swales told him. 'By the way, is the tea made?'

'Yeah. I just made it.'

Swales walked into the back room and Flossy followed him in, knowing that the manager always had a cup of tea before anything else. Curse that Bernie Gilchrist, he thought. The man had well and truly led him up the garden path. 'No problem. You're a cert to win. Then there'll be bookings galore,' were his words. The ten pounds prize money would have been enough to cover the cost of the suit, which he certainly would have needed for those engagements. As if it wasn't bad enough hearing about poor Meg Johnson and having to answer all those questions to the police, he now had to face the wrath of Ken Swales.

Monday mornings were always quiet and Moreland's store manager rolled and smoked two cigarettes before emerging from the back room. Flossy had busied himself meanwhile at the shirt counter and he said a silent prayer as Swales looked around the shop.

'Oh my good Gawd! Flossy, what's that suit still doin' 'ere?'

'Snake-eye said it just wasn't 'im when 'e tried it on,' the young man said meekly.

'Not 'im? Nuffing's 'im. The man was a liability from the off. Why you ever tried ter do business wiv the likes of 'im I'll never know,' Swales declared.

Flossy winced visibly. 'Snake-eye Monzarelli's not the sort ter say no to eiver,' he replied.

'But yer didn't 'ave ter tell the geezer you could get 'im a

281

white suit!' Swales raved. 'Wait till the boss finds out. 'E'll 'ave your cobblers in a box.'

'Don't talk about body parts, please,' Flossy appealed to him. 'I feel sick enough as it is.'

'Well, we can't send it back wivout a big fuss an' who the bloody 'ell's gonna want a white suit?'

'I would, if I could afford it,' Flossy said quietly.

Swales suddenly saw a way out. 'You could buy it. Yer'd get a staff discount.'

''Ow much would it cost me then?' Flossy asked.

'Right, let's see. Nine guineas less ten per cent. That'll be . . . er, eight an' 'alf quid.'

'I've got a fiver. Could yer stop the rest at 'alf-a-crown a week?'

'Flossy, yer beginnin' ter test my patience,' Swales growled.

The young man was shrewd enough to know how far he could go before Swales really did his pieces and he decided to fall back on another ploy. 'I'm really very sorry, Ken, but I was only tryin' ter be a good salesman,' he said sweetly. 'You 'ave to admit, even the boss was pleased. 'E said so 'imself. All right it didn't work out, but I am prepared ter take the consequences. I could afford three shillin's a week if I drew me 'orns in. Would yer consider three shillin's?'

Swales stared at Flossy's little-boy-lost smile and sighed deeply. 'All right, all right. We'll call it 'alf-a-crown a week,' he relented. 'An' don't ferget ter take it 'ome wiv yer ternight. I don't want the boss ter see it, understood?'

'Fanks, Ken. Fanks very much,' Flossy gushed. 'I'll go an' 'ide it straight away.'

Chapter Twenty-Eight

Kate Flannagan sat at the table in the quiet living room twisting her damp handkerchief between her fingers. It was late afternoon and her sister Mary had taken the children off her hands for the day. The shock of finding Meg's body had turned her blood to ice and it was only now that she was beginning to pull herself together. Amy had been very good. She had given her a strong black coffee laced with brandy, and it had helped steady her nerves somewhat, but she was still fighting to control her shaking and her feelings of nausea.

The knock made her jump and she felt nervous about opening the front door. No one would be safe now, she thought. Not till the beast was caught.

'Hello, Kate. Can I come in, or is it inconvenient?'

The young woman managed a smile. 'No, of course not. Come in, Pat.'

The policeman sat down facing her across the table and his hand went out briefly to touch hers. 'Are you all right?'

'I can't stop shakin',' she told him, fighting back her tears.

'Look, I could come back a little later if you want,' he said quietly.

'No really. In fact I'm glad yer called,' she replied. 'I was 'alf expectin' ter see yer last night when the police came round askin' questions.'

'I've been away for a few days,' he told her. 'I went down to see my kid sister in Wiltshire. I only heard the news when I got back this morning. It's nice to see you again, Kate, though I wish it was under different circumstances.'

'It's very nice ter see you too,' Kate replied. 'Will you be workin' on the . . .'

'Yeah,' he answered quickly on seeing her hesitate. He looked at her eyes and smiled. 'I've been thinking about you.'

'Me too.'

'Kate, I'm sorry but I have to ask you about last night,' he said slowly with a sympathetic frown. 'I've seen the statement you made and spoken to the officer concerned and he told me you were too distressed to be very specific. Are you up to it now?'

'Can I get us some tea first?' Kate asked. 'It'll 'elp me calm down a bit. I've got some coffee in if yer'd prefer that.'

'I thought you didn't drink coffee,' he remarked, giving her another smile.

'I don't as a rule, but after we met I thought it'd be nice ter get some in, in case you called again.'

'Did you expect me to?'

'I was 'opin' yer might.'

'I wanted to.'

Kate went into the tiny scullery to turn the gas up under the kettle and Pat followed her, leaning against the door-frame.

'I've bin drinkin' gallons o' tea since I – since I found poor Meg,' she said tearfully.

'Take it easy, Kate,' he said in a soothing voice. 'Most

people who stumble on a death react in the same way you did. A violent death is traumatic for whoever discovers it, especially when it's someone you know. It's better to let yourself go. Don't try and bottle it all up.'

Kate sniffed as she took the boiling kettle from the flame. 'You know, I didn't realise policemen were so carin' and understandin',' she said smiling.

'We're not all ogres,' he replied. 'But you're a special case anyway.'

'I'm touched,' she said, turning her back on him while she filled the teapot to hide her embarrassment.

'Don't worry about making coffee. Tea'll be fine.'

'Are you sure?'

'Yeah, I'm drinking too much coffee as it is,' Pat replied as he walked back into the room and sat down at the table. 'Where's the kids?'

'My sister's lookin' after 'em,' Kate told him. 'She came round this mornin' after she 'eard the news.'

He nodded. 'As a matter of fact I wasn't sure whether you'd gone to work but I thought I'd try anyway.'

Kate came into the room holding a tray with two cups of tea, a sugar bowl and milk in a small jug. 'I couldn't face goin' ter work this mornin', but I'm beginnin' ter feel better now,' she said as she set the tray down on the table and made herself comfortable in the chair facing him.

The policeman watched as she sipped her tea then he clasped his hands together on the white tablecloth. 'I understand you went to see Mrs Johnson about some dressmaking at nine o'clock,' he began, 'and that's when you found her body. Was that the exact time?'

'It was nine o'clock exactly when I left 'ere,' Kate replied. 'I remember 'cos I 'eard Big Ben strike on Amy's wireless. Amy's my next-door neighbour an' she always 'as 'er wireless on loud.'

'Tell me in your own time exactly what you remember about events yesterday,' Pat urged her. 'Any little detail could help.'

'Well, I'd already bin ter see Meg earlier about the pattern,' she recounted. 'It would 'ave bin round about four in the afternoon. I was 'avin' some difficulty in workin' the pattern out. Anyway, Meg sorted it for me then we agreed that I should go back later an' let 'er take a look at my efforts. I was there about three quarters of an hour. It must 'ave bin just before five o'clock when I left. That was the last time I saw 'er alive.'

Cassidy saw the tears beginning to form in the young woman's eyes and he touched her hand. 'Steady. Take your time,' he said quietly.

Kate gulped and dabbed at her eyes with the creased handkerchief. 'As soon as I reached 'er landin' I could see that the door was ajar,' she went on. 'I knew straight away that somefing was wrong. Meg was terrified o' bein' attacked an' she always 'ad the bolts across. I crept along the passage an' I was really scared. Then I saw 'er. She was slumped in the chair an' I'll never ferget 'er face. She was a pale-faced woman at the best o' times but when I saw 'er sittin' there she was all bloated, an' 'er face was scarlet. I could see this black string round 'er neck. I thought it was a bootlace but I didn't get close enough ter be sure.'

'What made you think it was a bootlace?'

'I remembered Amy next door tellin' me that Annie Griffiths was strangled wiv a bootlace.'

'Go on, Kate.'

'Well, I just stood there starin' fer a few moments then I ran down the passage and slammed the door shut be'ind me. I dunno why I did that. Anyway I must 'ave screamed out loud enough fer Mrs Smedley next door to 'ear. She came out an' I told 'er I'd just found Meg dead. She stood there as though she was struck dumb so I dashed down ter the street an' banged on the caretaker's door.'

'Did he answer?'

'After the second knock,' Kate said nodding. 'I must 'ave woken 'im up out of a sleep 'cos 'e looked all bleary-eyed. 'E stood there wivout sayin' anyfing fer a while, then 'e asked me if I'd called the police. That's when I ran up ter Dock Lane an' phoned up.'

Pat Cassidy took a sip from his cup. 'Did you notice anyone in the street when you went back to see Meg the second time? Anyone lurking about?'

'No, there wasn't a soul about.'

'I saw in the statement you made that you knew Meg only slightly,' Pat went on. 'The interviewing officer then realised that you were too distressed to continue and he entered that on his report. Do you feel able to carry on today?'

Kate gave him a brave smile. 'I can talk ter you quite easy.'

'I'm pleased,' he smiled back. 'Now, Kate, I want you to tell me anything that comes to mind which might have a bearing on who killed Mrs Johnson. Anything at all, no matter how silly or unimportant it might seem. Let's start by you telling me what you actually know of Mrs Johnson's habits. For instance, was she a heavy drinker? Did she have many visitors? Did she ever hint that someone was actually out to do her harm?'

'I got ter know Meg frew my son Jimmy,' Kate began. 'Jimmy an' 'is friend Charlie used ter run errands for 'er an' she told 'em ter let me know that she could do dress alterations and repairs if I needed any. That's 'ow I first came ter meet 'er. She altered a dress for me. A few days later I called ter see 'er about it an' she was drunk. I 'ad ter put 'er ter bed.'

'Did she get drunk much?'

'No, not ter my knowledge,' Kate replied. 'Apparently she used ter go out ter the pub quite a lot before Annie Griffiths got murdered but not since. Meg told me she was sure somebody was after 'er.'

'Can you be more specific?'

'Well, Meg was a friend of Annie's.'

'If I remember rightly from the interview I did at the time, Mrs Johnson told me that she hardly knew Annie Griffiths,' Pat remarked frowning. 'I'll have to go through the file to make sure. Sorry, Kate. Where were we?'

The young woman went on to tell him about Meg's meeting with Annie the night before Annie's death and about her finding the charm and slip of paper lying on the pavement.

'Was she certain it came out of Annie Griffiths's handbag?' Pat asked when she had finished.

'She said she was pretty certain,' Kate told him. 'Annie used ter keep a charm fer good luck an' Meg told me Annie was drunk when she was tryin' ter find 'er key.'

Pat drained his cup and Kate reached for the teapot. 'Like a refill?' she asked him.

'Yes, please,' he smiled. 'Right, let's see what we've got. Meg Johnson and Annie Griffiths were friends, or at least good neighbours. You said Annie had mentioned seeing someone, someone from the other side who had come back to haunt her. Now that could mean someone she thought was dead but in fact was very much alive. It could be someone with a grudge. Now Annie told Meg she intended

288

to confront this mystery person. The slip of paper she or someone else had cut out from a newspaper was a photo of a group of men, so it's quite possible that one of the men in that photo murdered Annie, and maybe Meg too.'

'D'you fink it's the same man?' Kate asked.

'I don't know yet but I strongly suspect so,' he replied. 'The autopsy report will probably help confirm it. Both women were killed with a black bootlace and the way the knots were tied might tell us something. That newspaper cutting would be a big help too, if it could be found. You say Meg told you that the devil was minding it. Have you got any idea at all what she could have meant?'

'Since last night I've bin puzzlin' over what she said. It just doesn't make any sense,' Kate said sighing.

Pat took another sip of tea. 'The devil could mean flames, as in hell,' he said half in thought. 'I wonder if she's hidden it in a chimney breast.'

'It's possible,' Kate replied. 'Maybe the bedroom. I remember when I put 'er ter bed that night there was a small screen in front o' the fireplace. It didn't look like she ever used that fire.'

'Well, that's a place to look for a start,' Pat said smiling. 'Right now, let's see where we are.'

Kate had recovered enough of her composure to chide him. 'Are yer supposed ter discuss this wiv me?' she asked with feigned severity.

He grinned. 'I'm sorry, I get carried away. But anyway, I think I can trust you not to repeat anything I say.'

Kate was serious now. 'I'm pleased that yer've decided ter take me inter yer confidence,' she replied. 'There's no need ter worry, I won't breave a word of it to anyone.'

Pat looked down at his notes for a few moments. 'There was no sign of forced entry,' he remarked. 'Now Mrs

Smedley from next door told us that Meg Johnson very rarely ventured out on Sunday evenings, and a Mr Walker who lives on the top floor of this block said that he was sitting in the window all evening and would have seen her if she had gone out. That can only mean that whoever killed Meg Johnson knew her well enough to be let in.'

'I'm sure Meg didn't go out,' Kate told him. 'She was expectin' me back anyway. She was a very nervous woman as I said, an' she was careful ter make sure who was knockin' before she slid those bolts.'

'She might well have opened the door to anyone from the Buildings, providing they had announced themselves,' Pat went on. 'But it might have been someone else who called. Someone from her past, or someone she'd met recently. In fact almost anyone.'

'Ter be honest, I don't fink she 'ad many friends away from the Buildin's, what wiv 'er not goin' out much,' Kate remarked.

Pat ran his hand over his face. 'I'll need to talk to the caretaker and as many of Meg's neighbours as I can,' he said. 'Will you be in tonight?'

She nodded with a smile. 'Will yer call in?'

'For sure,' he replied getting up.

She followed him to the front door and Pat turned to touch her arm in a friendly gesture. 'Don't dwell on this too much, Kate,' he told her quietly. 'Get out in the air. Go and talk to the neighbours. Who knows, you might even come up with something.'

As he made to leave Kate laid her hand on his arm. 'Good luck,' she said with a warm smile.

'It looks as if I'm gonna need it,' he replied before hurrying down into the street.

Chief Superintendent Baxter answered the phone and listened to the caller for some time, occasionally grunting in reply, then he raised his eyes to the ceiling irritably. 'We're a bit stretched at the moment, Frank, but at least we've got some men in the area. Yeah, the murder inquiry at Milldyke Buildings. Fine. Yes, I'll give you a ring if there are any developments. Cheers for now.'

Detective Inspector Grant looked up curiously and Baxter scowled. 'That was Carter Street,' he said. 'Can we keep a lookout for a Thomas Brindley, a thirteen-year-old who's disappeared. He was being looked after by his grandmother in Walworth and she's just died. They're sending a report through. Apparently the Brindley family used to live in Milldyke Buildings and he might have decided to go back there. Christ! As if we've not got enough to keep us occupied without searching for runaways.'

Chapter Twenty-Nine

The terrible murder on that summer Sunday had struck fear into the people of Milldyke Buildings. It brought back to mind the Sunday evening just eight months before when Annie Griffiths was found murdered on the bombsite in Dock Lane, and the general feeling was that both women had been killed by the same person.

Word had already spread throughout the area, and inevitably the ghouls came to look down Milldyke Street and shake their heads as they stared at the grimy tenement block. The word 'Milldykers' had taken on a new meaning now. All the bad rumours and memories of past incidents were rekindled in their minds and every outsider who went into the street, for whatever reason, felt ill at ease, as though some evil had manifested itself there and still lurked, waiting, biding its time.

All day long on Monday the police team knocked on people's doors to continue their investigations, and they were followed up by the team leader who verified details, confirmed times and generally checked the statements made. It was a painstaking task for all concerned, made more difficult by the various discrepancies and disagreements. According to some accounts, Meg Johnson had been in the habit of getting drunk, often frightening the street children by bawling down from her window to force them to run her errands, and she was an eccentric who sometimes spoke in riddles and had very few friends. On the other hand, different people described the unfortunate woman as a nice, cheerful person, though very nervous, and always ready to offer help and advice if needed. She hardly ever went out and drank very little.

Ernie Walker received the sergeant pleasantly and even offered to make him a cup of tea. 'I spend quite a lot o' time sittin' in that winder,' he said. 'I mean ter say, what else is there ter do at my age?'

Pat Cassidy saw the tall-backed chair with its tatty cushion positioned at the left-hand side of the open window and he went over to it. 'D'you mind if I take a pew?' he asked.

Ernie nodded. ''Elp yerself.'

From where he was sitting Pat could see the entrance to the turning and the bacon factory opposite. 'You've got quite a view from here,' he remarked.

'There's not much misses my eye,' Ernie replied. 'I can see everybody who comes in this turnin'.'

'You told the police officer that no stranger came in the street yesterday afternoon,' Pat reminded him.

'Yeah, that's right.'

'You saw the Buildings agent about during the morning and later the woman from the church went into the first block.'

''S right,' Ernie said, edging towards his favourite chair.

Pat had to lean forward and crane his neck to see the end wall and the entrances to the two last blocks but found that he could sit quite comfortably and see out into Dock Lane. 'It's a bit difficult to see the other end of the turning,' he remarked as he stood up.

Ernie settled himself in his chair once more and reached for his pipe. ''Ave yer talked ter Briscoe yet?' he asked.

'The agent, you mean? No, not yet.'

'A very nasty kettle o' fish, that one. Pig of a man. I dunno where they get 'em from, I'm sure I don't,' Ernie muttered as he unzipped his tobacco pouch.

'A bit of a tyrant, eh?'

'Tyrant's the word. D'you know 'e nearly caused poor ole Mrs Irons to 'ave a nervous breakdown? Plagued 'er somefing terrible over not cleanin' 'er stairs. The poor cow was in agony wiv 'er back at the time, but 'e never cared. 'E was gonna give 'er notice ter quit. Would 'ave done so too if it wasn't fer old Ferguson.'

'The caretaker?'

'Yeah. I don't like the man very much, but yer 'ave ter speak the trufe. Ferguson did a good job as far as Mrs Irons went.'

'Tell me, Mr Walker, was it possible that you dropped off to sleep on Sunday evening and missed someone coming into the street?' Pat asked.

'Definitely not,' he replied firmly. 'Sometimes I nod off, true, but not on Sunday evenin'. I was keepin' me eye out fer fings, yer see.'

'What things?'

'Well, I don't want it ter go any furver, but it's 'im an' 'er next door,' Ernie explained. 'Joe Sandford does night work at the sausage factory an' 'is wife Stella's bin gettin' up ter no good. Soon as the poor bleeder's back was turned she was at it. 'Avin' it orf wiv this long-'aired git from the market she was. Scruffy-lookin' bastard. I dunno what the attraction was. Anyway, Joe found out an' 'e give 'er what for. Blacked 'er eye an' give the bloke a good 'idin' inter the bargain. Long time since I witnessed a fight like it. If it wasn't fer Jack Dennis I reckon Joe would 'ave killed 'im. Anyway fings 'ave bin very quiet lately, but I've got a suspicion she's still seein' the geezer, though 'e ain't showed 'is face round 'ere since Joe 'ammered 'im. It was somefing Stella said that put me on me guard. She come in wiv me baccy an' some pipe-cleaners last week an' she said Joe's gone all moody on 'er an' she was finkin' o' leavin' 'im. That's why I was watchin' points. I was 'alf expectin' that 'airy sod ter come sniffin' round again on Sunday night.'

Pat hid a grin. 'But it was all quiet.'

'Like a morgue,' Ernie said sucking on his pipe before filling it with tobacco. 'It's changed round 'ere lately. At one time people would come back in the turnin' singin' an' makin' a noise every weekend after the pubs turned out, but now you can 'ear a pin drop. Mind you, it suits some people. Take that silly sod Barney Schofield under me. Bin a sergeant major an' 'e still finks 'e's in the bloody army the way 'e carries on. Marches out the turnin' like 'e's on parade, mumblin' to 'imself, an' 'e's always shoutin' at the kids. I done time in India way back before the First World War an' I come across people like 'im. Blighty sickness we used ter call it.'

Pat smiled. 'Well thanks, Mr Walker, you've been a great help,' he said amiably.

'Any time, son,' Ernie replied as he settled back in his chair and yawned widely.

The policeman left the flat willing to bet that the old man would be snoring soundly within the hour.

Kate was feeling lifted now despite the terrible shock of finding Meg Johnson's body, and she busied herself about the flat. Pat had promised to call back later and she wanted everything to be clean and tidy. She cleaned the windows

and changed the net curtains, put Jenny's box of colouring
books and crayons out of sight and then swept the kitchen.
She had other things to do but was prevented from getting
on with them when her next-door neighbour called in.

'Spiv was gonna bring me some jumpers but 'e can't just
yet, not while the coppers are still about,' Amy said. 'If 'e
showed up while they was 'ere they'd be all over 'is motor
like flies round a jam pot.'

Kate poured the tea and sat down facing her. 'The
policeman who called on me was the one we saw at the
station that time,' she told her.

'Yeah, I recognised 'im,' Amy replied. ''E's not bin ter
me yet. By the way, 'ow yer feelin'? Yer look a bit better
now. Yer got a bit more colour in yer cheeks.'

Kate afforded herself a brief smile. 'I am feelin' better.
I'm slowly comin' ter terms wiv it,' she replied. 'Meg's face
still keeps comin' back ter me though. It was 'er eyes, all
wide an' starin'.'

Amy shuddered. 'What frightens me is that it's someone
local who's done it, someone who lives in the Buildin's.
Meg wouldn't open the door ter strangers.'

'Yeah, but it could 'ave bin somebody she knew from
way back, somebody she trusted,' Kate pointed out.

Amy shook her head. 'I was speakin' to Ernie Walker this
mornin' an' 'e said that 'e was at 'is winder all day an' no
strangers came in the turnin'.'

''E could 'ave nodded off though an' missed 'em.'

'I don't fink so,' Amy said shaking her head. 'No, it's
someone she'd let in, or 'ave ter let in.'

'Like the caretaker, or Ted Briscoe.'

'Exactly,' Amy said quickly. 'I don't like that Briscoe.
Never did. I fink 'e's a real slimy git. Fancies 'imself wiv
the women too. Whenever 'e calls at my place 'is eyes are

everywhere. I'm gonna tell the coppers when they come an' see me.'

Kate sipped her tea thoughtfully. She had felt the same as Amy when the agent called on her. There was something about his eyes that made her cringe.

'Anyway, ter change the subject, my ole man's comin' 'ome termorrer,' Amy announced. 'I got a letter from 'im this mornin'. 'E'd posted it in Rotterdam. 'Is ship's dockin' in the Pool termorrer mornin'.'

'I 'ope Fred knows,' Kate said grinning.

'Yeah, I told 'im ter lie low,' Amy replied. 'It's bad enough the Sandfords gettin' at it, wivout me an' my old man 'avin' a stand-up fight in the street.'

'Is Fred still stayin' at the 'ostel?' Kate asked her.

'Yeah, but 'e don't like it.'

'Poor ole Fred,' Kate said with a smile.

'I dunno, 'e ain't doin' so bad,' Amy remarked. 'At least 'e ain't gotta put up wiv 'is wife's naggin' any more. She's up an' told 'im she don't want 'im back. Got 'erself a nice chap wiv plenty o' dosh by all accounts.'

'Still, Fred's got you,' Kate said supportively.

'Long as 'e appreciates it,' Amy replied. 'Do you know what? That ugly prat of a wife tore all their weddin' photos up in front of 'im. What a fing ter do. Mind you, she's silly as a box o' lights. It's no more than I'd expect from 'er sort.'

Kate put down the cup, her mind suddenly jogged by what Amy had just said. 'Did you ever go in to Meg's?' she asked.

'Once or twice,' Amy answered.

'Did you notice that photograph she 'ad on the side-board?'

'Can't say as I did. Wait a minute. Yes I did, come ter fink.'

'Did you ever take a close look at it?'

'No, I never did,' Amy said. 'Ter tell yer the trufe I was always glad ter get out o' there, what wiv that stale smell. The poor cow never 'ad a winder open.'

'I was just finkin',' Kate went on. 'Meg was about ter tell me somefing about that photo once, but like you I was makin' buttons ter get out o' the place. I wish I'd spared the time. It could 'ave bin a clue to who killed 'er.'

'I shouldn't worry, the police'll go over that flat wiv a fine toof-comb,' Amy told her. 'They'll be makin' inquiries about the picture anyway.'

'Yeah, I guess so,' Kate sighed.

Amy drained her cup. 'I'd better be gettin' back ter my gaff,' she said puffing. 'I've got some tidyin' up ter do before that pissy-arse 'usband o' mine comes 'ome.'

Once Amy had left Kate sat pondering over the photograph she had seen on Meg Johnson's sideboard. She remembered Meg saying that it was taken when she worked over at Poplar. She must remember to tell Pat Cassidy about it when he came back that evening.

At five o'clock the police team went back to a de-briefing at the station and Pat was shown the report that had arrived from Carter Street concerning Tommy Brindley. He remembered that Kate had taken the boy in when he ran away from school, and that it was her concern for the lad which had prompted her to call in at the station. Another minute or so and he would have missed her that evening. He smiled to himself as he remembered the chat they had at the cafe: it was the first time in a long while that he had let himself relax and open up. He recalled how her large hazel eyes had widened expressively and grown sad when he told her about losing his wife and child. She was some woman, he sighed. Slim yet shapely, and with a very nice pair of legs. Her hair was dark, almost raven, with a healthy sheen, and her oval face and little nose reminded him of a cheeky elfin.

'Cassidy, is there any chance of getting your thoughts on this?' Superintendent Baxter asked him in a sarcastic tone of voice.

The young policeman jumped visibly, to the amusement of his tired team. 'I'm sorry, sir, but I missed the question. I was on another tack.'

'Well, you were certainly somewhere,' Baxter growled. 'But just so we all don't miss out I'll say it again. Motive. Rational or irrational?'

Pat took a deep breath. 'It's my firm opinion that we have a very clever killer on the loose,' he said firmly. 'Motive rational. I believe that both killings were linked and carried out to silence the women, though I have to say that the gap between both murders does not altogether rule out the possibility that it was the work of a maniac.'

'Oh and why?'

'Mrs Annie Griffiths was murdered last November, on the last Sunday of the month,' Pat explained. 'Meg Johnson was also murdered on the last Sunday of the month, which, you may recall, follows the pattern used by the Hoxton Strangler back in eighty-nine who murdered all four of his women victims on the last Sunday of the month. His plea was that the moon's pull was at its greatest according to the lunar calendar and it affected him in such a way that he could not resist the urge to kill. All his victims lived alone and were all known to be partial to a drink. In other words, selective killings.'

'What are you getting at, sergeant?' Baxter asked testily.

'Simply that we have discovered through our questioning that there are one or two strange people living in Milldyke

Buildings,' Pat went on. 'Copy-cat killings are well attested to throughout the last hundred years or so, as we are all aware, and I think it might be wise to check with Scotland Yard and see if there are any similar unsolved killings on file, especially during the past eight months.'

Baxter nodded. 'Anything else you wish to grace us with?' he asked haughtily.

Instead of rising to the bait the young detective smiled. 'Yes, there is as a matter of fact,' he said quietly. 'The team have discussed their findings and we all conclude that the circumstances of the Johnson murder make it most probable that the killer is someone living in the Buildings, or at least closely linked to the people living there in some way.'

'Regular callers, tradesmen and so on.'

'Exactly, sir.'

There was a tap on the door and the desk sergeant looked in. 'The autopsy report you were waiting for, sir,' he said handing Baxter a sheet of paper.

The superintendent studied it for a few seconds then looked around at the gathered policemen. 'Well, the knots used in both killings were identical,' he announced. 'Furthermore, the ligature used was a black bootlace, the type used in heavy working boots. Gentlemen, all the signs point to it being the same killer. I want some results quickly, before some other poor soul gets strangled on our patch.'

The men dispersed and Baxter beckoned to Cassidy. 'I was impressed by your thoughts on this case, sergeant,' he said. 'By the way, where did you find out about the Hoxton Strangler?'

'The Trocette, I believe it was,' Pat replied. 'Fiction of course, but would that matter much to a deranged copy-cat killer?'

Baxter glared at him to see if he was being made fun of.

'Stay with it, sergeant,' he said tartly.

Pat Cassidy walked out of the station, his mouth parched and the urge to get a drink teasing at his insides. Must stay dry, he told himself. Forget the knotting pains in his stomach. Forget the mellow feeling that first drink always gave him. Concentrate instead on Kate Flannagan. Go and see her as promised.

'Time for a drink, sarge?' D.C. Crawley asked.

'Sorry, Larry. I've got another two people to see.'

'Tonight?' Crawley queried with a frown.

'Yeah, tonight. One's work, and the other, well the other's quite something again.'

'Good luck then, sarge.'

Pat caught the suggestive grin and waved to the policeman as he turned the corner. The urge to take a drink might soon begin to subside but the desire to see Kate Flannagan would still be burning brightly.

Chapter Thirty

Jack Ferguson the caretaker was busy frying rashers of streaky bacon when Pat Cassidy called on him on Monday evening and he wiped his greasy hands down the front of his trousers as he showed the policeman into his ground-floor flat. 'Just cookin' meself somefing to eat,' he mumbled.

'Don't let me stop you,' Pat told him affably. 'I'm in no rush.'

Ferguson showed him into the small room he used as his office. 'I won't be a few minutes,' he said, disappearing into the scullery.

Pat looked round the room. The bare table was strewn with papers and on the wall to the left he saw a pegboard hung with rows of keys, each numbered with a tag. There was a tall metal cabinet standing against the opposite wall and down by the unlit fire a large canvas bag lay open to display an assortment of tools.

The caretaker was soon back. 'No worry, I've stuck it in the oven ter stay warm,' he said.

'I take it you have keys to all the flats,' Pat inquired.

'Yeah, they're spares,' Ferguson told him as he flopped down in the only other chair. 'I'm obliged ter keep keys fer every flat. Sometimes the tenants lock themselves out an' then there's times I 'ave ter do repairs while they're out.'

'I saw in your statement that Mrs Johnson was followed home a week ago and she knocked you up,' Pat said, leaning back in his chair.

'Yeah, she was in a right ole state,' the caretaker replied. 'I let 'er in an' I went out ter look around but I couldn't see anyone. A few minutes later Flossy Chandler came down the street an' then Barney Schofield follered 'im in. Ovver than them two I didn't see anuvver soul. Anyway I finally calmed the Johnson woman down as best I could then I walked wiv 'er up to 'er flat. She got on ter me after that night about fixin' 'er up wiv a Yale lock, which I did. She was certainly a strange woman that one, Gawd rest 'er soul.'

'What do you mean?'

'Well, she was convinced someone was after 'er,' Ferguson explained. 'I couldn't get ter the bottom of it. She wasn't the sort who'd give yer a straight answer. I did tell 'er that if she was that worried she should go an' see the police but she nearly bit me 'ead off. All she would say was that the fewer people who knew, the better.'

'There seems to be some difference of opinion about her relationship with Annie Griffiths,' Pat prompted.

'I can't 'elp yer there, it was before my time,' the caretaker answered. 'I got this job a few weeks after the Griffiths woman was killed. I understand from people talkin' that the two women were friends of sorts. Apparently they used ter drink tergevver at times.'

Pat nodded then he sat up straight in his chair. 'Could I have the key to Mrs Johnson's flat?' he asked. 'I'd like to take another look around.'

The caretaker took the Yale key from the top row and handed it over. 'Rather you than me. It'd give me the creeps.'

Pat got up. 'Right then. Sorry to have disturbed your meal.'

'That's all right. Sorry I couldn't 'ave bin more 'elp,' Ferguson replied.

'Every little helps,' the policeman said in parting as he stepped out into the strangely quiet street.

With precision gained from long experience Pat Cassidy systematically examined each room of the dead woman's flat, and in the musty-smelling bedroom he moved the small fire-screen to one side and reached up into the chimney breast. Kate had been right. The fireplace showed no sign of a fire ever having been lit. The other rooms yielded nothing of importance and Pat scratched his head as he stood in the middle of the kitchen. According to what Kate had told him Meg Johnson had enlisted the devil's help in hiding that newspaper cutting, and whatever she had meant by it was a complete mystery now.

After going through all the sideboard drawers and the cupboard he sat down at the table and pulled on his bottom lip thoughtfully. One thing was puzzling him and he dwelt on it for some time. Then finally he sighed in resignation and left the flat.

Amy Almond was anxious to make sure that all of Fred Logan's bits and pieces had been removed from her flat before Bert came home and to her consternation she found one of Fred's cufflinks under her bed. Supposing there was something else that had been missed, she fretted, and with a nervous sigh she went over the place once more. Later when Charlie came in she sat him down and told him of her fears. 'Look, luv, yer know that me an' Fred Logan are good friends, an' yer know that people do tend ter talk. So what I want yer ter do is be very careful yer don't slip up an' mention Fred's name while yer dad's 'ome.'

'Nah, course not,' Charlie replied with a grin.

'What yer laughin' at?' Amy asked irritably.

'I'm not a kid any more, Muvver,' the lad told her. 'I know what's what.'

'Not so much of the "Muvver". I'm "Mum" ter you,' Amy replied quickly. 'Anyway what d'yer mean by you knowin' what's what?'

'Well, I can see fings,' the lad said hesitantly. 'Fred's a nice bloke an' I'm glad yer got 'im. After all me dad's never 'ardly 'ome, an' when 'e is 'e's nearly always drunk. 'E never 'as any time fer me or you, not like Fred. I don't mind Fred takin' me dad's place.'

'Yer a good lad,' Amy said ruffling his mop of fair hair.

Later that evening Fred called in, looking very upset. 'I just don't know 'ow ter say this,' he faltered as he sat down at the kitchen table.

'Say what? Out wiv it, luv,' Amy urged him.

'Last night I went ter the 'ostel as usual an' there was a crowd o' culshies stayin' there.'

'Culshies?'

'Yeah, culshey-mucks, Irish navvies who're workin' on mendin' the sewers down in Rovver'ithe,' Fred explained. 'Anyway they came in a bit rowdy an' kept us all awake 'alf the night. This mornin' I got up an' found me boots were gone. Someone must 'ave nicked 'em. I 'ad ter borrer a pair o' slippers off the 'ostel bloke ter get ter work. I can't take anuvver night in that place. It'd drive me round the twist.'

'So what yer gonna do, Fred? Yer can't stay 'ere. Yer know Bert's due 'ome termorrer,' Amy reminded him.

'I understand that,' Fred replied, looking uncomfortable. 'I took the afternoon off work an' went ter see Beryl. She'd left a message at work fer me ter contact 'er, yer see.'

'No, I don't see,' Amy said sharply. 'What yer tryin' ter tell me, Fred?'

'Well, I'm gonna go back 'ome fer the time bein'. Just fer the time bein', yer understand.'

'After all that bitch 'as done?' Amy raved. 'She's ripped yer bloody clothes up, chucked yer best shoes in the bin, slagged you off to all an' sundry an' now yer goin' back like a frightened little mouse. Where's yer pride?'

'She was quite calm when I went ter see 'er,' Fred said in a low voice. 'She wanted us ter try an' make a go of it once more.'

'Oh, I see it all now,' Amy scowled. ''Er fancy man's given 'er the elbow an' she's come cryin' ter you. Yer should 'ave told the ugly, schemin' prat ter go an' chuck 'erself in the river.'

'Yeah, an' then I'd be forced ter go back ter that bloody 'ostel again,' Fred countered.

'Yer could try fer private lodgin's. Lots o' people rent rooms out,' Amy told him.

'Don't yer fink I've already tried?' Fred groaned. 'It ain't as easy as yer fink. There's a lot o' labourers comin' inter the area what wiv all the rebuildin' goin' on 'ereabouts, an' most o' the lodgin' places 'ave bin snapped up. That's 'ow I ended up at the 'ostel.'

'So what yer sayin', Fred? Are yer tellin' me we're finished?'

'No, course I'm not.'

'So yer've got no intention o' tryin' again wiv Beryl?'

''S right. As I said, it's a temporary arrangement till that 'usband o' yours is out the way.'

'So yer won't be sleepin' wiv 'er?' Amy queried.

'Nah, I'm in the spare room.'

'I can't believe that,' Amy replied contemptuously.

307

'It's the trufe, sure as I'm sittin' 'ere,' Fred told her earnestly.

'Well, yer'd better be off then,' she said coldly. 'I wouldn't want yer ter keep Pratty Lil waitin'.'

Fred made an embarrassed exit and Amy sat staring down at the floor for a few moments as she mulled over all that he had said. Maybe he would be as good as his word, she thought, but on the other hand he might well be browbeaten into becoming the dutiful husband once more. What a mess.

Charlie walked into the room and saw his mother slumped at the table with her head resting on her arm. 'I wasn't asleep, Mum,' he said quietly as he came over to stand at her side.

Amy lifted her head and gave him a warm smile. 'We can manage, you an' me, Charlie,' she told him. 'We don't need anybody else.'

'Fred'll come back, yer'll see,' the lad replied quietly.

Kate had cleared away the tea things and coaxed Jenny into her nightclothes by the time Pat Cassidy called that evening.

'Hello, Jenny. All ready for bed I see,' the detective said smiling.

The young girl smiled back shyly. 'We're on 'oliday from school,' she told him.

'Yeah, an' I'm on the sand-man patrol,' he replied with mock seriousness.

'Are you gonna catch that terrible man?' the child said, clutching her favourite doll.

Kate gave Pat a despairing glance as she ushered Jenny from the room. 'Say goodnight ter the nice policeman, luv,' she bade her.

Pat Cassidy sat down feeling exhausted and he ran his

fingers through his hair while he waited for Kate to settle Jenny into bed. Jimmy sauntered into the room and looked at him with curiosity. ''Ave yer caught the murderer yet?' he asked.

The detective hid a smile. 'No, but it won't be long now. As a matter o' fact I've called to ask your mum a few questions that might help.'

The lad nodded and sat down at the table. 'Me an' Charlie used ter run errands fer Mrs Johnson,' he said matter-of-factly.

'What was she like?' Pat asked in a casual voice.

'She was a bit funny really,' Jimmy replied. 'She 'ad this stuffed squirrel in a glass case. At least, I fink it was stuffed. She told us she never went out an' it was good of us ter run the errands for 'er. We didn't mind 'cos she gave us money. We'd 'ave still got 'er fings for 'er though, even if she didn't pay us. We felt sorry for 'er.'

'That's nice to know,' Pat said smiling. 'Anyway we'll soon catch whoever killed her.'

Kate came back into the living room and gave the policeman a shy smile. 'I 'ad ter get Jenny settled down,' she said, 'or she'll be 'avin' nightmares.'

Jimmy was making himself comfortable but Kate gave him a warning glance. 'C'mon now, off ter bed or yer won't be ready when Charlie knocks termorrer mornin'.'

Jimmy gave the detective a cheeky grin as he left the room and Kate went into the scullery and returned with a laden tray. 'I thought you might be ready fer a drink,' she said. 'Tea or coffee?'

'Tea'll be fine,' he replied.

As soon as Kate handed him his cup Pat took a large gulp. 'That's the best I've had all day,' he said appreciatively.

'You look tired,' Kate remarked as she sipped hers.

'Yeah, it's been a very busy time,' he told her. 'As a matter of fact I got some bad news too when I reported in today.'

'Oh?'

'Young Tommy Brindley's run off again,' he said with a frown. 'Apparently he discovered his grandmother dead in bed a few days ago, and then the same day he learned that his mother had died in the sanatorium.'

'Oh my good God!' Kate gasped, covering her mouth with her hand. 'The poor lad. 'E must be distraught, wherever 'e is.'

'We've been told to keep a lookout,' Pat said sighing. 'The boy might try to come back here. At least he knows the people in these buildings, and I'm sure he remembers how kind you and your family were to him. He might try to contact you, Kate.'

'God, I 'ope 'e does,' Kate declared passionately. 'That lad needs a big cuddle more than anyfing.'

'I'm sure he'll show up before long,' Pat replied.

Kate clasped her hands together on the tablecloth as they both grew silent. 'Yer must 'ave bin very busy terday,' she prompted after a while.

'I've just come from Meg Johnson's flat,' he answered. 'I needed to take another look round. Kate, I want to ask you something. Would you think it strange if you searched through a home, any home, and could find no photos there?'

'Yeah, I s'pose I would,' she replied. 'There's always weddin' photos, old albums an' portraits buried away in drawers an' cupboards. I've got stacks o' photos in a shoebox in my bedroom cupboard.'

'There wasn't one photo in Meg Johnson's flat,' Pat sat quietly.

Kate thought for a few moments then looked up at his

serious face. 'Are yer sure yer didn't miss anyfing?' she asked.

'Certain.'

'Well, that's odd. I saw a photo in a frame,' she told him. 'It was standin' on Meg's sideboard in 'er livin' room.'

Pat shook his head. 'There was no photograph there when I searched the flat this evening.'

'Someone must 'ave removed it then,' Kate replied.

'Could you describe it?' he asked quickly.

'Well, it was of Meg wiv a group o' women,' she said stroking her chin. 'Oh, an' there was a man standin' at the end. 'E looked very small beside the women.'

'What else can you remember about it?' he pressed her.

Kate shook her head. 'Not much. I was just about ter leave 'cos I was worried about the kids bein' on their own when Meg showed me the photo. I do remember the women bein' dressed in white though, like factory aprons or overalls.'

'The background. What about the background?'

'It was just a brick buildin', I fink.'

'Are you sure there's nothing else you can remember?'

'I'm sorry, Pat, but like I say I wasn't takin' much notice at the time. I wish ter God I 'ad though.'

He smiled and shrugged his broad shoulders. 'It's one of those things.'

Kate got up and refilled his empty cup. ''Ave you eaten?' she asked.

'No, I'll get a bite soon as I get home,' he replied.

'Look, I've got some eggs an' bacon in. Let me rustle you up somefing,' she said willingly.

'No, I can't put you to that trouble. Besides . . .'

'Besides nuffing. It won't take me five minutes.'

'Well, if you're really . . .'

'Enough said. Take yer coat off an' sit over in that fireside chair,' she told him. 'It'll be more comfortable than that one. I won't be long. Yer'll find the evenin' paper under the cushion.'

He did as he was bid and opened the paper on his lap. He could hear the fat crackling in the pan and Kate's voice as she hummed to herself. A smell of bacon frying drifted into the living room and Pat closed his eyes. How long was it since he had last sat comfortably while his tea was being prepared by a pretty young woman? He forced his eyes open, hardly daring to surrender to the reverie or nod off in case the vision of his dead wife and daughter rose up to remind him of those few years of complete happiness.

Kate came into the room and laid the table, glancing over and smiling to herself as she saw the recumbent figure with eyes closed and the newspaper spread open on his lap. He was certainly handsome, she thought, even in sleep, but he looked pale and jaded, with his tie loosened, and the top button of his white shirt unfastened. How much was he still suffering over the tragedy in his life, she wondered.

A few minutes later the meal was ready and she gently nudged his arm to rouse him. 'Pat. Pat, yer tea's ready,' she said, jumping as he started awake.

'I'm sorry, I must have been in a deep sleep,' he said when he regained his composure. 'I was dreaming.'

While he ate the meal with relish Kate fussed about in the scullery, and as he wiped the last of his bread in the egg yolk she came in with fresh tea. 'There's some fruit cake if yer still got room,' she said smiling.

'No, really,' he replied. 'That was wonderful.'

Kate sat down facing him, watching diffidently while he sipped his tea. 'I've remembered somefing else about that photo,' she told him. 'I remember Meg sayin' that it was taken when she worked over in Poplar.'

Pat leaned back in his chair and sighed. 'Well, it's something to go on,' he remarked. 'It's puzzling though. Did Mrs Johnson throw the picture out, or did the killer take it? I'd bet on the latter. Like the newspaper cutting, I'm sure that photo would have given us some leads.'

'It might 'ave bin taken by a professional photographer, someone in the Poplar area,' Kate suggested.

Pat chuckled. 'Do you know you'd make a good detective. I was thinking the same thing.'

Kate felt her cheeks beginning to get hot and she got up quickly to clear the plates and teacups. Pat followed her into the scullery and picked up a tea cloth. 'Let me dry,' he said.

'There's no need.'

'Oh yes, there is.'

'Well, if you insist.'

'I searched that chimney breast by the way,' he told her as she handed him the first of the wet plates. 'There was nothing there.'

'It's a real mystery,' she replied. 'Whatever could she 'ave meant by sayin' the devil was mindin' it?'

'We have to consider that the newspaper cutting might be hidden somewhere outside the flat,' Pat reminded her.

'I don't fink it'll ever be found,' Kate said sighing.

'Maybe you're right, but a good policeman never gives up,' he said with a smile.

The last of the crockery was dried and safely back in the sideboard, and outside the evening was turning to dusk. 'Well, I'd better be off home,' Pat said.

Kate felt that she detected a note of reluctance in his voice and it caused her heart to flutter. 'Will you be about termorrer?' she asked him.

He nodded as he put on his coat. 'Would you mind if I call in some time tomorrow evening?'

'I'd be upset if yer didn't,' she said boldly.

At the front door he turned and quickly planted a kiss on the side of her mouth before she could react. 'Thanks for the meal, it was great,' he said smiling. 'Good night, Kate.'

'Good night, Pat,' she replied, hearing the nervous lilt in her voice.

He hurried down into the street and Kate watched from the landing window only to see him go into the first block. She went back into her flat and closed the door, still feeling his lips on her face, her mind buzzing with what had been said.

Chapter Thirty-One

Early on Tuesday morning the new bins arrived. Ada Champion looked down from her front-room window in response to the noise and saw that two large galvanised containers had been unloaded by the alley. There was a heated discussion going on between the two workmen as they prepared to put the bins back on the vehicle.

'Oi, what's your game?' she called down.

'We can't deliver 'em, missus,' one of the men shouted back.

'Why the bloody 'ell not?'

''Cos there's rubbish in the ovver bins, that's why.'

'Well, empty it out then.'

'No fear. We ain't bloody dustmen.'

Ada cursed under her breath and slipped her coat on quickly.

'Where you goin'?' Sid asked from behind his morning paper.

Ada's mumbled reply was lost on him and he went back to picking a few winners.

'These should 'ave come yesterday when the dustmen emptied the bins,' Ada reprimanded the two men.

'That's what I was just tellin' 'im,' the younger of the two workmen replied.

His older counterpart shrugged his shoulders. 'We don't make the rules, missus, we just do the donkey work.'

'So what yer gonna do then?' Ada inquired.

'Nuffing we can do, 'cept take 'em back.'

'Yer can't do that,' Ada growled at him. 'Those poxy bins in there are just about knackered. The lids don't shut prop'ly and the bloody smell's atrocious.'

Just at that moment Liz Fogan walked into the turning from her early-morning cleaning job. 'What's goin' on 'ere?' she said quickly.

'Yer better ask those two silly gits,' Ada scowled.

The younger man explained the situation while Liz stood hands on hips. 'So yer see, luv, we've gotta take 'em back, there's nuffing else for it.'

'You just wait there a minute,' Liz told him firmly. 'I'm gonna make a phone call.'

Ada had had enough and she went back to her flat to await the outcome. Some time later Liz knocked at her door. 'Well, I've sorted that out,' she said triumphantly. 'They're leavin' the bins outside the alley an' the dustmen are comin' later to empty the rubbish, then they'll put the new ones in place.'

'What about the old ones they take out?' Ada inquired.

'They're gonna leave 'em outside an' they'll be picked up termorrer mornin'.'

'Why can't the dustmen take the ole ones?' Ada went on. 'It seems a bloody arse-about way ter do fings, if you ask me.'

'That's what I said,' Liz replied. 'The bloke told me there's no room on the dustcart fer large bins.'

'You just watch,' Ada moaned. 'Those kids'll be all over them bins, mark my words.'

Liz had had enough of trying to talk sense to the

workmen and she wasn't going to get into another discussion about it so she merely shrugged her shoulders. Meanwhile the lorry drove out of the turning leaving the shiny new bins by the alley, and curious youngsters were already taking note.

Kate had returned to work on Tuesday morning and her workmates immediately besieged her with questions. 'Sounds like a maniac ter me,' Bet Groves remarked. 'One o' those evil gits who 'ave these visions.'

'Like Jack the Ripper,' Milly Tate piped in.

'Yeah, an' Charlie Peace,' the new young woman on the bench added.

'Charlie Peace was a burglar, yer silly mare,' Bet said with disdain.

'Yeah, but 'e was 'ung in the end,' Sarah persisted. 'When we was kids our mum used ter say if yer don't get ter sleep Charlie Peace'll get yer. Scared the life out of us she did.'

'Well, I fink it must 'ave bin terrible ter find that poor woman murdered,' Milly remarked as she deftly sealed a packed cardboard box. 'It's a wonder yer come in at all this week, Kate. I'd 'ave bin a nervous wreck by now.'

The arrival of the stern-faced supervisor on the scene prevented any further discussion, and as the workers toiled to the sound of lively music coming from the loudspeakers above their heads Kate's thoughts turned to the young policeman who had come into her life so unexpectedly. He was attractive, with sometimes a sad look in his pale blue eyes that touched her in a way she would never have anticipated. She had noticed it the first time she met him, and then again when he called round on Monday evening. It was fleeting, soon gone, but the moment had become imprinted deeply in her mind. In a troubled dream that night she had wanted to take him in her arms and hold him tightly, but he was out of reach, moving away into the blood-coloured mist that danced and swirled around and finally engulfed him.

'She gives me the creeps,' Milly said as the supervisor walked away.

'Dried up ole prune,' Bet growled. 'I know what'd do 'er good. Mind you, she wouldn't be any the wiser if one got plonked in 'er 'and.'

Milly started giggling and Sarah nudged Kate. 'I wish that big feller on the loadin' bank would plonk 'is in my 'and,' she chuckled. 'I'd know what ter do wiv it.'

'Oooh, Sarah, you are filfy,' Milly remarked, giggling even louder.

The supervisor was back, alerted by the hilarity on the packing bench. 'Milly, will you stop that silly giggling and watch what you're doing,' she said sharply.

The morning dragged on and Kate was glad when the factory whistle sounded at noon. She had been turning things over in her mind all morning and she needed the respite to pull all her thoughts together. Her divorce was going through and soon she would be a free woman, free to decide what path she would follow. Her children were her prime concern. She had managed to protect them from all the nastiness and trauma of the family split, but what difficulties would lie ahead if she should lose her heart to someone else – to Pat Cassidy? How would they react? They were growing fast though, and in a few short years they would be flying the nest. Was she to finally end up a grumpy old woman, living alone with only her memories, or would she have a chance to share the years with someone who loved her and cared for her? She smiled briefly to herself as she made her way home to Milldyke Street. Her bedroom was now a lonely place, with only fantasy and unfulfilled desire to haunt her sleep and restless hours. How nice it would be to have the man of her dreams putting his shoes under her bed.

Nobby Nolan earned a precarious living as a rag-and-bone man; he was a born sniffer, as it was called in the trade. Nobby could sniff out a good deal before his rivals were out of bed in the morning and he had the gift of knowing which streets to enter and which ones to give a wide berth to. Long Lane was a good bet, as were Abbey Street and the backstreets off the Tower Bridge Road usually, but Milldyke Street was one turning he avoided like the plague. He had learned the hard way that old iron did not come easily in that place, and any old bathtubs and mangles that there were would be falling towards his head from the top floors. The Milldykers didn't give old rags away, they wore them, that was one of the favourite gags he told his pals. The kids there would feed maggoty apples to his tired old nag and stuff its nosebag with sawdust, given half a chance, was another quip sure to raise a laugh.

Although Nobby Nolan never really believed all of this he flicked the reins as he drove down Dock Lane so as to send his nag trotting by the turning a little faster, until the glint of metal in the bright sunlight caught his eye. The horse clipclopped to a stop and looked round as Nobby suddenly pulled on the reins, no doubt surprised and confused by the sudden change of plan.

'Oi, you. You wiv the glasses. What's them doin' there?' Nobby asked.

The tubby lad gave him a disdainful look and walked away.

'The Council're changin' 'em, mister,' another lad told him.

Nobby climbed down from his cart and went up the alley to see if there was any cast-out junk worth having by the dustbins, and with a disappointed sigh he ambled back to his cart. 'Wassa matter wiv the bins then?' he asked the lad who was leaning against the wall.

'Nuffing. My muvver said it's a waste o' money.'

'I might as well take 'em away then,' Nobby replied.

Fearing that he might be asked to help, the shrewd youngster made a swift exit from the immediate locality, leaving Nobby scratching his head. The bins were large galvanised affairs too wide in the girth and too heavy for one pair of hands, he concluded.

'Where's the goldfish?' a young girl asked him as she came up sucking on a toffee.

'Fish? What fish?'

'The ovver man who usually comes brings goldfish fer ole rags,' the child told him, sucking back the toffee she had almost lost.

'I eat 'em all up meself,' Nobby said pulling a frightening face.

'Yer'll get poisoned,' the girl replied with concern.

'I eat nosy children too.'

'You're stupid.'

'Right then, stand back before yer get 'urt,' Nobby shouted as he climbed back on the cart.

'If you run me over my dad'll smash yer face in,' the child told him as she walked away.

The rag-and-bone man drove his cart up to the Woolpack where he sought out some assistance. 'Is Manny Jackson pissed yet?' he asked the barman as he looked into the snug bar.

'Give 'im time.'

'Ask 'im ter pop outside. I got a job for 'im,' Nobby announced.

The barman knew that Nobby could never be persuaded to go into the public bar for fear of having to stand someone a pint. 'All right, I'll send 'im out,' he replied.

Manny hoisted up his trousers over his large belly and screwed his eyes up at the sun as he walked out from the bar. ''Ow long's it gonna take?' he asked.

'About five minutes at the outside.'

'Will yer bring me back 'ere?'

'Sure fing.'

'What's it werf?'

'Two bob.'

'Make it 'alf-a-crown.'

'Done. Climb up.'

As Nobby had left Milldyke Street the dustcart had arrived, and by the time he returned the rubbish had been collected, the area in the alley disinfected with powder and the new bins set in place, while outside by the end wall the two tatty bins with their ill-fitting lids stood awaiting collection.

'What the bloody 'ell!' Nobby gasped as he pulled his horse up.

Manny Jackson was livid as he saw what his task was to be. 'You gotta be jokin',' he growled. 'Yer mean ter tell me yer dragged me out the boozer ter pick this load o' crap up? The two bins tergevver ain't werf 'alf-a-crown. You goin' orf yer 'ead or somefing?'

'They was brand new ten minutes ago,' Nobby said scratching his head in disbelief.

'You are bloody mad,' Manny laughed. ''Ere, take me back ter the pub an' you can keep yer poxy money. I'm quite likely ter pick up some disease touchin' them fings.'

Suddenly a metallic knocking sound startled the horse and it reared up. Manny gave Nobby a fearful look. 'There's a bloody rat in there,' he shouted. 'C'mon, let's get out of 'ere quick.'

As the cart rattled out of the cobbled turning the lid of one of the bins opened and a dirty face peered out.

'That was really good,' a young lad said as he ran up to the bins. 'Now get back in there an' kick a bit louder next time. We'll whistle when somebody comes.'

Flossy Chandler had been extremely careful to keep his new white suit from getting marked at the talent contest. If Bernie Gilchrist could be believed he would soon be playing in front of appreciative audiences and the suit was vital in promoting his image, he reasoned. To that end he steam-pressed the suit on Monday evening and lovingly hung it up on the clothesline he had strung up in his back room. The weather was humid and the bins had been emptied that morning as usual, so Flossy thought it safe to open the window a little. Unfortunately he overslept and forgot to close the window before he rushed out to work the next morning.

The new bins were now in place and the lids were much more sturdy than the old ones, resulting in loud clanging noises when people dropped them down. Now there was another irritation for the dwellers in the end block, and Ada Champion moaned about it to Freda Irons as they stood in the entrance on Tuesday evening.

'Wiv the ovver bins yer never really 'eard that much but these bloody great lids slam down like bombs goin' orf,' she grumbled. 'Scares the bleedin' daylights out o' me it does.'

'Yeah, me too,' Freda commiserated.

Just then Flossy hurried down into the street with a characteristic sway of his hips. ''Ello, ladies,' he said brightly.

'The new bins are in,' Ada remarked curtly.

'That's nice.'

'Yer won't be sayin' that when you 'ear the noise those lids make,' Ada warned him.

'If it's not one fing it's somefing else,' the young man replied with an exaggerated sigh.

''Old tight, 'ere comes the sergeant major,' Freda said quickly.

Barney Schofield came past carrying his polished dustbin and nodded as he went into the alleyway. There was a loud clang and Schofield walked out again with a satisfied look on his face. 'I see the new bins look clean and shipshape,' he announced.

'Silly ole git,' Ada growled as he walked away.

Flossy made his excuses and went in his flat, eager to see how his suit had dried out. A few seconds later he was back on the street. 'Me bleedin' suit! It's ruined!' he screamed out at the two women.

'What d'yer mean, ruined?' Ada asked him.

'It's covered in black spots!' Flossy ranted. 'I'll never get 'em out. After all the bloody time I spent on it. Gawd, I must be cursed.'

'The dustbin men were 'ere again terday,' Freda told him.

'Yer didn't leave yer winder open, did yer?' Ada queried.

'Yeah, I fergot ter close it this mornin',' the young man moaned, near to tears.

'Let's 'ave a look at it,' Ada said, raising her eyebrow at Freda.

When Flossy brought the suit out still on the hanger she chuckled. ''Ere, you could be one o' them there black an' white minstrels in that.'

'Don't mock, Ada, I'm really upset,' he wailed.

'Give us it 'ere,' she said, snatching it from him. 'I'll do it for yer.'

'It'll never come out, Ada,' he said holding his hand to his face in dismay.

'Now you piss orf in, an' leave it ter me,' she told him firmly. 'I'll do it ternight. It won't take me five minutes.'

'What yer gonna do, press it again?' Freda asked as soon as they were alone.

'Yeah, after I give it a good boil,' Ada replied.

Chapter Thirty-Two

Dockhead police station was a hive of activity on Wednesday morning and Superintendent Baxter gesticulated towards his paper-strewn desk when Pat Cassidy answered his call. 'Look at this lot,' he growled. 'I'm swamped with it. It's no wonder Tom Cox ended up in hospital.'

'How is he?' Pat asked as he sat down facing his superior officer.

'Doing well, I'm glad to say, but I'll be joining him before long if this gets any worse,' Baxter remarked as he reached for his mug of coffee.

'I need a car,' Pat said without more ado.

'Where for?'

'Poplar.'

'Am I to be enlightened, or is this a close-to-the-chest operation?' Baxter queried.

'I took the liberty of contacting Poplar police station,' Pat explained. 'I know a detective sergeant there and he's helping me trace all the photographers in their area. I'm following up a good lead as it happens.'

'So, do I get to know about it now or later?' Baxter said with a frown.

The young detective nodded towards the papers spread out on the desk. 'I feel I should wait, sir,' he replied. 'At this stage it'll just be wasting your time.'

'Thanks for the consideration, Cassidy,' the superintendent said with some sarcasm in his voice. 'But before you go swanning around Poplar you'd better take a look at this.'

Pat picked up the folder Baxter had tossed towards him and studied the contents for a few seconds, then he looked up wide-eyed. 'Very interesting.'

Baxter leaned back in his chair. 'They were unusually quick with that,' he remarked. 'Definite similarities there.'

'Can I take this?' Pat asked him.

Baxter nodded his approval. 'By the way, sergeant, that car you requested. It's one-way only, I'm afraid, just to get you there. I'm short of cars as it is. This friend of yours will no doubt be able to help you with some transport at that end. One other thing. I'm short of manpower too. Has the team finished talking to the tenants at Milldyke Buildings?'

'Yes, except Fraser and Samuels,' Pat replied as he got up. 'They're taking statements at the Woolpack pub and the surrounding area. They should be finished by this evening, all being well.'

'Study that file carefully, sergeant,' Baxter told him. 'It makes very interesting reading. By the way, I'd better sanction that car.'

Pat turned in the doorway. 'I won't need it for an hour, I need to call in at Chambers Wharf first to speak to a Mr Brightwell.'

'A suspect?'

'No, a scout master.'

Baxter shook his head in confusion as he picked up the phone.

Kate was anxious about the children while they were on holiday from school and she made a point of going home at lunchtime to check that they were all right. Amy Almond had been very helpful by getting them something to eat during the day as well as providing drinks and generally keeping an eye on them, but nevertheless Kate worried. 'You won't let them stray out o' the turnin', will yer?' she had fretted. 'Well, not Jenny, anyway.'

'Don't worry, they'll be fine.'

'There's some lemonade and fruit. Be sure that they don't guzzle that lemonade or Jenny'll be sick.'

'Look, I know what ter do, don't worry.'

'By the way, there's some crayons an' drawin' books in Jenny's bedroom an' Jimmy knows where fings are in case yer need anyfing.'

'Kate, will you stop worryin',' Amy said firmly.

The young woman hurried home on Wednesday lunchtime to find Jimmy and Jenny sitting together with Charlie Almond in her kitchen, tucking into pie and mash. 'You don't normally eat 'ere, do yer?' she queried.

'Me dad's come 'ome,' Charlie told her matter-of-factly.

'Oh, I see,' Kate replied with a frown.

'Me dad's 'avin' a private talk wiv me mum so she gave us the money ter get pie an' mash,' Charlie added.

Kate quickly made herself a pot of tea and a cheese sandwich and sat down at the table. The children had finished but they made no attempt to leave.

'Mrs Almond said we've gotta wait 'ere till she comes in,' Jimmy told her.

'I fink me mum an' dad are 'avin' an argument,' Charlie said as he twiddled with his fork.

Kate sighed sadly. 'When did yer dad arrive, Charlie?' she asked.

'About an hour ago, I fink,' he replied. 'We came in fer a drink an' they were shoutin' at each ovver. That's why me mum told us ter go an' get pie an' mash.'

'Was yer dad pleased ter see yer, Charlie?' she asked him with concern.

The lad shrugged his shoulders. 'I fink so.'

'Well, I shouldn't worry, everyfing'll be all right, I'm sure,' she said with a smile.

Just as she finished washing up the dirty crockery Kate heard Amy's front door slam shut and heavy footsteps on the stairs. There was no time to speak with her neighbour now, and in any case it might not be prudent at the moment, she decided. Time was flying and she quickly set off back to work, intending to see Amy as soon as she got home that evening.

Ted Briscoe called on the caretaker that afternoon. 'We've got permission ter clear Mrs Johnson's place out,' he said as he slumped down in a chair.

'Are the police finished wiv it then?' Ferguson queried.

'Nah, we gotta put all the stuff in our store,' the agent told him. 'By the way I'll need the key. I gotta make an inventory. The van's comin' ter clear the flat termorrer, then you can get on wiv the decoration.'

'I'm too busy wiv ovver jobs at the moment,' Ferguson replied.

'Well, it'll 'ave ter be done out before we can re-let it,' Briscoe said sharply. 'I got somebody comin' ter look at it Friday week an' it needs ter be finished by then.'

'That ain't givin' me much time,' Ferguson protested.

''Ow long's it gonna take yer ter put wallpaper up an' whitewash the ceilin's? It ain't as if yer need ter strip the old paper. Just bung the new stuff over the top.'

'I can't do that. It'll look a right poxy mess,' the caretaker said in disgust.

'Well do yer best. I can't be worryin' about the ins an' outs o' bloody decoratin'. That's your job,' Briscoe retorted irritably as he got up to leave.

Ferguson handed him the appropriate key. 'I'd better be gettin' back ter work,' he said curtly.

Briscoe hurried along to the Johnson flat and let himself in. He turned out drawers and ran his hand round the recesses, searched through cupboards and the wardrobe, examined the contents of the dressing table and then turned his attention to the trinkets. He upturned the vases and examined the scant ornaments, and finally ran his hand up the chimney breast and checked the floorboards in every room before he was satisfied that nothing had been missed. The inventory had been completed in a few minutes but the thorough search had taken him much longer, and as Briscoe left the flat he still fretted that there was something he might have missed.

Down in the street Charlie Almond sat with Jimmy Flannagan in the shade of the bacon factory while they talked in earnest.

'I wonder where Tommy Brindley's 'idin' out,' Jimmy was saying. ''E must be really upset over findin' 'is gran'muvver dead an' then the coppers tellin' 'im 'is muvver 'ad died. No wonder 'e run away.'

'Yeah, I'd 'ave gone too,' Charlie replied. 'When yer got no one ter look after yer they put yer in a children's 'ome.'

'If I was on me own I'd run away ter sea. They let yer be a cabin boy when yer pretty young.'

'I bet Tommy Brindley's run away ter sea.'

'Yeah, 'e told me once 'e was gonna stow away an' be a cabin boy.'

''E could be in China by now.'

'Shouldn't fink so. It takes ages ter get ter China.'

'Well, 'e could be in Africa or somewhere like that.'

'Yer know what I reckon?' Jimmy said suddenly.

'What's that?'

'I reckon Tommy's 'angin' around the docks tryin' ter get a ship ter one o' them places.'

'We could go down by Tower Bridge an' see if 'e's there,' Charlie suggested.

'Trouble is those ships only go ter places like Denmark an' Poland,' Jimmy replied. 'I fink 'e's gone over ter the East India Docks. That's where the Chinkie ships come in.'

'We could go over there termorrer mornin',' Charlie said grinning.

'I dunno,' Jimmy hesitated, scratching his head. 'I promised me mum I wouldn't go too far an' leave Jenny on 'er own.'

'My mum'll look after 'er,' Charlie said. 'We could tell 'er we was gonna look fer Tommy.'

'Yeah, all right. We'll go there termorrer,' Jimmy replied.

With the Scotland Yard file on the seat beside him and a vital bit of information gained from his visit to Chambers Wharf, Pat Cassidy sat back deep in thought as he was driven to Poplar. Wally Lyons had been adamant when shown the knot tied in the black bootlace taken from around Meg Johnson's neck. 'This is not yer usual slipknot,' he said shaking his head. 'I train my scouts in tyin' knots that are useful fer scoutin' an' I show 'em the type o' knots used by seamen, lorry drivers an' dockers, so yer'll believe me when I say that's a very strange knot.'

Pat nodded at the dock ganger. 'I wouldn't argue, Wally, but what are your thoughts on it?'

The big man stroked his chin with a gnarled hand. 'It's got a double loop in it, can yer see? Look just there,' he pointed out. 'If yer looped the lace over someone's 'ead an' pulled that knot tight yer'd never get it loose. It's more like a garrotte knot than one yer'd tie in a strangle cord, though the end result would be the same.'

'A garrotte knot?' Pat queried.

Wally smiled indulgently, happy to be consulted by the same policeman he had on one or two occasions invited along to talk to his scout pack. 'Let me tell yer,' he began. 'Years ago, way back in the eighteen sixties ter be exact, there was an outbreak o' particularly nasty violence in London. Highway robbery, where the victims were attacked from be'ind by 'avin' a cord slipped over their neck an' pulled tight. The knot was such that it couldn't be loosened, an' while they struggled they were relieved o' their valuables. Quite a few o' the poor sods died o' strangulation an' the practice got so prevalent that they brought out what was called the Garrotters Act. Those caught usin' that method o' robbery were automatically flogged. So that's anuvver bit of useless information yer've just learned,' Wally said chuckling.

'Not so useless, mate,' Pat smiled. 'Could this knot be the same type as the one used around that time?'

'Who knows? It could 'ave originally bin passed on by some foreigner, a seaman maybe,' the scoutmaster suggested.

'Garrotting is a Spanish method of execution. I just wonder—' Pat remarked almost to himself as he made to leave the waterfront.

'Well, good luck, Pat,' the big man called out after him.

Now as he neared Poplar police station the young detective was eager to get on with the painstaking and time-consuming task of talking to all the photographers in the area.

A tall ginger-haired man was chatting to the desk sergeant as Pat walked into the station and he looked round with a big grin on his ruddy face. 'Nice to see you again, Pat. It's been some time,' Detective Sergeant Don Ridley said as he held out his hand.

'You look well. How's the family?' Pat asked.

'All growing up,' Don said grinning. 'Look, I've got a car ready. Do you want to start right away or have we got time for a chat over a cuppa?'

'I'd like to get going right away if you don't mind,' Pat told him. 'We can chew the fat later.'

'Always the professional,' Don grinned as they made their way to the rear of the station to pick up the car.

The two policemen sat together on the back seat as the vehicle sped along the West India Dock Road, with Pat Cassidy explaining what progress he had made regarding the two killings.

'Well, let's see what transpires today,' Don Ridley said as they pulled up at the first call.

The photographer was of little help. 'We only do weddings and studio portraits,' he said, peering through his pebble-lensed spectacles.

The second photographer was even less helpful. 'Nah, we don't do anyfing like that,' he mumbled. 'In any case, we don't keep the negatives fer very long. Fire risk, yer see.'

The policemen got similar responses from the next two studios they visited and Pat sighed in frustration. 'It doesn't look too good, does it?' he said dejectedly.

'There's a few more yet, don't give up,' Don Ridley replied encouragingly.

The driver pulled the car up outside a dingy-looking shop in Chapel Street and Pat shook his head. 'I don't think we'll get any joy here,' he sighed, 'but you never know. Shall I do the honours?'

The old man behind the counter studied Pat over his gold-rimmed glasses. 'Well, we 'ave done a few outside jobs ovver than yer run-o'-the-mill weddin' parties an' functions,' he said. 'We done a nice one o' the local football team last season. Come out very nice it did. They were pleased wiv the results. I done some parties on VE day an' a few on VJ day as well.'

'Have you ever taken a group photo at a local firm or factory?' Pat asked him.

The photographer shook his head. 'Nah. Don't get much call fer that sort o' fing.'

'Well, thanks for your time anyway.'

''Ere just a minute, I did do one a few years ago,' the old man said as Pat made to leave. 'I almost fergot about it. Beginnin' o' the war it was. The church 'ostel in Merrydown Street. I was asked ter do it fer the church magazine.'

'A group of women in white aprons or overalls?' Pat said quickly.

'Yeah, that's right, aprons an' caps,' the old man replied.

'And was there a man standing at the end of the group?'

''S right. Vic Purvy,' the photographer told him. 'That's 'ow I come ter get the job, frew ole Vic. 'E used ter drink in the same pub as me, yer see.'

'Have you still got the negative?'

'Nah, 'fraid not. We only keep 'em fer a limited time.'

'This Vic Purvy. Is he still about?' Pat asked with bated breath.

'Yeah, as far as I know. Ain't seen 'im fer a few weeks though.'

'Can you give me his address?'

'Yeah. Twenty-four, Winsford Street. Just past the church on yer right.'

Pat thanked the old man and hurried back to the car smiling triumphantly. 'I got a result,' he said enthusiastically. 'Winsford Street.'

The sight of a police car pulling up in the middle of the row of terraced houses attracted a few curious glances, and one old lady standing at her door chuckled as the young policeman knocked at number twenty-four. 'What's ole Vic bin up to?' she asked.

'Just a social call,' Pat told her with a smile.

''E'll be gettin' a bad name, socialisin' wiv rozzers,' she remarked.

Vic Purvy came to the door and squinted as Pat Cassidy introduced himself and presented his warrant card. 'Yer better come in. I don't want those nosy ole cows to over'ear anyfing,' he growled.

When Pat explained the purpose of his visit the old man's face lit up. 'I got one o' the pictures yer talkin' about. We all got one,' he said quickly.

'Can I see it?' Pat asked.

'Take a pew, son, I won't be a minute,' Vic told him. He was soon back holding a framed photograph. 'There we are.'

Pat studied the picture. He had seen the body of Annie Griffiths when he was called to the bombsite in Dock Lane and Meg Johnson's body at the police morgue, and here they were, standing side by side in the photograph. 'Do you recall the names of these women?' he asked.

Vic Purvy seated himself in a high-backed armchair by the hearth. 'The one standin' next ter me is Alice Ford,' he pointed out. 'She was the 'ead cook. Next to 'er is Minnie Cole who 'elped in the kitchen. The one in the middle is

Rose Middleton from the church. She run the place. Next to 'er is Annie Griffiths, the assistant cook, an' that one at the end is Meg Johnson. She used ter make the beds an' clean the place out.'

'Those two at the end. What do you know of them?' Pat asked him.

'Why d'you ask?'

'They've both been murdered.'

'Oh my good Gawd!' Vic exclaimed, touching his hand to his head.

'You could help us catch whoever did it by telling me what you know of these two women, and about the hostel, and anything else that comes to mind which might give me some leads,' Pat explained clearly, leaning forward solicitously in his chair.

Vic Purvy filled his clay pipe with care and then he told his story. 'When my ole dutch died just before the war broke out I got ter drinkin' too much, an' me married daughter got worried over me,' he began. 'She wanted me ter go an' live wiv 'er an' 'er ole man, but I didn't get on wiv 'im so I stayed in me own place, till it got too much fer me, an' then out o' the blue I got this offer from the church. They said I could 'ave a room an' board at their workin' men's 'ostel in Merrydown Street if I'd be the 'andyman an' look after the boiler. That's 'ow I come ter be there. I didn't 'ave anyfing ter do wiv the blokes who stayed there. They were a mixed lot, mainly regulars, but some o' the women knew 'em well. Annie Griffiths used ter serve up the evenin' meal along wiv Minnie Cole an' they was always chattin' to 'er.'

'What about Meg Johnson?' Pat cut in.

'Meg was never there in the evenin' when the men booked in,' Vic recalled. 'She used ter do 'er work once they'd gone in the mornin'.'

'Is the hostel still in use?'

Vic shook his head sadly. 'It got a direct 'it durin' the back end o' the Blitz,' he sighed. 'Rose Middleton was workin' late that night doin' 'er books an' she was killed outright along wiv the lodgers.'

'All of them?'

'All but one,' Vic replied. 'The worst o' the Blitz was over an' the air raids were spasmodical at the time, so the men used ter stay in their beds when the sirens sounded. That particular night was a bad one though. Lucky fer me, our Peggy was in labour wiv 'er second an' I went round to 'er place ter see 'ow she was. I was only gone fer an hour an' when I got back the 'ostel was flattened an' burnin' like 'ell itself. Nuffing I could do. Nuffing anybody could do. Twelve beds in that place there was an' they ended up pullin' eleven charred bodies from the ruins. All the beds were filled that night as usual, accordin' ter Minnie Cole, so one man got out alive. 'E just disappeared. Never came back or reported 'imself safe. Very strange that.'

'What about records?' Pat asked. 'Names and such.'

'All the records perished in the fire,' Vic told him. 'Annie Griffiths an' Minnie Cole only knew the men by their Christian names or their nicknames, like Tubby an' Lofty, so they couldn't 'elp much wiv findin' out who it was survived.'

'Are Minnie Cole and Alice Ford still living local?' Pat inquired.

'Minnie died at the end o' the war an' I 'eard that Alice married a Yank an' went ter live in America,' Vic replied, sucking noisily on his pipe.

'I wonder how Annie and Meg came to live in Bermondsey,' Pat said thoughtfully. 'Can you throw any light on that?'

'Yeah, I can. Meg met a merchant seaman who lived over the water an' she moved in wiv 'im, accordin' to Annie Griffiths,' Vic explained.

'And what about Annie herself?'

'Annie was born in Bermon'sey, as a matter o' fact,' the old man went on, 'but she was put up fer adoption when she was just a little mite. That's 'ow she come ter live in Poplar. She told me all about it once. 'Er an' Meg Johnson were friends an' Meg told 'er about a flat goin' in 'er buildin's. Annie was keen ter find out who 'er real muvver an' farver were an' she thought it'd 'elp if she moved over there, yer see.'

'I wonder if she ever did find out,' Pat remarked.

'Gawd knows,' Vic replied, shrugging his shoulders.

The young detective thanked the old man for his help and took his leave. Later, after a few cups of coffee and a lengthy chat with Don Ridley in the police canteen at Poplar, Pat Cassidy caught a bus back to Bermondsey. The mystery was deepening, he thought with a sigh as he glanced once more at the photograph he had borrowed from Vic Purvy. Two women dead, the crimes possibly linked to another in Soho, and now there was the mysterious stranger who had survived the hostel bombing in Poplar.

A wave of tiredness assailed the young policeman, and with it came a strong urge for a few stiff drinks to help him relax properly, but an inner voice stopped him: his need to see Kate was even more compelling.

Chapter Thirty-Three

The warm summer evening was wearing on as Kate stared out of the kitchen window. Below, the bombsite in Dock Lane was full of ominous shadows and she shuddered as she thought about the poor woman whose life had been choked out of her on that desolate ruin. Since then the council workmen had put up corrugated fencing but this had already been breached in places, and the local children often played there amongst the rubble that had once been a busy factory. Beyond was the Jamaica Road, quiet at this time, and above the rooftops the western sky was full of red and gold, promising another glorious day. Tonight though there were other things to consider. Hopefully Pat would be arriving soon and the young woman wanted everything in place, the children in bed and coffee simmering on the stove.

'Come on, Jimmy, it's gettin' late,' she urged him.

'We're on 'oliday, Mum,' he protested.

'It doesn't matter. Now put that comic away an' get ter bed.'

Jimmy puffed as he untangled himself from the fireside chair. 'Mum?'

'Yeah?'

'Me an' Charlie were finkin' o' goin' over the docks termorrer.'

'What for?'

'Ter see if we can spot Tommy Brindley.'

'An' what makes yer fink yer'll find 'im over there?'

'Me an' Charlie was talkin',' the lad replied. 'We fink 'e's tryin' ter sign on as a cabin boy on one o' those Chinkie ships.'

'I don't fink yer'll find 'im over there, an' in any case I don't want you two wanderin' off an' leavin' Jenny on 'er own,' Kate said firmly.

'Charlie said 'is mum'll look after Jenny.'

'Mrs Almond's got enough ter do.'

'Can't I go then, Mum?'

Kate saw the disappointment in her son's eyes and she sighed deeply. 'Now listen, Jimmy,' she began. 'I know you're concerned about yer mate Tommy, an' I am too, but yer gotta look at this sensibly. Before a lad o' Tommy's age goes ter sea he'd 'ave ter have his parents' permission. It's not like the old days when anyone could run away ter sea. Besides, the police are aware that Tommy's on the run an' they'll be watchin' all the docks an' ports. It's more like Tommy's stayin' wiv a friend somewhere, like 'e did wiv us.'

''E might 'ave slipped 'ome 'ere when it was dark,' Jimmy said hopefully.

Kate shook her head. 'Mrs Almond told me that Tommy's gran'muvver gave permission fer the estate people ter clear the flat out. No rent 'ad bin paid fer some time an' it was obvious that Tommy's mum wasn't goin' ter get better.'

'I wonder where 'e could be.'

'God only knows,' Kate sighed. 'I just 'ope 'e's all right, wherever 'e is.'

Jimmy went off to bed reluctantly and Kate sat thinking for a minute or two. On getting home from work that evening she had knocked at Amy's door but Charlie had told her that his mother was out. It was unusual for Amy not to be home at that time and Charlie had not been able to explain, except to say that she had gone to see someone. Now, as she sat in the quiet living room, Kate suddenly heard Amy's door go. She wanted to go and talk to her, feeling that her neighbour might welcome a sympathetic ear, but it was a bit awkward at the moment, she thought, with Pat Cassidy due any minute.

The young woman sat agonising for a few minutes then she got up and looked into Jimmy's bedroom. The lad was in bed reading and he glanced up surprised.

'I gotta go next door fer a few minutes,' she told him. 'Can you let Mr Cassidy in if 'e knocks? Tell 'im where I am an' that I won't be long.'

Jimmy nodded and went back to his comic. Kate let herself out and knocked on Amy's front door to find her neighbour red-eyed and full of woe.

'I've bin sittin' in the bloody park fer an hour,' she declared. 'Fred wanted ter see me after 'e'd done work. What d'yer fink e' come out wiv?' Kate's expectant silence prompted her to go on. ''E said Beryl's changed. 'E said she's bin nice as pie an' she wants 'im back, fer good.'

'An' 'e said yes?'

'That's about the strength of it,' Amy sighed dejectedly.

''E'll soon change 'is mind, yer'll see,' Kate told her with an encouraging smile. 'Fred'll come callin', once yer 'usband's gone back ter sea.'

'That no-good git already 'as,' Amy snorted. ''E came 'ome yesterday an' 'e wasn't in the place five minutes before 'e ushered poor Charlie out the door. Said 'e wanted a private talk. I ask yer. Six months away an' not so much as a kiss-yer-arse ter the lad. Anuvver farver would 'ave made a fuss of 'is son. Not 'im though. 'E didn't even bring anyfing 'ome fer the boy, not that Charlie expects it, but yer'd fink 'e'd 'ave made the effort ter look pleased ter see 'im after all this time. Not that selfish git.'

'An' 'e's gone straight back ter sea?' Kate queried.

'Got a ship up in Liverpool,' Amy told her. 'Sailin' ternight by all accounts. I did give 'im some ear'ole bashin'. I told 'im it wasn't good enough an' that 'e wasn't bein' fair ter me or Charlie an' 'e said if I didn't like it I'd 'ave ter lump it. I let 'im 'ave it then. Called 'im everyfing from a pig to a dog, an' wiv a few choice words in between. I told 'im if 'e thought 'e was gonna share my bed fer one night 'e could fink again. I told 'im straight that 'e was treatin' me like a common tart. I could just see it. I'd wake up next mornin' wiv 'im gone an' a couple o' quid left on the dressin' table. I told 'im ter piss orf there an' then.'

'An' Fred knows all this?'

'Yeah, I told 'im but it didn't make any difference.'

'Poor Amy. Yer not 'avin' much luck lately, are yer?' Kate said warmly.

Her neighbour looked up from the table with large sad eyes. 'I'm firty-seven this year, Kate, an' what 'ave I got ter show fer it? An ole man who can't stand five minutes o' me company an' a bloke who's bin takin' me fer a ride. I'm livin' in this poxy 'ole, strugglin' from day ter day ter make ends meet an' I can't even take that lad o' mine away fer a week's 'oliday. I don't know 'ow I'd get on if it wasn't fer Spiv Copeland, I really don't.'

''Ave yer seen anyfing o' Len lately?' Kate asked her in an effort to cheer her up.

'Nah, 'e's bin wary o' callin' while the coppers 'ave bin round 'ere,' Amy replied. ''Ave you seen anyfing of 'im?'

Kate shook her head. 'I fink I let 'im know 'ow fings are, as far as I was concerned.'

'Yer could do worse,' Amy said. 'At least 'e'd treat a woman right. I only wish 'e fancied me. I'd soon let 'im put 'is shoes under my bed.'

The kettle started to sing over the flame and Amy made a pot of tea. Kate was anxious to get back to her flat but she thought it might seem callous if she rushed away too quickly and left the unhappy woman on her own.

'I wonder what progress they're makin' in catchin' that evil git,' Amy remarked.

'That detective's comin' ter see me again this evenin',' Kate told her.

'Who, Cassidy?'

'Yeah.'

'On friendly terms then?'

''E's very nice. Not like yer'd imagine a 'tec ter be,' Kate said, sighing to herself. 'You know 'ow 'e was over the two boys.'

'So is this a social call?'

'Partly.'

'That tells me a lot,' Amy grinned, regaining some of her buoyancy.

''E wants ter check up on a few fings but we are gettin' ter know each ovver a little bit,' Kate admitted.

'Well, best o' luck, luv, but just make sure 'e's the right man before yer go all the way,' Amy warned her. 'Just look at me. I'm the prime example of a scatty mare who falls fer the wrong fellers.'

'Don't worry, Amy, I've bin bitten once,' Kate said firmly. 'I'll be a bit more wary next time.'

The two women sat for a while chatting, but Kate was mindful that Pat might be waiting, and finally she made her excuses to leave. She let herself into her flat expectantly and found Jimmy sleeping soundly. What if Pat had knocked and got no answer? she fretted.

It was getting late when she heard footsteps on the stairs and she was at the front door waiting for his knock.

'I'm sorry, Kate, I've been over to Poplar,' he said with a tired smile.

She tried to look casual but inside she was glowing. 'I've got some coffee ready,' she told him. 'I know yer'd really prefer it ter tea.'

Pat's eyes widened appreciatively as he sat down in the fireside chair. 'I've got so much to tell you,' he said, stretching his legs out and sighing.

'Should you?' she replied from the scullery.

'If you'd sooner not.'

Kate came in looking anxious. 'I was only jokin',' she said quickly. 'I can't wait ter find out what yer've bin doin' an' what yer've found out.'

Pat smiled at her serious expression. 'I've made good progress and I know I can trust you to keep it confidential,' he replied.

'Let me get yer the coffee first,' she said excitedly.

They sat facing each other in the tidy living room and Kate was wide-eyed as she listened. Finally the policeman put down his empty cup on the floor beside him and ran a hand over his pale face before he told her the latest strand of the story. 'It was just a hunch but it came up,' he went on. 'Apparently this killing in Soho happened just after the war started. The victim was a pimp by the name of Gus Wesley, and the method used to kill him was identical to the one used on the two women, a black bootlace tied in the same way, but the killer was never caught. According to the file, the West End police put a dragnet on the area and rounded up as many prostitutes as they could. Many of them said they knew the victim very well. A few of the women even admitted that he had been their pimp, but they could throw no light on why he should have been murdered, although, as you would imagine, a pimp makes enemies and he was known to have been a violent character. The interviews uncovered a few things about him. He was supposed to have ill-treated his girls and he had been looking for a particular man who had got too familiar with one of the girls he ran. The problem was that prostitutes are not the best of witnesses at any time. They have an aversion to co-operating with the police, who after all are out to clear them off the streets, and also they live in fear of getting cut up by the very powerful gangs controlling prostitution and gambling in the West End.'

'So yer've nuffing much ter go on,' Kate cut in.

Pat looked thoughtful. 'One thing did emerge that might be of help,' he continued. 'The police had recently interviewed one girl who was coming up on two charges, one of soliciting and the other of assaulting another prostitute who'd apparently queered her pitch. She was looking at a prison stretch and she co-operated with the police, hoping for leniency by giving them information on the unsolved murder of Gus Wesley. The girl stated that a prostitute by the name of Nan Lynn, whose pimp was Gus Wesley, had told her that she had become involved with a man she referred to as Spanish Joe, who had been pressing her to give up the game and go away with him. Anyway, Gus Wesley had found out and beaten her up badly, and the girl felt that might have been the reason Wesley was killed.'

'By Nan Lynn's boyfriend?'

'Yeah, that's right.'

'Didn't the police pick up this Lynn woman fer questionin'?' Kate asked.

Pat shook his head slowly. 'Someone did some talking,' he explained. 'Whether it was the police or the girl herself we don't know, but all hell broke loose in Soho. Nan Lynn's friend got her face slashed with a razor and Nan Lynn herself disappeared. No one would say a word after that and the gangs now rule with an iron fist.'

'That's terrible.'

Pat shrugged his shoulders. 'All we've got to go on is the name Spanish Joe.'

Kate refilled his empty cup and sat looking at his tired, handsome face. 'You look exhausted,' she remarked quietly.

He smiled. 'It's been a long day.'

'Let me get yer somefing to eat,' she said with concern.

The detective shook his head. 'It's very nice of you to offer but I've eaten already, I promise.'

'So where d'yer go now?'

'It's a question of putting all the facts and information together and looking for some little thing that might make some sense of it all,' he told her.

'Some task.'

'It surely is,' he replied. 'I've been puzzling over that chat I had with the old man in Poplar. You remember I told you that he said one man got out of that bombed hostel alive. Could that man have been Gus Wesley's murderer hiding out in the East End? And could Annie Griffiths and Meg Johnson have discovered his true identity? Cast your mind back for a minute. Remember what Annie said to Meg Johnson about someone from the other side coming back to haunt her? Well she might have meant the other side of the river, which is a common enough expression in this area.'

'So it could 'ave bin someone who was stayin' at the men's 'ostel?'

'Exactly.'

'So 'e kills Annie, but why did 'e wait so long before 'e killed Meg?' Kate asked.

Pat leaned forward in his chair. 'Let's suppose the killer feels safe in the knowledge that the one person who could identify him is dead. Then one day he calls on Meg for some reason and sees that picture on her sideboard. He then realises that she was Annie's workmate and that Annie might have said something to her. He can't take any chances. And in any case they can't hang him twice, so he kills Meg as well.'

'Not many people visited Meg ter my knowledge, other than neighbours,' Kate recalled.

'When I left here last night I called in on the caretaker,' Pat went on. 'He told me he'd seen the picture on her sideboard when Meg invited him in for a cup of tea after he'd fixed her new lock. Like you, though, he couldn't describe it in detail. He told me he was anxious to get out of the flat.'

'Yeah, I can understand that,' Kate replied.

'We know that Meg Johnson must have let the killer in,' Pat reminded her.

'Ted Briscoe the agent goes in all the flats,' Kate said quickly. ''E invites 'imself in. 'E came 'ere just after I moved in. Fair gave me the creeps.'

'The caretaker also told me that Briscoe was around here on Sunday morning,' the policeman said, pulling on his chin with thumb and forefinger. 'I don't think there's any love lost between those two.'

'Ferguson's a lazy sort, accordin' ter the neighbours, but 'e keeps 'imself to 'imself,' Kate replied. 'Briscoe always

347

seems ter be nosin' around an' chattin' the women up. 'E treats it as a slight if 'e doesn't get offered a cup o' tea. It's common knowledge.'

'I'll be speaking to Ted Briscoe again tomorrow,' Pat told her. 'In the meantime I'd better get off home.'

'You look really shattered,' Kate remarked. 'Why don't you stay the night? I've got a chairbed an' I can set it up in 'ere, if yer'll 'elp me. Besides, we'll all feel safe 'avin' a detective as a guest.'

Pat Cassidy smiled. 'What about the neighbours? Won't they talk?'

Kate leaned over and rested her hand on his forearm. 'I'm doin' nuffing wrong so why should I care what they fink?' she said calmly.

'As long as you're sure.'

'I'm sure. Now relax an' I'll get us some supper. D'you like cheese?'

'Perfect,' he replied smiling.

A young lad slipped into the dark turning unseen, even by the usually alert Ernie Walker, and as he made his way to the end block he puffed with exhaustion. All day long he had trudged through the hilly streets of Hastings, recalling the happy week he had spent there before the war. He recognised the fishermen's huts where they hung their nets and the little playground by the sea where he had turned round and round on the carousel until he was nearly sick. His father and mother had laughed happily as they whisked him up by his hands and ran over the rough stones to the water's edge, telling him that they were going to throw him in, and he had laughed too at the mad fun of it. They loved him and he loved them. A happy child lost in a timeless moment with no thought to the future. But they were gone now, as was his grandmother, and there was no one left. Now he was older and he thought about the years ahead. At first they would put him in a children's home, and then a hostel for young men. Better the sea, and a life of adventure and travel. Tomorrow he would go and sign on, but tonight he had to sleep.

Tommy had the key ready as he reached the first landing and he eagerly slipped it into the lock. What was wrong? It wouldn't turn. They must have changed the lock. Well, the landing was better than the street, he decided as he curled up outside the front door.

'Oh my good Gawd! Yer frightened the bleedin' life out o' me,' Flossy gasped.

Tommy stood up slowly. 'Sorry, Flossy,' he said sheepishly. 'I didn't fink anybody'd know I was 'ere.'

'I 'eard yer go up the stairs,' Flossy told him. 'I thought, that's a strange tread, so I said ter meself, Flossy, don't be a coward, go an' see who it is. Good job I did. The bleedin' coppers 'ave bin on at us ter keep a lookout for yer, yer little perisher. Where yer bin 'idin'?'

'I bin down the coast,' Tommy replied.

'Sorry to 'ear yer bad news, dear,' Flossy said, putting a hand up to his face. ''Ere, I bet yer starvin', ain't yer?'

Tommy nodded. 'I've only 'ad some apples.'

'Well, you can stay wiv me ternight,' the young man told him. 'We'll worry about termorrer when it comes. In the meantime yer need some food in yer belly an' a nice warm place ter lay yer 'ead. C'mon, luv, foller me.'

Night settled over Bermondsey, and a full moon shone down on the mean backstreets as Kate quickly undressed and slipped on her dressing gown, knotting the cord around her slim body before she went back into the living room.

'That chairbed's a bit rickety,' she said shyly. 'I 'ope yer'll be comfortable.'

Pat approached her and gazed into her eyes. 'I'm sure I will, and thanks again,' he said quietly.

She made no attempt to move away, wanting him to kiss her, and she sighed as he took her by the arms and pulled her to him gently. He leant down towards her, inclining his head and then she tasted his lips. The kiss was soft and tender, almost delicate. As he lifted his head she saw the look in his eyes and knew that he desired her. 'Goodnight, Pat,' she said softly.

'Goodnight, Kate. Sleep tight.'

She lay awake for hours, listening to her daughter's shallow breathing as she relived the kiss and remembered the passion in his eyes.

In the next room Pat Cassidy sat for a while in the darkness, his thoughts confused. She was beautiful and very desirable, but like him she had lived alone for some time and it showed in the way she trembled at his touch. He was still trembling now. With a deep sigh he climbed into bed and was asleep almost as soon as his head touched the pillow.

Chapter Thirty-Four

A tapping noise had invaded Kate's muddled dreams and she struggled to rouse herself, turning over on to her back and raising her hand against the bright sunlight that was streaming through the partly drawn curtains. She heard his voice and eased herself up in bed, pulling the sheet up around her neck. 'Come in,' she croaked, suddenly aware that she had overslept.

Pat smiled as he handed her a cup of tea. 'I took the liberty. Hope you don't mind.'

Kate could see that Jenny was still sleeping soundly beside her and she felt a little embarrassed as she reached out her bare arm and took the cup from him, but he discreetly turned his head and sat down at the bottom of the bed. 'I thought I'd better wake you,' he said, 'it's ten past seven.'

'This is lovely,' she replied. 'I can't remember the last time I got a cuppa in bed.'

'I slept like a top,' he remarked. 'I need a shave though.'

'Sorry, but I don't 'ave a razor,' she told him with a smile.

'No worry, I can get a shave at the barber shop.'

'What about some breakfast?' Kate said quickly. 'Let me get yer somefing. It'll be no trouble.'

'I've had some toast,' he said sheepishly.

Kate took a sip of tea. 'Will you be around 'ere terday?' she asked.

He nodded. 'There'll be the usual meeting at the station first thing, and then I've got to see the estate's agent and one or two other people. After that I'm going over to West End Central police station. I need to check a few things out.'

'I appreciate yer tellin' me all those fings last night,' she remarked. 'Yer don't need ter worry though. What was said won't go no further.'

'I know that,' he smiled. 'It was nice to share some thoughts with you. My usual routine is to go home and sit there for hours with a few drinks while I mull over the day, but last night was different. In fact it was very nice.'

'I'm glad yer fink so,' she said smiling. 'Will I see yer ternight?'

'Would you mind if I called? It might be late, though,' he replied, adding quickly, 'but I won't presume on you again.'

Kate wanted to say that he would be more than welcome but held back. 'I 'ope yer get some good news about Tommy Brindley,' she said.

'Yeah, the longer it gets, the more worrying it becomes when youngsters go missing,' he frowned. 'Anyway let's hope he's been found safe and well.'

'Jimmy and Charlie Almond wanted ter go over the West India Docks ter see if they could spot 'im,' Kate told him. 'They thought Tommy might try ter get a ship.'

Pat shook his head. 'The port police would soon spot him and they have a list of missing children. No, I've a feeling he'll show up here soon. He might even call on you after the kindness you showed him.'

'I just 'ope 'e does,' Kate sighed.

Pat Cassidy stood up. 'Well once again, thanks for the hospitality, Kate,' he grinned shyly. 'Look forward to seeing you tonight.'

As soon as he had left Kate dressed quickly. She guessed that there might well be a few knowing glances and a few words exchanged by her neighbours on seeing the policeman leaving, but it didn't matter. She was happy, happier than she had felt for a long time, and was looking forward to seeing him again that evening.

Flossy Chandler sat facing the young runaway at the kitchen table. 'I've gotta go off ter work soon,' he said. 'Yer must go an' give yerself up, Tommy. People are worried.'

'What people?' the lad said sharply. 'I've got no family ter worry over me. I'll be off soon.'

Flossy watched as Tommy finished the last of his marmalade-coated slice of bread and he sighed in anguish. 'Look, I'll get in trouble if the coppers find out yer stayin' 'ere.'

'Well, I'm not, am I?'

'Yeah, but yer did.'

'No one's ter know.'

'I do.'

'But you won't grass me.'

'Where did yer learn that sort o' language?' Flossy said quickly.

Tommy shrugged his shoulders and then looked at the young man with anxiety in his eyes. 'Would yer want me ter be put in a kids' 'ome?' he asked.

'I 'eard they're quite nice,' Flossy told him kindly, 'an' besides, it wouldn't be fer long.'

'I don't care, I ain't goin',' Tommy said firmly.

'Well, yer can't stay 'ere wiv me, that's fer sure.'

'Why not? I could pay yer six bob.'

'I wouldn't let yer stay 'ere fer six quid.'

'I thought you was a kind bloke but yer just like all the rest,' Tommy growled as he got up quickly from the table. 'I don't care anyway. I'm gonna run away ter sea.'

'That's the biggest mistake you ever made finkin' I'm like everybody else, you ungrateful little sod,' Flossy replied angrily. 'I'm different, an' that's why yer can't stay 'ere.'

'I don't understand,' the lad said frowning.

'Sit down an' listen,' Flossy told him in a stern voice that surprised himself. 'You used ter live in this block. You remember the names I got called be'ind me back, an' ter me face as well at times. Pansy boy, big queer, Queeny. D'yer remember when that big bully Palfrey kicked me all the way up the turnin'?'

Tommy nodded. 'Yeah, I remember.'

'Well, I've lived a lot of it down, but if anyone knew you was stayin' 'ere I'd be 'ounded out o' the street.'

'But why?'

'The innocence o' the boy, it's really touchin',' Flossy groaned as his eyes went up to the ceiling. 'Just because.'

'Yer mean they'd fink you were interferin' wiv me?'

'Good Gawd, the penny's dropped at last,' the young man sighed.

'I'd tell 'em we were just friends,' Tommy replied.

'Yeah, an' you could say I was the King's muvver fer all they'd believe yer,' Flossy growled. 'Be sensible. Somebody would shop us an' I'd be put away fer 'arbourin' a juvenile or worse.'

'Don't worry, I'm off now,' Tommy said, getting up again. 'If yer get in trouble over last night I'll just tell 'em the trufe. It was very late when yer found me so yer fed me an' let me kip down on the floor.'

'Look, I can't sit 'ere arguin' all day,' Flossy told him sharply. 'Why don't yer go an' see Mrs Flannagan? She looked after yer last time. She'll know what ter do.'

'I'll fink about it,' Tommy replied nonchalantly.

''Ere, there's a few bob,' the young man said, reaching into his trouser pocket. 'Don't tell anyone I gave it to yer or they'll fink the worst.'

'Fanks, Flossy. I never called yer names.'

'No, yer never did.'

'Well, goodbye.'

'Cheerio, luvvy, an' fink about what I said,' Flossy urged him, tears coming to his eyes. 'Now piss off before yer get me all upset.'

Barney Schofield bought his morning paper in Dock Lane as usual and marched back at a quick pace. Good for the constitution, he reminded himself. Just like the barrack square drill. Guaranteed to blow away the cobwebs.

'Mornin', Mr Schofield,' Freda Irons called out to him as they passed at the corner of Milldyke Street.

'Mornin', em . . .' he mumbled.

Tommy Brindley came running past and Schofield stopped to watch his progress.

'Yer know who that was?' Ernie Walker called down. 'That was the Brindley kid.'

Barney Schofield glanced up at Ernie's window. 'The police told me the boy's gone AWOL. They should be informed at once.'

'Well, yer'd better go an' tell 'em then,' Ernie replied.

'Where did the boy come from?' Schofield called up.

'Gawd knows.'

Mary Enright came out of the last block in the street and

walked quickly towards Dock Lane. 'Mornin', Mr Schofield.'

'Mornin', em . . .' he mumbled.

'I've just seen Tommy Brindley,' she told him.

'Me too. Where did 'e come from?'

'Out o' my block,' Mary replied. ''E was standin' on the front step when I came down the stairs.'

'Somebody's bin 'idin' 'im out, I've no doubt,' Schofield said sharply. 'Capital offence, 'arbourin' deserters.'

'I don't fink 'e's actually desertin',' Mary remarked, grinning at the man's flushed face. 'More like 'e was runnin' away.'

'Same meat, different gravy,' Schofield said quickly. 'The police should be informed.'

'Well, you've got more time than I 'ave,' she replied. 'You tell 'em.'

'Don't fink I won't.'

'Nuffing would surprise me where you're concerned, yer silly ole git,' Mary mumbled to herself as she left the turning.

Joe Sandford was coming home from his night shift and he nodded pleasantly to Schofield as he passed him. 'Mornin', Mr Schofield.'

'Mornin', Sandford. Just seen the Brindley boy. Leggin' it from the turnin'.'

Joe was tired and eager to get to bed. 'Is that right?' he replied. 'Yer'd better tell the police then.'

Barney watched him go into the block. 'Good God Almighty, am I expected ter do everybody's biddin'?' he called out.

'Someone's gotta,' Joe called back as he trudged up the stairs.

Flossy stepped out into the sunshine and strode off down

the street. 'Nice mornin',' he said on passing.

'The Brindley boy's just run out o' the turnin',' Schofield told him.

'Oh my good Gawd. Better let the coppers know then,' Flossy replied as he hurried off.

Emily Drew from A block had been having a lengthy chat with Ada Champion by the communal bins, and as she traipsed round to the front of the building she saw Tommy Brindley come out of Flossy's ground-floor flat. Without more ado she hurried back just as Ada was emerging from the alley. ''Ere, what d'yer fink?' she said in a shocked voice. 'I just seen the Brindley lad comin' out o' Flossy Chandler's.'

'Oh my good Gawd,' Ada gasped. 'Surely 'e ain't bin keepin' the boy there.'

'Looks that way.'

'It's disgustin'. I'll 'ave a word or two ter say to 'im when I take that suit of 'is back ternight,' Ada growled.

Emily Drew was in the habit of calling on her special cronies for elevenses and on that particular morning she had much to say. Ruth Palfrey was outraged when she heard the news, as was Aggie Dolan. 'My ole man'll kill the dirty git,' Aggie raved.

'So will my Alan,' Ruth scowled. ''E nearly done it last time.'

'Wait till I tell my ole man,' Janice Miller cut in. 'My Richie can't stand the dirty little git.'

The women of A block were united in deciding that Flossy Chandler should be dealt with severely and they fumed as they sipped their tea noisily.

When the news of Meg Johnson's murder reached the church Father O'Shea was momentarily shocked into sobriety and he agonised over what to do. He had a busy parish to minister to and he knew he had neglected parts of it. 'I tried, Sister, I really did,' he lamented piously. 'I even played football with the children there. I spoke to people and made myself known and offered my services, but my rewards were very scant. I felt as though I was making a little progress nevertheless, but now this terrible thing has happened. I blame myself. I should have persevered.'

Sister Claudine was a forgiving soul, and being acquainted with the reverend father's weaknesses she smiled sympathetically. 'You did your best,' she replied. 'No one could ask more.'

'I was brought in to save souls but I've neglected the vast majority of my flock,' he wailed, 'allowing the most hopeless reprobates to take up my time.'

Sister Claudine was all too aware of the fact that Father O'Shea spent most of his time battling the same vice as the heathens at the Woolpack and other dens of iniquity but she smiled again. 'It's never too late,' she told him in a quiet voice.

'No, you're right,' he said stoutly. 'I'll try again. I'll beard the lion. Today I'll go to Milldyke Street and offer my condolences to the poor people there for the terrible crime perpetrated on their doorstep.'

The sister nodded her head slowly. 'And in doing so you'll find great comfort I feel sure. I will pray for you, Father.'

At eleven thirty that morning Father O'Shea stopped off to wish the landlord of the Bell a good day, and two hours later he emerged feeling that there was something he had to do. The feeling nagged at him and he went into the church gardens to ponder, only to fall asleep within minutes.

Alan Palfrey had been primed by his wife Ruth after he got

home that evening and he went out to call on Richie Miller. The two of them went to see Mickey Dolan who had also been fired up.

'Let's work somefing out,' Richie said.

'Yeah, up the Woolpack,' Mickey replied, licking his lips.

Armed with a pint apiece the three men laid their plans.

'We'll get 'im ternight,' Mickey urged them.

'We'll get rid o' that dirty poof once an' fer all,' Richie replied.

'I should 'ave done the job prop'ly last time,' Alan growled.

'We'll give 'im a good pastin' then we'll strip the dirty git an' 'ang 'im up from the lamppost wiv a placard tied round 'im,' Mickey said malevolently. 'Time we're done wiv 'im, 'e won't 'ave the gall ter show 'is face round 'ere again.'

Father O'Shea went back to the vestry feeling very down at heart. 'I should have been a publican or a farrier,' he groaned to himself. 'As it is I play at saving souls and I can't even save my own. I'm doomed. Destined to be laughed at and reviled and exiled for ever from the parish. Why didn't I stay on the lemonade?'

Sister Claudine looked very cheerful when she came back from the mothers' meeting. 'Well, Father, did you minister to the poor souls in Milldyke Street?' she asked him.

'May the good Lord be praised, Sister,' he said in a loud voice on finally being jogged into remembering.

'May He indeed.'

'Tonight I will go to Milldyke Street and endeavour to practise my calling, Sister.'

'Good for you,' she replied, feeling very slightly guilty for thinking that he would get no further than the Woolpack.

Chapter Thirty-Five

Ada Champion took the white suit down from the back of the kitchen door and examined it. 'I'm sure the bloody fing's shrunk,' she remarked.

'Well, what else did yer expect,' Sid replied, 'puttin' it in the bloody copper, yer silly mare.'

''Ow else was I gonna get the black marks off it?' she retorted. 'Anyway, at least it's clean.'

'Fat lot o' good that'll be if it don't fit 'im,' Sid mumbled caustically from behind his paper.

'Well, we'll soon find out,' Ada told him. 'I'm takin' it down now.'

'If it 'as shrunk an' 'e gives yer an ear'ole bashin' don't expect me ter come ter yer rescue,' Sid said quickly. 'Yer shouldn't 'ave volunteered ter clean it in the first place. What's wrong wiv 'im doin' it 'imself? 'E washes 'is own curtains an' sheets. I've seen 'im 'angin' 'em out round the back.'

'Shut yer noise, yer grumpy ole git,' Ada growled as she walked down the passage.

Flossy looked pleased when he opened his door and saw the suit. 'Fanks very much, Ada. It's come up like new,' he said with a happy smile.

'Yer better save yer fanks till yer try it on,' she cautioned

361

him as she passed it over. 'I fink it's shrunk a bit.'

'It was a bit loose on me anyway,' he replied. 'I'll 'ang it up in the bedroom.'

Ada gave him a steely look. 'I've 'eard from someone that you've 'ad that Brindley boy stayin' 'ere,' she said abruptly.

The colour drained from Flossy's face. He looked over her shoulder at the landing to make sure no one was listening, then he put his hand up to his chest. 'Ada, as God is my judge there was nuffing goin' on,' he replied. 'Last night I 'eard a noise on the stairs an' I got worried, 'specially after what's 'appened. Anyway I took a look an' found young Tommy curled up outside 'is old flat. What was I ter do? The poor mite looked ill. I gave 'im somefing to eat an' drink, made a bed on the floor an' then I gave 'im some breakfast this mornin'. I told 'im 'e'd 'ave ter go ter the police or the welfare but 'e wouldn't listen. 'E's 'opped it. Gawd knows where, but I couldn't stop 'im.'

'Yer should 'ave knocked at my door,' Ada told him. 'I'd 'ave took 'im in.'

'Maybe I should, but I wasn't finkin' straight,' Flossy said sighing. 'All I could see was 'is poor little face starin' up at me like a scared rabbit.'

'Anyway, I thought I'd better put yer on yer guard,' Ada warned him. 'Some people round 'ere can't keep their traps shut fer five minutes.'

'Well fanks, Ada, an' fanks fer doin' me suit,' he said with a big smile.

As soon as he closed the door on his neighbour Flossy took the suit from the hanger and examined it. It was certainly spotless and well pressed, he thought. Better try it on though.

At seven o'clock the angry trio left the Woolpack and made

their way back to the Buildings. They had managed to scrounge a coil of rope and the landlord had provided a square of cardboard and a black crayon.

'Now remember what we agreed,' Alan Palfrey said burping loudly. 'No one's gonna talk us out of it, an' if anybody tries ter stop us we'll sort 'em out good an' proper. That dirty little queer's gotta be taught a lesson 'e won't ferget.'

The three men marched along to the end block and were immediately spotted by Ernie Walker who got up quickly and knocked on the Sandfords' front door.

'Joe's gone ter work,' Stella told him.

'It looks like trouble,' Ernie remarked. 'I bet they're after Flossy Chandler.'

'What for?'

'Didn't you 'ear about it? Flossy's bin up ter no good wiv the Brindley kid,' the old man explained. 'That Drew woman told me.'

'Yer don't wanna take no notice of 'er,' Stella replied quickly. 'She's a troublemaker.'

'There's no smoke wivout fire, that's what I always say,' Ernie told her firmly. 'Anyway I'm goin' back ter keep an eye out.'

Curtains had been pulled back and people stared down from open windows. Children had been called in and one or two people stood chatting together at the block entrances. Amy and Kate stood looking down from the landing anxiously. 'I wish Pat was 'ere,' Kate sighed.

'Someone's gotta stop 'em or they'll kill 'im,' Amy said urgently. 'That Mickey Dolan's a nasty bit o' work.'

'What can we do?' Kate fretted.

'I'm gonna knock an' see if Jack Dennis is in,' Amy told her. ''E ain't frightened o' the likes o' them.'

HARRY BOWLING

'I'm gonna run up ter Dock Lane an' phone the police,'
Kate said quickly.

'It's too late!' Amy gasped. 'Look!'

They stared down at the sad spectacle of an utterly terrified
Flossy being dragged into the street by Palfrey and Dolan
with Miller bringing up the rear, carrying the rope over his
shoulder. The victim had his white suit on, the trouser bottoms
two inches above his ankles and his coat sleeves halfway up
his arms. Kate ran down the stairs and along the turning only
to be stopped by Janice Miller and Ruth Palfrey. 'Where d'yer
fink you're goin'?' Janice asked her nastily.

'It's none o' your business,' Kate replied with spirit.

'We're makin' it our business,' Aggie Dolan said as she
stepped forward.

Kate realised that it was hopeless and she looked past
them to see that a crowd had gathered around the men.

'What yer gonna do wiv 'im?' Freda Irons asked.

'We're gonna take 'im on the bombsite an' work 'im
over, then we're gonna string 'im up,' Dolan snarled.

'You can't do that,' Ada shouted.

'Oh can't we? Now you listen 'ere, muvver. You or
nobody else 'ad better try an' stop us,' Palfrey shouted back.

'Leave me alone. I ain't done nuffing,' Flossy pleaded.

'Shut yer dirty trap,' Dolan told him.

'Leave 'im alone, yer bloody great bullies,' Mary Enright
shouted at them.

Everyone from the Buildings seemed to be out in the
street now, even the reclusive Mr and Mrs Thomas. People
were milling around the ever-growing circle with the terrified figure of Flossy Chandler cowering in the centre.

'String 'im up,' someone called out.

'Shut yer poxy noise, you,' came the retort.

'Give the dirty little git what for,' another urged them.

364

'Yeah, give it to 'im.'

Flossy was grabbed by the arms and frog-marched along the turning, his face white with fear and trembling uncontrollably. 'Someone 'elp me!' he cried out desperately.

Tommy Brindley had spent the day at Blackheath, walking across the wide expanse of grass and strolling down the twisting village streets. At midday he went to the coffee stall on the edge of the heath and bought a hot meat pie and a lemonade with the money Flossy had given him; then later, when he grew tired of tramping around, he sprawled out on the warm grass with the hot sun on his face. In the distance he could see the gates of Greenwich Park, and he suddenly remembered that his father had once taken him through those gates and down the steep hill to where the river curved in a wide bend and huge ships moored up at the wharves. He climbed wearily to his feet and retraced their journey, down the long straight road to General Wolf's proud statue by the old observatory walls, gazing down at sunlight glittering on the surface of the Thames and bleaching the white stone walls and colonnades of the Maritime Museum. That was the place they had made for, his father and him. Through the high-ceilinged rooms with portraits hanging and glass cases full of treasures, the blood-stained uniform of the fleet admiral Lord Nelson and artefacts from a heroic bygone age.

The museum guide, dressed in a black suit and a peaked cap, was standing beneath a huge painting of a naval engagement, and people gathered around him as he invoked the glory of the past. 'The battle of Trafalgar took place on October the twenty-first, eighteen hundred and five,' he boomed out. 'The British fleet, consisting of twenty-seven ships of the line, took on the Franco-Spanish force of thirty-three ships, and the battle commenced at noon near

Cape Trafalgar. By five o'clock it was over. The enemy had been routed, but during that afternoon Lord Nelson had received his mortal wound, a musket shot fired from the main top of the *Redoubtable*. Admiral Lord Nelson was given a state funeral and a memorial was erected in his honour in what is now known as Trafalgar Square.'

The young lad had slipped into the hall unnoticed and he stood behind the visitors, hoping he wouldn't be challenged. He walked along behind them as they converged on another relic of the island's history, and now the guide was describing the lives and feats of the naval heroes Collingwood, Rodney, Hawke and Howe.

'Yer Lord Nelson was the best o' the lot,' one elderly man said to his wife loud enough for Tommy to hear. 'One eye, one arm an' one ambition.'

'Shh, be quiet, Bert,' she reprimanded him.

People looked round and the young lad decided it was time to leave. Out in the warm sunshine once more he made his way down to the water's edge, past small shops selling souvenirs and the vast hull of the Cutty Sark. The tide was turning and in midstream he watched the timber-laden ships ride at anchor. One day he would be a seaman and sail the oceans looking for adventure, but now he was tired and dreaded the thought of sleeping on the street. Jimmy's mother had given him a bed for the night once and she might do so again, if he asked her nicely.

Father O'Shea reached the Woolpack, to the dismay of the landlord who was tired of subsidising the priest's drinking habits.

'I can't stop, but I will partake of a small whisky, just to fortify myself for the task in hand you understand,' Father O'Shea said with a smile.

'One small whisky, on the house, Father, as yer've got fings ter do,' the landlord said pointedly.

True to his word the priest left the pub and made his way along Dock Lane, unsure as to the proper way to approach the poor sinners of Milldyke Buildings. Door-knocking had never appealed to him, but he did quite favour the public fire and brimstone approach that left no one in doubt of what was in store for sinners who did not repent. A public sermon at this time of night might not be received very well though, he realised, and it might have the effect of undoing anything he had achieved so far, which was very little, he had to admit.

Another visitor to Milldyke Buildings had arrived a few minutes earlier but hesitated to enter the turning when he saw the frenzied activity taking place there. Watching cautiously from the corner, Tommy Brindley soon became aware that Flossy was being persecuted. He caught a glimpse of the terrified man and saw the rope slung over another man's broad shoulder. Immediately he remembered the film he had seen recently, in which a horse thief was hanged from a tree. People protested in the film, but it made no difference, the thief was still strung up. They were going to hang Flossy, and it was all his fault. With his heart threatening to burst from panic and sheer desperation Tommy ran towards the phone box, straight into the frocked figure with untidy ginger hair and bleary eyes.

'Whoah there. What's the big hurry?' Father O'Shea asked as he clutched the lad.

'Let me go! I gotta tell the police!' Tommy shouted.

'And what for, might I ask?'

'They're gonna lynch Flossy an' it wasn't 'is fault. It was me. I went there of me own accord,' Tommy blurted out breathlessly.

'Show me,' the priest said, taking the boy by the arm in a strong grip.

They reached the street and Father O'Shea held up his arms to the heavens. 'Halt! In the name of Holy Mary, Mother of God!' he shouted in a deep voice.

For an instant there was complete silence, then Mickey Dolan stepped forward. 'Stand aside, Farver. This don't concern you.'

The priest's eyes flared. Coaxing and cajoling were arts he found hard to master, but thumping the tub of the Lord and channelling His unadulterated wrath was what he excelled in. He was stirred and roused, as if the dragon had once again forced contemplation of forbidden pleasures of the flesh upon his mind. Confrontation was the clarion call and he roared aloud. 'Stand aside? And who are you to tell a messenger of God to stand aside? Are you he who spills sin from the cracks of the night?'

'This man interfered wiv a kid an' we're gonna teach 'im a lesson,' Palfrey cut in.

'Oh ho! So now there are two,' the priest said in a mocking voice. 'Step forward, filth spawn of the pit, if you dare. Tell me with your tongues of demons that you are prepared to take a man's life to placate your black, evil souls. Answer me, or be forever ripped apart in hell.'

'Who said anyfing about killin' 'im?' Aggie Dolan called out.

'Come the harlot, a whorish maw spread open to the slime of Satan,' the priest boomed out. 'Holy Mother of God! Forgive these sinners.'

'All right, enough o' yer preachin', Farver,' Dolan said as he faced him. 'We got business ter do.'

'Take one more step and I'll visit the molten wrath of the

Lord upon your sorry head,' Father O'Shea told him with blazing eyes.

Tommy pushed his way to the fore. 'Flossy never done anyfing, 'cept feed me an' let me sleep there fer one night,' he shouted, his voice shaking with emotion.

'You heard the boy. Release this unfortunate at once,' the priest commanded.

'The boy's lyin'. The nonce must 'ave give 'im money ter shut 'im up,' Dolan growled. 'Out o' my way, Farver.'

As he stepped forward Dolan was smashed down by a massive punch that shot out swiftly and accurately.

'May the Lord sanction and give me strength,' Father O'Shea said, raising his eyes to the evening sky as he shook his stinging fist.

Aggie Dolan had bent down to comfort her husband and she looked up with eyes of flint. 'Yer can't take us all on,' she snarled. 'Not one man on 'is own.'

'What about two though?' Jack Dennis said calmly as he stepped forward and stood at the priest's side.

'I wondered 'ow long it'd take 'im ter do somefing,' Muriel Dennis said with pride.

'We still outnumber yer,' Palfrey growled.

'What about takin' on a woman, 'cos that's what yer'll 'ave ter do,' Kate said as she moved out of the crowd.

Ada Champion, Freda Irons and Mary Enright went to Kate's side.

'I might be an old woman but I'm still more than a match fer you lot, an' yer busybody ole women,' Ada said with passion.

Flossy stood with shoulders bent, his face chalk-white. 'Why don't yer listen ter the boy? 'E's tellin' the trufe,' he gasped.

Suddenly the loud voice of the ex-sergeant major

boomed out. 'There's a time fer prayin' an' a time fer battle. Ignore the priest. Take him away. Tie him to the gun wheel. Flay 'im within an inch of 'is life.'

The tirade was heard by everyone present, but far from inciting them it had the opposite effect. Barney Schofield had finally stepped across the thin red line, and in that eerie knowledge all present were stunned to silence. They turned to stare at the solitary figure twitching in his madness.

''Elp me get 'im in,' Aggie said to Ruth Palfrey as Mickey Dolan started to come round.

'C'mon, Richie, it's all over,' Janice Miller told her husband.

The crowd moved away to allow Flossy Chandler room and he trudged along to the end block, looking a sorry sight in his soiled white suit.

'You'll be all right now, son,' Ada told him.

'Course yer will,' Freda added.

'Look at me. Just look at me,' the young man groaned. 'I look like a music 'all turn.'

'Yeah, well I fink yer brought the 'ouse down,' Ada said smiling.

The night was balmy, with a moon breaking through scant cloud. It shone down over a quiet Bermondsey and lit up the old buildings. Tommy Brindley slept soundly next to Jimmy, his belly full, his fears gone till morning. In the quiet living room, Kate waited, anxious now that the hour was late.

At ten o'clock Pat tapped lightly on her door, tired and drained but eager to see her, to kiss her and hold her tight.

She stood back in the darkness of the passage and as she closed the door he took her in his arms. The kiss was soft and tender, then as she moulded herself to him it became intense.

Chapter Thirty-Six

The street outside was empty and quiet now as the two young people sat holding hands across the kitchen table.

'It was terrible,' Kate said with a shudder as she finished telling him about what had happened earlier that evening. 'I really thought they were gonna kill 'im. I was prayin' yer'd show up an' put a stop to it.'

'From what you've just told me it seems you all managed things quite well on your own,' Pat remarked with a smile. 'Is Tommy all right?'

'Yeah, 'e's sleepin' like a top,' she replied. 'Will 'e be able ter stay 'ere fer a while?'

'I don't see why not. Anyway, I'll try and get things sorted out tomorrow,' he told her.

Kate smiled at him. 'I'm glad yer called ternight, Pat. I've bin finkin' about yer all day.'

'Me too,' he replied, squeezing her hands. 'There I was, in the middle of an important meeting with the superintendent at the West End station, and all I could think about was you.'

'I bet yer didn't even give me a thought,' she laughed, looking down at his strong hands resting over hers.

Pat smiled, his eyes twinkling, then he let go and eased back in his chair. 'It was a discouraging meeting anyway – I didn't learn much.'

'You look tired,' Kate told him. 'I saved yer some stew. Eat first an' then yer can tell me all about it.'

The young policeman's eyes lit up when Kate placed the hot meal in front of him and he looked up at her with amusement as she put two very thick slices of bread beside his plate.

'The kids love dippin' bread in their stew,' she said almost apologetically.

'So do I,' he grinned.

She busied herself while he ate, occasionally casting discreet glances at him, and then when he had cleared his plate she faced him across the table and smiled. 'Any room fer a sweet? I've got some apple pie. I made it meself.'

He nodded. 'Yes, please. The stew was perfect.'

Kate went into the scullery and came back with a wedge of apple pie covered in steaming custard on a small plate. 'I'll make some tea, or would yer prefer coffee?' she asked him.

'Tea'll be fine,' he replied.

Kate hummed happily to herself as she waited on the kettle. His embrace in the dark passage had set her aglow and she remembered that delicious feeling when his arms went around her. She had been nervous and shaking after the confrontation in the street, but now she felt desired, completely safe in his arms, and she wanted him to know it.

Pat leaned back and rubbed his midriff. 'Kate, I have to say that was the best meal I can remember.'

'Yer don't eat well, I can tell,' she told him with motherly severity.

'Does it show?' he asked.

'No, just intuition.'

He gently caught her arm as she passed. 'I really appreciate the meal, Kate,' he said sincerely.

She put her arm around his shoulder. 'Why don't yer sit over in the armchair an' make yerself comfortable,' she urged him.

'Look, I'd better be goin' soon,' he said quickly.

'It's late. Why don't yer stay? It's no 'ardship, really,' Kate said with an encouraging smile.

'I'm putting you out, especially now that you've got young Tommy staying here,' he reminded her, 'and besides, I'm most likely giving you a bad name with your neighbours.'

Kate's smile grew wider. 'After what's 'appened ternight I don't fink anybody'll be too worried about what's goin' on 'ere. Anyway it's none o' their business. I want yer ter stay ternight. Yer look all in. Get a good night's sleep.'

'If you're really sure you don't mind.'

Kate went over to the sideboard and picked up a small paper bag. 'That's fer you,' she said brightly.

'A razor. You bought me a razor.'

'There's a packet o' blades there too.'

He stood up and pulled her to him. 'I think I'm falling in love with you, Kate,' he said huskily.

The kiss was tender, and she wanted it to last for ever, but with a supreme effort she broke away. 'I'd better get the tea,' she said quickly.

They sat facing each other as the night came on, with only the muted sound of a tug whistle to disturb the quietness. They sipped their tea and then Pat put his cup down at his feet as he saw the look of expectancy in her large hazel eyes. 'I told you about the meeting this morning over at West End Central,' he began. 'The superintendent there let me go through the files and then I spent this afternoon and early evening checking up on a few of the statements on the Gus Wesley killing. Everywhere I went it was the same thing. A complete brick wall. The super had warned me about the response I'd get, but I had to try. No one's talking, Kate. The street girls are running scared and when I did manage to have a word with one or two of them and mentioned the name Nan Lynn they scurried off. A local grass told the police that he thought the Lynn woman had been looked after by some of the girls and then spirited out of the area. According to him Nan Lynn has become a danger to the criminals who are running the area. It's a sophisticated organisation headed by the Mendoza brothers and they control all the prostitution and gambling in Soho. As it happens there's a big clean-up campaign been promised by the new Chief Constable, and very soon Soho's going to be turned upside down. Every dubious establishment will be raided and there are a lot of arrests in the offing. The Mendozas know this and they want to get to Nan Lynn before the police find her.'

'But what 'as she done ter them?' Kate asked him.

'Nothing at the moment, but once she's brought into the station she'll be put under a lot of pressure. Apparently there's a prostitute serving a long sentence in Holloway for manslaughter and she's bargaining for some remission. She's already made a statement that Nan Lynn was present when her boyfriend Spanish Joe killed the pimp. Once the police confront her with this information she'll know that the game's up. Either she co-operates or she'll be charged as an accessary with the prospect of a long spell behind bars. The organisation realises that if she talks it could mean them being put away instead for a very long time. The simple truth is, Kate, if they get to her first they'll most certainly kill her.'

'That's terrible,' Kate almost whispered.

'Regardless of all the implications, though, it's vital we get Annie and Meg's killer as soon as possible,' Pat replied. 'The trouble is we've got so little to go on.'

'By the way, did yer talk ter Briscoe?' Kate asked.

Pat nodded. 'He told me he was on business in the street on Sunday morning but left around noon and spent the rest of the day at his home.'

'Where does 'e live?' Kate asked.

'Rotherhithe.'

'What did yer fink of 'im?'

'I can't put my finger on it but there's something about the man that doesn't ring true,' Pat said thoughtfully.

'Do yer fink 'e could be the killer?' she asked.

The detective was silent for a while, then he shifted in his chair. 'Briscoe's dark and swarthy so I suppose he could be taken for a Spaniard,' he remarked. 'He's only been with Harris Estates for three years, which could place him at Poplar during the Blitz, but he told me that he'd been living in Bermondsey for years and used to work in the office of an engineering firm that was destroyed in the early days of the Blitz.'

'Wouldn't the labour exchange be able ter confirm that 'e actually worked there?' Kate asked helpfully.

'I've already tried,' Pat said smiling. 'They lost most of their records when the exchange was bombed. Anyway, during the interview I asked Briscoe about his habit of calling on the tenants at odd times, and he explained that he has other properties to look after and he fits his time in at weekends to allow him time off during the week. He told me he preferred it that way. He said it was easier to catch the tenants at home at weekends.'

'Amy told me that 'e's separated from 'is wife,' Kate cut in.

'Yeah, he mentioned it to me,' Pat replied. 'Apparently she left him before the war.'

'Briscoe's one person Meg would 'ave let in,' Kate reminded him.

'I actually saw him at his office this morning,' Pat went on, 'and while he was talking I noticed a small china ornament on the windowledge behind him. It was a beautiful thing, about six inches high, a matador holding a cape and doing a pass with a bull. It was quite lifelike and the colours were outstanding. I remarked on it and Briscoe looked a bit embarrassed. He told me that it originally belonged to one of the tenants who had died and that the estate manager had given him permission to keep it when it was time to dispose of the tenant's belongings. He said that it wasn't the sort of thing the Salvation Army would be interested in, as they only wanted furniture and bedding. No doubt he was telling the truth, but I wondered why he had chosen that particular ornament? Could it be a reminder of his past, perhaps? That would put Briscoe in a whole new light.'

Jenny suddenly called out in her sleep and Kate went in to settle her, and while she was gone the young policeman sat in deep thought. That morning Chief Superintendent Baxter had told him to report back to Dockhead police station at five o'clock for a meeting with the murder investigation team but he had been too busy in Soho. He knew he would have to face flak the next morning but at the moment he was more concerned with that day's events. He had approached one young street girl who looked no more than sixteen and she had gone as white as a sheet when he mentioned Nan Lynn. She had warned him that it was dangerous to mention her name and then run off. He had had the same reaction when he tried Spanish Joe's name, which at least told him that the mystery man was known in the area. In the coffee houses, bars and shops the response was the same, a shake of the head and a frightened glance around. It seemed as though the organisation had everyone running scared, but someone out there had to come forward sooner or later: someone wronged, or with a grudge, who could supply vital information on either Nan Lynn or Spanish Joe.

Kate came back to the kitchen and sat down facing him. 'She's all right. I think she was 'avin' a bad dream.'

'It's understandable, considering what's been happening around here,' Pat replied.

Kate leaned forward in the chair with her hands clasped in her lap. 'I was finkin' terday about when I found Meg,' she remarked. 'The front door was open. Wouldn't the murderer 'ave closed it after 'im? I did, instinctively.'

'I gave it some thought,' Pat replied, 'but we have to try and put ourselves in his position. The killer had tricked his way in and from what you've told me Meg Johnson would have replaced the bolts.'

'She did when I called in,' Kate said quickly.

'OK, so it was her custom,' Pat went on. 'It was Sunday evening and from what we know Meg Johnson very rarely went out on Sundays. Her next-door neighbour Mrs Smedley hears footsteps on the stairs, Meg's door opening and shutting and then the bolts being replaced. Later she hears the door opening and shutting again, but no bolts being shot. That tells her that Meg has gone out, and her curiosity is roused. She might well look out of the window to see if it really is her neighbour going out. We're assuming that this is what the killer was thinking.'

'So after killin' Meg 'e silently slides the bolts an' opens the door, then creeps out of 'er flat,' Kate finished for him.

'And Mrs Smedley would have no reason to suppose anyone had left,' Pat said raising his eyebrows.

Kate nodded her head slowly. 'If we're assumin' right it means that whoever killed Meg knew about 'er 'abits an' those of 'er next-door neighbour too.'

'I'm certain in my mind that Mrs Johnson was murdered by someone she knew very well, someone she would have had no hesitation in letting in,' Pat replied with conviction.

'Someone who lives in the Buildin's, or Briscoe,' Kate said wide-eyed, seeing him nod. 'It's scary. I've gone all cold.'

The young policeman gave her a reassuring smile. 'We'll get him soon, don't worry,' he urged her.

Kate wanted him to hold her, kiss her and make her feel safe once more, but he looked exhausted and his eyes were heavy-lidded. 'Look, I'll make us anuvver cup o' tea an' then yer must get some rest,' she told him firmly.

The chairbed was narrow but softly sprung and comfortable and sleep came easily. He was there again, in the camp that defied all ideas of humanity. All around him starved and tortured souls stared at him pleadingly with hollow eyes, their shrivelled bodies twisted on the ground as he walked past to the hut. He could see him, the monster responsible for all the horror, the monster of his endlessly recurring nightmares. He reached down for him as he had so often before, but as before his arms were like lead and he was transfixed, his anger rising up to choke him as he saw the leer of defiance, the yellow teeth and the crudely shaven head. The inmates were gathering, pointing and nodding as they shuffled slowly across the yard, and he was behind the hut, staring down at the bowed figure with the revolver clasped in his hand. The barrel was pointed at the back of the monster's head but his trigger would not move and he screamed out at the sky in sheer desperation.

His head was bathed in sweat and his heart was pounding furiously but as he woke he threw his arms around the sweet-smelling body and let his head rest on the warm soft breasts. Her voice was a reassuring whisper and slowly the thumping in his chest subsided.

'You must 'ave bin dreamin',' she said as she held him to her. 'I 'eard yer shout out in yer sleep.'

He could feel her fingers caressing his wet hair and neck and he closed his eyes for a moment to clear his fevered mind. 'I'm sorry, Kate, I was having a nightmare,' he told her quietly. 'I hope I didn't wake the kids.'

Kate smiled, her white even teeth flashing in the darkness. 'It's all right. Go back ter sleep,' she coaxed him as he lifted his face to her.

He lay down on his back with one arm behind his head, watching her as she tightened the cord of her dressing gown.

'Are you OK, Pat?' she asked quietly.

His answer sent a shiver of pleasure through her whole body. 'You're a beautiful woman, Kate. I've been wanting to tell you from the first day we met.'

She looked down at him, feeling the strong urge to let herself go and smother his body with kisses, but instead she stepped back a pace and gave him a smile full of promise. 'Go back ter sleep,' she told him. 'I'll see you in the mornin'.'

Chapter Thirty-Seven

Friday morning had dragged on interminably and Kate sighed with relief when the factory whistle finally sounded. The day was warm and sunny with a slight breeze moving the air, and as she made her way home she saw a car draw in to the kerb beside her.

'Jump in an' I'll run yer 'ome,' Spiv Copeland said cheerfully.

'It's all right, it's only a short distance,' Kate replied.

'Jump in an' save yer legs,' he persisted.

She slipped into the passenger seat, quickly adjusting her dress but not before he had caught a glimpse of her thigh. He made no attempt to drive off. 'I've not seen anyfing of yer, Kate, but Amy told me about you findin' that poor ole gel's body. It must 'ave been a terrible shock for yer.'

Kate nodded. 'Yeah, it was 'orrible. I keep seein' 'er face in me mind.'

Spiv slipped the car into gear and eased up on the clutch. 'I've missed seein' yer, Kate,' he told her as he pulled away from the kerb. 'I 'ad some gear but I couldn't bring it round, not wiv the boys in blue buzzin' about. They know me face too well.'

Kate glanced at him with a smile. 'Still the same ole Spiv.'

'Yeah, still in the market fer a nice little bargain.'

'Did Amy tell yer Fred's gone back to 'is wife?' Kate asked as they drove along Dock Lane.

Spiv nodded without taking his eyes off the road. 'She deserves better,' he said quietly. 'I'd put my cap in the ring, if I wasn't otherwise engaged.'

'You courtin'?'

'No, but I'm lookin' in anuvver direction.'

'Oh?'

'Come on, Kate, yer know what I mean,' he said quickly as he pulled up on the corner of Milldyke Street. 'I've still got the sweats over you. I fink about yer all the time. I want yer ter come out wiv me one night, say yer will.'

She sighed as she reached for the door handle. 'I can't, Len. Yer know the score.'

'I don't. That's just it,' he replied. 'OK, I know what yer said, but I put it down ter yer marriage problems. I thought yer'd change yer mind once yer sorted fings out.'

'I told yer at the beginnin' me marriage was over an' done wiv,' she answered firmly. 'It's just that I don't feel the way you do. I like yer a lot, Len, yer know I do, but that's as far as it goes.'

He looked at her with anxious eyes. 'Amy tells me that yer've bin gettin' cosy wiv one o' the 'tecs.'

Kate stared back at him. 'Amy tends ter dramatise everyfing,' she said sharply.

'So it's not true then?'

'I've gotta go, the kids'll be expectin' me,' she told him.

'Well, is it?'

'Is it what?'

'True about what Amy said?'

'It's none o' your business, Len,' she said with irritation in her voice. 'But if yer must know, yes, I 'ave bin gettin' cosy wiv this detective, as yer put it.'

Spiv Copeland shook his head slowly. 'A 'tec of all people.'

'Detective or not, 'e's a nice feller,' Kate said defensively.

'Don't expect me ter give up on yer, Kate,' he told her with narrowed eyes.

She slipped out of the car. 'Fanks fer the ride, Len. I'll be seein' yer.'

'Yer can bet on it,' he replied.

Kate walked into the street, observed by Ernie Walker, who was in his usual position, staring down from his open window.

That morning Superintendent Baxter was waiting impatiently. 'Where did you get to yesterday?' he said angrily as Pat Cassidy answered his summons.

'I'm sorry, sir, but I got a bit tied up in Soho.'

'This is your manor, sergeant, not Soho,' Baxter reprimanded him.

'I was following up a lead and meeting with the head of division there, as you were aware,' Pat reminded him.

'Don't you get on your high horse with me,' the superintendent said furiously. 'I wanted you back here last night. We had a de-briefing, in case you've forgotten. If we're not careful this murder investigation is going to come to a full stop. We should be pulling people in, putting the pressure on, making a few waves.'

Pat looked hard at his superior officer. 'Granted, sir, but where do we start? Who do we pull in? So far all the statements taken and all the follow-ups have led us nowhere. If you'll pardon me, we'd be better employed following up positive leads.'

'Like swanning about up West, I suppose.'

'If that's where the break's going to come from, then yes.'

'Now you listen to me,' Baxter said impatiently. 'I've been put in charge here on a permanent basis as from yesterday, and from now on things will be done my way. In future I want a daily report on your progress. I want you and your team to go over all those statements and come up with something. That's where the break will come, not from trying to find this mysterious Spanish Joe. Once you've cross-checked everything, I want you to start bringing in a few of those with unsafe alibis for further questioning. I'm giving you two more weeks, and if there's no progress by then I'm going to request help from the Yard. Now get to it, sergeant.'

Pat left the office feeling totally frustrated at not being able to make the superintendent see sense. Going over the statements yet again was a pure waste of time. Another day or two with a free hand and something would come up, he felt sure. The young prostitute in Lisle Street was worth another try and there were still a few visits to be made in the seedy quarter of London's West End. As it stood, valuable time was being wasted.

'Well, if it's not Sherlock himself,' a voice called out.

Pat turned to see Sergeant Bill Murphy grinning at him. 'I've just been talking with our new boss,' he growled. 'What's this about him taking over?'

'Didn't you hear? Tom Cox has applied to retire on medical grounds,' Murphy told him.

'We should talk. Time for a drink?' Pat asked.

'Surely.'

The two policemen made themselves comfortable in the saloon bar of the Bell and Murphy smiled across the table as he picked up his drink. 'We've got a good result at

Tooley Street,' he said. 'Things have quietened down considerably and Baxter's very pleased. Not so with you though, by all accounts.'

Pat pulled a face. 'The super's a pain,' he scowled. 'We're now confined to cross-checking the statements again. What a way to do business. You're well out of it, Bill.'

'Yeah, it seems that way,' Murphy replied. 'Take my advice, Pat, and nick a few days' leave. You've got plenty due. It's holiday weekend anyway. Let the team do the spade work for a change. You look like you're ready for a break.'

'I might just do that,' Pat told him, taking his notepad from his pocket.

Early that evening the people of Milldyke Buildings saw a horse and cart come into the turning and pull up outside the last block. A short while later Flossy emerged from his flat and stood fussing as the men loaded his furniture and personal belongings on to the cart. Ada Champion came out of the block and walked over to him. 'I 'ope there's no 'ard feelin's about me ballsin' up yer suit, Flossy,' she said.

'It's all right, luv, don't upset yerself. White suits don't look good on me anyway,' he replied with a disarming smile.

'I'm sorry ter see yer go,' Ada told him. 'I fink some o' the people round 'ere 'ave got a lot to answer for.'

The young man who had been helping with the loading gave Flossy a smile then turned to Ada. ''E'll be all right wiv me, luv. I'll look after 'im.'

'You see as yer do,' Ada replied. 'That boy's bin frew enough.'

The two young men climbed on to the tailboard and

waved to her as the cart moved away from the block entrance. As it reached C block they saw Kate standing alongside Amy Almond, and Flossy called out to the driver and the cart pulled up. Flossy jumped down and went over to the two women. 'I'd just like ter say fanks fer what yer did last night, Kate,' he said quietly. 'I didn't 'ave the chance ter get ter know yer very well an' that's my loss. Maybe we'll bump into each ovver again. I 'ope so. I'm only movin' over ter Weston Street.'

Kate smiled. 'Good luck, Flossy, an' keep up wiv the pianer. It'll come good for yer one day, I'm sure.'

'Yeah, good luck, luv,' Amy joined in. 'We're gonna miss yer.'

'Fanks, Amy,' the young man replied with a wan smile. 'I'm gonna miss you too. Yer know, up till last night I loved livin' 'ere, silly as it may sound. I felt safe. I got used ter the smell o' those poxy bins an' Ada's naggin'. I even got used ter Mrs Drew peepin' in me winder every time she emptied 'er bin. I liked ter see the kids kickin' the tin can about, the smell o' that bacon factory, Mary Enright wiv 'er dead rat an' Freda Irons goin' on about 'er bad back all the time. I loved the support I got wiv the talent show an' the way people stopped ter talk ter me. I know 'alf of 'em laughed at me be'ind me back but they're good people who gotta live 'ere frew no fault o' their own. Last night though I saw the ovver side. I saw the bigotry, the prejudice and intolerance that comes ter the surface when people are faced wiv somefing they don't understand. I 'ad to ask meself, will we ever learn ter live tergevver, despite our differences? 'Cos if we can't, then the war we've just bin frew counts fer nuffing. Anyway I've said me bleedin' piece, ladies. Good luck, an' God bless yer.'

Amy wiped a tear away and Kate stood sad-eyed as the

cart drew out of the turning, and then they saw Father O'Shea. He waved to the two young men and marched quickly into the turning, looking very determined as he went into the first block.

'I bet 'e's gone up ter see the Dolans,' Amy ventured a guess. 'Aggie Dolan always used ter go ter church at one time. I reckon there'll be a few 'Ail Marys floatin' around ternight.'

The two women walked back into the block and as they reached the first landing Amy gave Kate a sly grin. 'Spiv's callin' later,' she said with a wink. ''E's got some more gear.'

Kate went in and set about tidying the living room, thinking all the while about Flossy and the ordeal he had undergone. What he said made sense. The Dolans and their cronies had behaved like animals, and driven a harmless, likeable young man out of the street with their bigotry. It was sad and depressing but she felt pleased at having stood up to the bullies.

The knock on her door brought her out of her reverie and she was surprised to find that it was Pat Cassidy. 'Is somefing wrong?' she asked on seeing his serious face.

'Kate, I wanted to speak to you for a few minutes,' he replied as she let him in.

She led him into the kitchen and looked at him expectantly as he sat down at the table. 'What is it, Pat?'

He gave her a reassuring smile. 'I got to thinking this afternoon,' he began. 'Seeing as it's a bank holiday weekend I thought maybe it'd be a good idea to go down to Wiltshire for a couple of days. You remember I told you about my sister's farm. She's always pressing me to visit her more often, so I phoned her.'

'That'll be nice for yer,' Kate smiled. 'The rest'll do yer good.'

'That's why I called,' he went on cautiously. 'You see I told her that I'd met someone and she was delighted, and said I should bring you along. She'd love to meet you. I told her it was difficult because you had two children and were looking after another young lad too and she laughed it off. She wants you all to come, Kate.'

'That's very nice of 'er, but 'as she got the space?' she reminded him. 'What about the work involved in puttin' us all up?'

Pat's smile grew more broad. 'You've got to see the place and know my sister to understand,' he told her. 'Gilda and Norman are very down-to-earth. They've got a rambling farmhouse with two extra bedrooms that they occasionally use for bed-and-breakfast guests. They've also renovated a dry barn and turned it into a dormitory for use by rambling clubs and the like. The space won't be a problem, and as for the work involved, Gilda's a dynamo, and she loves it when I visit her. She'd be very happy for us all to go. She told me so in no uncertain terms. You'd love her, Kate, and Norman too. Say you'll come.'

She looked bewildered. 'Pat, it's lovely of yer ter fink of us all, but I dunno. There's the train fares fer a start, an' I couldn't go there wivout offerin' yer sister somefing fer our keep.'

The young policeman leaned across the table and clasped her hand in his. 'Now, listen to me, Kate,' he said firmly. 'Forget the money for fares. I wouldn't consider you paying anyway. As for offering Gilda money for board, don't even think about it. She'd feel insulted. You and the children would be her guests, just like me. You'd love it there and so would the kids. We can go first thing tomorrow morning and come back on Monday evening. Just think of it. Two whole days in the glorious countryside, with the children getting clean air in their lungs and sleeping in the barn, tired out after an exciting day. And you and I can sit together on the log bench outside the farmhouse and watch the sun go down over the hills, and then enjoy a few drinks with Gilda and Norman. Honestly, Kate, you'll love it.'

She looked down at her clasped hands. 'You make it sound wonderful.'

He squeezed her fingers gently in his. 'We need this time together, Kate,' he said quietly. 'I've got things to say, things you need to know about me, and I want to get to know you really well too. It's important to me. Please say you'll come.'

'Put like that, 'ow could I refuse?' she answered with a smile.

He stood up and pulled her to him. 'I promise, you and the kids will really enjoy it,' he said as he took her into his arms.

Chapter Thirty-Eight

Kate was up very early on Saturday morning, closely followed by the children who were eager to get going. 'Eat yer breakfast an' then go an' get ready,' she told them. 'Mr Cassidy'll be 'ere soon.'

''E said I could call 'im Pat,' Jimmy reminded her.

'All right, Pat'll be 'ere soon. Now don't dawdle, I've still got fings ter do.'

The children needed no coaxing. 'It'll be marvellous sleepin' in a barn,' Tommy said excitedly.

'Yeah, an' there's sure ter be an owl in it,' Jimmy told him.

'Is there gonna be pigs an' sheep, an' cows?' Jenny asked.

'I expect so,' Jimmy replied. ''Ere, I wonder if they'll let us milk the cows.'

'I see 'em do it on the pictures once,' Tommy remarked. 'I wonder if it 'urts 'em.'

'Nah, they get used to it,' Jimmy said grinning.

'I wonder if they've got a sheepdog,' Jenny said with her chin cupped in her hand.

'If they've got sheep they're bound to,' Jimmy replied with a superior look. 'Stan's ter reason.'

Kate hustled the children from the table. She had stayed

up late getting things ready, rushing about like a mad-woman: clothes needed ironing and boots and shoes needed cleaning; woollies had to be sorted out for the early morning country chill; and to cap it all she had discovered that the one suitcase she possessed had a broken clasp and a big split along the stitching. Fortunately Amy had come to her rescue, and she had also revealed over a cup of tea that Spiv Copeland's visit earlier that day had been a little more than business only.

'I tell yer, Kate, I was really surprised,' Amy had told her. ''E brought me a bundle o' stuff, some more o' those nightdresses an' a few blouses an' skirts, an' I gave 'im a cup o' tea as usual, an' I sensed that 'e was makin' 'imself comfortable. I noticed it 'cos normally 'e's got itchy feet. This time it was as though 'e 'ad all the time in the world. "Yer need a break, Amy," 'e said. "Yer workin' too 'ard." I was wonderin' what 'e was gettin' at an' then 'e comes out wiv it. "Why don't you an' Charlie come ter Margate wiv me fer the weekend," 'e ses. I tell yer, I was really surprised. Then 'e tells me that 'e'd always fancied me but never showed it 'cos 'e knew I was tied up wiv Fred Logan. I got a bit shirty an' said that if 'e thought I was a loose woman then 'e'd got anuvver fink comin'. I told 'im straight that I wasn't the sort ter sleep wiv every Tom, Dick or 'Arry an' 'e was most upset. "Amy, I fink too much of yer to dream of askin' yer ter sleep wiv me," 'e said. "Well, that's all right then," I told 'im. "Long as yer understand." Anyway the upshot was that 'e's bookin' me an' Charlie in separate rooms. Apparently it's a place 'e's stayed at before, right on the seafront.'

'I'm pleased for yer, Amy,' Kate replied. 'Len's a nice bloke, an' Charlie loves 'im.'

'I just 'ope the rooms are adjoinin',' Amy laughed. 'I'm

not a prude, it's just that I don't like bein' taken fer granted. As a matter o' fact I've always 'ad a soft spot fer the feller.'

Now, as Kate hurried to get ready, she felt excitement building up inside her.

'Mum, the taxi's 'ere,' Jimmy called out from the front bedroom.

Kate was waiting at the front door with the large suitcase as Pat ran up the stairs and soon they were off, with Jenny squeezed between her mother and the young detective and Jimmy and Tommy occupying the pull-down seats. The taxi took them over the wide Westminster Bridge past Big Ben and the Houses of Parliament and into St James's Park, with Pat pointing out places of interest. On to Hyde Park they went and out into the Bayswater Road, with the traffic quite light at that time of the morning. Soon they reached Paddington Station and the children gazed wide-eyed at the bustling activity. Uniformed servicemen and women mingled with holiday travellers and porters went to and fro wheeling luggage on large barrows. The tender spat out pressurised steam with a noise that startled the children and they looked up in awe at the smutty-faced fireman as he leaned nonchalantly over a brass rail high up on the footplate.

They found an empty carriage and settled in minutes before the train pulled away from the platform, and as soon as it gathered speed Kate sighed with relief.

'A penny for your thoughts,' Pat said as he laid his hand on her arm.

'Pleasant thoughts, werf a shillin' at least,' she told him with an impish smile.

He smiled back at her and stretched his legs out. 'What a relief to get away from everything for a couple of days,' he said with a deep breath. 'The super wasn't too happy about me dropping it on him at the last minute, but I've got so much leave outstanding he couldn't very well refuse me.'

''Ave yer bin put under pressure?' Kate asked.

Pat nodded. 'My going over to Soho didn't go down too well with him, but I'm certain that if we're going to make any progress at all it'll originate there. I've got a few leads to follow up and people to see, but for now I'm going to put it right out of my head. I'm going to concentrate on you, Kate.'

'That sounds nice,' she replied, resting her shoulder against his.

The balmy day had turned into a cool starlit night, with the smell of pinewood drifting down from the copse beyond the valley to mingle with the scent of roses and clematis growing round the farmhouse entrance. The four of them sat together around an ancient, heavy table, sipping mulled wine and chatting comfortably.

'The kids were so thrilled,' Kate remarked. 'That barn is lovely. They couldn't wait ter get ter bed.'

'They certainly wore themselves out,' Norman said smiling.

Gilda looked at her brother as she raised her glass to her lips and noticed the way he glanced at Kate. They were obviously lovers, she thought. That look said it all. How naive of her to assume that they would want separate rooms. It would have been more sensible to broach the subject plainly; after all Pat was her brother and they had always been very open with each other. Never mind, she would sort things out tactfully, at an opportune moment.

Norman engaged his brother-in-law in conversation while the women got up and moved away from the table.

'I've always had a yearning to go to Canada,' he said. 'Our ship called in at Vancouver for repairs during the war and we stayed over for a few days. I'd palled up with a Canadian who was serving on my ship, and he took me to visit his family's fruit farm in the Okanagan Valley, which is in British Columbia. There's so much potential there. It's a new country, Pat. Gilda and I have talked about emigrating and I think I've sold her on the idea.'

'You'd give up your law practice?'

'For Canada, yes, bearing in mind that I could set up there if need be.'

Gilda was eager to learn more about the attractive young woman who appeared to have stolen her brother's heart, and linked arms with her as they strolled outside to the edge of the gravel area. 'I've been very concerned about Pat,' Gilda said quietly. 'We've always been close and since he came back from the war I've noticed the change in him. It's hard to put my finger on it, but he seems almost haunted. Maybe I'm just being naive; after all, none of the servicemen who actually saw action will ever be the same, will they?'

They had reached the fencing and they stopped to watch the mist rising from the valley to enshroud the pine copse on the dark skyline.

'Losin' 'is wife an' baby must 'ave bin so 'ard ter bear,' Kate said with a sad sigh.

Gilda nodded. 'It must have been a terrible experience.'

'There's somefing else though,' Kate replied as she leaned on the fencing. 'When Pat first told me about 'is loss I saw the sadness in 'is eyes, which was only natural, but I've seen anuvver look, a kind of distant look, as if 'e's not 'ere any more.'

Gilda smiled. 'I think you and I are on the same track,'

she said. 'I'm pleased Pat's found you and I hope you find happiness together.'

Kate turned to face her and noticed her straw-coloured hair moving in the breeze, her blue eyes full of concern and she warmed to her. 'It's very nice of yer, Gilda,' she replied. 'You an' Pat are so alike.'

'It's getting quite chilly, let's go inside and make ourselves comfortable,' Gilda said, taking Kate by the arm. As they walked back from the shadows into the light coming from the farmhouse door she stopped suddenly. 'Kate, I don't want you to take this the wrong way, but before we go in I want to say something. I put you and Pat in two different rooms without finding out first if you preferred to stay together.'

Kate smiled disarmingly. 'I couldn't take it the wrong way, Gilda,' she replied. 'Where I live there's a lot less room than 'ere. Me an' the kids share two small bedrooms an' Jenny sleeps in my room. On both occasions that Pat stayed overnight 'e used a chairbed. We're not lovers.' She smiled as she added, 'Not yet.'

'Thanks for being so frank,' Gilda replied grinning. 'Let me tell you that I hope you soon are. A word of advice though, for your own piece of mind. The floorboards between those two rooms squeak somewhat. There's no need to worry though. Norman sleeps like a top. I don't think an earthquake would wake him. As for me, a floorboard creaking in the middle of the night will tell me that romance is afoot.'

Kate squeezed Gilda's arm as they carried on back to the house. 'Pat told me I'd like you,' she chuckled.

Norman got up from the table. 'Shall we check on the children before we go in?' he suggested.

'So you are serious about Canada,' Pat said as they walked towards the barn.

'Deadly so.'

'What about this farm?'

'We'd put it on the market.'

'Wouldn't it be better to rent it out?'

Norman shook his head. 'Once we go we'll burn all our bridges, Pat. It's the only way, and Gilda agrees with me.'

The evening chill was noticeable in the rambling stone sitting room and Gilda lit the log fire. 'What about some supper?' she asked them. 'I've cheese, pickles, some ham.'

Pat slipped his arm around Kate's waist as they stood in front of the burning logs. 'This is really something,' he said happily. 'Sometimes I really envy you and Norman, Gilda.'

'Would you like to live here permanently?' she asked him.

'It would be a lovely place to retire to,' he replied.

High in the rafters of the dry barn a tawny owl sat observing the intruders below, and as it ruffled its feathers Jenny nudged her brother. 'Are you asleep, Jimmy?' she whispered.

'Yeah.'

'Well, can yer wake up?'

'Wake Tommy.'

'But you're me bruvver.'

Jimmy turned over to face her across the wide gap between their camp beds. 'What is it?' he asked irritably.

'I just 'eard a noise.'

'It's the country.'

'So what?'

'There's always noises in the country.'

'I fink there's an owl up in the roof.'

'Well, it won't 'urt yer.'

'Promise?'

'I promise.'

'Jimmy?'

'Yeah?'

'Do yer fink Mummy's gonna marry Pat?'

'I dunno.'

'I like Pat, 'e's nice.'

'Yeah, so do I, now get ter sleep.'

'Jimmy?'

'What now?'

'I like Tommy.'

'Well, tell 'im, not me.'

'But you're me bruvver.'

Jimmy sat up in bed. 'Look, Jenny, I'm tryin' ter get ter sleep. We've got fings ter do in the mornin'. Gilda's gonna let us watch 'er milk the cows so we gotta get ter sleep quick.'

'All right. Night, Jimmy.'

'Good night.'

A pale moon climbed up in the starlit sky and shone down into the end bedroom. Kate lay awake, her hands behind her head as she glanced up at the oak-beamed ceiling. As she waited her thoughts turned to what she and Gilda had discussed earlier that evening. One thing was for sure: whatever devils Pat was struggling with, she would help him drag them into the light and conquer them.

Out in the dark a low breeze was blowing across the sky, rustling the foliage of the old sycamore and sending shadows dancing on the whitewashed wall that faced her bed. The shadow-branches shifted and twisted in the dim moonlight and now she saw a figure, crouched and cloaked as he entered the block. Meg take care, she almost mumbled aloud, Meg take care.

Outside a floorboard creaked and then came the faint sound of the door latch being lifted. Light from the passage-way shone briefly into the room and then left it to the shadows once more. Pat stood there, dressed in his heavy dressing robe. 'Kate, are you awake?' he whispered.

'I knew yer'd come ter me,' she said in a voice she hardly recognised.

With a quick movement he slipped off his robe and stood before her, his lean nude body eager with arousal, and then he was beside her in the bed. She turned to him, letting him feel her warmth, urging him to caress her, and she sighed with ecstasy as his experienced hands moved over her. She felt his lips and the urgency building as he pressed against her and she drew on him, breathing faster with him. He moved on top of her, leaning on his elbows. 'The thought of you has been driving me crazy, darling,' he said huskily.

'I've wanted yer so much,' she gasped as his hands strayed down to her most intimate flesh.

His thighs were hot against hers and she wrapped her legs around his waist as he entered her, wanting to feel him thrusting deep inside her. He was tender in his hunger, and as the delicious sensations grew she moved in rhythmic unison with him. Slowly, the fuse of mounting ecstasy burned, and with a stifled cry she trembled at the peak. He was ready too, she could tell, then an explosion of love carried her away, off into a fantasy world of lights and sparkling shapes as she squeezed her eyes tight. She could hear his rapid heartbeats, or were they her own? She felt the hot softness of his lips on her breast, closing over her hard nipple and she shuddered. 'Darling. Was I good?'

'I can't tell you how good,' he gasped, his arms shaking as he held himself above her.

Her arms went up to his neck and she pulled him down

on top of her, still locked in love.

They lay close, Kate's fingers finding the slight indentation in his back. 'Is that a wound? Were you wounded in the war?' she asked him with concern.

He smiled, his white teeth catching the pale light from the window. 'Yeah, but it wasn't much. I've been critically wounded tonight though. Cupid's arrow, right through the heart.'

Chapter Thirty-Nine

The sun had climbed high in the clear sky over Blaydon
Mere Farm and the sound of children's happy voices carried
up from the valley beneath them as Pat and Kate stood hand
in hand on the ridge. They could see the tiny figures below
by the white-stone farmhouse, and beyond the vast expanse
of Wiltshire countryside.

'It's like a patchwork quilt of lovely colours,' Kate
sighed. 'I could stay 'ere fer ever.'

Pat slipped his arm around her. 'I could too, with you,' he
replied in a quiet voice. 'Last night was beautiful. And
today? Well, what can I say.'

She leaned her head on his shoulder. 'I'm so 'appy, an'
the kids too. This is like a fairytale ter them.'

He smiled. 'They were up with the lark this morning.
Gilda said all their eyes were popping when she milked the
cows. They've helped feed the pigs and goodness knows
what. She's really taken by them, Kate. Gilda loves kids,
but she can't have any of her own. She told me the last time
I was here. I think she and Norman have come to terms with
it, because they're so happy together, but I wonder if that's
why they want to emigrate to Canada and sell up here.'

'Sell this lovely place?'

'Yeah, it does seem a shame, but they've both got big

plans. Fruit farming, so Norman told me.'

The tall slender trees swayed in the light breeze and scattered the sun's rays by where the two young people stood on a deep carpet of pine needles. The sweet-smelling aroma was intoxicating, the cooler air invigorating and they savoured the peaceful moment. She could feel the reassuring pressure of his arm around her and he was thrilled by her nearness.

'It's like the 'ole world's standin' still, it's so quiet,' Kate remarked with a happy sigh.

'I've walked up here and had that same feeling,' he replied. 'If the wind is in the right direction, you can hear the sound of tractors and machinery from the farms way off in the distance, and the bells of Blaydon church on Sunday mornings. One day I climbed up here when the sky was threatening and got caught in a thunderstorm. To be honest I was a bit wary of sheltering under the trees but I waited to watch the lightning. The eye of the storm was some way away but the forks of lightning seemed to be moving nearer as they hit the valley, then suddenly a lightning bolt struck that end tree. You can see the one from here, the one with the split bole. For a moment I was rooted to the spot, then I turned and ran full pelt back down the valley and up into the farmhouse. I was soaked to the skin, gasping for breath, but boy was I relieved.'

Kate turned to him and slipped her arms around his neck. 'Kiss me, Pat,' she whispered.

He lowered his head, and as their lips met she closed her eyes. She felt the warmth of him and the urgency of his kiss, the tingling sensation down her spine and the special feeling deep inside her that had not left her since they became lovers. She could feel the hardness in his loins and the beat of his heart and her breath came fast and hurried as he suddenly lifted her bodily and laid her down on the pine needles. She wanted him desperately and knew that he felt the same.

Jenny sat a few yards back from the mere, warned severely by her protective brother about falling in, and she sang to herself as she picked the petals from a wildflower. Nearer the water's edge Tommy looked into the murky depths. 'Will I be able ter stay wiv yer?' he asked. 'Fer good I mean?'

'Yeah, I should fink so,' Jimmy replied as he probed what he thought to be a lazy fish.

'Would yer mum mind?'

'Course not.'

'I could 'elp wiv me keep. I could get a job.'

'Yer gotta finish school first.'

'I mean a paper round or 'elpin' a milkman on Saturdays.'

'Nah, there's no need ter do that.'

'I wouldn't mind.'

Jimmy moved the stick in the water. 'If it was down ter me yer could stay fer ever but I fink me muvver's gotta get permission from the welfare people first.'

'I'd never go in one o' them 'omes, Jimmy.'

'There's no need.'

'They might try an' make me.'

'Nah, they won't.'

'Are yer sure?'

Jimmy sat down on the tall grass and lobbed the stick out into the mere. 'If they try to we'll run away tergevver,' he said in a manly voice.

Tommy seated himself alongside his friend and clasped his hands around his knees, and a casual observer might have taken them for brothers. Both were fair and blue-eyed, though Jimmy was more robust. A noticeable difference, however, was that one wore a confident look while the other had a frightened expression.

'Would yer really?' Tommy asked anxiously.

'What, run away wiv yer? Yeah, course I would. We're mates, ain't we, an' mates 'ave gotta stick tergevver,' Jimmy told him.

'I wanna do a wee,' Jenny complained.

'Well, go be'ind that tree,' Jimmy growled.

'I'm frightened o' snakes.'

'Well, look first.'

'I wanna go back ter the 'ouse.'

Jimmy got up and took her by the hand. 'Come on then,' he sighed in resignation.

Tommy followed a few yards behind, thinking about what had just been said. Jimmy was his best friend now, and mates should stick together.

'You don't need ter come back ter the 'ouse if yer don't want to,' Jimmy told him.

'It's OK,' the lad replied with a wide grin.

The sun had dipped down now, a huge blood red orb that seemed to be speared on the sharp tips of the tall pines, and the valley was darkening with misty purple shadow. Inside the farmhouse Norman and Pat sat talking together by the log fire while the two women busied themselves in the large kitchen.

'It's something to consider,' Norman was saying. 'We'd love to keep it in the family. After all this house has been special to us, and there's a good feeling about the place.'

Pat Cassidy looked thoughtful. 'I love it here, but I've got a career that's ready for a shot in the arm. I've applied for a promotion to inspector and I'm hopeful, providing I can come up trumps with the case I'm working on.'

'The Milldyke murders?'

'Yeah. The problem is we've got a new super and I'm on the rack at the moment,' Pat explained. 'I've got two weeks to solve the killings or the big boys from Scotland Yard will come in.'

'Two weeks doesn't seem long enough to me,' Norman remarked. 'One or two of the cases I've been involved with recently were only cleared up after years of detection and perseverance.'

Pat sat up straight in his easy chair and leaned forward as he made his point. 'I'm certain I can get a breakthrough, given a free rein, but with my superintendent it's impossible,' he replied. 'He's of the old school. Everything must be done by the book.'

'Well, I hope it works out for you, but if it doesn't, remember we'd love you to buy this farm,' Norman emphasised.

The large stove was alight with pots of vegetables simmering over a low heat. A joint of beef sizzled in the oven and Gilda used the back of her hand to push the hair from her forehead as she checked the rising Yorkshire pudding. 'We can make a start soon, Kate,' she said as she gently closed the oven door.

'We'll all be sorry ter leave termorrer,' Kate said sighing. 'It's bin really lovely.'

'We've enjoyed your company, Kate,' Gilda replied, giving her a warm smile. 'It's been lovely having kids around and I've noticed how happy and relaxed Pat is. That's down to you of course. You make a very good couple.'

Kate leaned back against the large Welsh dresser. 'Pat

told me about 'is back,' she said quietly.

'Did he tell you everything?'

She nodded. ''E told me that there's a small piece o' shrapnel still lodged near the spine an' they don't want to operate, unless it starts ter move.'

'I know it gives him pain at times, but he said he can cope with it,' Gilda replied with a slight frown, and she seemed to hesitate for a moment. 'Did he tell you about Malthausen?'

Kate's face looked pained as she nodded. 'You know the story?'

'He told me everything, but he made me swear that I wouldn't tell another soul, not even Norman.'

'On the second night 'e stayed at my flat,' Kate went on, 'I 'eard this shout in the middle o' the night and I found Pat bathed in sweat. 'E passed it off then as just an ordinary nightmare, but last night 'e told me about when 'is unit overran the concentration camp. I cried buckets when 'e told me the full story. 'Ow can 'e blame 'imself, Gilda? After comin' across such terrible fings it was only natural that 'e reacted in the way 'e did, 'specially when yer consider what the war 'ad taken from 'im.'

'I told him to put it out of his mind,' Gilda answered. 'Many a soldier would have done exactly what he did, and maybe in a more brutal fashion. At least that monster of a guard had a more human end than thousands of the poor wretches who were imprisoned there. I think it's a very good sign that he confided in you. He must feel really close to you.'

'I love 'im dearly, Gilda.'

'I know. It shows.'

Kate smiled as she laid her hand on Gilda's arm. 'I'm glad you approve. I can see you an' Pat are very close.'

'I'm absolutely delighted,' Gilda replied, then with a saucy smile she said, 'Don't let him creak that floorboard tonight, Kate. Take him with you and keep him warm and happy.'

Pat came in with the children who all looked a little tired. 'I had to carry Jenny part of the way back,' he said smiling. 'Anyway I gave them a guided tour of Blaydon and I'm sure they'll all sleep soundly tonight.'

The bank holiday Monday was hot and sunny after the early morning mist had cleared and the children strolled about the farm, watching the cows munching the lush grass in the upper meadow and then going off to stare curiously at the fat pigs slurping messily at their trough. They went to the dry barn and rolled in the hay, climbed the pole fence and ran down to the mere to hunt for frogs, and then finally, reluctantly, they came back to the farmhouse to get ready to leave.

'I feel sad,' Jenny said gravely as she sipped her lemonade.

'Never mind, we'll come back soon,' Kate told her reassuringly.

'I wish we could stay 'ere fer ever,' Jimmy said, looking up towards the ridge from the doorway.

'Where's Tommy?' Pat asked as he came in from the kitchen.

''E's gone ter see the cows again,' Jimmy told him.

Kate glanced quickly at Pat and then went out to find Tommy. She saw him standing by the fencing and went up to him, gently putting her arm round his shoulder. ''Ave you 'ad a nice time, Tommy?' she asked.

The lad nodded and looked up at her long enough for her to see that his eyes were brimming. 'I wish we could stay 'ere fer always,' he said in a tiny voice.

Kate saw the lone tear setting off down his flushed cheek and her heart melted. She pulled him close, her other arm going around him. He buried his head against her and sobbed, his shoulders heavy.

'It's all right, Tommy. Everyfing's gonna be fine,' she said softly as she stroked his head. 'We're gonna do our best ter keep yer fer always. Pat's gonna try too. We'll talk ter the welfare. I'm sure they'll let yer stay wiv us. Yer'd like that, wouldn't yer?'

He looked up and Kate took him by the shoulders. 'Now listen ter me. Whatever 'appens you're part of our family now. I promise we'll fight 'ard ter keep yer, an' it's important you understand that.'

Tommy brushed the tears away with the back of his hand. 'I understand, Mrs Flannagan. I was just sad we've gotta leave.'

'So am I,' Kate told him quietly, 'but we'll be comin' back very soon, all of us, an' 'opefully fer longer.'

They had all gathered together outside the farmhouse to say their goodbyes as the taxi drove in and Gilda gave her brother a big hug. 'You're a lucky feller, Pat. Take care of her.'

There were hugs and handshakes and last-minute quips, watched by the patient driver, and then they were off, gazing back at Gilda and Norman standing close together and waving as they disappeared from sight.

'Auntie Gilda's lovely,' Jenny remarked. 'She let me go in 'er room an' try on 'er earrin's an' brooches. She put some powder on me face too.'

Jimmy was smiling to himself, recalling the sight of the pigs wallowing in the muddy sty, but Tommy looked very serious as he stared out of the taxi window.

'I can't tell yer 'ow much I enjoyed it, Pat,' Kate said

softly as she slipped her hand into his.

His pale blue eyes twinkled and the corner of his mouth moved in a secret smile as he looked at her. 'I'll never forget it,' he replied.

Chapter Forty

The fate of Tommy Brindley had been held in abeyance over the holiday period by the brief phone call Pat Cassidy had made to the welfare services on Friday evening, but their representative was due at the police station soon and the young detective glanced repeatedly at his wristwatch as he worked through the files of the Milldyke murders.

'Where should this suspect go? On red or blue?' Detective Constable Fernley asked scratching his head.

Pat looked up at the blackboard Superintendent Baxter had prepared with the coloured strips and shrugged his shoulders in disgust. 'Francis Chandler? On white,' he replied quickly.

'There's only red and blue,' Fernley reminded him.

'Exactly.'

The detective smiled briefly and picked up another file. 'Mr Schofield,' he said sighing. 'Now let's see.'

Pat reached across the desk and grabbed the file from him. 'Schofield's gone out of his mind,' he growled. 'He's a white too. We're just wasting our time. Look at this lot. Mrs Irons, Mrs Champion. Mrs Drew. God Almighty!'

The detective stared past Cassidy's shoulder for a short moment before lowering his head quickly.

'I see there's some disagreement over my methods,' the superintendent said tartly.

Pat spun round in his chair. 'Just making a comment, sir,' he replied with a pained expression.

Baxter was about to respond when the desk sergeant looked in the room. 'Sergeant Cassidy, there's a Mr Brown from the welfare services to see you,' he said.

Pat hurried out with relief and shook hands with a thin balding man in his early forties. 'We'll use the end office; we won't be disturbed there,' he said smiling as he led the way.

Harold Brown made himself comfortable at the fixed metal table and opened his briefcase. 'Ah, here we are,' he said in a reedy voice. 'Thomas Brindley, thirteen years old in September. Mother recently deceased. No father. No other known relatives.'

Pat wanted to correct the assumption that Tommy had been an immaculate conception with a sarcastic remark, but he held back. 'Tommy's father died in captivity during the war,' he stated plainly. 'Far East.'

'Yes, we have it all here,' Harold Brown replied officiously as he flicked a page over. 'Absconded from grandmother's home. Later reported safe and being cared for by a Mrs K. Flannagan of Milldyke Buildings, Milldyke Street, Bermondsey. Phone call from Detective Sergeant P. Cassidy, Dockhead police, stating that the boy would be joining her family for a trip to Wiltshire on Saturday and would be returning on Monday evening. Now then. Let's see where we are.'

Pat wanted to reach across the table and put his hands around the man's thin neck to shake him till he rattled, but instead he breathed in through clenched teeth to calm himself. 'The boy's fine,' he said. 'Fit and well, and happy with the family, who have a son his age.'

'I see there's no mention of a Mr Flannagan,' Brown remarked, looking over his tortoiseshell glasses.

'Mrs Flannagan lives alone. She's divorcing her husband.'

'Um . . . I see. Could pose a problem.'

'I don't see why.'

'A woman alone with a son of her own.'

'And a daughter of nine.'

'Um . . . I see. That adds to the problem.'

'Why?'

Harold Brown took off his glasses and proceeded to clean them with a grubby handkerchief. 'One wage coming in. Already has two children to feed. Unsanitary housing conditions. Sleeping arrangements. Obvious upset in taking in an unstable boy. The list goes on.'

The desire to reach out and throttle the man grew more urgent. 'I'd like you to know the full facts before you make any rash judgements,' Pat began.

'Oh, I can assure you we're not in the habit of making rash judgements,' Brown replied quickly.

'If you'll just let me go on,' Pat said sighing. 'Tommy Brindley ran away after having found his grandmother dead in her bed, and then that same day being told that his mother had died in hospital. That would be enough to make any young lad unstable, as you put it, but it's important you understand that Tommy Brindley is definitely not unstable.'

'That would have to be determined by a psychiatric doctor,' Brown cut in.

'Will you please be quiet until I've finished,' Pat said in a raised voice. 'I'm a good friend of Mrs Flannagan and can vouch for the fact that she keeps her home spotlessly clean. Her children are well fed and she takes her parental responsibilities very seriously indeed. Tommy Brindley has been made welcome and he shares the large bedroom with Mrs Flannagan's son. As for the financial considerations, I will be providing any support that's needed.'

'But the buildings are unsanitary.'

'Well, in that case why don't you concern yourself with all the other children living there already?'

Harold Brown was not used to being talked down to and he was beginning to sweat. 'I'm afraid we haven't the time or the staff to monitor the situation, except when it concerns one of our charges,' he replied in a subdued voice.

'Then I suggest you find the time,' Pat told him sharply. 'Go and take a look at the children living in Milldyke Buildings. They're as healthy there as in any other part of the borough, which says something about the efforts made by their parents. Make no mistake about it: Tommy Brindley will thrive with the Flannagans, which is more than can be said for the lad if he's put into a children's home.'

'Our children's homes are first class,' Brown said a little indignantly.

'Oh, I'm sure they are, but Tommy's had to deal with two tragedies already in his young life and now he finds himself without a relative in the world. All he's got is the Flannagan family, who love him like he's one of their own. Would you sanction taking that away from the lad?'

'Certainly not, sergeant, but I would have to visit Mrs Flannagan and talk to the boy himself.'

'That's fine, Mr Brown,' Pat replied, laying it on slightly. 'I'm sure you'll have no reason to feel concerned, and I believe you're a fair-minded man.'

The syrup in Pat's voice seemed to mollify the welfare officer and he smiled briefly. 'I'll write to Mrs Flannagan right away to arrange a visit. I'm sure we can resolve this matter to everyone's satisfaction.'

'I'm very pleased to hear it,' Pat replied.

When Harold Brown left the station the young policeman made a quick decision, 'Joe, cover for me, will you? I've got someone to see.'

The detective nodded. 'I'll do what I can,' he replied.

Kate had spent the morning hard at work in a warm, happy trance, which Bet Groves had been quick to latch on to, and there was more than a little repartee passed back and forth across the workbench. Kate rode it all with the occasional smile and a look of detachment on her pretty face. They could make all the assumptions and allusions they liked, she told herself. They didn't know the half of it. Now, as she hurried home at lunch-break in the warm sunshine she was impatient to see Pat again.

Amy was eager to hear all about the trip to Wiltshire and she had much to tell as well, but there was little time to talk just now.

'They're all fine,' she said as Kate looked in on her. 'Jimmy an' Charlie 'ave gone wiv Tommy over the park an' Jenny's in the bedroom wiv Elsie Burton's gel. I got such a lot ter tell yer, Kate. I'll pop in ternight.'

Kate put her head round the bedroom door to see Jenny and Laura Burton sitting at the dressing table. 'I 'ope yer not makin' a mess, Jenny,' she said.

'We're tryin' on earrin's, Mum,' Jenny said grinning. 'Look, I've got the pair on that Auntie Gilda gave me.'

'They look nice,' Kate smiled. 'Now look, I've gotta go back ter work. You be'ave yerself fer Mrs Almond, an' don't keep runnin' in an' out.'

Amy came up behind her. 'Don't worry. They're no trouble,' she remarked, looking over at the children. 'Laura, if you keep makin' them faces in the mirrer yer'll 'ave the_ devil jump out after yer. Now come on, I'll give yer both some lemonade.'

Kate reached the door. 'We'll 'ave a chat ternight, Amy,' she said as she hurried out of the flat.

Outside the hot sun reflected up from the pavements and children sat in the shade of the bacon curer's. A few boys were playing football by the end wall and a lorry was parked by the factory gates with the driver snoozing in his cab while he waited to get his consignment of greenbacks unloaded. Kate stepped out of the block and suddenly stopped as she thought about the two young girls seated at Amy's dressing table. What was that Amy had said about the devil jumping out of the mirror? 'Why of course!' she said aloud. That was it. Why hadn't she thought of it before? It was a common expression she had often heard herself as a young child when she pulled faces at the mirror.

Jack Ferguson was taking a nap when Kate knocked loudly at his front door and before he could reach it she rapped against it urgently once more. 'All right, all right, I'm comin',' he growled. 'What's the bloody rush?'

'Mr Ferguson, I'm sorry ter trouble yer but there's somefing I gotta do an' I need your 'elp,' she blurted out.

'What's wrong?' he asked, rubbing a gnarled hand over his face.

'Meg Johnson's furniture. Where did it go?'

'The store. Why?'

'What store?'

'The estate office store.'

'I need ter see it.'

'The furniture?'

'Yeah, an' as soon as possible.'

The caretaker's brow creased. 'Look, d'yer mind tellin' me what all this is about?' he asked irritably.

Kate took a deep breath. 'Meg Johnson 'id a cuttin' from a newspaper in 'er flat an' I've got good reason ter fink it'll 'elp solve 'er murder, an' that of Mrs Griffiths.'

'But the police 'ave already searched all frew Mrs Johnson's fings. Twice ter my knowledge,' he told her.

'They would 'ave missed the 'idin' place,' Kate said excitedly. 'But I'm sure I know where it is. Can yer 'elp me?'

'Yer mean go ter the store now?'

'No, I don't want Ted Briscoe ter know. It's important 'e don't get ter know.'

'But 'e'll 'ave ter know. After all 'e's the agent, gel, not me.'

'Can't yer let me in ternight, after I get 'ome from work? Please, Mr Ferguson.'

'Well, I 'ave got a key ter the store but the trouble is Briscoe often stays late,' the caretaker said stroking his chin.

'We could leave it till late.'

'We might not 'ave to,' he replied. 'Briscoe works in the end office facin' the street. I should fink 'e'd 'ave a winder open if 'e was there, 'specially with this weavver.'

'So yer'll 'elp me? Let me in?'

'If it's as important as yer say, I got no choice, 'ave I?' he said with a rare smile. 'By the way, I 'ope you ain't told Emmy Drew or that Irons woman anyfing about this. They're both well in wiv Briscoe.'

Kate shook her head. 'I 'aven't told a soul,' she replied quickly.

'I'll wait fer yer ter give me a knock then,' he said.

Pat Cassidy took a train to Charing Cross and walked through Trafalgar Square and into Soho full of trepidation.

He knew only too well that his whole career would hinge upon his making good progress today. Once Baxter realised he was missing he would put two and two together. The promotion application would be on its way to the bin and he might well end up back in uniform as a beat bobby.

The seedy cafe in Lisle Street was empty when Pat walked in, apart from two foreign-looking individuals sitting together in the far corner. 'Seen anything of Zoe Lestor?' he asked abruptly.

'What's it ter you?' the cafe owner replied, his wide ugly face screwing up menacingly.

'I'm told she uses this establishment. In fact I know she does,' Pat said in a measured tone of voice.

The owner could smell trouble and he briefly glanced over to the two men in the corner. 'I ain't seen 'er fer weeks,' he growled.

Pat walked over to the two customers, who seemed to be taking a mild interest in the conversation. 'Do you speak English?' he asked.

One of them nodded. 'Whadda yer want?'

'I've got the best trick ever,' he said smiling as he took a pack of playing cards from his pocket. 'I bet you a pound I can tell you what card you're thinking of. Just shuffle the pack and pick a card without touching it. Just keep it in your mind.'

The man did as he was bid and then Pat smiled amiably. 'Now you shuffle them,' he told the other man, who looked at him blankly. The first man muttered a few words and then his friend shuffled the cards. 'Right, I'll be back,' Pat told them with a large wink.

'What's goin' on?' the proprietor asked irritably.

Pat walked back to the counter and took hold of him by the string of his grubby apron. 'This is a police matter,' he hissed as he flashed his warrant card. 'Now are you going to co-operate, or do I shut you down for gambling?'

'Who's gamblin'? I ain't gamblin'.'

'Yeah, but those two are.'

'I can't see no cards.'

'I've got the cards in my pocket with their prints all over them,' Pat said narrowing his eyes. 'Now, what's it going to be?'

'Zoe doesn't start work till ternight,' the cafe owner replied grudgingly.

'Where do I find her now?'

'Twenty-four, Sale Place. It's along on the left.'

Pat strolled out of the cafe and suddenly dived into a nearby shop doorway. His hunch proved correct, for almost immediately one of the men hurried from the cafe and walked quickly along the street, turning into Sale Place after first glancing left and right. Pat slipped out of the doorway and ran towards the narrow street, just in time to see the man enter a delicatessen. The policeman took a deep breath and trotted along the pavement looking for number twenty-four. It was situated at the far end and by the door there were four or five bells with women's names printed underneath them. He rang on Zoe Lestor's bell and waited anxiously, his eyes fixed on the food shop. He heard footsteps on the stairs and as the door opened he saw the hunted animal look in the young girl's eyes. She recognised him immediately and tried to slam the door in his face but he was too quick for her. 'Don't give me any grief, Zoe, your life's at risk!' he shouted. 'Just do as I say. Is there a fire escape?'

She nodded dumbly. 'I don't want no trouble,' she said in a dry voice.

'You'll get it in spades if you don't do exactly as I say.

Now come on,' he shouted as he hurried her up the steep flight of stairs. 'Which is your flat?'

'Top one.'

'It would be.'

A minute or so later they were walking warily through the back alley that led out into Charing Cross Road.

'It's a long story, but there's no time to tell you now,' Pat said as they came out into the brightly lit thoroughfare. 'Suffice it to say that there's a street woman doing time in Holloway Prison who's keen for a deal. She's talking her head off at the moment and she named you. She said you'd know where Nan Lynn's hiding out. So what's it going to be? Me, or the investigation team at West End Central?'

''Ow can I trust yer?' she asked fearfully.

'I give you my word, and I don't give it lightly,' he replied with an earnest look in his eyes. 'Trust me, or take your chances with the organisation after you. Listen to me, Zoe. I'm certain they've got someone on the inside at West End Central nick. You've got to realise that if they pull you in the mob'll get to know straight away.'

'I don't seem to 'ave much choice, do I?' she said with a sigh of resignation. 'We'll need a cab.'

Chapter Forty-One

All afternoon Kate worked automatically, her mind else-where. Why hadn't she realised much earlier what Meg Johnson was trying to say to her, she fretted. If only she had pressed her more at the time. It couldn't be helped, but at least she now had something for Pat to work on. She had tried to phone him at the station but he had been out, so she had left a cryptic message with the desk sergeant. Pat would understand what she meant, and she hoped he would get the message in time to join her at the estate office that evening. At least Jack Ferguson had been helpful in agreeing to open up the store, even though he had doubts about Briscoe being around.

The noise of the machinery and the women's chattering voices seemed far away as Kate puzzled over what she might find. With a bit of luck Pat would be able to add another piece of the jigsaw and hopefully bring the case to a swift conclusion. She felt proud of herself for being able to help. From what Pat had told her he was under a lot of pressure from the chief at the station and time was running out.

When the factory whistle sounded the end of the working day Kate breathed a huge sigh of relief. She hurried home with excitement building inside her, stopping to make another phone call to the police station. The desk sergeant told her that Sergeant Cassidy had still not returned but assured her that he would get the message as soon as he arrived.

As she walked into the street she saw Jack Ferguson standing in the entrance to the block looking a little agitated.

'Briscoe's in the Buildin's,' he said quickly. ''E's up at Mrs Enright's. Somefing about water comin' in.'

'It won't make any difference, will it?' Kate asked him.

'I dunno,' the caretaker replied scratching his head. ''E might need ter go back ter the office later. We'll 'ave ter be careful. Anyway 'e's callin' in before 'e leaves. I'll try an' get some info out of 'im. Just as long as yer don't breave a word o' this to anybody.'

'Jack, I swear I 'aven't, an' I don't intend to,' Kate said emphatically. 'I've not even told Amy Almond. It's too important.'

'That's all right then. Look, we better wait till seven,' Ferguson told her. 'Briscoe should be gone by then.'

The taxi weaved its way through the afternoon traffic in London's West End and soon it pulled up in a wide street in Bloomsbury.

Pat looked puzzled as he helped Zoe from the cab. 'Where are we going?' he asked.

The young prostitute led him into an alley. 'We're goin' in the back way,' she told him.

At the far end of the alley Zoe pushed open a door and Pat followed her into what he discovered was a bookshop. It was a cramped little place and as Zoe edged towards the counter she caught the elderly shopowner's eye. He nodded briefly and then bent down again over the large tome he was examining.

'Follow me,' she whispered.

Behind the counter a door led off into a tiny passage with a flight of stairs leading up into darkness.

As they reached the first landing the young woman tapped gently on a door. 'Mamma Reeves, it's Zoe Lestor,' she called out.

There was a lengthy pause and then the sound of a chain being freed. The door creaked open and Zoe immediately embraced the rotund woman. 'Mamma, I've brought some-one wiv me. I'm in trouble an' 'e's 'elpin' me,' she said breathlessly.

'Well show him in, girl,' Mamma Reeves said in a deep voice. 'Let him sit facing me. I want to touch him.'

Pat could see that the woman was blind. She moved with accustomed confidence to her armchair and sank down with a deep sigh. 'I'm getting old, dearie,' she chuckled. 'My old bones are beginning to protest.'

Pat took the seat opposite her and Zoe sat to one side in the dingy but well-furnished room. Around him he could see draperies, cushions and what looked like an expensive tapestry tablecloth that almost touched the floor. The walls were adorned with paintings and on the very large side-board there were framed photographs and knick-knacks of all shapes and sizes.

'Lean forward, young man,' Mamma Reeves said in her loud voice. 'I want to feel your face.'

Pat felt a little foolish as he allowed her to run her ice-cold fingertips from his forehead, around his eyes and down his cheeks to stop at his chin.

'This is Detective Pat Cassidy from over in Bermondsey, Mamma,' Zoe told her. ''E's investigatin' the murder of two ladies an' 'e wants ter talk ter Nan Lynn.'

Mamma's head moved sideways and she seemed to

ignore what Zoe had just told her. 'The young man's got a strong face and I can tell he's under pressure,' Mamma replied. 'Those worry lines on his forehead are very pronounced.' She smiled cannily. 'An honest enough face though.'

Pat studied the elderly woman and saw that her eyelids were closed tightly and flatly, which suggested that she had had both her eyes removed at some time. Her large flat face and forehead were marbled with burn scars, and her grey hair was thin and wispy.

'Mamma, it's important,' Zoe pressed her.

'You won't be able to talk to Nan Lynn,' the large woman said quietly. 'She doesn't exist any more.'

Pat's heart sank. 'Doesn't exist? You mean she's dead?'

'To all intents and purposes, yes.'

'I don't understand.'

'Lean back in your chair, young man, and relax. I can hear you fidgeting. Hand me your warrant card please.'

Pat took it from his pocket and passed it over. He watched as the old lady ran her fingers over it, feeling the indentations. 'Zoe, are you happy for me to talk to this man?' she asked.

'I fink we can trust 'im, Mamma.'

'You know where the things are, girl. Go and make us some tea,' she told her. Then turning her head at an angle she leaned back against the cushions. 'Tell me why you want to talk to Nan Lynn,' she bade him.

Pat took a deep breath and quickly told her about the probable link between the two murders in Bermondsey and the murder of Gus Wesley.

'So you're searching for Spanish Joe in connection with the three murders,' Mamma replied with a slow nod of her head. 'Well, I can tell you that you are on the right track.

But first you should know why Zoe brought you here. Are you sitting comfortably? It's a long story.'

The large woman breathed heavily and adjusted her hands. 'I suppose it goes back to the twenties,' she began. 'I was working the streets in Soho, a very different place at that time from what it has become, I might add. In those days we had our pimps and ponces, but they worked independently, not in the pay of a criminal organisation like they do today. Don't get me wrong, it wasn't an easy life. There were times when pimps fell out with each other and with the girls they controlled. We sometimes lived on a knife edge, and I was getting old in the tooth as far as streetwalking was concerned. The girls were getting younger every week and I decided it was time to call it a day. My pimp saw things differently and we rowed. He wanted me to carry on for a few years more, but he flew into a furious rage when I refused and threw acid in my face. You can see the results. I nearly died.'

'I'm very sorry,' Pat said.

'It doesn't matter,' Mamma went on. 'I'm an old woman now, but what does matter to me is that I've been able to take on another role in my autumn years. My name still counts for something in Soho and street girls come to me when they're in trouble. That's why you can never meet Nan Lynn, young man. She has a new name, a new life, and apparently she's recently got married to a nice young man who works in the City. What I can do, however, is put you in the picture. Nan Lynn was crazy over this Spanish Joe. He came into her life before the war and she intended marrying him. He wasn't a Spaniard. He got his name from serving in the Republican army during the Spanish Civil War. He was a revolutionary in those days, and used to hang around the cafes and coffee bars talking politics. As a matter of fact his trip to Spain was arranged by an organisation which had its headquarters in Soho at the time.'

Zoe Lestor came in with a laden tea-tray. ''Elp yerself ter milk an' sugar,' she said, setting it down on a low stool by Mamma Reeves's chair.

'I'm listening, Mamma,' Pat said as he stirred his tea.

'I never got to find out his surname,' the old lady continued. 'He was a braggart, always boasting about his exploits, but Nan loved him. Unfortunately Gus Wesley found out and confronted her. He told her to get rid of him and when Nan began to rave at him he attacked her. I'm sure he would have killed her but for Spanish Joe. He arrived on the scene just in time and promptly throttled Wesley with a bootlace. He even had the gall to tell Nan that he had learnt the technique whilst serving in Spain. Anyway he had to go into hiding and he left Soho in a hurry. That was the last time Nan ever saw him. Apparently her love for him was much more intense than his feelings for her. He made no attempt to get in touch with her and she was heartbroken. She worked the streets throughout the war, but times were changing. The organisations have taken over all the prostitution and gambling in the area. Anyone who objects is dealt with and I have to tell you that there are a few girls who've had their looks ruined in the process.'

'Did Nan Lynn fall foul of them?' Pat asked her quickly.

'She dropped out of sight when the police started their clean-up campaign,' Mamma told him. 'You see, word got around about what had happened, and the organisation were scared that if Nan was pulled in for questioning she would talk and give details of their operations. She had no choice but to go into hiding. The mob were out to silence her and the police wanted her as a witness. Either way she was doomed, unless she disappeared. That was where I came in.

I helped her start a new life, but don't ask me to tell you where she is now, because I don't know.'

Pat sipped his tea thoughtfully. 'Do you know if any of the people who recruited the likes of Spanish Joe are still about?' he asked.

Mamma shook her head. 'When the war started the Socialist Fighters as they called themselves disbanded, but I have a name and address you could try. There might be some information forthcoming. Don't bank on it though.'

'I need every lead I can get,' Pat replied quickly.

'I'm sure you do, young man,' Mamma remarked. 'As a matter of fact I have a friend who comes in daily to read the newspapers to me. I was very interested to learn about those two poor women getting murdered in Bermondsey, especially when I heard that they were both strangled with a black bootlace. Spanish Joe is your man, but the motive is a mystery to me, just as it must be to you.'

'I can only suppose that he killed them to silence them,' Pat ventured. 'I believe that they discovered his true identity when they were working at a men's hostel in Poplar, where Spanish Joe had decided to hide out.'

'Would you like some more tea, young man?' Mamma asked.

'No, but I'd like the name and address you have for me,' he replied.

'Zoe, fetch me that handbag from the sideboard,' the old lady requested. 'Our guest is in a hurry. You will stay here though, for the time being at least.'

Pat said his goodbyes, thanking Mamma for the information and hoping that she would be able to help Zoe start a new and better life, then he caught a taxi back to Soho, feeling that at last things were beginning to move.

Chapter Forty-Two

The church clock of St James's was striking seven as Kate hurried along beside Jack Ferguson. She breathed deeply, trying to control her excitement, and smiled to herself as she recalled Amy's puzzled frown and obvious irritation at being kept in the dark. She had promised to tell her everything later, but even then Amy had tried to worm a few details from her.

'I got a pair o' pinchers an' a screwdriver,' the caretaker announced.

Kate smiled at him. 'I'm sure they'll do,' she replied.

When they neared the estate office in River Lane, Kate could smell the sour Thames mud and the aroma of spices wafting from a nearby warehouse.

'It looks quiet enough,' Ferguson remarked. 'There's no winders open. I take it Briscoe's left. 'E said 'e was goin' ter see someone in Abbey Street this evenin'.'

They reached the old building which housed the estate offices on the first floor and the caretaker put his key in the padlock on the ground-floor store beneath. The large wooden doors swung open and they stepped inside. Ferguson closed the doors behind them and slid the bolts across. 'We don't want no one nosin' in,' he told her. 'Now, where do we start?'

Kate led the way through the assortment of building materials, bags of cement and plaster, tins of paint and metal piping to the pile of furniture standing in the far corner by a flight of stone stairs. The place smelled musty but cool after the warm day and Kate pointed to the dressing table. 'Can yer get that big mirror off?' she asked him.

The caretaker gave her a puzzled look before doing as she asked. 'There we are,' he said as he lifted it off and laid it down on the surface of the dressing table.

Kate looked along the edge of the mirror. 'I need the back off,' she told him.

Ferguson turned it face down and prised the retaining clips away from the thick plywood backing, and as he lifted it free Kate saw a small piece of paper flutter to the floor. With a shout of triumph she crouched down and picked it up. It was a newspaper cutting showing a photograph of five men in scruffy clothes standing together outside a building, with a caption below that read, 'Home From Home'. Below the heading the first name was clear, that of a Tim Arrowsmith, but the rest of the names were obliterated by an ink stain. 'I knew it,' she said smiling with satisfaction. 'I'll need . . .'

Her voice broke off as she looked up at Jack Ferguson. He was standing a few feet away from her, his face grey and his eyes wide and staring.

'What is it?' she said getting up slowly.

'You couldn't leave it alone, could yer?' he growled. 'You 'ad ter play the detective.'

'What d'yer mean?' she replied sharply, her face flushing up.

'The man in the middle o' that picture,' he said, his eyes unblinking, 'is Jack Ferguson – the *real* Jack Ferguson. So yer see, I can't let yer show that ter the police.'

Kate suddenly felt icy fingers gripping her spine and she gulped. 'I don't understand.'

'No, I don't suppose yer do,' he said with a ghost of a smile on his thin, stubbled face. 'The police won't 'ave no trouble findin' out what newspaper that cuttin' came from an' they'll find the name Jack Ferguson. That's why I can't let yer give it to 'em.'

Kate's heart thumped loudly in her chest and her eyes were bulging as she saw the movement of his hand. He had slipped it deftly into his coat pocket, and as he withdrew it she saw that he was holding a black bootlace.

'You! It was you all the time!' she gasped. 'But why? Why did yer kill them two 'armless old ladies?'

Ferguson slowly twisted the bootlace around his finger as he closed in on her. 'Does it matter?' he said in a low voice.

'I want ter know,' Kate answered defiantly, playing for time.

'I bumped into Annie Griffiths quite by chance in the pub an' she reco'nised me.'

'From the 'ostel in Poplar. You stayed there, didn't yer?'

'Yeah, I was on the run from the police.'

'Over the pimp murder.'

'You seem ter be well informed.'

Kate was slowly backing away from him. 'Annie told yer she 'ad proof you wasn't Jack Ferguson so yer killed 'er.'

'Right again.'

'Then yer saw the photo on Meg Johnson's sideboard an' realised she'd worked at the 'ostel too, so yer did the same to 'er.'

'I 'ad to. The Johnson woman was a bundle o' nerves an' she was sure someone was after 'er. She was weakenin'. She could 'ave gone ter the police wiv that bit o' paper at any time. I couldn't take the chance. She 'ad ter be silenced.'

'So yer knew she 'ad this,' Kate said, thrusting it out in front of her.

'No, I never,' he replied. 'But she mentioned that she 'ad somefing they should see. It must 'ave bin that.'

He was getting closer to her and Kate glanced over his shoulder at the stairs. It was her only chance. 'So the real Jack Ferguson died in the 'ostel fire an' you took 'is identity.'

Ferguson jerked on the bootlace wrapped around his hand and smiled. 'It was a stroke o' luck really. The Blitz was on, yer see. The East End was gettin' it bad at the time an' one night I slipped out o' the 'ostel durin' a lull in the bombin' ter see a woman I was friendly wiv. By the time I got back the bombs were fallin' an' the 'ostel 'ad copped it bad. It was a right mess but I managed ter get inside before the fire took 'old. Jack Ferguson was lyin' near the door an' I could see 'e was dead. They were all dead. I was the only one out o' the dozen ter survive. Anyway I saw me chance an' I went frew Ferguson's pockets. I found 'is identity card an' ration book an' the rest was easy. When they finally pulled the bodies out o' the ruins o' that place they were burned beyond reco'nition, an' I was safe. I was the new Jack Ferguson an' I came over this side o' the water ter start afresh. I wasn't ter know that Annie Griffiths 'ad moved over 'ere too, till she confronted me. After I killed 'er I applied fer the job o' caretaker. I saw it as a good ploy. Who'd fink that the killer would move inter the area instead o' gettin' as far away from the scene o' the crime as 'e could? It worked too, till I spotted that photograph on Meg Johnson's sideboard when she invited me in after I put a new lock on 'er door. Yer see, I knew Annie Griffiths, she used ter chat ter me when she served the evenin' meal, but I'd never met the Johnson woman. She was just a cleaner. But, like I said, I couldn't take a chance wiv 'er, so she 'ad ter go.'

'An' now yer gonna kill me,' Kate said, fighting to keep her wits about her.

'If I'm caught, it's the rope, so I can't let yer live, much as I want to,' he said calmly.

'Yer'll never get away wiv it,' she gasped. ''Ow d'yer know I didn't lie ter yer. I might 'ave told Amy where I was goin' an' who I was goin' wiv.'

He shook his head slowly. 'I've worked it all out,' he replied. 'You asked me to 'elp yer an' I did. We didn't find anyfing, then I left yer outside this office 'cos yer told me you was gonna meet somebody.'

'But they'll find me 'ere. 'Ow yer gonna explain that?'

'But yer won't be 'ere,' Ferguson said with an evil smile. 'There's a balcony upstairs that overlooks the river. They'll find yer body right enough, a few miles downstream.'

'I knew it 'ad ter be someone who was aware o' Meg's funny ways,' Kate told him as she backed up to the brick wall. 'After killin' 'er yer left 'er door open so no one would 'ear yer come out. I'm right, ain't I?'

'Yeah, that's right.'

'Tell me somefing,' Kate said, praying for some divine intervention. 'Why use the bootlace? It's a giveaway. It links the three murders.'

He chuckled from deep in his throat. 'A Spanish garrotting method that works well wiv a bootlace. I was taught it over there durin' the Spanish Civil War. Who'd suspect a quiet, inoffensive caretaker of 'avin' any connections wiv Spain. When they find you in the river wiv this lace round yer neck they'll end up addin' one more unsolved murder ter their list.'

'What's yer real name?' she asked as she prepared herself.

'Joe Gains.'

'Fanks fer tellin' me.'

Suddenly he leapt forward and grabbed her by the shoulders but she brought her knee up sharply and caught him in the groin. He doubled up crying out in pain and she dived towards the stairs. He reached out and caught her by the ankle, pulling her shoe off but she managed to reach the stairs and dash up to the dark landing. She had no idea where the lights were and guessed that the front stairway would only lead down to a locked front door. Her only chance was to elude him, make a dash back downstairs to the store and let herself out before he caught her.

'There's no way out, Kate,' he called out as he came slowly up the stairs. 'Don't let's prolong this. It'll be quick. I'll make it quick.'

She was sure he would hear the beating of her heart as she pressed herself back into a doorway and she prayed madly, frantically, for Pat to help her.

'I'm comin' for yer, Kate. Just come out wherever you are an' let's get it over wiv. I promise it'll be quick.'

Kate knew that he was trying to panic her and she bit hard on her lip. He was coming closer and soon he would get her. She would never see her children again. She would never see Pat again nor feel his strong arms around her. There must be something she could do. As he reached the landing she charged out and threw herself at him, hoping to bundle him down the stairs but he had braced himself and caught her up in his arms. She could feel the strength in his wiry frame and she struggled in vain. The bootlace went around her neck and with a quick move he pulled on it. Her throat felt like it was clamped in a vice and a red mist swam before her eyes. There was no one to save her and she knew it was the end.

Pat Cassidy was feeling pleased with himself as he made his way back to Bermondsey. Mamma Reeves had given him the one lead he needed and now he could finally bring the case to a conclusion. For a while though it had seemed as if he had come up against yet another brick wall. Pedro Valdez had been very helpful. He had delved through old records in his comfortable flat above a barber's shop in Dean Street and come up with a list of twenty names, all of whom had been recruited and assisted financially to join the International Brigade in nineteen thirty-six. Valdez had gone on to explain that during their first engagement at the defence of Valencia eight of the volunteers were killed. Two more died later from their wounds and another from typhus. Of the nine survivors, one was killed during the London Blitz and the remaining eight had gone their separate ways.

Pat stared out of the window as the tram trundled over Westminster Bridge. Down below he could see the Thames shimmering in the early evening sunlight and laden barges moored midstream. Eight names, but where to start? he had thought. The search could take for ever. Another brick wall, and still more confrontations with the station superintendent. But then Valdez had mentioned how he and his colleagues had had to beg for funds wherever possible to pay for each volunteer's passage to France and train ticket to Spain, as well as paying for a passport and accommodation. That was it. The Passport Office held the key, the final piece of the puzzle. They held copies of all photographs used in passports.

The young policeman smiled to himself as he recalled the dash to Petty France and the pained look on the office manager's face when asked to hunt through his files. The result was conclusive. The photograph of Mr Joseph William Gains depicted a lean-faced man with dark hair. He might be grey now, but the likeness was unmistakable: it was Jack Ferguson, the Milldyke caretaker.

At five minutes to seven Pat Cassidy walked into the police station at Dockhead and was confronted by one of his team. 'Baxter's running up the wall, sergeant.'

'Don't worry, I'll go and see him right away,' Pat told him with a wide grin.

'Sergeant Cassidy?' the desk sergeant called out. 'There's a . . .'

'Later,' Pat said as he strolled to his superior's office.

Superintendent Baxter's face was hot and flushed as he looked up. 'And where the bloody hell have you been all day, or should I not ask?' he growled.

'I needed to see someone over at . . .'

'Did it ever occur to you that I might have required your assistance here?' Baxter raved. 'I warned you once and I don't intend to repeat myself. It's about time you realised this is not a one-man band. I've had a full team out there scratching themselves while you've been away on some fancy fling. Not content with that you have the gall to submit a promotion application. Well, I can tell you now that . . .' The insistent ringing of the phone interrupted Baxter's diatribe and he clenched his teeth as he snatched up the receiver. 'Wait outside, I'll deal with you later.'

Pat deliberately slammed the door behind him as he left, his face dark with anger.

'There's a message for you,' the desk sergeant said quickly as the detective was about to storm past.

'Sergeant Cassidy!' the superintendent's voice rang out. 'In here!'

Pat's face had gone chalk-white as he read the message. 'Later, damn you!' he shouted back as he dashed from the outer office.

Baxter was speechless with rage but the detective had already forgotten him as he sprinted down the steps of the station. River Lane was only a short distance but the empty police car parked outside was an opportunity too good to pass up. Pat slipped quickly behind the wheel and with a screech of tyres set off at breakneck speed. As he reached the estate office he jammed on the brakes and was out of the car almost before it stopped. He shouldered the heavy store doors and cursed aloud as they resisted his frenzied attempts to get them open. There was no time to lose, he told himself, goading himself on as he jumped back behind the wheel and the next moment he sent the car careering into the store. Splintered wood flew everywhere and he was out of the car once more, glancing round in panic. He heard noise up above and tore up the stone stairs.

Jack Ferguson was about to apply the final pull on the tightened bootlace when he heard the crash and he dropped his victim on the floor as he turned and quickly lifted a window, climbing through on to the balcony. Down below the muddy water ebbed and flowed and he searched feverishly for a safe way down.

Pat saw Kate lying face down on the bare floor and knew instantly that he had only seconds to act. With a quick movement he reached the window and put his elbow through the glass. Using a long shard he quickly cut through the thick knot of the bootlace before pulling Kate up into a sitting position. She started to cough and her hand came up to her neck.

'Thank God!' he cried.

'The caretaker,' she croaked.

'I know. Just stay still,' he told her as he made for the open window and clambered through. 'It's over, Gains. Don't make it any harder on yourself.'

The fugitive had one leg over the rail and he looked up in panic. 'Don't come near me or I'll take yer wiv me,' he shouted.

Pat edged forward. 'Don't be silly, Gains.'

Suddenly there was a loud crack and the whole railing gave way. The murderer screamed as he fell backwards and Pat heard a dull thud and then a splash. Ripples from the agitated water spread out in a widening ring and bubbles burst on the surface. Pat knew that Spanish Joe would never come back this time. The thud he had heard had been his head against the concrete sea wall below and he would most likely have been dead before he hit the water.

Kate was on her feet when he climbed back into the building. 'It's all over, darling,' he said softly.

'I knew yer'd come fer me, Pat,' she said with a brave smile, 'but yer left it a bit bloody late.'

'I promise I'll never be late again, Kate, not even for breakfast,' he said with a deep sigh of relief as he slipped his arm around her waist and led her from the building.

Epilogue

On the fifth of August, merchant seaman Albert Almond was killed in a drunken brawl outside a pub near the Liverpool Docks. Amy Almond's grief was short-lived, for on the first Saturday in September she married Spiv Copeland at the Bermondsey Register Office. It was a quiet affair, attended only by her close friends, and she hugged Kate tightly on the steps outside. 'You keep a tight grip on that man o' yours, luv,' she said smiling. ''E's a cracker.'

Kate stood beside Pat Cassidy with her children close at hand as the car drove off to Margate. Charlie was beaming as he waved from the back window and everyone waved back.

'Where are we goin' now?' Tommy asked his new brother.

'We're gonna see our Aunt Mary an' Uncle John,' Jimmy informed him. 'They're all right, you'll like 'em.'

The Flannagans and Pat Cassidy made their way to Abbey Street and were soon feeling at home. Kate chatted and gossiped with her sister while in the backyard Pat and John lazed in the warm sunshine, sharing a quart bottle of light ale.

'Kate was tellin' me yer got into a bit o' trouble over the case,' John remarked.

Pat grinned sheepishly. 'You could say that,' he replied.

'I was prepared to take whatever the superintendent intended dishing out, until I found out that he'd been sitting on my promotion application. That was the final straw.'

'So yer told 'im where ter put it,' John said chuckling.

'Sort of,' Pat replied, his grin getting wider. 'Anyway, there was no going back after that. My resignation was on the desk next morning.'

'I 'ear yer lookin' ter buy yer sister's farm.'

Pat nodded. 'They've offered me a very good deal, as a matter of fact. I can rent it for a year with an option to buy.'

'Sounds very nice.'

'Too good to turn down.'

'I can just see Kate an' the kids. They'll love it there.'

The ex-policeman smiled. 'It'll be a dream come true for them.'

In the small parlour the soft sounds of piano music came from the wireless as Kate held out her hand for Mary to inspect her engagement ring. 'I felt it was a bit too much ter pay, ter tell yer the trufe, but Pat insisted,' she said. 'It's really lovely. I'm so excited.'

'Do yer remember the last time we sat 'ere talkin' about rings, when I wanted ter give yer Mum's ring ter pawn,' Mary reminded her with a warm smile. 'So much 'as 'appened in these last few months.'

'I know,' Kate said quietly. 'An' now I'm gonna be a farmer's wife.'

'I'm so pleased for yer,' Mary replied. 'I can't wait ter see the place.'

The music stopped and then the voice of the announcer came on. 'That was a musical interlude by our special guest today, the very talented Francis Chandler.'

Kate looked up at the wireless in surprise. 'Well well. Someone else 'as 'ad a change o' luck,' she said happily.

A selection of bestsellers from Headline